wasteground

by
dennis apperly

authorHOUSE®

AuthorHouse™ UK Ltd.
500 Avebury Boulevard
Central Milton Keynes, MK9 2BE
www.authorhouse.co.uk
Phone: 08001974150

First published by AuthorHouse 3/4/2008

ISBN: 978-1-4343-5886-8 (sc)
ISBN: 978-1-4343-5885-1 (hc)

Printed in the United States of America
Bloomington, Indiana

This book is printed on acid-free paper.

In memory of 'Midnight' Steve Long who died on the streets of Gloucester in December 2001 aged 40.

foreword

I SAW my first beggar in 1972 in Glasgow when I began working with homeless people. I contrast this with today when sadly they are a common sight in most cities and large towns.

What happened? So-called 'Care in the Community' happened. 'Care' that shifted people from one institution (hospital) to another (prison) or took the homeless off our streets and put them in prison.

Around one third of those about to be released from prison report having nowhere to stay and around 28,500 people are homeless on leaving prison each year (*Crisis Statistics on Homelessness*).

Where is the 'care' for the alcoholic who was discharged onto the streets from hospital with a note in his pocket which read 'if you drink again you will die'? When they found him dead by Gloucester Cathedral the day after his hospital discharge, in his other pocket was more than £400 back pay in disability allowance.

This man was one of the 81% of homeless people who are addicted to either drugs or drink. Heroin comes top of the league, followed by alcohol (*Crisis, Home and Dry? 2002*).

Unfortunately, his was one of the many funerals I attended in the course of my working life. He was also younger than the average age of

42 years the street homeless can expect to live to (*another Crisis statistic*) and the doctors with whom I work would say that this average age is falling, given the increase in intravenous drug use.

The problem with 'Care in the Community' is that it is done by 'professionals' and we, the community, only get involved when something goes wrong and then we have a witch-hunt to find someone to blame for not caring properly on our behalf. Perhaps only 'Care *by* the Community' can be effective. Care that has each of us taking the moral responsibility which is truly ours, instead of leaving it to others.

This year (2007) I walked from Glasgow to Gloucester, where I now work with the homeless. I did it for two reasons: to raise funds for the homelessness charity I represent and also to raise awareness of street homelessness.

The real tragedy outlined in *Wasteground* is that the characters in the book could be people I have met living on the streets of Glasgow, Gloucester or Leeds. Dennis writes about the "ravages of street life," but he also paints a picture of the story behind the face. And there is always a story behind the face. To me these faces are real because I have met and lived with them in so many places.

Fen, in the book, grew restless when faced with kindness and he reminded me of the many people who have expressed this sentiment in a hundred different ways.

"When people are good to me, I get confused; when they are bad to me, I understand."

Yes, there is indeed a story behind every face. Stories that need to be told and to be listened to.

Dennis's book does just this.

Brian Jones, director of Gloucester Emergency Accommodation Resource (Day Centre and Night Shelter). August, 2007.

prologue

They gather in soulless bus stations, in unfrequented corners of urban parks, in derelict buildings, in forgotten railway sidings, in lonely churchyards, in the alleyways and the underpasses.

They beg, they steal, they forage and some sell copies of the Big Issue.

They live and die on the streets of our cities and towns – day and night, spring, summer, autumn and winter, in all weathers.

Most are alcoholics, many are drug addicts, all are homeless and seemingly without hope.

They scratch a kind of living on the fringes of our society, they are the outcasts, the untouchables.

But they are also human beings with feelings; they were new-born babies once, born pure and innocent, on the threshold of life, with the whole world in their hands.

So what happened, what went wrong, how and why did the likes of The Professor, Midnight Sam, Scots Robby, Lady Jane and Fen end up on the wasteground?

This is their story.

I

THE PROFESSOR yanked apart a length of coarse string around his waist, fumbled inside a voluminous navy blue overcoat and pulled out a two-litre bottle of White Lightning.

The bottle was half-empty and glinted in the firelight. The Professor grunted with relief; he hadn't been certain there was any left. After all, it was gone nine o'clock and several bottles had bit the dust since his first drink some twelve hours ago. But, just to be sure, he bent his head forward, slightly to one side, and scowled.

Rubbing his hands for warmth, The Professor unscrewed the top slowly and deliberately, forehead creased with concentration, and tilted the bottle to his mouth. Eyes closed, he took a long pull at the cider, licked his lips and wiped his mouth carefully with the back of his hand. He shifted his position to a squat, hugging his knees underneath the skirts of the vast, over-sized overcoat which engulfed him.

A quick and vicious breeze laced with a stinging mist of November drizzle swept the wasteground, flattening the flames of the fire and swirling smoke into the faces of the four men. The Professor shivered and his unkempt, straggly grey hair danced in the wind.

"Fuckin' cold," a young man, cocooned in a threadbare sleeping bag opposite The Professor, whined, squirming closer to the fire like a slow snake. He broke into a fit of harsh coughing. He cleared his throat noisily and spat into the fire. The Professor looked up briefly, shook his head and then corrected himself and nodded, the day's build-up of alcohol confusing him. "Do you want a smoke?" he asked, coughing in sympathy with the younger man, who shuffled into life at the offer. The other two men – their flat, expressionless faces flickering in the firelight – rustled.

"Thought you didn't have none. Been smoking mine all fuckin' day. Cost me a fortune." The young Brummie grumbled, but then he always grumbled. The Professor reached into the inside pocket of his overcoat, produced a respectably lengthy dog-end – the remains of a Benson and Hedges – and tossed it across the fire.

"Found it outside the One-Stop Shop when I got the cider. Not bad for a doggie. You're welcome to it. I'm all smoked out. Mouth like a vulture's crutch."

The young man picked up the cigarette reverently and prepared it for use, which included the addition of a small quantity of cannabis resin. When he had reshaped the half-cigarette into a semblance of roundness and flamed the end with an ember from the fire he manoeuvred himself into a sitting position, legs together with his knees pulled up to his chin, still wrapped up in his sleeping bag. His face glowed orange in the firelight, giving him a bizarre (and inappropriate) angelic appearance, despite the surly expression and the grimy, unshaven face. He was 23 years of age but his eyes were old, old and suspicious and dead. They betrayed the ravages of street life and some dark secret. His name was Mark Fenemore, but only he knew that. People called him Fen.

Fen was a recent addition to the group and not an entirely welcome one. He had a bad disposition, a short fuse and a long memory. He

2

bore grudges. None of the group spoke much about their past lives, nobody asked questions, but Fen was particularly secretive and aggressively so. The most innocent of questions would send him into a rage, often a violent rage. And life on the street was difficult enough without courting unnecessary violence. So naturally nobody asked Fen questions, nobody argued with him, in fact nobody spoke to him hardly at all. And, to add to the mystery about the man, he drank very little alcohol. An occasional can of lager, but nothing to match the vast consumption of the others. Cannabis was his thing, but even that was in modest quantities.

Having a virtual non-drinker in their midst was a novelty but it also had its practical uses. When the others were too drunk to stand a cat in hell's chance of getting served at the One-Stop Shop, Fen would begrudgingly oblige. And if one of them were to collapse in a comatose heap, invariably exposed to the elements or at risk of being arrested, then Fen would kick or drag the vulnerable creature out of harm's way.

"Gissa drag, Fen," a slow and gentle voice whispered from the shadows and Midnight Sam edged into the circle of firelight. He pushed out his hands from the flapping sleeves of his donkey jacket towards the flames. The fire was beginning to lose its battle with the rain, which was now falling steadily, petulant and persistent. Nobody bothered much with the fading fire, not even Midnight Sam, who was usually in charge of such things. They all knew that it would fizzle out soon enough and they were too drunk to do anything about it, apart from Fen, who would do nothing about it because he was Fen. Four pairs of eyes stared with a weary inevitability at the sizzling embers and when thick palls of smoke billowed out from the dying embers, stinging their eyes, the men merely inched back to the edge of the circle, coughing and clearing their throats. Fen curled a lip nastily and gave Midnight Sam an unpleasant, sideways glance.

"No fuckin' way," he whined, his Birmingham accent sharp and cutting. He pointedly drew on his joint, exhaling in the direction of the others. A vulgar and challenging gesture. "You never give *us* any fags, you're always on the fuckin' bum. No way."

Midnight pulled a mildly indifferent face and shrugged. He turned over on to his back, hands behind his head, and yawned. His large, watery eyes shone from his smooth, brown face and he smiled that warm and secret smile of his. The rain glistened on his forehead and his donkey jacket fell open, exposing a hopelessly ripped pullover.

The Professor scrambled over to Midnight, a bottle of cider in one hand and a fully-fledged cigarette in the other. He tossed the cigarette on to Midnight's chest.

Scowling at The Professor, Fen muttered: "And where the fuck d'you get that from? All I get's a poxy dogend and that fuckin' 'alf-breed gets a proper fag, It ain't fuckin' right, it ain't. Black bastard," he added as an afterthought.

Ignoring the foul tirade, Midnight Sam inspected the cigarette, placed it gently into the middle of his mouth, wormed his way back to the fire and stretched his head towards a glowing ember. He frowned as the heat stung his forehead but he managed to get the cigarette going.

"Thanks Prof," he said, patting the older man on the shoulder. "You're a real gent, you are, a real gent."

The fourth man, who had been squatting several feet away from the others, suddenly sprang to his feet and pulled the hood of his three-quarter-length anorak over his head. A lock of ink-black, curly hair question-marked down the centre of his forehead to the bridge of his nose. He tilted a bottle of cider to his lips. His small, hazel eyes, set too close together, flicked over his companions and rested on the fire. Scots Robby hugged himself ostentatiously for warmth and blew hard into his cupped hands. His breath steamed silver in the cold night air.

He stamped his feet and picked up a draw-string army kitbag, heavily stained, soaking wet and bulging.

"This fuckin' weather has set in for the night – it's not going to let up now." He gazed into the cascading rain, his strong Scottish accent lending the words authority. "There's no way we're going to keep this fire going and my kitbag's getting fuckin' soaked." He clasped the bag protectively underneath his left arm and stood to attention. Rivulets of rain dripped from the torn, imitation fur lining of the anorak hood on to his nose and trickled down into his neat, black moustache.

"I don't know about you three, but I'm going to give the night shelter a go," he said brusquely, accusingly, but with veiled invitation in his voice. Scots Robby stood with his legs apart and waited for the others to get up. But nobody did, although The Professor scratched his small and wayward beard thoughtfully and looked up at the Scotsman.

"I think we're too late for the night shelter, Robby," he ventured. "Supposed to clock in by eight-thirty and it's gone nine already. You know how strict Welshie is and the place is bound to be full by now anyway. Best bet, I reckon, is the bus station. If we get moved on, then there's always the underpass. At least it'll be dry. Might even get a fire going, eh Sam."

Scots Robby smoothed his moustache and pursed his lips as if he were considering some complex metaphysical problem. He frowned, shook his head, turned sharply on his heels and marched off into the gloom, hitching the army kitbag over his shoulder: "I'm going to give the night shelter a go."

The others watched his disappearing back without comment. After about half an hour, they got up and fussed with an assortment of bags which had been strewn around the fire. When they had gathered their belongings, which included three depleted bottles of cider, they scattered the remains of the fire with their feet (out of habit as it hardly posed a danger) and shambled off in the direction of town, a faint glow a mile-and-a-half distant.

"Scotch prat, thinks he knows it all," snarled Fen, leading the trio across the wasteground. Long, troubled, lurching strides, hooded head sunk into narrow, hunched shoulders. His holdall bumped across the ground as he picked his way through the flotsam and jetsam, but he didn't seem to notice or to care.

The Professor and Midnight Sam walked comfortably together, if unsteadily, some way behind, sidestepping the large, glistening puddles of rainwater which were forming. Fen, on the other hand, splashed his way through, sometimes kicking at the water. The Professor tilted a bottle to his lips and drained the contents, tossing the empty container on to the ground. Midnight gave his friend a lopsided grin, eyes sparkling, and produced another bottle of White Lightning with a flourish. He offered it to The Professor, who shook his head and lifted the skirts of his overcoat to avoid the mud.

When they reached the road, Fen had already crossed to the other side where a narrow pavement wound towards the city lights. He was walking quickly ahead of the other two. He glanced over his shoulder with a quick jerk, said nothing and carried on, but a fraction slower.

The Professor stopped several times on their way into town to get his breath back. He would stand for a while, head bowed, hands pressed on to his hips, gasping deep and hurting breaths. He would stare intently at the pavement, fighting to slow down his breathing and regain his strength. The constant ache across his stomach was making itself felt again – sharp and deep pulses of frightening pain. He would wince and rub his stomach cautiously, experimentally. Midnight Sam, not knowing what else to do, would proffer his bottle of cider, genuine if drunken concern written on his face. The Professor would shake his head, steady himself with a hand on his friend's shoulder and set off again. Although a good fifty yards ahead by this time, Fen would instinctively pick up on the hiatus and slow down again.

When they got to the town – when cold street-lights illuminated the rain-black asphalt and affluent shop windows were pearled bright but unwelcoming – the trio at first became subdued and nervous. Suddenly there were people – albeit huddled and welded to their umbrellas – but people all the same. They were leaving the safety of their world – dark and despairing though it was – for an alien world, a world above the wasteground, a world which no longer belonged to them.

Fen allowed the other two to catch up and they walked into town together, pretending to be drunker than they really were. It was better that way; it was their defence mechanism. It alienated them from the rest, afforded them space, distanced them from so-called 'respectable' folk. Most people try to ignore drunks and this group of street-drinkers were well aware of that. So they began to make slightly more noise than they normally would, sufficient noise to encourage the public to leave them alone, but not enough to attract the attention of the police. It was a fine balance, but they were experienced at striking it.

Fen, hunched and irritable, kept two or three paces ahead and kicked a beer can until it clattered out of reach. Every so often he would stop, turn around, survey the other two with mild contempt, cough and spit into the gutter, before carrying on. Midnight watched him with a sad expression on his face; he tried, unsuccessfully, to engage the young man in conversation and thrust his big hands deep into the pockets of his donkey jacket. The Professor brought up the rear, quickening his pace doggedly now that the bus station was a mere quarter of a mile away. His breathing was rasping and his shoulders were slumped, but determination gleamed in his bloodshot, once china-blue eyes. Determination to get dry, to get out of the rain.

A police patrol car slowed as it passed them. The two officers inside looked over at the trio, registered recognition – one even nodded a cursory greeting – before the vehicle accelerated away. Fen scowled at the disappearing rear lights but Midnight Sam raised an arm in friendly acknowledgement. He was a kindly man to all the world and ever keen to show it. Mostly this paid dividends. His infectious kindness would invariably be reciprocated; people would smile back in return. But there were those, albeit a few, who did not like Midnight Sam. They feared and disliked him. They disliked him because he was kind and they were not, and they feared him because they did not understand kindness. They were restless in the presence of kindness. Such a man was Fen.

They heard Scots Robby long before they saw him. His loud and challenging voice, Scottish accent even more pronounced in anger, boomed out from the depths of the bus station just around the corner. Other voices could be heard, measured and patient voices, and then the sound of breaking glass.

The police car which had passed them earlier was parked at the taxi rank which ran parallel and behind the bus station. The two officers were standing at the head of one of the bays and Scots Robby was perched precariously on a bench, waving a broken bottle of whisky above his head. The front of his jacket was stained with the spilled contents and a two-inch, horizontal gash decorated his forehead. A trickle of blood ran down the side of his nose and into his moustache.

"If I want a fucking drink, I'll have a fucking drink and you fucking Sassenach bastards are no going to stop me," Scots ranted, pointing the jagged, broken base of the whisky bottle at the two patient policemen and swaying dangerously. "And I'm not fucking drunk," he added as an afterthought, his voice descending to a growl.

"Come on Robby, calm yourself down," one of the policemen raised placating hands. "Calm down, there's a good chap. Give me that bottle and come on down. And mind your language."

Scots Robby frowned, more at himself than at the police officer; he was primed for confrontation and not for reason. He needed something or somebody to hit out at, to react to, to kick off at, and he wasn't getting the feed from this understanding policeman. And he was extremely drunk, the whisky having had an interesting reaction with the cider. Nevertheless he stood (or rather swayed) his ground, but he suddenly lost interest in the broken bottle. He let it fall on to the bench, where it broke again. Very sensibly, the police officers said nothing. They simply waited for the Scotsman to run out of steam, which he did rapidly, mumbling incoherently and gesticulating without much enthusiasm.

Midnight Sam strolled easily, if a shade unsteadily, up to the bewildered Scotsman, raised an apologetic eyebrow to the policemen and beckoned his friend to step down. The Professor provided sort-of back-up by shuffling closer, but Fen was nowhere to be seen. It was not that he was scared, he simply hated the police. At first glimpse of the parked patrol car he had bolted, probably to the underpass, but you never knew with Fen: he could be gone for days, even weeks. And he could be anywhere. He would reappear eventually, surlier than ever, with no explanation and the others knew better than to ask.

Scots Robby faded fast and sank into a heap on the bench, his mouth working but no intelligible sounds resulting. Midnight sat down besides him and put an arm around his shoulder. The Scotsman wriggled feebly – he didn't like being touched – but he gave up the struggle and fell asleep.

"You're going to have to get him home," one of the officers said, inwardly kicking himself for using the word 'home' – an alien concept for such people. "We're going to have to take him in if you don't get him out of here and we just don't need the hassle tonight. We go off duty in half an hour. Get him out of the bus station and don't bring him back and we'll be on our way. Okay?"

The Professor came quietly to the rescue, not engaging with the police officers but somehow taking control of the situation without uttering a word. He sat down on the other side of Scots, nodded to Midnight and together they hefted the dead-weight man to his feet. Midnight gathered up the army kitbag, which had fallen to the ground, and tightened the draw string. The Scotsman's eyes half-opened and he registered consciousness with a protracted baritone belch. He moaned and complained but allowed the other two to support him as they zig-zagged from the bus station. Relieved (they wanted to go home to their wives) the two policemen followed the struggling trio back towards the taxi rank and returned to their patrol car. With inadvertent tact, Scots waited until the patrol car had vanished around a corner before he vomited copiously and colourfully on to the pavement. Feeling at once better he sloughed off the supporting arms of Midnight and The Prof and marched forward with an exaggerated military gait.

"I was in the fucking army, you know … forward, fucking march, left-right, left-right," he announced, swinging his arms and swivelling his head in mock eyes-right. The other two watched him blankly and followed, waiting for him to slow down, which they knew he would. They also knew he had been in the army; he had told them often enough.

The three street-drinkers hugged the shop window side of the pavements, where it was fractionally drier, as they made their way across town, their destination the underpass. The Cathedral loomed with sombre beauty. The intricate masonry, with its myriad statuettes and carvings, mighty windows and soaring square tower, glowed golden from the array of ground-based arc lights which surrounded the building. Glowing with indestructible grandeur, aloof and forbidding, severe and disapproving, the Cathedral rose from the clutter of shops, roads, pavements, alleyways and multi-storey car parks – a miserable mess of plastic, concrete, steel and glass.

When they reached the *via sacra* and took the path through the Cathedral gardens, The Professor stopped briefly, not to get his breath this time but to look up. He put his hands on his hips, screwed his face against the rain and gazed at the Cathedral tower, a small smile on his face. Things had been so different then, he thought without rancour. The time for bitterness – and by God he had been bitter – had long gone. Now he only had time for survival and he was barely managing that. He turned away from the House of God and trudged along after the other two. Midnight instinctively allowed The Professor his private moment (although not having the faintest idea what it was about) but Scots Robby was oblivious to anything else apart from the lure of the underpass, where at least the rain could not get to him. Midnight Sam slowed until The Prof caught up, wheezing with the effort, while the Scotsman lurched ahead.

On the other side of the Cathedral the town petered out to a typical inner city sprawl. Gloomy blocks of housing association flats, a sheltered accommodation development of apartments, depressing rows of 1930s terraced houses and a poorly-lit car park bordering the northern by-pass. An articulated lorry, spray fanning from its wheels, thundered by, while a double-decker bus, almost empty, groaned along in the opposite direction. A lone cyclist in luminous yellow waterproofs struggled down the cycle path, red rear light flashing bleakly. A sporadic stream of cars, windscreen-wipers working overtime, roared passed, just catching the gutter puddles, much to the fury of Scots Robby, who resolutely remained on the edge of the pavement, waiting for a chance to cross the road.

The Professor and Midnight Sam, on the other hand, sensibly stood well back.

"Fuck off!" Scots yelled at each offending vehicle and stood his ground, far too proud and obdurate to retreat to safety. "You did that on fucking purpose, you bastards." He gave two-finger and one-finger salutes with tremendous feeling, but the passing cars continued to splash him, without malice but with great success. Finally the three men found a gap in the traffic and scuttled across the road, their coats flapping. Scots Robby subjected a motorist who dared to sound his horn to a torrent of abuse and The Professor held on to a street lamppost while he recovered from the spurt of energy.

Ironically the rain eased to an intermittent drizzle by the time they reached the underpass. One large puddle, in the middle of which lay a Tesco shopping trolley, barred the entrance. Without comment, they tugged off their shoes and socks and waded through the cold, black water, holding their belongings at waist height. Midnight Sam righted the trolley and pushed it out of the puddle. Others had been there not so long ago. The charred remains of a fire were banked against the base of the curved inner concrete wall of the underpass. Two empty plastic flagons of GL cider lay on their sides, crushed, and dozens of tiny, twisted dog-ends were scattered around like maggots.

Scots Robby, sobering up, removed his wet anorak and draped it, along with his evil-smelling socks, over the shopping trolley. He touched the gash on his forehead lightly and inspected his fingers. It was only a superficial wound and had stopped bleeding. He rummaged inside his kitbag and extracted a greasy grey blanket and a well-worn black, roll-neck pullover, which he struggled into before sinking down against the wall in the foetal position. He pulled the blanket around his body and over his head until it covered him completely and almost immediately fell into a noisy sleep. Scots not only snored and bubbled when he slept, but he mumbled and cursed, often convulsing with rage at some great indignity he imagined had been done to him.

Midnight Sam sifted through the dead embers and pushed them into a pile, making a little hole in the middle. He pulled a plastic bag from his holdall and extracted a bundle of neatly-sawn kindling wood (obtained from a hardware store, unbeknown to the staff, earlier that day). He collected the scattered but dry pages of several discarded newspapers, bunched them into tight balls and built a small fire which took very quickly. Midnight Sam could get a fire going anywhere.

Midnight and The Prof pushed the shopping trolley, festooned with its dreary array of dripping clothes, close to the fire. They crawled into their sleeping bags and curled up close together for extra warmth. Midnight was asleep in seconds, that familiar half-smile on his unblemished, handsome face. But The Professor turned over on to his back, hands clasped behind his head and stared up at the low, vaulted ceiling. The ache in his stomach was steady and he concentrated on the pain – a little game of his – to try to make it go away. He looked across at the fire, fierce and cheerful. Hopefully he would be able to get to sleep before it went out.

By the morning the rain had stopped, but grey clouds scudded across the sky and a gusty wind had whipped up from the north-east. Scots Robby had gone but Midnight Sam was sleeping like a baby. The clothes on the shopping trolley were dry apart from Midnight's donkey jacket which had fallen off and somehow ended up in the large puddle, some two or three yards away. The Professor climbed out of his sleeping bag, rubbed his eyes with the backs of his balled fists, retrieved Midnight's donkey jacket from the puddle and draped it back over the trolley, careful to keep it apart from the dry clothes. He pursed his lips and stroked his chin: Scots Robby was quite capable of such motiveless spite.

The Professor donned a dark green pullover which had a hole in the left sleeve exposing the elbow and his overcoat and wrapped the string twice around his slender waist. He dug deep into one of the pockets and brought out a squashed packet of Benson and Hedges. He took out two cigarettes, which left him four, and laid them on the ground next to Midnight Sam. Without waking his friend The Professor left the underpass, sidestepping the puddle which had shrunk during the night.

Rush-hour traffic growled by, nose to tail, stop-starting towards the city centre. Businessmen tapping irritable tattooes on steering wheels or mouthing conspiratorially into mobile phones. Mothers in gleaming people carriers takingtheir children to school – normally one child per vehicle – and diesel panel vans screaming with pointless bursts of speed. Buses seething with unsmiling commuters. An occasional articulated lorry, lit up like a Christmas tree, juddered through the jam. The Professor threaded his way across the grid-locked bypass, earning a couple of car horn blasts for daring to touch the bonnets of vehicles – touching them to steady himself and only touching them gently at that. He would raise both hands in an apology but the motorists would never smile back at him. It was rush-hour, but The Professor was in no hurry.

He headed for the Post Office. It was Thursday, around ten o'clock he guessed, and he was going to pick up his weekly Incapacity Benefit. Situated in one of the only tree-lined streets in the centre of town, the 1920s, austere building had miraculously escaped the redevelopment architectural vandalism of the 1960s and although ugly boasted a comforting permanence.

"Hi Prof," a young man, swaddled in drab and damp clothes, with a placid mongrel dog curled beside him on the pavement, looked up from a small pile of Big Issues and grinned. "How you doing"? The Professor crouched down with difficulty and stroked the dog.

"Bloody foul night," he said and immediately broke into a paroxism of coughing, It was the first time he had opened his mouth to speak that day. After several seconds he continued: "I got soaked to the skin. Missed the night shelter and Scots Robby got us kicked out of the bus station."

"Where d'you end up?"

"The underpass. Sam got a fire going. Wasn't too bad. You haven't seen Fen, have you Paddy?"

"Not if I can help it," said the young Irishman, frowning.

The Professor straightened and stepped into the Post Office, cautious and self-conscious. There was quite a queue which he joined without making eye contact with anybody else, a rare feat in a crowded room, but street-drinkers were well-versed in the art. After around 15 minutes it was his turn and he gave a sigh of relief as the automated, sugary voice announced that he should go to "cashier number four please." Cashier number four was a bright and bubbly girl in her late teens who had a smile and a kind word for everybody, especially The Professor. He collected his £53 and counted the money carefully. He bought a first-class stamp before leaving the counter with a nod and a wave to the cashier.

Once outside the Post Office The Prof steeled himself for what he knew would be a mildly humiliating experience. It always was. He knew he should be used to it by now but it still niggled him. Going into a shop like WH Smiths in East Street for 'the likes of him' invariably involved weathering a forest of disapproving eyes, ignoring the close attention of store detectives, the thinly-veiled disgust of the shop assistants and the overt disdain of other shoppers. But it had to be done. Once a year in mid-November it simply had to be done. Keeping his head down and his hands thrust deep into his pockets, he made his way to the birthday cards section. A store detective, who had latched on to him the moment he had walked through the doors, pretended to be looking at greetings cards at the end of the same stand.

The Professor chose a card, borrowed a biro at the till and started to write. He noticed that his hands were shaking. Was it the cold, was it the damp, or was it a hangover? Probably all three.

He wrote in a laboured, thin and spidery script: 'All my love as always. Be happy, my little girl. Dad.'

2

MIDNIGHT Sam was born in a private hospital in Bristol on October 4, 1974. He was a bonny baby, weighing in at 8lbs 6ozs, with a little fuzz of black hair and big brown eyes. A contented child from day one, he hardly ever cried. The mid-wife commented that he was one of the easiest babies she had delivered and the doctor, who kept tabs on Samuel for the first few months of his life, marvelled at how calm and well-adjusted the boy was. He woke for his feeds as regular as clockwork with little more than a mild whimper and invariably settled back down again after he was replete to an unflustered sleep. He was indeed a contented child, which was ironic, since the circumstances of his conception and entry into the world were far from conventional.

In January, 1973, Jennifer Crawley, bitter and weakened by an acrimonious divorce, fled cold and depressing England for a two-week holiday in The Gambia. She had read about the tiny West African country, which was just beginning to open up to tourists, in one of the Sunday newspapers. Off the beaten track; a million miles from her sadness and perceived failure; hot, basic, remote and perhaps romantic. She desperately needed to get away after a lonely and unhappy Christmas, made all the lonelier by friends and family determined to 'include' her. Their well-meaning kindness had only reinforced the fact that she was on her own.

The ten-year marriage had produced no children – Jonathan's biological failing and not hers – and, at 29, she felt so confused, hurt, worthless and lonely that it physically hurt. She would awake in the middle of the night, automatically stretch her arm to where her husband used to be, momentarily forgetting that he was not there anymore. She cried herself to sleep many times only to wake up in the morning, nailed to the bed with a cold and black despair. Jennifer contemplated suicide a number of times, normally after Jonathan had telephoned to say he was "so sorry" but also to confess how he had finally found true happiness with whatever her name was. And of course he hoped that she too would also find true happiness one day.

Jennifer switched onto auto-pilot and went through the motions of living. And it was working – she was beginning to feel more settled, less bleak, less aching, less suicidal – until Christmas reared its 'happy families' head. The jollity was too much for her to bear. It made her want to scream.

So, with a healthy bank balance and a mortgage-free house – the result of a generous divorce settlement – she headed for Thomas Cooks in the High Street and booked a fortnight's full-board at the recently-opened Atlantic Hotel in Banjul. With "you deserve it, you go and enjoy yourself" platitudes ringing in her ears; the sympathetic, firm hand of a friend gripping her arm; the sorrowful shake of the head; and the "you're so brave" remarks making her want to punch someone, Jennifer Crawley fastened her seat belt and counted the seconds before the aeroplane swept off the runway at Heathrow Airport and headed south to the sun.

The Gambia was everything she had hoped it would be. Basic apart from the hotel which was luxurious (thank God, she had to admit), very African and of course very hot. From the moment she collected her room keys from reception and followed the porter in his fetching red fez she felt the mantle of misery which had weighed her down for so many months lifting from her shoulders. Bristling with excitement she set about rearranging the room, making home. And then she threw open the windows which overlooked the swimming pool and the palm-fringed beach beyond, stepped out onto the balcony, took a deep breath, closed her eyes and absorbed the sheer, delicious foreignness of it all.

England, winter, guilt-ridden but gone Jonathan, sympathy and that big, empty house in Congresbury, ten miles south of Bristol, suddenly seemed very distant, very small. But this was here and now and so was she. She rang room service and, after a bit of confusion, successfully ordered a large gin and tonic.

Jennifer pampered herself: she changed into a pure silk dressing-gown which Jonathan had bought her the previous year while on a 'business trip' to Thailand (actually he had taken his new love there). She stood on the balcony and leaned against the wall to enjoy her drink. The shadow of the hotel crept across the swimming pool, now empty apart from one overweight, elderly lady who was halfway through her regulation ten lengths a day. Beyond the hotel grounds the sea was flat, pearly and translucent. It was a magical moment and she savoured it. So much so that she ordered another gin and tonic and settled down to watch the sunset sink swiftly into night. Suddenly the sky was black with a hazy moon sitting just above the horizon – hazy from the high clouds of sand constantly wind-borne from the distant deserts of Mali and Algeria to the east. A warm breeze – or was it the gin? – softened her cheeks. For the first time since Jonathan had walked out on her almost a year ago Jennifer felt happy. And a flutter of excitement too.

She carried this happiness around with her for the next couple of days while she built up her confidence to venture outside the confines of the hotel grounds – a gilded cage, but a cage nonetheless. When she mentioned her desire to explore Banjul on her own to the hotel-based Thomas Cooks agent – a loud, flashy man in his mid-forties – she was treated to an exaggerated and condescending frown.

"Not at all advisable, madam, at least not on your own," he shook his head and handed her a brochure. "Excursions every day, organised coach and boat trips, experienced tour guides. That's the way to do it, madam." He pronounced the word 'madam' as if she hardly deserved the title. "Certainly not on your own, especially not a woman, not in The Gambia."

The agent sat back in his chair, beaming a false smile, and shuffled a pile of papers on his desk. "Surely they told you that when you booked the holiday in the UK?" he asked, an accusing tone in his voice. But Jennifer stood her ground and persisted until she was given begrudging directions and an 'on your own head be it' warning from the hotel rep.

But as soon as she had skipped confidently down the grand, marble steps, crossed the sweeping driveway and turned sharp left out of the bougainvillea-bedecked entrance gates onto a dusty track, her heart sank. She was immediately assailed by a group of children from one side of the road and by three determined-looking young men, who trotted towards her from the other side. One of them grabbed her arm, not too gently, and told her that he was her guide. The other two men shouted angrily and pushed the man away. They then turned on Jennifer and told her that they were to be her guides and the first man was a thief and a rapist. They positioned themselves either side of her, hands on her elbows, and virtually frogmarched her along the track. Meanwhile the group of children pranced about in front of her, skipping backwards and demanding money. Two mangy mongrel dogs, tails low and ears flat to their heads, bared their teeth at the rare sight and odour of a white woman. They began to growl and crab their way cautiously but unerringly towards Jennifer. One of the men holding onto Jennifer's elbow bent down and picked up a large stone with his free hand. He feigned to throw it at the dogs. They backed off reluctantly, snarling, hackles raised, before flopping down in the hot dust with sudden boredom.

"No thank you, I'm quite all right," she said and wriggled her elbows free. "I don't need a guide, thank you very much." But the impoverished citizens of Banjul were not to be rejected as easily as that. A comparatively fabulously rich, lone Englishwoman, wearing a watch worth more money than they could hope to earn in a year, was not going to escape their clutches without a fight. And fight they did – alternatively smiling and glowering, sweet-talking or threatening, shouting or whispering – all the way passed the run-down soccer stadium and the State House. They finally got the message and sauntered away when Albert Market thankfully came into sight.

Jennifer, whose previous travel experiences were confined to the South of France, the Swiss Alps and the Italian Riviera (and even then always with Jonathan in the driving seat), was proud of herself. Amazed, more likely. For although not a timid person, she had led a fairly sheltered, predictable, middleclass life. Holidays were about sunbathing, browsing around souvenir shops, dining out in style and embarking upon the occasional sleekly organised but lifeless excursion. They were not about dodging rabid dogs, fending off the unwanted attentions of aggressive, six-foot-tall Africans and sidestepping dozens of demanding, equally aggressive, street urchins. And they were most definitely not about being the only white woman to be carried along on a seething roller-coaster of black humanity amidst the crazy clutter of Banjul's colourful market.

But this holiday was always going to be different and the ever-present edge of uncertainty was beginning to excite her. She owed a lot to that smug travel agent in the yellow Calypso shirt, no-doubt still sitting pompously behind his tidy desk in the Atlantic Hotel. She might well have turned back the instant she left the safety of the hotel grounds, had it not been for the inevitable smirk the irritating man would doubtless have subjected her to upon her hurried return.

Albert Market was the first of many adventures for Jennifer in The Gambia and her confidence grew daily. After the initial euphoria of staying at a swanky hotel on the edge of a palm-fringed African coast under a tropical sun had worn off, the Atlantic became a tiresome trap to her. It merely reinforced the fact that she was alone. There were couples, families and children everywhere. Shared dining tables, husbands and wives, boyfriends and girlfriends, self-conscious illicit lovers, groups of girls, groups of men, an ageing gay couple and three middle-aged, rather stern women reluctantly having a good time. No, the hotel made her feel lonely, but Banjul and The Gambia did not.

Jennifer ventured further afield and soon discovered that the 'sights' referred to by that annoying Thomas Cook agent were easily (and far more cheaply) accessed by going it alone. So, just four days after she arrived in the country, she found herself bouncing about in the back seat of a battered old Peugeot estate car, driven by an off-duty policeman who had propositioned her with a day trip to Lamin Lodge, moments after scolding other beach-bum touts for trying to do exactly the same thing!

The arrangements for the trip were deliciously clandestine and involved meeting up with the officer (who'd borrowed a 'brother's' car for the day) underneath a distinctive palm tree three hundred yards down the beach. She was under strict orders to get into the unlocked and empty vehicle and wait for her unofficial guide to arrive, which he did several minutes later. Timing appeared to be of the utmost importance and she entered into the cloak-and-dagger subterfuge with glee.

The drive south, through the dusty market town of Serrakunda and out onto the flat, burnt-brown countryside, was an eye-opener for Jennifer. Straw huts, mud huts, unmade, rutted roads; rag-arsed toddlers racing after the car and waving frantically; slow and sleepy oxen wearily drawing carts laden with coconuts or melons or pineapples or bananas. An old man with a crooked stick taller than he, stopped to watch the passing car and raised an arm in a solemn, not entirely approving salute.

Lamin Lodge was about three kilometres east of Lamin village, a bizarre restaurant and guest house built entirely of wood, on stilts and overlooking a vast and inviting mangrove creek. The owner – a hunchbacked Indian in his mid-sixties with serious attitude – indicated a creaky seat and took their order. Beer for Jennifer and a coke for the policeman-cum-guide. Jennifer paid, naturally. She sipped her beer, which was warm but she didn't mind, and shaded her eyes to look out over the creek, green tongues of mangrove snaking across the still, sparkling water. Below, next to the stilts, was a dodgy jetty and moored to the uncertain wooden construction were three dug-out canoes. Four half-naked young men were sprawled in the shade of a vast baobab tree on the bank nearby, sound asleep.

"Will they take me for a trip?" Jennifer asked the policeman. He nodded, shrugged his shoulders, tipped the bottle of Coke to his lips and drained the contents in one long, gurgling draught. He leaned over the rickety wooden walls of the lodge and harangued the sleeping men in Mandinka. One of the four men pushed himself up onto an arm and squinted at the lodge, trying to work out where all the shouting was coming from. He saw the policeman, yawned and replied sleepily. The other three stirred, opened their eyes briefly and promptly went back to sleep. A deal of sorts had been struck.

The policeman took charge, flashing his identity card and bristling with self-importance. Jennifer squatted in the prow of the crude, narrow craft, the policeman sat upright and 'in charge' in the middle and the young boatsman, with an unusual-smelling, home-made cigarette dangling from the corner of his mouth, was fluid at the stern, spearing his wide-bladed paddle into the water. They crossed the creek in fifteen minutes and slid into the world of the mangroves, which grew thick and tall and silent, a dark and dusty green which hid the sun. A myriad tantalising channels twisted this way and that - a watery maze, a wonderland - and Jennifer was in heaven. It was pure African Queen. She dragged a hand in the cool water, dabbed her forehead and hugged herself with sheer pleasure. The policeman frowned, but the boatman beamed.

Jennifer evaluated her situation: here she was squatting in a dugout canoe with two complete strangers, one moonlighting policeman and one half-naked, and she had to admit, rather dishy African oarsman; she was gliding enigmatically through an uncharted mangrove swamp in Darkest Africa, alone and, to her growing amazement, quite unafraid.

It was a magical day, a life-changing day (or so she felt at the time) and when she got back to the Atlantic Hotel, having missed dinner, her heart was full and the emptiness of that long, bitter, post-divorce year a mere memory, a thing of the past. Lamin Lodge, she decided over a gin and tonic on her hotel room balcony later that evening, was a turning point in her life.

The next morning Jennifer breakfasted early, ordered a taxi to the Barra ferry terminal, south of Banjul on the banks of the River

Gambia, and embarked on her next adventure. The Thomas Cook agent was inconsolable: for some reason he had taken it upon himself to bring this wayward young woman into line, to save her from herself. He warned her, hinting strongly that her travel insurance would not cover such foolishness, that she caught the "notorious" Barra ferry at her own risk. "That old rust bucket is just waiting to sink," he said, this time with a degree of truth in his voice. Mister Wet Blanket (as she had privately dubbed him) only succeeded in fuelling Jennifer's determination to give it a go.

But when the taxi-driver dropped her off at the terminal, giving her a disbelieving and bewildered look, she had immediate misgivings. She had barely taken a step away from the taxi when she found herself surrounded. Two men - typical Gambian spivs - swaggered up to her and offered their services as guides once they got to the other side. They tried to physically drag her to the ferry terminal waiting room. Jennifer reacted instinctively. She wrenched her arm free with a ferocity which surprised her, shouted "no" in a voice which surprised her even more and marched imperiously into the waiting room alone. She joined around three hundred people, all locals, a number of sheep, goats, chickens and one unhappy, long-horned cow, who bellowed mournfully and occasionally defecated on the stone floor. Nobody seemed to mind, so Jennifer chose not to mind either. She stood shoulder-to-shoulder in the stifling, airless room and waited, although she was not entirely sure what she was waiting for.

Suddenly the doors were hurled open and the passengers, along with their livestock, surged forward, shouting and waving their arms about. Jennifer was literally carried along by the human tide and saw no reason to object.

The Barra ferry was in a class of its own and for once Jennifer had to concede that Mister Wet Blanket at the hotel had understated the situation. The boat was the literal definition of a rust-bucket. Covered in orange-coloured flakes of rust which came away at a touch, the ageing tub was falling apart in all directions. Sagging beneath a staggering overload of vehicles, produce, animals and people, it groaned agonisingly into the river, listing heavily to starboard. Strange and ominous noises filtered up from the engine room and the boat demonstrated a semi-circle in the wrong direction before heading vaguely out towards the town of Barra on the north side of the river.

Jennifer spent the one-hour journey politely but firmly resisting the determined advances of a tall, far-too-tactile Sudanese man in a white turban and a not-too-clean jellabiyya. He said he was a university student (unlikely at the approximate age of forty) and that he wanted to practise his English (again unlikely as he spoke in the region of ten words of the language). But, as Jennifer was to discover, he had his uses.

Barra, the port town on the north side of the river, was a bedlam of confusion and noise. It made no sense whatsoever. Her plan was to explore the town, the river, the villages where natives were seized by European and American slave-traders in the 19th century, but where on earth was she going to start? Suddenly the allure of the swimming pool at the civilised Atlantic Hotel with its safe and sugary luxury was pretty powerful. But she could not have turned back had she wanted to. She found herself squashed and pushed down the iron gang-plank and out onto the concrete jetty, which itself had seen better days. And all the while her Sudanese admirer was there, too close for comfort, steering her through the crowds. Steering involved a long, thin hand drifting down to her bottom or resting on her upper body, perilously close to her breasts.

A small herd of goats, rubbing against Jennifer's thighs, mingled happily with the crowds, and she nearly got run over by a dilapidated lorry, festooned with colourful motifs, which inched passed her. Bulging sacks of groundnuts on the back of the lorry miraculously stayed in place. Her self-styled guide was thankfully now in front, weaving a useful pathway through the thick wedge of people, a pathway which Jennifer followed gratefully.

When the crowds fanned out through the dock gates, scurrying in all directions, the pressure eased and Jennifer tapped the Sudanese man on his shoulder: "Thank you, thank you very much but I'll be fine now." She nodded encouragement for him to go away, but he was not to be dismissed that easily.

"You want hotel?" he asked gravely and picked his nose, without embarrassment and without hurry. Jennifer was on the point of refusing, politely of course, but she surveyed the criss-cross of sandy streets, mud, concrete and corrugated iron huts and stalls, the total lack of order, the dust, the noise and the heat and she changed her mind.

"Why yes, thank you," she smiled.

When they reached the concrete steps to the ambitiously named Paris Hilton, Jennifer turned, took several bank-notes from her purse and held them out, standing her ground. For some obscure reason, Jennifer's self-styled Sudanese guide galvanised into a quick fury. There followed an unintelligible tirade in Arabic, before he snatched the money. He folded the bank-notes, thrust them somewhere into the folds of his jellabiyya, tossed back his turbaned head and was gone, absorbed into the mellifluous ebb and flow of the streets as if he had never existed.

Puzzled, Jennifer smoothed the sides of her dress, rumpled from the mayhem, adjusted her sun-glasses, hoisted her handbag over a bare shoulder and strode into the dingy hotel with more confidence than she felt. The reception area was deserted. To the right was a small and drab and empty dining room but to the left was a surprisingly pleasant, if cluttered, bar. Faded sepia photographs of Paris – the Eiffel Tower, Sacre Couer, Versailles, the Arc de Triumphe, Place de la Concorde and romantic night cruise boat scenes on the Seine - vied with optimistic oil paintings of Banjul. Several tatty mock-Chesterfield sofas were scattered around.

At a long, ornately-carved wooden bar, on an equally ornate wooden stool, sat an African in his early twenties. He was engrossed in deep conversation with the barman, an old man with an almost right-angled hunchback and an involuntary twitch which kept his lower jaw ever busy.

Midnight Sam's father-to-be turned his head slightly to one side as Jennifer walked into the room. He saw her out of the corner of one eye but carried on talking to the barman.

Jennifer sat down in the middle of one of the sofas and fanned herself with a large, dog-eared menu which lay on the huge and heavy coffee table in front of her. An overhead ceiling fan creaked and wobbled ineffectively. It appeared to be on the point of working its way free from the ceiling and plunging onto Jennifer's head. She savoured the whackiness of it all and looked at her reflection in a six-foot square mirror set in an elaborate, carved wooden frame – ebony she supposed – which hung on the wall opposite. The glass was smeared with past accidents and coated with recent dust and a pronounced crack zig-zagged from the top, left-hand corner to the bottom, right-hand corner. A pair of almond-shaped, wide-set, grey-blue eyes – large eyes – looked back at her. Not bad, she thought, raising her eyebrows at her reflection and squirming cat-like, despite herself, into the lumpy but comfortable sofa.

The hunchbacked barman materialised beside her, a battered tray hanging from his left hand, by his side. He inclined his head and widened his watery eyes in silent inquiry.

"Coca-cola, please," she smiled up at the old man. "Oh, and have you got any peanuts?"

The barman nodded and shuffled back to the bar, the tray tapping against his leg. Jennifer noticed that he walked with a limp.

"That is one thing we have plenty of," the young African on the bar stool called across, laughter in his voice. He swivelled on the bar stool to face her, a bottle of beer in one hand and a cigarette in the other. His face was kind and full of humour, his skin as shiny and smooth as plastic, eyes big and brown and steady, lips thin and a full Negroid nose. He wore a red and black checked shirt and a pair of faded, blue jeans. The collar and cuffs of his shirt were frayed and his left knee poked through a hole in the jeans. He was barefooted.

"Groundnuts – Gambia's national agricultural identity, our biggest and one of our only exports," he said. He took a small sip of his beer – a rather elegant and prim action – and slid, equally elegantly from the bar stool and strolled over to where Jennifer was sitting. He settled easily into the sofa opposite, placed the bottle gently on the coffee table and smiled across at the Englishwoman. He stubbed out his cigarette in a battered, tin ashtray: "I hope you don't mind me joining you. Honourable intentions, I assure you, madam. I would just like to talk, practise my English a modicum. No advances, I give you my word." Jennifer smiled back, smiled at his quaint English, and he went on: "You are, dare I say, a rare sight in Barra. An Englishwoman on her own and …," he paused and gestured around the bar expressively, "enjoying a drink in the magnificent Paris Hilton."

Jennifer suppressed a giggle and waited for him to continue.

****

His name was Sadou Midaka. He was a Mandinka, with a touch of Fula and an ancestral thread back to the Serahuli of Mali. At the age of 22 he could speak and write English, French and three African

29

languages – all fluently. He was self-taught, having spent countless hours poring over various books in Banjul's sad and depleted library and, with mixed success, cajoling tourists into sending him literature when they got home. He lived in a one-storey, concrete hut midst the rabbit-warren shanty town suburbs which housed the vast majority of Barra's population. He shared the three-roomed home with two elder brothers, an arthritic grandmother who ruled with a rod of iron, and a sick cousin.

The three men scratched a living from growing groundnuts on a miserable, hard and dry small-holding five miles up the River Gambia and by acting as unofficial tourist guides whenever they could. Sadou was best at that; he had natural charm. The grandmother and the sick cousin spent most of their days begging in Banjul, after having cadged rides across the river on one of the numerous canoes which plied the route.

Sadou's mother and father had both died of blackwater fever – a virulent strain of malaria which attacked the kidneys – and a sister had died during a localised cholera epidemic two years beforehand, when she was 14 years old.

Sadou possessed a natural dignity. He stood straight and walked with a measured stride. When he spoke, the words were delivered with care and precision, as if he were acting out some Victorian period drama. He always thought before he spoke and he always listened intently to what others had to say. Despite his pitifully frayed, hand-me-down clothes – which were spotlessly clean – he was one of those people who never appeared to be untidy. A torn T-shirt and tatty Levis on Sadou Midaka compared favourably with a suit from Savile Row on most other men. He had natural style.

Over the next few days Sadou showed Jennifer The Gambia. Borrowing a series of battered vehicles from friends or from members of his vast, extended family and on one occasion an outboard motorboat which let in the water, he treated her to a magical insight into his country. He took her up-river, through jungle, across arid savannah and into remote villages. He showed her where the slave ships had weighed anchor, where the luckless slaves were "processed," where the deep and mysterious jungle gave out onto semi-desert – the advancing Sahel – and where plump and prehistoric crocodiles slid fatly into the narrow creek which separated the mainland from the long, thin island of Ginak.

They crossed the creek in a dug-out canoe, Sadou pointing out the periscopic eyes of the crocs and chuckling with delight as Jennifer shuddered with revulsion and gripped the sides of the boat. Jennifer followed in Sadou's footsteps as they traversed the little island, in single file on narrow paths which wound through the undergrowth. They passed clusters of straw huts, miniature rows of dusty crops, women bent double to the ground as they hacked at the bare earth with crude hoes.

On the north side of the island, which they reached in an hour, the thick vegetation ended abruptly and a dazzling expanse of white-gold sand spread out either side of them. The Atlantic Ocean, an impossible blue, stretching far, far beyond its knife-edge horizon to the Americas. The unblemished beach was deserted save for one long-horned cow lying in the sand, head lazily high at the sound of the two humans and tail flicking nonchalently at the flies. The creature was a beautiful golden-brown colour, with a pure white face and a black tip to her tail. Her dumb, soulful eyes gazed unblinking at Jennifer and Sadou, her head following them lugubriously as they walked up the beach. But her body did not move. Several dusty coconut palm trees yearned low from the edge of the undergrowth towards the distant sea.

"Madiyanna Lodge is not far, less than a quarter of a mile away," said Sadou, slowing down for Jennifer, conscious of the heat and the flies. "We can have a cold drink and we can dine there," he added as if referring to lunch at the Savoy.

Madiyanna Lodge was built of wood and thatch on the edge of the beach behind a clump of palm trees. An open-sided restaurant-cum-bar surrounded by three grass huts. An old hammock slung between two of the palms twitched in a sea breeze.

After lunch – yassa poulet (grilled chicken in an onion and lemon sauce) accompanied by the ubiquitous boiled rice and a slightly-corked bottle of Muscadet – they strolled down to the water's edge. Sadou told Jennifer about the wildlife on the island – the hyena, the wild boar, the crocodile and even the occasional, bold leopard – and he told her his hopeless dream of somehow acquiring the island and turning it into a national park, which he and his brothers would of course run. And he would rename it Paradise Island.

As they stood, barefoot and ankle-deep in the frothy, warm water, looking out to sea, Jennifer felt for Sadou's hand. She was in love with him. And later that hot, sweet night, on a lumpy mattress in one of the three grass huts, Midnight Sam was conceived.

3

IT WAS a recurring dream, one he had had since childhood. He was lying in a huge hammock, swinging slowly to and fro and laughing into a high, hot, hazy blue sky. His father's face seemed to fill the sky, smiling and safe and looked down at him. It filled his world.

But suddenly the smiling face darkened with fear. And Midnight followed his father's stare over the hammock and out to sea. Midnight Sam's mother, dressed in a bright red, tight-fitting ballroom gown and gleaming brown fur stole, was wading straight out into the ocean. She kept on walking, her head held high, until she disappeared under the water. Midnight Sam looked up at his father and tried to scream but there was no sound; he tried to climb out of the hammock but he was unable to move. And then his father's beautiful, strong, round face began to shrink until it became the size of a pinhead before it vanished altogether. The sky turned black and cold rain hammered down and Midnight Sam woke up, his eyes brimming with tears. He lay perfectly still, eyes wide open, blinking the tears away, while he waited for the despair of the dream to lift.

When he saw the two cigarettes which The Professor had left him, he smiled. He climbed out of his sleeping bag, stood up with his legs apart, yawned, broke wind loudly and pleasurably, bent down and picked up the cigarettes. He tucked one behind an ear and the other in the breast pocket of the thick, tartan shirt he was wearing. He pulled a bottle of White Lightning from his holdall and took a long, medicinal swig, wiping his lips with a shirt-sleeve. He went to put on his donkey jacket, recoiled from the soaking wet garment, turned back to his holdall and found a thick, dark blue pullover with a two-inch hole bang in the middle.

Midnight threaded the donkey jacket through the straps of his holdall and walked out of the underpass, along the oily grass verge which ran alongside the road. A Number 46 double-decker bus lumbered by completely empty, close to the verge and splashed him. He stopped and gazed at his wet jeans without anger, found the bottle again and had another drink. The warmth of the alcohol spread across his stomach and up to his chest: he felt able to face the day, dark, damp and dismal though it was. It started raining again before he reached the Post Office. Stinging, spiteful, slanting rain driven by an unforgiving north-east wind.

As soon as Midnight Sam had drawn his benefit he headed for the day centre. Besides meeting up with The Professor, Scots Robby and possibly with Fen, he needed to get his donkey jacket dry and the day centre was the only place he could think of where that could be achieved. On the way there he called in at Tescos, weathered a close, unsubtle inspection by two store detectives, smiled directly at a CCTV camera and bought two bottles of strong cider, the supermarket's own brand.

Scots Robby was sitting, hunched and morose, in the reception area of the day centre in South Street, scowling at the floor and clutching a mug of tea in both hands. The gash on his forehead had crusted black and the front of his anorak bore the evidence of the night before – blood, vomit, whisky and cider. He had a deathly pallor and took tiny, distasteful sips at the tea.

"How you doing?" Midnight clapped the Scotsman on the shoulder and sat down beside him. "How's the head?" He peered at the wound and gave an encouraging nod. Scots Robby said nothing, but he wriggled his shoulders to escape Midnight's hand. He blew into his steaming mug and glared at the far wall. At 40 and with ten years of alcoholic wallowing on one wasteground or another to his debit, every hangover was becoming one too many. He had discovered that whisky and cider mixed were even more unpleasant the following morning.

"Seen Prof ?" Midnight asked. Scots Robby pecked cautiously at his tea but then decided to have a proper, manly gulp. Sadly the tea was having none of it: some of it went up his nose, some went scalding down his throat but the majority joined the mess on the front of his anorak. He coughed and retched.

"Fuckin' 'ell," he growled, reluctantly adding, "he's up there with the doc."

Midnight frowned: "I don't know what's wrong with him. He's getting worse, seems like he's never well these days. Runs out of breath all the time and that pain in his guts is getting worse. Don't know what's wrong with him. Never well these days ..."

Scots Robby shrugged, yawned and managed a successful gulp of his tea. He busied himself with a roll-up, which involved quite a few "fuckin' 'ells," and threw the tobacco pouch onto the coffee table, looking around for somebody to blame. Midnight squirreled inside his pullover and extracted one of the cigarettes The Professor had left him. He gave it to Scots Robby, who accepted with an ungracious grunt and waited for a light. Midnight obliged.

****

Sadou Midaka and Jennifer Crawley spent the rest of the divorcee's holiday together, every day and every night, sleeping on the lumpy mattress on the bare ground in the grass hut where they had first made love. Sadou had insisted she return to the Atlantic Hotel and explain that she would not be staying there anymore – she had made "alternative arrangements," he instructed her to say – but he was also adamant that she should spend the last night of her holiday at the hotel "for decency sake." Of course the Thomas Cook agent was a nightmare, but Jennifer was in no mood to argue and told him it was her holiday and she would spent it any way she wished.

Banbuna, the owner of Madiyanna Lodge, entered into the love triste with enthusiasm. He knew Sadou and he had an eye – albeit a distant eye – for the Englishwoman. Sadou earned his keep by working the sleepy bar, collecting supplies from the mainland and entertaining the other three guests – a young, evidently rich black American couple on an 'ethnic' discovery trip and a very shy, pathologically polite German in his mid-thirties. Meanwhile Jennifer flirted tastefully with Banbuna, token-tidied the occasional table, lazed in one of the hammocks and wandered along the beautiful, inevitably deserted beach. She would don her bikini (much to the prurient but secret delight of the desultory staff at the lodge) and strike out, in a respectable crawl, close and parallel to the shore. She was in heaven. Not only was she with a good man – and Sadou was the epitome of a good man – but she felt free, and more important, she felt strong again. And of course the delicious naughtiness of it all. What on earth would her Middle England, middleclass, Conservative – with a small or a big C – friends and family think of her?

But Jennifer did not care. She was happy at last and she no longer felt that aching loneliness, even when she was on her own while Sadou ran his numerous errands. She could hardly believe it but she realised, with delicious amazement, that she was over Jonathan, really over him.

Despite his intellect and intelligence, Sadou was basically a very simple man. He had found a woman – a beautiful white woman, which admittedly and unashamedly gave him kudos – and he decided that he loved her. But what did the word 'love' really mean to him or, for that matter, to Jennifer? It was the archetypal 'holiday romance,' but in their case it crossed a number of boundaries, which made it all the more exciting. Jennifer was in love with being a desired woman again, but Sadou was in love with what he, with sweet and flawed innocence, perceived to be his future.

"I love you Jennifer (never Jenny, despite her protestations) and I want us to be as one together, to be man and wife, to start a family and to prosper. He looked out over the night sea, eyes half-closed, as he imagined and planned their dynasty. A full moon gleamed on his dark brown forehead. Jennifer shivered to the sexual thrill of his big, safe hands on her shoulders, but she did not feel what he felt, she did not feel the future or the dynasty. She only felt the overpowering sexuality of his big, safe hands on her shoulders.

On the last day of her holiday, Sadou borrowed a friend's beat-up old Toyota half-truck to drive Jennifer to Banjul's sad and silly airport. The rest of her Atlantic Hotel group had arrived by coach earlier. Apart from one or two gossips who made valiant and unsuccessful attempts to discover the gory details of what she had been up to, the outrageous Englishwoman who had disgraced herself in the worst possible way was indignantly snubbed. And it delighted her: she had never felt so important.

They exchanged addresses (c/o The Paris Hilton in Sadou's case) and they both made declarations of undying love (solemn and serious, again in Sadou's case). There was the inevitable tearful promise of a return visit and the final hug.

****

When Jennifer discovered that she was pregnant her mind went into turmoil. She had spent 12 years married to Jonathan, desperately yearning for the regulation 2.4 children like all other respectable married women she knew. But it was not to be and she was just beginning to adjust to diverting her attention and her affection from the idea of having babies back to her husband when he upped and left her. Admittedly very apologetically, very tearfully – he even claimed to be broken-hearted on one traumatic occasion – but he left her just the same. And now here she was, unarguably pregnant with a black Mandinka 'holiday romance' foetus growing in her white, middleclass womb.

Friends and family suggested that the only "sensible" thing to do was to have an abortion. Her doctor, who she thought and hoped might have talked deeply about the sanctity of life and the rights of the unborn child, surprised and disappointed her by suggesting the same.

But Jennifer surprised herself. Still aglow with the moonlit magic of Sadou's Paradise Island, his mellow voice, the quaint turns of phrase he used, the physical beauty of his being, his dreams and the innate kindness and decency of the man, Jennifer told them all, including the doctor, to go to hell. She was going to have Sadou's baby and that was that. The future would take care of itself.

But when she took baby Sam home after a two-day stay in hospital – a cool and calm private ward (and why not? she could afford it) – a little dark cloud followed her. She was troubled and she could not fathom out what the problem was. The baby was lovely, a truly beautiful boy, and the birth itself had been remarkably easy. Very quick and not as painful as she had imagined it was going to be. That she was unable to breast-feed was unfortunate, she felt, but hardly unique. It didn't really bother her. What did bother her though was the fact that she felt relieved, glad even that she was unable to breast-feed. She did not want to breast-feed Sam, had no desire to, and that bothered her. Secretly and greatly.

Jennifer had had the third bedroom transformed into a baby boy paradise. Walls painted in alternate bright and pale blue, an impractical but irresistible shag-pile blue carpet scattered with nursery rhyme rugs on the floor; tinkling mobiles dangling from a ceiling painted like the night sky, complete with a smiling man-in-the-moon and shooting stars; an expensive, hand-made, mock-Victorian cot and teddy bears and cuddly toys everywhere. She introduced little Sam to the nursery from heaven and she had spared no expense. But there was something missing, something important, hugely important, and she did not know what it was. Not at first.

It was only later, when Sam was one month old, that she began to suspect what was wrong. The knowledge niggled at her and she would try to push it away, shake off such unpleasant nonsense and get on with the business of looking after her baby. Because that was what good mothers did and she was determined to be a good mother, And, in every way but one, she was a good mother.

Jennifer Crawley did not possess the maternal instinct, she did not feel that the baby was part of her, belonged to her. Everything she did for Sam was an act, an act of duty, a very good act but an act all the same. She fed him, she bathed him, she cuddled him, she settled him down to sleep, she watched and cared for him every inch of the way. But that deep, all-consuming, fierce heat of maternal love was not there. She fought valiantly against this lack, fought against herself, often pretending that what she felt (or rather what she didn't feel) was the same for other mothers. But in reality she knew differently. Like a dull but persistent early cancer it was always there, often beneath the surface but always there and growing.

Many mothers discover they do not have the maternal instinct and yet they still love their progeny. But Jennifer suffered a worse deprivation – a deprivation which would do great damage to Sam in years to come: she did not love her child. She did not hate him, dislike him or resent him. She even liked the adorable baby. But that indomitable, indestructible and fearless Mother's Love was not there. And it never would be.

When Sam was six months old Jennifer found a good and very expensive nursery nearby, returned to her old job as a PA to the boss of an advertising agency and got on with her life.

Jonathan telephoned her several times to see how she was, to be magnanimous and patronisingly encouraging about Sam, but the real reason was to ask her out "to talk about the old times." Jennifer had already heard that the course of her ex-husband's new love was running far from smooth and she took some pleasure in turning him down, politely of course. He only wanted a shag anyway.

A new and quite amazing thought crept into her mind one cold and windy March afternoon. It was a Sunday and she was taking Sam out in his pushchair to the park. The baby was wrapped up warm and wore a big, blue dummy, like a badge, in the middle of his mouth. His brown eyes peered pleasantly up into the grey, fretful sky and he smiled either side of the dummy.

Jennifer sat down on a park bench, idly pushing the pushchair to and fro with her left hand and stared at the friendly but freezing lake. A dozen ducks, making a ridiculous noise and, averting their eyes from Jennifer, closed in vaguely, sensing the possibility of food. When none was forthcoming, they made a pretence of exploring the lakeside, some waddling clumsily out of the water and petulantly pecking at each other.

A fantastic thought occurred to Jennifer and spread, within seconds, throughout her whole being. She slumped her shoulders, exhausted by the enormity of the idea, and her stare at the lake was suddenly unseeing. She was looking deep into her new thought, examining it with ruthless and indulgent honesty, tossing it over in her mind, finding flaws and mending them, arguing and then counter-arguing, swelling inwardly with the excitement of the thing.

Jennifer decided, there and then on the park bench beside the frozen lake, that she would take her baby boy to The Gambia, not for a holiday, not for the purpose of showing Sadou his son, but to stay. They would be married and they would be a family, a family living together as they should. She knew that Sadou would be ecstatic with the idea and she hoped – although she hardly dared admit it to herself – that perhaps with Sadou at her side the elusive Mother's Love would materialise.

Since Jennifer's return to England they had kept in regular contact – dreamy, sensual letters from her and rather courtly, poetic love letters from him – and the memory of that blissful, magical and supremely cathartic holiday still burned bright in her. But what she did not realise was that the flame was the holiday, the holiday romance, and not a lot to do with Sadou. Although the irritating truth had tugged at the shirt-tails of her mind on many occasions in the past, this time she scared it away with self-delusion. Sadou was the man of her dreams, he was the father of her beautiful baby boy – the child she would love the moment she embraced his equally beautiful father – and the three of them would live happily ever after in a grass hut at Madiyanna Lodge on Paradise Island.

Her next and most important letter to Sadou was going to be a tricky one. First of all she had to tell him that he was a father (she had studiously dodged that one for the past six months). She also had to tell him that his firstborn was a son (high value to an African, especially to such a proud and traditional African as Sadou) but she then had to explain that the boy she had named Sam (and was that the right name to have chosen?) was already six months old.

As it turned out it was not as difficult as she had thought. She decided to write a letter explaining how she had not wanted to impose on him, to make demands which he might have found hard to meet (tactfully and sweetly worded) and how she had wanted him – a young and vibrant man on the brink perhaps of some great destiny – to be free to follow his dream. It was not an *entirely* truthful letter, but then it was not entirely untruthful either.

When Sadou Madika, swinging idly in the hammock outside the lodge where he now worked full-time, read Jennifer's apologetic but brave words, his heart swelled. He swung his legs off the hammock, held the letter in front of his face like a shield and trotted down the beach towards the water's edge. He had a son! He was the father of a baby boy. Tears filled his eyes as he waded out from the shore, still scrutinising the letter as if he couldn't believe its contents, until the warm water reached his waist.

He had a son.

****

Jennifer Cawley married Sadou Midaka in a small Protestant church in Banjul two weeks after she and baby Sam arrived in The Gambia. Sadou's brothers, his ailing cousin and crabby grand-mother were there, as was the affable and faintly bemused owner of Madiyanna Lodge, his staff of five, several strangers who saw the unlikely couple enter the church and were curious as to what was going on and a seven-month-old baby boy, who grinned and gurgled throughout the ceremony. No member of Jennifer's family, not one of her friends, nobody from 'her side,' was present. And it wasn't distance or convenience or cost that kept them away.

4

AFTER fumbling the operation twice and dropping the envelope on to the pavement, The Professor finally managed to post his daughter's birthday card through the letterbox in the wall outside the city centre post office. He stared at the postbox for a long time before he turned away, trying to make himself invisible, and headed for the day centre in South Street.

It was always difficult for him at that time of the year and it never got any better. Nevertheless he set his jaw to the predictable day ahead and remembered with a physical start that he would have to divert to an off-licence for the obligatory bottle of White Lightning. Once he had bought the cider, scurrying from the shop like an unwelcome rodent, he darted into the first alleyway he came across – grey, littered and puddled from the previous night's rain – and tilted the bottle to his lips. The cold liquid warmed his insides and began to dull the sullen pain in his stomach, a pain which had been increasing over the past three months. He leaned back against the wall, the bottle dangling from his right hand and quietly fought to regulate his breathing. He needed to get more drunk than usual that day; he needed to blur out the birthday card, to blur out the past, to blur out the tragedy of his life.

But first he needed to pay a visit, albeit a reluctant visit, to the day centre. It was open surgery from 10 o'clock until midday with Doc Dawes and the stomach pains and breathlessness had been getting worse. The doctor was gentle and discreet, compassionate and non-judgemental, a good man. Nevertheless The Professor always felt uneasy in his presence. Doctor Dawes looked a little too deeply at him, listened perhaps too intently, asked a few too many questions and always in the tone which said 'why are you here? what is your sorrow? what has happened to you?' The Professor knew – and the knowledge unsettled him, upset his fiercely-guarded anonymity – that this young medical man was close to him and worse, that he wanted to get closer.

"Same problem?" Doctor Dawes asked. "How is the pain?"

The Professor shook his head, a nervous, dismissive twitch, and stared straight ahead, over the doctor's shoulder, his own shoulders hunched with stubbornness. The doctor fiddled with his stethoscope, got up, lifted The Professor's shirt and listened to his chest. He returned to his desk, leaned back in the chair, head to one side and closed his eyes.

"You know what the problem is, don't you? You do know what's wrong with you, how ill you are?" The Professor said and did nothing. "I've been telling you for the past three months, but what good does it do? You need to go into hospital, you need to undergo tests, you need access to serious medical care. You are a very sick man and living the way you do will, quite frankly, kill you. You are only 45 years old but …"

"I know how old I am," The Professor snapped, still staring straight ahead. "I do know how old I am," he added, softening his tone apologetically. "I just want something for the pain. Please, doc, just something for the pain."

Doctor Dawes was accustomed to dealing with the homeless, the alcoholics, the drifting drug addicts, the street drinkers. He had been volunteering his services to the day centre for two hours every Thursday for the past five years. And for free. But there was something about The Professor which unsettled him, some secret tragedy. They all had their own secret tragedies, he knew that, but The Professor's appeared to be darker, more despairing, more agonising than the rest. The doctor felt an urge to ask him. He wanted to know how this clearly well-educated, well-mannered and intelligent man had ended up on the street, how he had ended up slowly killing himself. But he knew better than to ask.

Doctor Dawes was one of the good guys and The Professor would have been perfectly safe to confide in him, but that was not the point. What made such a relationship impossible was the vast chasm which so quickly opened up between the homeless and so-called normal society. Three weeks on the streets was all it took, so the experts reckoned. And The Professor was six years down the road. Six irretrievable years. His mind, his intellect might be the same, but his world had changed. He was on the other side of the fence now and he had neither the will nor the means to scale it.

The doctor wrote The Professor a prescription, tore it from the pad and handed it across the desk with a helpless smile. There was so much he wanted to say, but the firm, ironic expression on The Professor's face warned: don't ask, don't waste your breath, don't bother with me, because I won't tell you.

As The Professor struggled to his feet and steadied himself with both hands on the back of the chair, Scots Robby burst into the room unannounced, an expression of thunder on his face. The superficial gash on his forehead had started to bleed again (he had been picking at the scab) and a rivulet of fresh blood trickled down his left temple into a corner of his moustache.

"How long do I have to fuckin' wait?" he shouted, ignoring The Professor and glaring at the doctor. "I could be bleeding to fuckin' death for all you care. I got set upon last night, beaten up by a bunch of Sassenach bastards for no fuckin' reason whatsoever and you expect me to wait around all fuckin' day."

"You clouted yourself on the head with a bottle of sherry, Robby, self-inflicted wound, I'm afraid," The Professor cut in wearily and with a degree of irritation. "In case you don't remember, Sam and I were there, we met up with you at the bus station. Remember?"

Scots Robby saw The Professor for the first time and he bristled with inexplicable indignation. He puffed out his chest in readiness for an argument but Doctor Dawes took control of the situation: "Come and sit down Robby. Prof and I are through, you'll be delighted to hear (the doctor could not resist a touch of sarcasm). Let's take a look at that head of yours. When did you do it?"

"Like I said, bunch of Sassenach bastards laid into me. Didn't stand a chance. Just laid into me they did."

Doctor Dawes rubbed his chin thoughtfully, stepped out from behind his desk and examined the Scotsman's forehead. The Professor shook his head and left the room quietly, clutching his prescription. As an afterthought he poked his head back around the door and asked mischievously: "You don't know what happened to Midnight Sam's coat I suppose Robby? It had somehow lifted itself off the shopping trolley, floated for about eight feet and landed bang smack in the middle of a big puddle of rainwater. Amazing really."

Scots Robby whirled, brushing the doctor with an elbow, his face contorted with an even mix of anger and guilt: "What the fuck d'you mean? Nothing to do with me. How the fuck do I know what happened to his jacket. Nothing to do with me."

The Professor nodded with a wry smile, raised a hand to the doctor and left the room, closing the door behind him. He descended the stairs slowly and carefully, holding onto the single bannister with his left hand. He sat down on a sofa in a corner of the restroom, breathing heavily, and stared at the wall opposite. A National Health poster explaining the symptoms of Hepatitis A stared back at him. At least that was one thing he hadn't got, he thought.

A gaunt young man, red-eyed and pale, brought The Professor a mug of tea, spilling a good deal. He hurried nervously away. People were always doing things for The Professor. He never asked, he never expected it, but it always happened. Actually it embarrassed him but he was too weary to protest. And, after all, a mug of tea was a mug of tea, embarrassment or no embarrassment. He clamped both hands around the hot mug, blew weakly at the surface, drew in his breath and took a cautious sip.

Midnight Sam strolled into the day centre, draped his donkey jacket over a radiator and joined The Professor on the sofa. The sudden warmth made him shiver but the smile on his face was faraway and real. He looked affectionately at the older man and asked: "You okay, Prof? How you feeling? Been to see the doc?"

The Professor nodded. He was fond of Midnight Sam: there was a deep goodness, a serenity, an inner peace about the man.

"Fine, Midnight. I'm just fine. Doc says that I'm alive, which is a relief, but he's not sure for how much longer."

Midnight Sam's face darkened and The Professor added quickly: "No, no, I'm only joking, Sam. Doc Dawes gave me the magic pills, well at least he gave me the prescription, so everything's going to be okay. How about you?" he asked, changing the subject.

Midnight was not to be wrong-footed quite so easily: "I'm okay, Prof, apart from my jacket. Bloody soaked it was. Got it on the radiator now. It'll soon be dry." A thoughtful pause. "You sure you're okay. You were breathing pretty bad last night, coughing bad too. What did the doc say?"

"Gave me a prescription, like I told you." The Professor fumbled in his trouser pocket and produced the piece of paper, waving it as evidence. He drew a packet of cigarettes from his other trouser pocket. The smoking ban had not reached the day centre. "Never smoked when I was younger, never touched them. Only took it up six-seven years ago. Smoke like a trooper now ..." He lit Midnight's cigarette and then his own, inhaled deeply, stifled a cough and leaned back into the sofa. "Smoke like a bleedin' trooper now," he repeated, mimicking a Cockney accent and failing to stifle a cough a second time. It was a painful coughing fit: he bent almost double, spluttering a string of saliva onto his knees, red-faced, his cheeks shuddering with the strain, eyes watering.

Midnight looked anxious and impotent. He didn't know what to do so he put an arm around The Professor's shoulders and waited for the coughing to stop. "You're not well, Prof, you're not well at all. Doc's a good bloke and all that, but he can't be much of a doctor, Prof, not if he don't know what's wrong with you. Why don't you get yourself down to the hospital, see someone there? They'd sort you out, good and proper. I could come with you, make sure they know how ill you are."

The Professor gulped a couple of deep breaths, punched Midnight Sam lightly on the arm and looked around the room, wide-eyed as if he was seeing it for the first time.

"Nothing wrong with old Droopy-Dawes, Midnight. He's a damn fine doctor. I just don't want to go down to the Royal. It scares the shit out of me. Once they got their hands on me, sticking tubes everywhere,

I don't think I'd ever get out again, not alive that is. Nothing wrong with Doc Dawes, Midnight. Honestly. He knows his stuff, but I don't think there's a lot he can do for me."

Panic flashed across Midnight's face again, his eyes started and his kind mouth suddenly drooped, like a child's. The Professor recognised the fear, inwardly rebuked himself and ruffled the back of Midnight's head: "I'm only taking the piss, Sam. Just a touch of asthma and a bit of an ulcer. Nothing to worry about. It'll be fine, soon as I get down to the chemists."

Scots Robby thundered down the stairs, scowling at the world, a crisp white bandage (he had insisted on a bandage) impressively wound around his forehead. His long, lank, black hair, curtained by the bandage, gave him the appearance on an Apache warrior, an image spoilt by the moustache. He sat down heavily on a chair opposite The Professor and Midnight Sam and glowered at them.

"And where the fuckin' hell did you two get to last night?" he demanded accusingly. "One minute you were there and the next … nowhere to be fuckin' seen."

They were used to this, to the Walter Mitty world of Scots Robby. It happened all the time. Whenever the Scotsman went over the alcoholic edge he would surface the next day, even more argumentative than before and with serious attitude. It was always somebody else's fault and his version of events, fanciful to say the least, would become set in Scottish stone – forever.

"How's the head?" asked The Professor. "Doc appears to have fixed you up pretty well. Fancy a smoke?"

The Professor tossed a cigarette towards Scots Robby, who caught it deftly and stuck it into his mouth. He craned forwards for a light, without a word of thanks and Midnight Sam obliged.

"I think I've fractured my skull. I know about wounds. I've been in the fuckin' army, you know. The quack doesn't agree, told me it was only a wee bang. What the fuck does he know?"

When there was no response, Scots Robby sought for something else to say, something conciliatory. "What you two up to today?"

"Dunno," answered The Professor. And then, with a touch of mischief: "We'll have to wait for Midnight's coat to get dry first." He couldn't resist revisiting the incident which had been bugging him all day. "Like I said, it fell into a big puddle of water in the underpass last night. Must have got there all on its own accord. Magic. Bloody amazing."

Midnight Sam fought a smile and Scots Robby grunted, beaten and confused, but cagey. He sprang to his feet, inspected a wristwatch that had not been there for six-and-a-half years and mumbled something about the Post Office before marching out of the building. The Professor and Midnight Sam exchanged glances.

****

Sadou Midaka sat on the side of a crumbling, derelict jetty in a quiet corner of Barra's river port and stared out to sea. The stern of the ferry, listing and groaning under its ludicrous load of humanity, produce and machinery, had just disappeared from sight on its laboured way back to Banjul on the south side of the river. The setting sun stained the sky above the horizon a myriad shades of red and gold – stunningly beautiful – and a balmy early evening breeze came in from the Atlantic. But Sadou felt none of the magic; he was a puzzled and a sad man. And lonely. He called a curt warning in English to the little boy who was trying to climb onto a beached fishing canoe some 20 feet away. The boy pretended not to hear his father and he hooked one leg over the side of the pirogue and tumbled inside with a muffled thump.

Sadou stood up, shook himself out of his mood and walked over to the 40-foot long vessel which lay on its side near to the water's edge. Sam's head popped up and he grinned at his father. Sadou tried to appear cross but failed, melting as usual under the warmth of his son's smile. Nevertheless he hoisted the boy out of the boat and the pair walked back up the beach, hand in hand.

Samuel Midaka was three-and-a-half years old when his mother went back to England. Jennifer had returned several times before for what she referred to as her "UK fix" and Sadou had graciously kept his own counsel, although he was not altogether happy about the situation. Privately he did not approve of his wife's ever-more-frequent trips home. She would return with a false gaiety, armfuls of expensive presents for Sam and a cheerful monologue about who had got divorced, who was sleeping with whom, who had got married, who had left who and for whom and how everyone was "oh so delighted" to see her again. Sadou would smile politely and try to say the right things. The euphoria of her trips would keep her going, like a drug, for a week or so. She would busy herself around the large, thatched rondavel Sadou had built for her, unaided and with his own hands, near to Madiyanna Lodge. She would clean, wash and cook and play diligently but awkwardly with Sam. And she would make love to her husband.

But something had gone, something which Jennifer reluctantly had to admit to herself might never have been there in the first place. It was one of the oldest stories in the world: the difference between falling in love and loving someone. But in Sadou's case it was different. His expectations of their relationship were very simple: Jennifer was attractive and good company and he liked her and she had given him the most precious gift of all, a son. And she was a white woman. His status locally had grown. He was contented, proud and determined to give Sam all the advantages he had never had. And the boy already had one advantage, one huge advantage: a British passport, that all-important British passport. It was, for his son, a passport to education, opportunity and prosperity.

Once the romantic illusion of living in a grass hut on a palm-tree fringed beach of shining white sand with a handsome, gentle and kind young man had worn off, harsh reality set in. The mosquitoes bit, and they bit with a vengeance, the heat was unrelenting and she had no friends to gossip with. In reality she had nothing to do apart from look after Sam, which she found a dreary and depressing bore. She was trapped. Trapped in a grass hut with a man she did not really love and a child she could not bond with.

Jennifer had tried to be honest with Sadou and had, on many occasions, broached the subject of them all resettling in England. She had money and contacts, baby Sam had a British passport, Sadou was intelligent, young and hard-working and could apply, with some justification, for residence. But her integrity was flawed, her powers of persuasion half-hearted, her words empty of heart and without conviction. Sadou saw through his wife's pusillanimous reasoning and felt sad at what he accurately began to predict was going to happen. He was nevertheless indignant and morally outraged.

"But how can you leave your son, your own flesh and blood?" he asked her on one occasion, when his patience finally ran out. "He is a part of you, a part of us, he is our future. He is of your blood. You are his mother. How can a mother leave her child?"

Jennifer had no answer. She had no idea how she could leave her son. All she knew was that she was going to and that she would probably not shed a tear. To her Sam was a sweet and innocent little boy, but the filial bond was not there and it never would be. And that worked both ways. For the child felt the same, although not yet being capable of expressing or understanding such a feeling. Jennifer knew that. It was the only secret, the only bond they ever had: the mutual indifference they felt towards each other.

"When he is bigger you must bring him to England," she said with false brightness as they stood outside the doors of the departure lounge at Banjul International Airport (a grand title for such a rundown, hotchpotch of buildings). "I could show you both the sights …," she closed her eyes for a second and put her hand to her mouth. "I'm sorry," she said, shaking her head, her eyes suddenly full of tears. She extended a hand to Sadou. He took it briefly and ushered Sam forwards: "Say goodbye to your mother, Sam. She is going away."

Sam looked levelly at his mother. Both of them understood. Jennifer bent down, kissed Sam lightly on both cheeks, gave Sadou a soulful, despairing look, shook her head and walked through the swing doors into the departure lounge. Sadou placed both hands on this son's shoulders, turned the boy gently around and led him out of the airport to where his old and borrowed Fiat was parked.

5

BISHOP'S Palace is an austere three-storey 17th century building some two hundred yards from the Cathedral, enclosed by a 12 foot high wall. Next-door and attached to the Palace is the boarding house of King's College. The Cathedral and the college have always been inextricably entwined, both temporally and spiritually.

Midnight Sam waited self-consciously at the doorstep, aware that a small group of college schoolchildren had gathered around the entrance and were watching him and giggling. He buttoned up his donkey jacket, remembered the dog-end behind his left ear, removed it and tucked it into his shirt pocket and took a short step backwards. When the door opened he ducked inside.

Bishop John fussed around Midnight in the spacious hallway, accidentally elbowing his elderly and stern housemaid out of the way and immediately apologising profusely. Accustomed to the confusion (he was a regular and welcome visitor) the street-drinker handed his coat to the housemaid and shook the 73-year-old cleric enthusiastically by the hand.

"If it's not convenient, your honour, I'll call back later." He made the same apology every time he called and it always received the same response.

"Of course it's convenient, Sam, you know you are always welcome here," said the bishop, a six-foot something, thin and angular man, with huge feet and hands and a long, grey, boyish face. He took Midnight Sam by the arm and ushered him across the hallway and into a cosy, hopelessly untidy room – Bishop John's private retreat. The walls were lined with books and the room was cluttered with three ageing armchairs (a large, fierce-looking tabby cat immovable in one of them), a mahogany drinks cabinet and a round coffee table in mismatching rosewood. The room wreaked of tobacco (Bishop John favoured a pipe) and wood smoke from the small, open fireplace which boasted a small but tinglingly hot blaze. Although the bishop was married with three grown-up children this was very much a bachelor's room. A man's room. His room.

Midnight Sam squirmed into one of the armchairs with a contented sigh and settled into the corner of one of the wing-backs with child-like delight. He loved visiting the bishop, he loved the room and he rather loved the bishop. Despite the apparent absurdity of the situation – an alcoholic, homeless street-drinker being entertained by a bishop – Midnight Sam felt completely at ease.

Bishop John liked Midnight Sam. He considered the young man to be a true Christian, to be what he believed his chosen religion was, or perhaps should be, all about. Listening to Midnight quietly expressing his concern for The Professor or for some "young kid" he'd seen sleeping rough on the street the night before or for anybody in need or in distress (anybody apart from himself, of course), filled the bishop with awe, guilt and a deep sense of shame. Bishop John enjoyed ecclesiastical respect, position and comfort – he was a professional Christian at the pinnacle of his career. He had always tried to do his best and to adhere to standards of conduct and care which he held dear. But, being a good and questioning man, he placed Midnight Sam on a higher plane. He regarded his regular guest – a man who had known no respect, had no position and had experienced no comfort whatsoever – as a far better Christian than he could ever hope to be.

"So how is The Professor?" the bishop asked, handing Midnight a generous schooner of sherry, belligerently charging a glass for himself, despite the fact that the 'yard arm' was a good ten minutes away. One of his 'flock' was more important than convention, he reasoned with himself.

"I'm worried about him. He's coughing much more these days, your honour. And that pain in his stomach, it seems to be getting worse and I reckon …"

"What does Doctor Dawes say?" the bishop interrupted.

"Don't know. He won't tell me. I've asked him but he goes on about patient confidence or something."

"Patient confidentiality," Bishop John corrected.

"Yeah, that's it, patient confidential."

Midnight Sam reached for his schooner of sherry and heroically resisted the urge to drain the glass in one. He took a small sip and replaced the glass on the coffee table.

"Sam, I've asked you before, but why don't you try to get him to come here? I'm not going to preach at him, you know me too well for that. It's just, it's just …," he paused, fighting some inner battle, "it's just that I think that maybe I could help him," he finished lamely.

"With respect, your honour, you don't know him like I do," said Midnight. "He's stubborn, Mister Bishop, he won't take charity from nobody. D'you know, he's got to be the only Big Issue seller in the world who won't take money unless the punters actually buy a copy of the frigging magazine. He's unreal. No, I'm sorry, your honour, but you don't know him like I do." An element of pride in the comment.

But it was not entirely true: Bishop John knew more about The Professor's past than Midnight Sam did, a great deal more. But he would never let on, not in a million years. He had sworn himself to secrecy several years ago and he was an honourable man.

Two schooners of sherry later and with four fivers in his shirt pocket – for him, The Professor, Scots Robby and Fen (wherever he was) – Midnight Sam took his leave of Bishop John, who felt that £20 was a small price to pay for a slice of reality. Midnight never had to ask and the bishop always insisted.

****

It was Thursday, benefits day, the only day of the week that the likes of Midnight Sam, The Professor, Scots Robby and Fen had money in their pockets. And they would spend it unwisely, though maybe not unwisely as far as they were concerned. For what was the use of wisdom? Surely it was too late for that.

Midnight collected an armful of Big Issues, gravitated to his pitch in a boarded-up doorway in the pedestrianised city centre, sat down and spent the next three hours trading his wares. A few regulars dropped their pound coins with a kindly word or two into the scarf he had fashioned into a circle, some passers-by winced an embarrassed apology and gave nothing, most strode purposefully by without a word, two men growled "get a job" comments and three young, hooded and troublesome teenagers poked fun at him before snatching some coins from his scarf and bolting down an alleyway. Midnight was not overly perturbed: the pound coins and 50p pieces he had already stashed away, out of sight. Two principal reasons for this: firstly to provide leaner pickings for young, hooded and troublesome teenagers and secondly not to deter potential customers by appearing to be doing too well.

The highspot of Midnight's business day was when he was approached by a middle-aged American couple who were looking for "your historic church" but were intrigued by the whole Big Issue issue. "What a great idea, hey Marjorie," said the man expansively before he knew what the idea was.

Midnight, feigning awkwardness in his tutorial role (he'd handled American tourists before), mumbled, pretending to be unable to meet the candid gaze of the man and woman: "The magazine is sold by homeless people like me – it's the publisher's way of giving us a hand up.

"We have to register as homeless, we buy the magazines for 50p a copy and then we've got to stick to our pitch and sell them for £1 each. But people can give us whatever they want of course, so long as it's at least £1," he paused, waiting for the implication to sink in. "Big Issue bosses are trying to make us stand on our own two feet, getting us back into the way of working for a living. Earn our keep, pay our way, so to speak." That did the trick. That and Midnight's irresistible smile. Twenty pounds was a sizeable profit for a 50p magazine.

It was four o'clock, the light was beginning to fade and low, rain-grey clouds hurried across the sky. Midnight Sam gathered his belongings and ambled off down South Street. It took him an hour to cover less than a quarter of a mile. A pair of friendly policemen wanted to know what he and The Professor had done with Scots Robby the previous night and a dozen yards further on a chatty newspaper vendor beckoned him over to discuss the latest mugging in the Park – it was front page in the Evening News – followed by an elderly couple who knew and adored Midnight and insisted he join them on a street bench and share an egg mayonnaise sandwich. Which he did, since he hadn't eaten all day. Two-and-half flagons of White Lightning, but no food.

The end of the pedestrianised zone was in sight and Midnight was quickening his step when a little girl, about six years old, marched up to him under the encouraging eye of her mother, thrust her hand out and gave him 50p. "My mum says get yourself a cup of tea," she blurted, red-faced, adding: "My mum likes you, she says that you're nice. But she says that you don't look after yourself. Why don't you look after yourself ?" she demanded. Midnight shook his head, made a fuss of looking around before beckoning the girl to come closer. He then pulled a funny face and crossed his eyes. The little girl giggled delightedly, spun on her heels and skipped back to her mother, harbouring some secret she thought she now shared with him. Children loved Midnight Sam, despite his appearance. He knew how to be with them – himself – and they knew that too.

Scots Robby was about to bluster his way through the swing doors into The Mitre, when he saw Midnight Sam turning the corner. He dropped his arm and shouted: "And where the fuckin' 'ell 'ave you been? Been waiting for you at The Tree most the fuckin' afternoon. I'm getting inside this fuckin' pub, before it rains again. Goin' to piss down any minute." Nevertheless he waited for Midnight to catch up.

Secretly Scots Robby had been lonely all day and was glad to see his fellow down-and-out. But he would never have admitted it, least of all to himself and he would never have admitted that he was a down-and-out. Midnight Sam, The Professor, Fen – they were down-and-outs. But not him, not Robert Sinclair. He was merely temporarily down on his luck, fallen on hard times, going through a difficult patch. Things would improve soon, very soon, and he would be back to where he belonged. But sadly he had no idea where that was. Scots Robby was always going to show *them,* he was always going to teach them all a thing or two. It was always *their* fault, but the problem was that he didn't know who *they* were.

Midnight Sam and Scots Robby walked into the pub together, Midnight in front because there was always a danger of them being refused entry if Scots Robby crossed the threshold first. It was important that did not happen as The Mitre was the only pub in town where they could get served. And that was only because Bobby, the landlord, liked Midnight and The Professor. Scots Robby and Fen, he did not like much, least of all the surly young Brummie, who hardly drank, spoke not a pleasant word to anybody and had the unsettling habit of staring long and hard at every customer who walked in.

Scots Robby, having heard via the tramps' bush telegraph about the generous American couple, made a beeline for an alcove surrounded on three sides by the frosted and engraved front windows of the pub. He puffed and grunted his way onto the corner of a wooden bench, which had long lost its varnish, not bothering to remove his anorack.

"Large whisky … please," Scots Robby shouted his order from the alcove, the 'please' a reluctant afterthought only added when he saw a quick frown darken the landlord's chubby face.

Midnight, who assumed that Scots Robby knew about the Americans, had taken up his position at the bar, a £10 note in his hand. "And I'll have a glass of sherry," he said with a touch of defiance.

The landlord twitched his eyebrows and stood back, suppressing a grin, but Scots Robby suppressed nothing. He cackled loudly from the alcove: "Sherry? You come into a pub and ask for a fuckin' glass of sherry? Who the fuck d'you think you are? Lord fuckin' Muck? Mister Midnight Sam would like to partake in a glass of your finest sherry, my good man," he mimicked a posh English accent with surprising accuracy and shook his head, the excitement bringing on a noisy and unfortunately productive fit of coughing. "Fuckin' sherry!"

"That'll do, Robby," the landlord snapped. "I've told you before about your language." He turned back to Midnight, who had taken no notice of Scots Robby and was still tendering the £10 note. "Would that be the dry, medium or the sweet?" he asked with admirable control.

Midnight stroked the corners of his mouth and scratched the back of his head: "I had a couple of snifters with the Bish this morning, lovely it was, and in one of those funny-shaped, curvy glasses."

"Schooners?" suggested Bobby.

"Yeah, that's what he called them. Schooners."

Bobby bent down and disappeared behind the bar. He rummaged about for several seconds, wheezing with the effort, before his beefy arm snaked up and placed a large, dusty sherry schooner with a chipped rim on the bar. His head popped back into view, a triumphant expression on his face.

"That's it," cried Midnight, inspecting the glass.

Bobby stretched up to the top shelf above a row of well-used optics where nothing had happened for years. He tilted the bottles forward to read the labels until he found a three-quarters empty bottle of Harveys Bristol Cream. He wiped the dust off with his hands, swilled the schooner under the tap and poured Midnight Sam his sherry.

Feeling quite grand but looking quite ridiculous, he took the two drinks over to the alcove, where Scots Robby had decided to sulk. "Got the taste for it with the Bish, nice and sweet," he said apologetically. Scots Robby grunted, muttered something about "poncy, fuckin' sherry" under his breath and reached for his tumbler of whisky.

"Now that's a drink. That's what I call a drink, a man's drink." He inspected the tumbler with reverence. "All the way from Bonnie Scotland. That's what I call a drink. Not any of your poncy, poxy Sassenach sherry."

The differing merits of sherry and whisky occupied the conversation for a quarter of an hour until The Professor struggled wearily through the swing doors, dripping wet and shivering from the cold. His rambling overcoat was jewelled with rainwater and his grey hair was plastered across his forehead.

"Got this bloody lot dry at the day centre," he looked down disgustedly at his drenched coat, his chin touching the lapels. "Got caught on the corner of South Street. Heavens damn well opened. Bloody soaked." He undid the string belt, flicked the coat from his shoulders and let it fall to the ground. Midnight leaped to his feet, picked up the overcoat and draped it over the back of a chair in front of a coal-effect gas fire which was fixed to the wall. The Professor shook the lapels of his old and frayed, dog-tooth sports jacket, hitched up his corduroy trousers, also too big for him, and slowly straightened himself at the bar, breathing heavily.

"All right, Bobby?"

The landlord, busy polishing a beer mug with a tea towel, nodded and frowned at The Professor's wet clothes: "You'll catch your death, Prof. You don't want to be wandering about in this sort of weather."

"Two more of what they're having and I'll have a pint of Olde English," he said.

Bobby gave The Professor an exaggerated wink: "You'd better go and get Midnight's glass then – or should I say schooner – I don't think I've got another one. Not much call for them in The Mitre."

This was their Thursday treat, initiated a year ago by The Professor and, barring illness or Scots Robby's occasional holidays at Her Majesty's Pleasure or Fen's mysterious walkabouts, they had never missed. Midnight, The Professor and, after a bit of persuasion, Scots Robby would each part with £10 of their benefit money and enjoy a 'civilised' drink or three in the only pub in town which would have them. And Bobby, beneath the gruff, no-nonsense exterior being a decent chap, would invariably throw in a drink on the house.

The rules were simple but etched in granite: don't arrive drunk, don't get too drunk and don't drink your own stuff on the premises. Scots Robby was the only one to struggle with sticking to the rules, but most of the time the others managed to keep him out of trouble. When Fen was around he would join in the ritual, but on his own terms. He never put £10 in the kitty and he rarely joined them for a drink; he simply turned up and played the fruit machine and, as often as not, disdainfully slapped a £10 on the bar for Bobby to get the others a drink before leaving without a word.

"Fen done his usual disappearing act?" Bobby asked. "Gone a-wandering?"

"He took off when we got to the bus station last night," said The Professor. "One look at the police car parked at the taxi rank and he was gone. It's not as if he doesn't see cop cars all the time. Sometimes he gets an idea in his head and he takes off."

"Odd bugger," said the landlord, his mouth down-turned. "Can't make him out at all. Always on edge, about to blow. Makes me nervous, he does." He took a £10 note from The Professor and handed him the change. The Professor slid the coins back into the little brown envelope which contained the remainder of his benefit money. He shuffled the envelope into a trouser pocket and carried the three drinks over to the alcove. Midnight went to get up and give him a hand but The Professor shook his head. Concentrating hard, he spilled nothing.

Scots Robby tried to crank up the sherry versus whisky argument again but he petered out when the other two drank in silence and stared pointedly out of the window.

"What's Fen's fuckin' problem?" the Scotsman changed tack, focussing on another subject but, ever-aware of the landlord, keeping his voice low. "Why the fuck does he take off like that? Beyond me."

Midnight Sam and The Professor did not know either and they didn't care very much. It was something Fen did and there was no point in challenging him about it. He would only subject them to a torrent of abuse, even lash out – he'd done that before. But he would come back, as bad-tempered as ever but with money in his pocket. And, by way of apology for being such a pain in the arse, he would buy the cigarettes and the booze for the next day or two. But without a word. He was secretly relieved that they were still there and that they still allowed him back in their company, although he would never have said so.

Bobby continued polishing the freshly-washed glasses on his bar and he watched the three men in the alcove out of the corner of his eye. He looked at the clock on the wall above the fireplace and pursed his lips. Five-forty-five. Fifteen minutes before the advent of the usual, 'on-the-way-home' brigade, who would loudly proclaim what a relief it was to have "a real pint in a good, old-fashioned pub." Bobby didn't mind being patronised: he could be as ethnic as they wanted so long as they paid his prices.

The Professor and co. had picked the time of their weekly pub treat with care. Between four o'clock and six o'clock in the afternoon was a time when The Mitre was unlikely to be busy. This they did for two reasons: firstly they knew that should they venture into the pub at any other time they would be stared at, sniggered at and subjected to implied or even verbal abuse and they didn't need that. All they wanted was a quiet drink in the warm, with chairs to sit on and a table to put their glasses on. The second reason was that they were perfectly aware Bobby was doing them a favour, a huge favour, and they didn't want to embarrass him or for him to think twice about letting them in.

A silence fell upon the three men, as inevitably happened after about an hour-and-a-half in the pub. These men were used to drinking on the move, in corners of The Park, in alleyways, shop doorways, the bus station, The Docks, down by the Railway Triangle, in bus shelters, on the wasteground. They were not accustomed to sitting down in a warm and intimate group around a table and in front of a roaring (albeit imitation) coal fire. It was always the same. The first half hour was luxury; the second half-hour confusing and the rest of the time downright uncomfortable. But it was always worth it for that first half hour.

Midnight Sam watched the flickering flames of the gas fire, deep in thought, finished his schooner of sherry and got up.

6

TEN-YEAR-OLD Samuel Midaka collected the dirty plates from five cluttered tables in the open-air restaurant at Madiyanna Lodge, stacked them neatly and hurried importantly into the kitchen. The diners, apart from one Australian couple on honeymoon, had left and the chef – a light-skinned Fula who vehemently but impossibly claimed he had been trained in Paris – occupied the hammock between the two coconut palms on the edge of the beach. He hummed in rhythm with the swing of the hammock and smoked an interesting, home-made cigarette.

The rows of 'tomato plants,' which took up most of the middle of Paradise Island, surprisingly enough never bore the familiar red fruit you would have expected. But what they did bear was extremely popular and, as far as the islanders were concerned, it beat the hell out of tomatoes.

Samuel could already read and write and speak in three different languages – English, French and Mandinka. Sadou had insisted on the first two out of practicality and the third out of pride and ethnic duty. Samuel was older than his ten years in many ways. Besides being bright and interested, he was capable of unusually deep thought for one so young. People took to him quickly and he enjoyed the attention and yet he was, in truth, a shy and private individual.

Samuel tried and failed to understand why his mother had left them (it was never 'him' but always 'them'). He spoke seriously to his father about it on many occasions and Sadou had never prevaricated, he had never insulted his son with candyfloss explanations. But he himself was puzzled and not entirely sure what had gone wrong.

Samuel attended to the lone Australian lovebirds – another bottle of red wine – cast a quick and adult eye over the otherwise empty and now tidy dining area and, satisfied that all was in order, he walked away from the lodge, down the sweeping beach to the crust of small wavelets which frothed their way over the sand. He stood, ankle-deep in the warm water and, small hands on slender hips, he looked out to sea, squinting in the blinding sunlight.

"You must learn, and I will teach you, because education is the key to your future," Sadou would say solemnly as they walked along the shoreline of Paradise Island. A small breeze whispered through the coconut palms and a rind of surf tickled their bare feet. "This is your country, Samuel, and it is a beautiful country. But you are privileged to have another, a country you have not seen yet, a country where a man can become rich in body, mind and spirit. England is your other home and one day very soon I will take you there. And when we are there, you will be able to learn much more than I could ever teach you. You will have such great adventures, you will make such great discoveries and meet so many different kinds of people ..."

"But I like it here, father, and I don't know this England," Samuel would interrupt softly, without rudeness, kicking the little wavelets as he walked. "Why do we have to leave? I have all my friends here and my uncles. I like my home, father."

Sadou would rest his arm gently around his son's shoulders and bend his head down to speak to the boy.

"We are poor, Samuel, and in The Gambia we will always be poor. One day you will want to take a wife, you will want to have children of your own. And you will want what is best for them. Then you will understand. You will have an opportunity to be happier, more content, more successful than you could ever be here, my son. Trust me, Samuel, I know what is best."

And Samuel, trusting his father as he did, would nod in agreement with the words but in his heart he was never sure. He loved his life, he loved Paradise Island, and he did not want anything else. He knew intimately the habitat of the wild animals – the bushbuck, the otters, the various species of monkey, the duiker and the hyena. He knew where to find crocodile and even where the occasional leopard was likely to wander into his country from Fathala Forest, over the border from Senegal. He had friends in the village on the opposite side of the island on the banks of the narrow creek which divided it from the mainland; and there were one or two older boys he knew in Barra.

Samuel was one of those rare human beings who was emotionally self-sufficient and spiritually content. Despite his tender years, he was a thoroughly rounded and balanced person. He did not possess that restlessness, that questing, troubled, angry and insatiable restlessness so common to the human species. Interest, wonder and curiosity, yes, there in abundance, as with intelligence and a desire to learn. But, unlike his well-meaning father, he had no ambition beyond knowledge itself, beyond his home, beyond what he already knew, understood and loved. He was certainly a self-sufficient and contented boy.

Even the circumstances of his estranged mother's behaviour – the blunt fact that she had abandoned him at the age of three – did not appear to have done the devastating damage one would have expected, at least not then. Samuel had not pushed her desertion away, suppressed his feelings, refused to accept what was, after all, the unacceptable. No, he had faced the situation head-on. He had discussed it with his father, with his closest friends and, to their initial embarrassment, with their mothers. Samuel, wiser than his years by a long way, came to the correct conclusion that his mother had never loved him. Never mistreated him, liked him in her own way, but that was all. He also realised that he felt the same about her.

On the other hand he loved his father passionately, unreservedly, with his whole being. Sadou was Samuel's world and Sadou felt the same about his son. You only had to see them together, the way they looked at each other, how they touched each other. Their bond, besides being forged of steel and unbreakable, was a thing a beauty.

Jennifer wrote on a regular basis, both to husband and son, enclosing money, a great deal of money, which Sadou deposited in a bank account he had opened in Banjul. Her letters were falsely gay and self-deprecating – "you're much better off without me" – and sad. Sad because they made Sadou realise that the woman he loved was superficial and without substance. She was living in London and, in her own words, "having a whale of a time" socialising, doing the scene, "the season" (whatever that meant). She babbled on interminably about Ascot, Henley, Wimbledon, about society parties where she rubbed shoulders with authors, actors and even minor royalty. She wrote of things her Mandinka husband did not, and had no desire to, understand.

A couple of hastily and dutifully penned paragraphs at the beginning and end of each letter would pay lip-service to the well-being of her husband and son. Obligatory and polite concern but without an ounce of honesty. And those separate letters to her son – agonising struggles of obligation – were embarrassingly formulaic.

Asking the right questions, making the correct noises, going through the motions. But the boy was never fooled.

By the time Samuel was ten years old his father had built up a sizeable bank balance. Besides Jennifer's regular 'guilt' cheques he had earned money anyway he could. Sadou had a number of jobs: full-time safari guide and bar tender at Madiyanna Lodge, small-holder on his tiny groundnut farm along with his two brothers, freelance guide and taxi-driver at Barra (whenever he could borrow a vehicle) and a stallholder selling fruit in Banjul's Albert Market.

Sadou had dedicated seven years of his life to making his dream come true: to take Samuel to England in time for his beloved boy to begin his secondary education. Jennifer had agreed to go through the pretence of their marriage and act, on paper at least, as the 'responsible adult' in order to get Samuel registered and settled into a school. Not just any school of course, as Jennifer was financially able and willing to go distinctly up-market. She put his name down for a place at Brentford College in Wimbledon – a private, boarding school with a diverse ethnic mix and, according to Jennifer, with an excellent academic reputation. Sadou was excited, Samuel less so.

Sadou had applied for and been granted a six-month visa, during which time he would get a job and apply for status to enable him to stay in the United Kingdom. He had saved up enough money for them both to live fairly comfortably for a while, especially as Jennifer had insisted on paying the school fees (which were considerable) and buying the uniforms, sports kit, books and the multifarious bits and pieces associated with school life. She had also volunteered to find Sadou a small flat in Wimbledon and to pay the deposit. But Sadou had insisted, in his courtly, old-style English, on providing "sufficient monies to satisfy all rental requisites."

On the day of their departure – it was two weeks before Christmas – Samuel got up early, just before the sun rose, blood-red over the arid deserts of Mali far inland to the east. He had said his goodbyes, all bar one. It was a solemn 10-year-old boy who sat in the middle of the hammock which creaked between the two coconut palms. The sea was pearl grey, awaiting the sun, and the light was cool and silver. Behind him the eastern sky was burned pale lemon, then gold, until it flamed orange as the Earth turned for another day. Tall palm trees were silhouetted black against the rising light and tiny dawn birds darted between the shivering palm fronds, chattering with excitement.

Samuel said goodbye to Paradise Island.

****

It was midway through December and Midnight Sam was a troubled man. Christmas was around the corner and this year he wanted it to be different. For the past seven years the festive season had gone largely unnoticed within the city's homeless community. To be fair to Brian Davies, who ran the day centre and the night shelter he always tried his best, even digging deep into his own pocket to try to make the day a bit special. A hot turkey dinner, a Christmas cracker apiece, a batch of mince pies donated by the Women's Institute and out would come the rather tired-looking, four-foot, artificial Christmas Tree with its built-in baubles (some cracked, others minus the original paintwork) and temperamental flashing lights.

"What have you got in mind, Sam?" asked Brian when the rumours which had been buzzing around the day centre for a few days had got too much for him. Midnight stroked an imaginary beard, cocked his head to one side, shifted deep into a corner of his chair and waited theatrically for a few seconds before he spoke: "I fancy a real tree, a big one, one of those Norwegian spruce things and I reckon we should get some holly and mistletoe and all that sort of stuff."

"And?" Brian could tell from Midnight's tone that there was an 'and.' Midnight inspected the centre boss out of the corner of his eye and made a quick but risky decision.

"Well, I thought, it being Christmas and all that and everybody in the world celebrating … well, I thought it wouldn't do any harm if, just for the one day of course, we could have a glass of wine … perhaps?" Midnight shook his head in anticipation of a negative response. "Toast the birth of Jesus, so to speak?" he ventured, over-egging the cake.

"You know the rules, Midnight. No alcohol in the centre or the shelter. I've chucked people out before now for bringing alcohol in. You know how strict we are about that."

Brian saw the deflated expression on Midnight's face and added gruffly: "I'll think about it. We'll have another talk about it tomorrow." But he knew that he was going to agree and he also knew that he was going to buy the booze himself. He was already doing the sums in his head: how many bottles of wine, maybe a quarter bottle of whisky for Scots Robby and perhaps something a bit more classy – port or brandy – for The Professor.

"If I do agree – and I haven't said 'yes' yet – it would be strictly for the one day only, Christmas Day, it would be a one-off. And …," he paused and frowned beneath his bushy, black eyebrows, " … it would be our big secret. Nobody outside the centre would have to know anything about it, nobody. City council, not to mention the press, would crucify me." He knew that he was wasting his breath, that the city council (his major funders) and the local rag would get to hear of it, sooner or later.

But he was also fairly confident that he was able to weather the storm. After all, without his day centre and night shelter – and they were morally his – how would the local authority cope with the city's homeless?

Brian Davies had been in the city for twelve years. Before that he had worked as a probation officer in Cardiff. But when he had read an advertisement in the South Wales Echo for somebody to set up and manage a night hostel for homeless men in an English city many miles to the east, he knew that he wanted to be that 'somebody.'

He soon won the confidence of the city council, who initially employed him, and built up invaluable relationships with the police, the probation service, various charities and housing associations. The city council gave him his head and became principal funders, freeing Brian to seek extra funding for a dream he had of launching a 'one-stop-shop' day centre.

The night shelter was one thing (and one very valuable thing at that) – somewhere for the homeless and the lost to find a warm, dry and safe bed for the night – but a day centre was altogether different. It would be a place where the forgotten people could go during those long and lonely days and meet like souls; where they could be seen by unjudgemental doctors and dentists; where they could get their benefits and other problems sorted out; where they could have a bite to eat and a hot drink for free; where they could be themselves, out of the disapproving glare of the outside world; where they could be cared for by the likes of Brian Davies and Doctor Dawes.

Brian lobbied a number of charitable trusts, the National Lottery and a whole range of local and national businesses. He was persistent and it paid off. Within four years he had expanded the night shelter and opened his longed-for day centre, ironically located in a former public house at the bottom of South Street. It had taken dedication, doggedness and damn hard work to make his dream come true.

"What did he say?" Scots Robby grilled Midnight Sam later the same day. "Are we or are we not going to have a true, Scottish, fuckin' Hogmanay this year?"

They were sitting on a wooden bench in the park, next to The Tree, a magnificent oak where the city's street-drinkers and homeless frequently assembled. They were into their second flagon of White Lightning.

"He said he'd think about it, but he'll be all right, I know him," said Midnight. "And it's not Hogmanay. It's not a New Year's Eve party. It's a Christmas party, it's on Christmas Day."

"Fuckin' Sassenach shite," Scots Robby retorted viciously. "Hogmanay – now that's a real, fuckin' celebration for you. Something worth having a party for, worth getting fuckin' pissed for. Not your poxy Sassenach Christmas." Midnight ignored his friend and rummaged about in his donkey jacket for a cigarette. He lit up and offered the flagon to Scots Robby, who took it ungraciously and drunk more than he wanted. Midnight cleaned the top of the bottle with the palm of his hand and screwed the cap back on delicately.

The weather had taken a turn for the better over the past few days. The wind had dropped, the skies cleared and the temperature had risen. It was unseasonably mild. As dusk began to creep across the park, the sky glowed clear blue, with a smudge of yellow where the sun had been.

Two men and a woman joined them. Barry Morgan, a garrulous Welshman, boring and boorish when sober and an absolute bastard when drunk, and two strangers. The man, thick-set with a full black beard, did all the talking and the woman, a willowy, delicate creature who looked much older than her 27 years, sat nervously on the end of the park bench.

She darted Midnight a quick smile. A hint of refinement lurked behind her red-rimmed eyes and in the set of her angular jaw; it glimmered faintly through the ravages of street life which were etched on her pale, sombre face. She wore a haunted expression.

The man introduced himself as Gordon Blacklock and waved a hand at the woman, who was leaning forwards, rocking rhythmically with her hands clasped on her lap. "She needs a drink," he said dismissively and Midnight Sam shifted closer to her on the bench and held out his bottle.

She looked up at Blacklock for permission, he gave a curt nod and she reached for the flagon tentatively with both hands.

Blacklock was 43 years old and "from up north." His accent was strong and harsh, his mannerisms challenging, aggressive and rude. But he was better dressed, better kept than the usual street-drinker. When he spoke he had a habit of leaning his head back and to one side and of narrowing his eyes. He never smiled.

Jane – nobody ever knew her surname – was a once-pretty young woman, but a broken nose, two missing front teeth and a scar which ran from the centre of her left cheek to the top lip had marred her appearance. That and years of abuse at the hands of a succession of violent men, men for some reason she found herself attracted to. And of course the booze. The mind-numbing, mind-scrambling, mind-bending booze.

"You'll need to get down to the night shelter by 8.30pm if you want beds for the night," said Midnight. "Better get there a bit before – fills up pretty quick this time of the year. I'll show you where it is if you like. Not far from here. About 15 minutes."

"They got themselves a fuckin' bedsit," said Barry Morgan with a nasty sneer. "Fuckin' jammy, I calls it. Only been 'ere five fuckin' minutes an' they got a bedsit."

Blacklock, who was leaning against The Tree, turned from the group and scratched the back of his head.

"Nothing jammy about it," he said. "Bought the local paper and knocked on a few doors. Cash in hand," he turned and gave the others a disdainful look, leaning his head back and tapping his right temple with a thick forefinger. "You've got to use your head. Cash in hand. That's what does it. Every time. All done and dusted within the hour. Eh, Jane?"

He swivelled around and looked at her impassively, his eyes cold and mocking. Jane nodded, ringing her hands in her lap but no longer rocking. Midnight tapped her on the thigh with the flagon. "Thanks," she whispered and took another drink, steadier, less desperate than the first. Blacklock stared at them, mouth downturned, and strode over to the bench. He prodded Jane roughly on the shoulder and she got up quickly.

"See you later," he said, leading her away by the elbow.

They didn't have to say where or when: street-drinkers, tramps, the inner-city homeless automatically knew where to meet and when. They gravitated to the same places – bus stations, bus shelters, railway sidings, parks, alleyways, doorways.

"Thanks for the cider ...," Jane said, looking over her shoulder and pausing for a name.

"Sam," he said. "People around here call me Midnight Sam. Oh and it's no problem, no problem about the cider. Any time." Blacklock tightened his grip on Jane's elbow and quickened his pace.

"I'm Jane," she added, raising her voice a little but without turning around this time. She had to trot to keep up with Blacklock, whose head was sunk bullishly into his broad shoulders.

"How did he get a fuckin' bedsit?" Barry Morgan whined, not willing to leave the matter be. "Where the fuck did he get his money from? Must have put down a deposit and all that. 'Ow the fuck did he do that?"

"He's from up north," Scots Robby said sagely, as if that explained everything. "We look after our money over the border, not like you fuckin' Sassenachs."

"You're a fine one to talk, you're always on the bum, you've never got no money," Barry Morgan protested. "Anyway he's not Scotch, he's from Newcastle. He ain't from Scotland."

"Scottish, not Scotch," Scots Robby corrected the Welshman indignantly. "Scotch is the fuckin' drink."

The argument clicked effortlessly into cruise control; it bore all the hallmarks of a morning-long exercise. Desolate, pointless but time-consuming. That all-important ingredient: something to occupy an hour or two, something with which to fill the endless days. Until the welcome oblivion of alcohol-induced sleep filled the yawning gaps. But Midnight was more self-sufficient than the other two and ten minutes of Scots Robby and Barry Morgan settling down to a marathon argument was more than enough. He got up from the bench, stuffing the near-empty bottle of White Lightning inside his donkey jacket, and drifted off into a chill grey mist which had started to gather across the grass. Scots Robby watched the back of Midnight's donkey jacket until it disappeared into the gloom.

Midnight Sam had something else on his mind, as he ambled towards the off-licence on the corner of Wellington Street. All he could see was the expression on Jane's face as that unsmiling, brutish bloke of hers frog-marched her away. She was clearly terrified of him, but there was more than fear in her eyes. There was a pleading, a begging for help, it seemed. And for a second she had looked straight into Midnight Sam's soul.

7

A FLOTILLA of ducks busied themselves across the water towards an elderly woman who stood patiently by a weeping willow tree, a carrier bag of bread over her arm. A squadron of scavenging seagulls wheeled ever closer, practising their swoops. As soon as the woman tossed handfuls of bread towards the ducks, the blitz krieg began. The ducks paddled furiously in circles, their bodies half out of the water, heads craned forwards, beaks snapping at the air, while the gulls dive-bombed, screeching and snatching pieces of bread literally from the ducks' mouths. The woman, who wore a red head-scarf and a grey, ankle-length raincoat despite the warm, late May sunshine, tried to favour the frantic ducks but it was not an easy task.

Sadou Midaka and his 17-year-old son sat close together on a fallen and rotting tree trunk at the side of the lake in Wimbledon Park. Sadou picked up a small stone and skimmed it across the water. Three ducks detoured to the splash but quickly about-turned. "How do you think you faired?" he asked.

"English, French, German, Latin pretty good, I think," Samuel replied, leaning back on the bench to let the sun warm his face. He had grown into a fine young man, with strong good looks and an inviting, open face. He had his father's eyes and his mother's wide, up-turned mouth. He possessed a measured depth, close to serenity, like his father. "Not so sure about the others. I should pass, but don't expect miracles in the sciences. Chemistry was an absolute stinger."

Sadou chuckled to himself at the private school lingo but, as ever, he warmed to his son. He knew how hard his boy had worked, how much he deserved the excellent marks he confidently expected him to achieve. His confidence was shared by Samuel's housemaster, a scatty but impassioned Irishman, known to both pupils and teachers, including the headmaster, as 'Spud.' Spud had Samuel down for an inevitable university place. He secretly favoured Oxford or Cambridge and had already made covert noises in those directions.

"Do you still want to enter the teaching profession when you have gained your degree?" Still the quaint English, the old-fashioned turn of phrase.

Samuel turned to face his father: "That's what I want to do. More than anything else, it's what I want to do." He stared out over the lake and added, speaking more to himself: "And I am going to do it, I am going to teach and …"

Sadou finished the sentence with a good-humoured but resigned sigh: "… and you are going back home to do it. To be a teacher in The Gambia. I know, I know."

Samuel frowned: "Father, you know that besides always wanting to be a teacher, I have always wanted to go back home. It is where I belong and it is where I can be of most use. You have always known that."

"But this too is your home – England, all this, this is your home now," Sadou spread his arms expansively to encompass the lake, warm and buzzing with flies, but Samuel shook his head solemnly. So Sadou left the subject. They had had the same conversation on numerous occasions and Samuel was always politely immovable. Sadou privately admired his son for his stance; he also knew in his heart that his desire for Samuel to remain in England was motivated by selfishness. He did not want to be apart from the boy. He loved England and he did not want to return to The Gambia, where his memories were of poverty and hardship and of a marriage that had foundered. But his respect for Samuel and the boy's high ideals outweighed his filial desires and he knew that when the time came he would give his son his blessing.

The woman who had been feeding the ducks folded her carrier bag and dropped it into a waste bin; she waddled off towards the road, a bit duck-like herself. Her captive audience turned and fanned out towards the middle of the lake, ever-seeking fresh pickings, and the seagulls disappeared, although their cries could still be heard.

Father and son had come a long way since they had arrived in the United Kingdom six years previously, as apprehensive and fearful as each other. Samuel temporarily moved in with his mother in her cottage in Hampton Wick and Sadou went about making home in a one-bedroomed flat in Wimbledon, courtesy of his estranged wife. In a matter of days, Sadou got a job as a junior porter in the local hospital.

The school term started a few weeks later and what was to be their routine for the next five years began. Jennifer had been kind, generous in the extreme and accommodating; and Samuel had been polite and appreciative. Nevertheless he was relieved when the taxi arrived to transport him, two suitcases of clothes and uniforms and several boxes of expensive 'essentials' from his mother's cottage to Brentford College. Sadou and Jennifer accompanied the 11-year-old boy to boarding school. Samuel was naturally nervous, but he was not scared. He trusted his father but more importantly he trusted himself.

Every weekend Samuel would spend with his father in the tiny flat. Sadou would make up a bed on the sofa in the living room (initially for himself but Samuel steadfastly refused the privilege) and for two golden days he would fuss over his son. And they were golden days. Sadou would pump Samuel about his progress at school, encouraging and positive where there was uncertainty and self-doubt, admonishing where there was arrogance. But all the time interested. There were few secrets between them. Even when the pubescent lad's sexuality began to emerge with customary clumsiness there were open and candid discussions. It was a rare relationship.

While Samuel progressed at college – a popular boy, helped greatly by his prowess at sport – his father gained respect and quick promotion at the hospital. Within two years he had been appointed head porter. But in the meantime he had enrolled as a trainee teacher at an English language school for foreign students in the neighbouring district of Southfields. From the outset it was obvious that he was a natural. Friendly, understanding, thorough and communicative. His students liked him and listened to him and he was encouraged by the principal to study for a full-time position.

Sadou's life was a constant juggling act: he had to manipulate his hospital shifts to free him for eight hours every Friday at the English language school and to give him Saturdays and Sundays off, so that he could spend the weekends with Samuel. That meant working on average for 70 hours a week, often more. He spent most evenings studying for his teaching qualifications.

The weeks turned into months and the months into years and Sadou's son became a young man. Sadou passed the necessary examinations and left the hospital to take up an appointment as full-time lecturer at the language school. Having successfully applied for residence status, his future was stable in the UK, his son was going from strength to strength and life was good. Samuel was en route to university and beyond and Sadou was carving out his own latent academic career.

****

The Professor bought a two-litre bottle of strong cider and 20 Benson and Hedges cigarettes from the One-Stop Shop at the bottom of London Road. He thrust the bottle into one of the deep pockets of his overcoat and fumbled with the cellophane on the cigarette packet. He tore at the irritating packaging, pulled out a cigarette with a shaky hand and lit up, using a lighter Midnight Sam had given him that morning. He coughed harshly into his cupped hands and the cigarette fell onto the floor. A string of saliva dangled from his lower lip. Pain stared out from reddened eyes as he stooped, hands braced on his thighs, and fought for breath.

The Professor was alone. Midnight was busy preparing for the forthcoming Christmas party, Scots Robby had gone on a bender with Gordon Blacklock and Fen was nowhere to be seen. It had been three weeks, but that was not unusual.

When the coughing fit subsided The Professor bent down with difficulty and picked up his cigarette; it had dropped into a puddle and had gone out. He undid the string belt of his overcoat and tucked the damp cigarette into the breast pocket of his thick, woolly shirt, sank back into a doorway and drank some cider. He waited for the anaesthetic glow of the alcohol to work, pushed the bottle back into his coat pocket and made his way wearily towards Station Crescent. It was four o'clock in the afternoon and night was beginning to fall. A chill north-easterly wind chased dark clouds across the sky but the rain had stopped.

Having already secured a bed at the night shelter (Brain Davies tended to give him preferential treatment and nobody, not even Scots Robby, complained about that), The Professor decided to kill time by paying a rare visit to a derelict area known as the Railway Triangle, half a mile out of town. It was somewhere different, a change of scenery.

The Triangle was a dreary testament to those great days of railway glory. A profusion of track, red-rusted and overgrown, leading nowhere any more; piles of rotting sleepers in readiness for use, frozen in time and rendered useless; dilapidated sheds; long-abandoned signal boxes, a few lone carriages, faded and sullen and with broken windows, skulking in abandoned sidings.

But The Professor liked the place. It was sad and melancholy, which often fitted his mood, and it was normally deserted, which also often fitted his mood. And the bleak view back over the city was, to him, strangely beautiful - lonely and dismal, but beautiful. The bus station, three ugly multi-storey car parks, a hideous, recently-constructed leisure centre, the ominous chimney which rose from the Royal Hospital, the austere Station Hotel and the backs of terraced houses. A thousand white lights glittered and the hum of traffic bore testament to the other world.

The Professor slumped gratefully to the ground, his back resting against the wheel of a goods wagon, out of the chill of the wind. He arranged his cigarettes, lighter and flagon of cider around him, tugged the lapels of his overcoat together and turned up the big collar against the cold. A three-quarter moon pulsed white-gold through a sudden break in the clouds and bathed the railway lines in a hard, silvery light.

The moonlight also picked out three figures coming from the direction of town, three men walking down the middle of a curving railway track, hunched and silent. The Professor, whose eyesight was not what it was, failed to spot them, but they had seen him. In fact they had seen him quite a while ago. The teenagers – two white and one black – had followed him from London Road, where he had stopped to take a drink of cider in a doorway. All three were hooded, high on crack cocaine and on a mission. And they had found their victim.

"What you doing here, old man?" said the taller of the two white youths, standing over The Professor, legs apart, hands flexing in readiness. The black youth bent down, picked up The Professor's flagon of cider, inspected the label and shook his head with mock disapproval: "Shouldn't be drinking this stuff, old man, not at your age."

The third teenager, short and thick-set and with bad acne, sank down onto his haunches and put an arm around The Professor's shoulders. With his other hand he pinched The Professor's cheek hard, the smile on his face changing instantly to a scowl. He looked up at the other two and nodded.

The Professor saw the nod out of the corner of his eye and the cold, sinking grip of fear was on him, suddenly blotting out all else. He knew what was coming and instinctively curled up into a ball.

The black youth struck him first – a hard kick in the ribs – and the youth with the bad complexion grabbed his hair with one hand and punched him on the side of the face with the other. The Professor, winded and in agony, sagged forwards and rolled over onto his back, gasping for breath.

"Got any money, old man, where's your mobile, old man?" demanded the black youth and the other two giggled, taking it in turns to kick The Professor as hard as they could. They measured their kicks as if they were taking penalties in a football match. The Professor bunched himself into the foetal position and took the blows. It seemed to go on forever until he ceased to feel the pain anymore, only the jarring thud of feet into his body. He started to lose consciousness.

"Look, he's got a watch," The Professor heard the distant words of one of his attackers and a rough hand tore the timepiece from his wrist.

"Christ, it's a fuck-off watch, worth a fuckin' fortune. How much is it worth, you old bastard?"

But The Professor was unable to speak. Two front teeth and his nose were broken, his lower lip split and his jaw was fractured, along with three ribs. He lay on his side, staring at a pair of white trainers, and registered vaguely that they were stained with blood. It took him a couple of seconds to realise that it was his own blood before he passed out. One of the teenage thugs reached down for The Professor's flagon of cider, took a small, token swig and then slowly poured the remainder over his body. The other two found that vaguely amusing and chuckled. They bent down and picked up The Professor's packet of cigarettes and the lighter Midnight Sam had given him, delivered a couple of half-hearted, parting kicks to the small of his back and, suddenly realising how badly they had hurt him, hurried away from the scene. They pulled their hoods down over their heads and hunched their shoulders defensively.

They no longer spoke to one another – they had their own private demons tumbling about in their heads – and as soon as they reached the main road, without a word, they split up. The Rolex watch – a graduation present to The Professor from his fiancée all those years ago – was not mentioned – and it weighed heavy, heavy with unwelcome guilt, in the pocket of the youth who had stolen it. He almost, but not quite, wished it was not there.

****

Midnight Sam lay on his dormitory bed in the night shelter, hands behind his head, and stared into a darkness dappled with city lights. He was beginning to worry. It was ten o'clock and The Professor should have been back by 8.30pm. At eleven o'clock the worry turned to panic. Midnight knew The Professor, knew his street habits, knew how dependable, how reliable he was. Something must have happened, something bad. It was always something bad.

He swung his legs off the bed, reached for his donkey jacket, wriggled his feet into his boots and crept out of the dormitory, careful not to disturb the other residents who snored, snuffled, coughed, farted or even sometimes softly wept the night away. He spoke to the shelter worker on duty and explained his concerns for The Professor. The volunteer, a former resident who had turned the corner and found his feet, shook his head: "I can't let you back in if you go out, Sam. You know the rules. If you're that worried why don't you let me ring the police? They know The Prof and they could keep an eye out for him. Why don't you go back to bed and leave it to me?" But he saw the obdurate expression on Midnight's face and knew that he was onto a loser. "Oh for Chrissake do what you like, but don't you expect me to let you back in," he grumbled. But they both knew that he would.

The wind had dropped and a faint drizzle had started to fall, cold and stinging and unkind. Midnight Sam buttoned up his donkey jacket, instinctively felt for his cider but remembered that he had hidden it underneath his bed at the night shelter. He did not bother to go back for it. His mind was sluggish. It was the end of a typical alcoholic day and his brain was at its worst – saturated with four or five two-litre flagons of strong cider and hardly a morsel of food. But he fought hard and somehow managed to martial his thoughts. The wasteground a mile-and-a-half down South Road; the bus station; the Cathedral grounds; the underpass on the far side of town; The Tree at the edge of The Park; or perhaps the Railway Triangle. The Professor would be at one of those places ...

It was four o'clock in the morning before Midnight Sam, drenched from the steady drizzle and bitterly cold, picked his way across the railway sleepers, tripping several times, and stumbled upon his friend, lying near the giant, rusted wheels of a long-forgotten goods wagon. He took a step backwards, shuffling his feet with horror but then craned his head forward to be sure. He looked down at the crumpled body, recognised the massive, dark blue overcoat and sank onto his knees alongside his friend. The Professor lay perfectly still, eyes closed, lips slightly parted, globules of blood bubbling down onto his beard with every shallow breath.

"Prof, can you hear me?" Midnight whispered, shaking his friend gently by the shoulder. The Professor groaned, flickered his eyelids briefly, and Midnight Sam recoiled.

The drizzle matured into a steady downpour and Midnight Sam, panic and sorrow in his eyes, tore off his donkey jacket and covered The Professor with infinite care. He stroked the older man's forehead and brushed the hair from eyes which were already starting to puff up. On all fours, staring down at the ground, he gritted his teeth and made a Herculean effort to clear his cider-softened brain. He spoke his muddled thoughts out loud until they somehow fought their way through the fog of alcohol and took form. With a surge of relief he knew what to do.

When Midnight Sam reached the flyover, some two hundred yards from the Railway Triangle, he stood in the middle of the road, feet apart, hands on thighs, and waited. It was 4.30am before the first vehicle came along, an articulated lorry, the front of the cab done up like a Christmas Tree. Midnight stood his ground but the lorry slowed a fraction and then manoeuvred around him on the wrong side of the road, sounding its throaty klaxon. An hour and eight vehicles passed, their drivers staring fixedly ahead, while Midnight Sam tried in vain to flag them down.

He was shivering uncontrollably from the bitter cold and terrified that his decision to wait for help was the wrong one, when a police patrol car pulled up.

8

DOCTOR Dawes was standing by the hospital bed, talking to a nurse, when The Professor regained consciousness. The swirling mists cleared and the disjointed, terrifying dreams receded. In their place came blurred vision, a distant, echoing sound of voices and an overall physical sensation of heat. He was unable to move, apart from a tentative turn of his head to the right and a limited flexing of both hands. And even that hurt. He murmured and the doctor swivelled round at the sound and stared down at the swollen eyes, mere slits in the mashed and blackened face. The Professor slid his eyeballs from left to right, without moving his head, and settled his vision upon the doctor, drawing a shallow breath in readiness to speak.

"Don't try to talk, keep still, don't move," said Doctor Dawes. "They've had to wire up your jaw. It's broken in two places. And you've got three fractured ribs. Lost a couple of teeth as well, I'm afraid and your nose is broken. Your kidneys are badly bruised. You took one hell of a beating. Thought we'd lost you."

The Professor tested the pains throughout his body, concentrating hard to acclimatise himself to the new situation, working out what he could or could not do. The penetrating ache in his head beat steadily;

his chest reacted to the slightest movement – anything more than the shallowest of breaths – with a vice-grip of agony; his genitals throbbed and his left kidney pulsed with a deep and frightening, internal pain. But he could move his feet without hurting, so he wriggled his toes for comfort. Out of the corner of one eye he saw a saline drip, which he presumed fed into his arm; he sensed that one tube was keeping his mouth open and another, smaller one was inserted into a nostril. He was unable to see the morphine drip inserted into his other arm, but he felt that something was there.

Three days beforehand, an ambulance had screeched up to the flyover, blue lights flashing, and two paramedics jumped out and scampered down the embankment on to the Railway Triangle, following the police officer over a criss-cross of redundant tracks to where The Professor lay. They carried a stretcher with them. Midnight Sam, wide-eyed, overawed but relieved by the attention, struggled to keep up, tripping once or twice over the railway lines (he had drunk a lot of cider that day). The paramedics checked The Professor's pulse, applied an oxygen mask, slid the stretcher underneath the inert, curled-up body, replaced Midnight Sam's donkey jacket with a silvery thermal blanket, inserted a plasma drip and picked their way quickly but with concentrated care back over the tracks to the main road. Midnight followed, clutching The Professor's cigarettes and one of his friend's laceless boots which had come off during the attack.

"Can I stay with him in the ambulance?" Midnight muttered, head down, shuffling from foot to foot. The two paramedics looked at the soaking wet tramp who wreaked of alcohol and was unsteady on his feet and then they looked at each other. They both winced and began to shake their heads, when the police officer butted in: "It's all right fellas, I know him. He's okay. Victim's a real close friend of his. He was the one who found him, the bloke who flagged us down …," the officer trailed, the unspoken words making it clear that Midnight Sam had probably saved his friend's life. Midnight sat in the back of the ambulance with The Professor, stroking the injured man's forehead. He made no attempt to wipe away the big, slow tears which rolled down his cheeks.

The Professor spent three touch-and-go days in intensive care before he was transferred to a general ward where he remained for two weeks. His jaw was healing well but the broken nose had knitted awkwardly, bending to the left. He had lost two front teeth and a third tooth at the back, which had split in half, had to be removed. He required 18 stitches to a three-inch gash across the back of his head. The thumb and forefinger of his left hand were broken, the thumb in two places, and he was heavily strapped for the three rib fractures.

****

While The Professor was recuperating in The Royal, Brian Davies had been busy back at the night shelter. With help, he had converted a seldom-used, basement storeroom into a tiny bed-sit. A local builder who owed Brian a favour or two (and had been a 'resident' himself a few years back) damp-proofed, skimmed and painted the walls and sealed and carpeted the concrete floor. He also converted a narrow but deep alcove into a mini-bathroom, installing a toilet and wash-basin. Modest but adequate furniture and furnishings had come from the Furniture Recycling Project (at a pittance). And a variety of niceties – framed pictures, ornaments, glassware, rugs – found their way to the bedsit, courtesy of Midnight Sam. Or, to be precise, courtesy of Debenhams, Marks and Spencer, British Home Stores and Furniture World, although the stores were not aware of their generous contributions.

Brian, trying to convince himself that the bedsit was not just for The Professor but for subsequent similar emergency cases – secretly chipped in £500 of his own money. And that was in direct defiance of his own cardinal rule never to become personally involved. But with a man like Brian Davies in a job like his, that was often easier said than done.

Nobody complained about the preferential treatment that The Professor was getting, not even Scots Robby, who even visited him several times in hospital. The Scotsman, not known for his generosity, on one occasion tried to smuggle in a half bottle of cheap, blended whisky. Fortunately one of the nurses spotted him trying to secrete the bottle underneath The Professor's pillows. A loud and abusive argument ensued.

"It's only a wee dram or two and it won't do him no fuckin' harm," Scots protested, bracing himself defiantly and hanging onto the bottle, which was still half-hidden beneath the pillows.

"Best medicine in the world. You Sassenach nurses haven't got a fuckin' clue. Drop of Scotch, drop of the hard stuff, that's what my mate needs. Not none of that poxy, fuckin' orange juice of yours."

Still protesting, but still clutching the bottle of whisky close to his chest, Scots Robby allowed himself to be escorted from the ward by two smiling but determined porters, who were clearly going to stand no nonsense. And, only for The Professor's sake, Scots Robby knew when he was beat. Better that way than for the coppers to get involved. At least he got to keep the whisky.

Brian Davies took Midnight Sam with him when he drove to the hospital to pick up The Professor. It was a difficult journey, not because The Professor was still in a great deal of pain (which he was) but because he did not want to go to the little bed-sit which had been created for him.

"I don't want anywhere permanent, Brian, you know that for God's sake," he said. "I don't belong anywhere permanent." He took a deep breath, which hurt like hell. "I'm not going Brian, you can't make me stay there!" He lowered his eyelids and squirmed painfully into the corner of the back seat of the car. "I'm sorry. I don't mean to sound ungrateful, but I'm terrified of the thought of settling down anywhere. It scares the shit out of me, Brian. I can't go there, I just can't. You know how impossible it is for people like us to get back."

Brian Davies sagged his shoulders as he negotiated the city centre traffic and half-turned his head to The Professor behind him. Midnight Sam – his once-fine brain softened with alcohol – was unable to say anything. He looked ahead and tried, unsuccessfully, to marshal his thoughts.

"I know what you're saying, Prof, but it'll only be for a short while until you get back on your feet again, I promise you," said Brian. "Give it until after Christmas; see how you feel then. You're still very weak. For Chrissake, you nearly died. You really can't look after yourself at the moment.

"Hospital said you had to be looked after and I've got a reputation to keep," Brian lied with a flash of inspiration. "Just until after Christmas, Prof. See how things are after Christmas."

The Professor sank his head onto his chest, temporarily forgetting his wired-up jaw and gasping with the pain: "Okay, okay, okay. I haven't got the strength to argue … and you're probably right. And thanks, Brian. Until after Christmas then."

****

Sadou Midaka was a very proud man. Not only had his 18-year-old son passed ten GCSEs with flying colours but he had excelled in his four A-level subjects, topping Brentford College with splendid grades in English, History, French and Geography. And the eager young man had gained a place at university. Not Oxford or Cambridge as his father and his housemaster had secretly hoped for, but Edinburgh, nonetheless a highly respected establishment. Sadou was well-pleased with Samuel:

his son had achieved what to him, a poor Mandinka native born in a mud hut, represented the unachievable, an impossible dream. Who knew what the future held for his beloved boy?

But Sadou himself had not been idle: he had studied for, taken and passed his own examinations and had rapidly risen to the position of senior lecturer at the English Language School in Southfields. His income had increased dramatically and, being a frugal and determined man, he had managed to put enough money aside to treat his son to a very special reward for his endeavours.

"But how on earth can we afford it father?" Samuel asked, wide-eyed with disbelief and delight. "It's not mother is it?" Sadou flashed his son a stern frown, shook his head and stood up. He indicated his son's empty glass: "Another beer?"

And so they caught the plane to Banjul, a Boeing 747, from Heathrow Airport at 8am on December 20th, 1990. It was a stone-cold, windless day, dark and dismal, with the faintest flurry of snow in the air. After three hours, Samuel, who was sitting in a window seat, looked down at the scattered islands of The Canaries, volcanic and barren. An hour later he followed the sharply defined coastline of West Africa, yellow-brown desert on one side of the plane and endless, pale blue sea on the other. A tiny fringe of white divided the two. His chest heaved with excitement and wonder: he was going home, going back to Africa. He willed the plane on with his eagerness and gazed down, transfixed, at the deserted coast five miles below.

Samuel had become thoroughly anglicised – the first eleven years of his life a half-forgotten dream – and yet, the moment he stood on the portable steps which were pushed manually up to the plane when they landed at Banjul airport, his re-encounter with the smell, the sound, the raw beauty of the continent was overwhelming. The harsh heat, the primeval thrill of Africa, his heritage, told his heart where he really belonged. Samuel descended the steps and strode out onto the baking tarmac, his father some way behind. He stood perfectly still, absorbing the complicated marvel of his homeland. Sadou understood and allowed his son the moment before catching up and clapping Samuel on the shoulder: "Welcome home, my boy, welcome home," he said in Mandika.

The next two weeks were magical, despite elements of sadness, more for Sadou than his son. Sadou's grandmother had reluctantly died, grumbling and belligerent to the end, as had his cousin, who had never drawn a well breath in her 37 years. One of his brothers had turned his back on groundnut farming and had sought fame and fortune on the dubious streets of Banjul. But Kano, his older brother – a dour and disapproving man – had stayed on at the smallholding, doing far better than he would ever have admitted. The international demand for peanuts was on the increase. Kano had moved out of the crumbling family hut in Barra and built himself a much larger home three miles to the east on the banks of the River Gambia, where he, his two wives and four children lived.

After three polite but not entirely relaxed days with Kano and his family, Sadou and Samuel returned to Paradise Island, the true purpose of their Odyssey. And thankfully little had changed. The narrow creek between the mainland and the island was still infested with crocodiles and the dugout canoe trip across was as irregular as ever. Once on the island things were again much the same. The hotchpotch village of grass huts, the ageing women bending double to their work in the fields, the rows of flourishing 'tomato plants,' the happy sleepiness.

But there were alterations to Madiyanna Lodge. Three more rondavels had been built and gardens, with lawns, exotic plants, bushes, shrubs and fountains, had been created. And, to Sadou's disapproval but not to Samuel's, a swimming pool now flanked the restaurant. A cork noticeboard was festooned with information about excursions and the like.

Both father and son were nevertheless relieved that the hammock between the two coconut palms was still there, exactly as it had always been, as was the sweep of virgin sand, and the distant hiss and gurgle of the powder blue sea.

Samuel was home and his heart swelled as if it would burst from his chest.

It was the loveliest Christmas he had known, the loveliest Christmas he would ever know. And he never forgot it.

****

It was two weeks before Christmas and Midnight Sam embarked upon a serious shopping spree. The phrase 'shopping spree' is normally associated with spending a considerable amount of money in a relatively short period of time, but in this instance not a penny had actually changed hands. Nevertheless the generosity of a goodly number of city shops had known no bounds, doubly admirable considering the recent bruising they had suffered for the benefit of The Professor's new bedsit.

If only the city's retail trade had realised how generous it had been. Had the various shopkeepers been aware of their philanthropy, in light of the plight of a certain impoverished couple in Bethlehem who had long ago been refused a room at the inn, they would surely have felt honoured to have been able to contribute so generously to Midnight Sam's seasonal plans for the homeless.

Candles, crackers, boxes of biscuits, mince pies, multifarious decorations, a Santa Claus outfit complete with beard and eyebrows, Christmas puddings, three free-range and organic turkeys, a sack of potatoes, four nets of sprouts and two substantial Ponsiettas from Marks and Spencer.

Most impressive of all was an eight-foot Norwegian Spruce Christmas Tree, with an attached label guaranteeing that no needles would drop for at least three weeks. Scots Robby had assisted with that particular acquisition by causing a drunken scene at the tills of Sainsbury's Homebase, while Midnight, wearing his amiable, I'm-not-doing-anything-wrong expression, side-stepped the gathering crowd of curious onlookers and staggered off with the tree.

Thankfully Brian Davies was spared the finer details of Midnight Sam's preparations, but even if he had guessed the truth he had chosen to exercise man's ability to hold two contradictory beliefs at the same time. Doublethink, courtesy of George Orwell, still had its uses. What the centre manager did not (or did not want to) know he could not be blamed for. But he did make one thing very clear.

"I'll provide the beverages – the drinks – and the smokes, Midnight," he said pointedly, glaring at Sam and lowering his eyebrows. "Nobody apart from me buys the booze. Do you understand? Nobody but me. Not a single drop."

Midnight Sam was actually relieved since acquiring alcohol carried with it distinct dangers of getting caught: "If you say so. No problem … and thanks. You're a real gent, you are, a real gent." The kindly but very street-wise Welshman wore a wry smile and asked himself for the umpteenth time whether a Christmas party was a good idea.

From time to time during his frenetic and stressful 'shopping' excursions, Midnight Sam would negotiate the concrete spiral staircase down to what had already been dubbed The Parlour to check up on his friend. The Professor was making slow but sure progress, although his left kidney and his ribs still ached horribly. He had had a dental plate fitted, his nose had all-but healed, if a touch lopsidedly, and his jaw had knitted together well. Eating and talking were no longer agonising exercises but yawning still hurt like the devil and the prospect of sneezing could not yet be contemplated.

The Professor had started listening to Radio Four (courtesy of Dixons), sitting back, eyes closed, in his comfortable but tatty, wing-backed armchair, which the Furniture Recycling Project had delivered. A second-hand, coal-effect electric fire warmed the room.

He indulged himself such rare comfort with confusion. Confusion at the fact that such pleasures were alien and frightening to him and yet he could not deny that warmth and comfort had their advantages. But he treated the situation much as would a holidaymaker savouring those two, make-believe weeks in the Mediterranean sunshine once every year. The Parlour was no more to him than a holiday destination, but unlike the two-week tourist, miserable at the thought of going home, The Professor masochistically yearned to return to the world he had become accustomed to. He wanted to be back out in the cold, where he felt he belonged.

He missed the wasteground.

9

THE lorry-driver sat on the verge by the side of the road, head in hands, rocking to and fro and muttering to himself. A small, wiry man in his late-forties, balding and with a thin grey moustache. His nostrils were caked with blood and a large lump was rising on the left side of his forehead.

The police officer who approached him from behind coughed before resting a hand on his shoulder, a comforting hand. The lorry-driver did not look up.

"Are you hurt?" the policeman asked, sniffing for alcohol and detecting none. "You the driver of the lorry?"

The lorry-driver nodded and slowly swung his head around, an expression of pleading and despair on his ashen face.

"Are you hurt?" the officer asked again and the lorry-driver shook his head vehemently.

"Banged my head on the steering wheel, that's all," he whispered, breathing deeply and staring sideways at the ground. "What about the other chap? The driver of the car? How is he? Is he badly hurt?"

On the other side of the road, opposite the jack-knifed articulated lorry, lay a red Ford Fiesta, on its roof, halfway down a deep ditch. It looked ridiculous, like a giant metallic beetle on its back, impotent and obscenely toy-like. Three paramedics, one holding a powerful lamp, were huddled together several yards from the overturned car, kneeling down over something in the grass and working hard. After ten minutes they stood up, two returned to the ambulance and the third walked over to the lorry-driver. He shook his head briefly for the benefit of the police officer and bent down to speak to the lorry-driver.

"Let's take a look at you, sir." He examined the man's face closely, his forehead knitted in a professional frown of concentration. "Do you feel dizzy, disorientated?" The lorry-driver shook his head. "Can you see my finger, now follow it." He obeyed sluggishly, without a word but to the paramedic's satisfaction.

The other two paramedics, in not too much of a hurry anymore, wheeled a stretcher to where the body lay. And when the ambulance left the scene and headed back to the hospital, there were no flashing lights, no blaring klaxons. An emergency had become a tragedy.

****

Samuel Midaka was well into his first year at Edinburgh University and was having the time of his life: settling into the cramped but friendly Halls of Residence, working hard for his English degree (much to the jealous derision of his peers), meeting girls – one in particular – tentatively enjoying his independence and generally testing his wings in readiness to fly. The first few months convinced him beyond any lingering doubt there might have been that he wanted, above all else, to teach.

And Sadou's own life was becoming more rounded, more complete. He was well-respected and well-paid at the English Language School; a colleague had persuaded him to try his hand at squash and he discovered that he had a natural aptitude for the game; he was seeing a nurse he had met while working at the hospital (a cautious relationship on both sides to begin with); and even Jennifer – distant but eternally generous Jennifer – had become a surprisingly pleasant bit-part in his world. She telephoned on a monthly basis, occasionally met up with her husband for dinner at some swanky restaurant and reminisced with genuine fondness. And, as regular as clockwork, she sent her son money.

****

The lecture was an interesting one – the influence of the two World Wars on English and American writers – and Samuel was studiously making notes (mental one's too) when the classroom door opened and the university principal stepped in, almost on tiptoe, and approached the lecturer who was in mid-flow at the lectern. The expression on the principal's face was sombre. The lecturer raised a hand to the students, bent his head to the principal and nodded slowly, his eyes closed.

"Would Samuel Midaka please step outside for a moment, the principal would like a word," he said, his normally jolly and enthusiastic tone flat and weary. Samuel got to his feet, puzzled and fearful. Something about the subtle but unmistakeable change in the atmosphere in the room, a sadness and a coldness, frightened him. He hurried down the aisle steps, forgetting his books, and followed the principal out of the classroom.

"There has been an accident, Samuel," said the principal, striving to control his own sorrow. The young Gambian student was very popular, much-loved by fellow pupils and staff alike. "I'm afraid I have some very bad news for you …," he paused, Samuel's widening eyes almost choking the head teacher. "Samuel," he rested both hands on the young man's shoulders, "your father was involved in a motor car accident last night. I'm really sorry. He was killed instantly, he can't have suffered. His car collided head-on with an articulated lorry. It appears to have been an accident, not anybody's fault. An accident, a tragic accident. I'm so sorry."

At that moment Samuel Midaka's world stopped. He felt physically and mentally numb and his emotions, in instinctive self-preservation, immediately shut down. Or, to be more accurate, they shut their doors to the outside world. He heard his own questions – "when did it happen?" "where did it happen?" even "what happened to the lorry-driver, was he all right?" and "where is my father now?" – but the questions came from somewhere else, somewhere outside his own brain, beyond his own mind.

It was as if a programmed machine, a robot, had clicked into action. The words came out all right and in a calm, level tone, but the speaker was not Samuel Midaka, not the young man who had just lost the reason for his existence. Even while he was asking the obvious questions, going through the motions, he could not help but view the scenario with a detached curiosity, as if the nightmare was purely an academic exercise. What does one say in such a circumstance, what are the right questions to ask, the right words to utter? How should one react, how should one behave? Deep inside his heart had broken and it would take him a long time, several months, before he realised that fact.

****

Jennifer organised and paid for the funeral and that included flying Sadou's two brothers and the proprietor of Madiyanna Lodge over for the service. She took Samuel to one side and reassured him that the flat in Wimbledon would always be there for him and he need never worry about money. He should carry on with his studies and become a teacher – Sadou would have wanted that. Samuel was polite and appreciative on the outside, but on the inside the lights had gone out. There was only darkness now; a numbing, ringing, unfillable void of darkness.

Two days after the funeral Samuel returned to Edinburgh, with a vague notion of 'losing himself' in his studies. The notion lasted for a month, during which time not one morsel of learning penetrated his brain. He would sit, somewhere near the back of the class, rigid and distant, and try to listen to what the lecturer had to say. He heard the words but they meant nothing. His friends (of whom he had many) at first tried to comfort him, to help him, to cheer him up, but after a while the force field of grey grief which surrounded him became too much of an obstacle for them. They were young and they had their own lives, their own futures, their own dreams. The girl he had been seeing tried harder, patient and tender, trying to coax the young man she was on the brink of falling in love with to get over his grief, to build bridges back to his own world. But what she did not and could not be expected to understand was that Samuel's world had revolved around his father.

She and all Samuel's friends began to avoid him, to avoid the black cloud which he carried around with him, to avoid the aura of misery which threatened to envelope all those who came close to him.

And one day – it was a bright, breezy day in early May – one day, Samuel was gone. His room was left tidy, his books stacked neatly on the bookshelves he had assembled himself many months beforehand, his bed was made and the desk where he had studied so hard boasted two-and-a-half A4 pages of an unfinished essay.

Only one holdall, packed with clothes, was missing. There was no note, no letter, nothing to explain where he had gone or why. The police later discovered that he had drawn £500 in cash from his building society savings account, which left a balance of £6.52p. After routine enquiries, which included three meetings with Jennifer Crawley, Samuel Midaka's name was added to the missing person's list.

10

THE Christmas Party at the day centre was a remarkable and memorable occasion. Nobody who had the dubious fortune to be there was likely to forget it for a long time. Brian Davies was likely to remember the day for the rest of his life.

Midnight Sam excelled himself and besides acquiring large quantities of festive goodies he had embarked upon a decorations campaign the like of which the humble drop-in centre in South Street had not witnessed before. Boxes of paper chains, king-sized sprays of mistletoe, dangerous bunches of holly, several miles (or so it seemed) of tinsel – silver, gold, green and red – hundreds of party poppers, and a vast assortment of glittering Christmas paraphernalia. Midnight's pride and joy was a six-foot wide by four-foot high by three-foot deep, glass-encased Nativity Crib, complete with Mary and Joseph, shepherds, three Kings of Orient and assorted livestock, all gathered dutifully around Baby Jesus in his crib.

It was far too late to do anything about it, but Brian's heart sank. Had he known the last-minute crisis which now faced St Gregory's Church in the nearby parish of Abbeywood, his heart would have sunk even lower.

Brian drove the short distance from the night shelter to the day centre to pick up The Professor. Scots Robby went along to help The Professor up the spiral staircase as Midnight Sam, resplendent in his Santa Claus outfit, was too busy with last-minute preparations. It was 11am on Christmas Day and the town was predictably deserted. When they reached the night shelter they found The Professor standing outside the building, in the doorway, engulfed in his navy blue overcoat. The beard was gone and his hair had been neatly trimmed. A plate to replace the missing front teeth was in place. Although still painfully thin, over the past couple of weeks he had put on some weight and there was a touch more colour in his cheeks. Brian had gently but firmly insisted that The Professor eat something hot every day, even if it was only beans on toast. And Midnight Sam had vigorously policed this routine.

"You should have waited in the Parlour," Brian frowned, taking The Professor by the arm. "You're still very weak, you know. You've got to take more care of yourself."

The Professor pulled a face and Scots Robby flustered out of the front seat of Brian's car and made a military meal out of holding the door open. He all-but saluted and The Professor all-but returned the all-but salute.

"How are you feeling?" Brian asked, starting the car.

"Ribs are still sore, jaw aches a bit, but I'm not too bad, considering."

"And the other stuff – the coughing and those stomach pains – how about that?" Brian broached the no-go subject tentatively.

The Professor grimaced: "Still there, I'm afraid, but you'd be amazed at the power of mind over matter. Would you believe it but it is possible to stop yourself from coughing or from sneezing if you know in advance that it's going to be agony. It's been nearly six weeks since I was beaten up and I've only sneezed once. A bloody miracle!"

Scots Robby, almost knocking The Professor over in his determination to lead the way, marched into the main reception lounge of the day centre, waving his arms about: "Give us some fuckin' space, we've got The Prof here. First time he's been allowed out since he got out of hospital. Make way!" He jerked his head from left to right until he spotted Gordon Blacklock, lounging back in the only armchair in the centre. He was holding a paper cup in his left hand, which was resting on one of the chair's bulky arms, and abstractly smoothing his beard with his other hand. It was his fourth large whisky since the party had begun at 10.30am.

Although Brian was determined to monitor the drinking, most of the partygoers had taken advantage of the 20 minutes it had taken him to collect The Professor and they had downed a few quick ones. Brian had insisted on paper cups: no drinking from bottles and definitely not out of glasses. Midnight was mildly disappointed with the latter instruction as he had acquired six cut crystal red wine goblets from British Home Stores especially for the occasion.

"Hey Blackie, why don't you let The Prof sit down?" Scots Robby boomed across the room, but the unsmiling northerner took no notice. He continued to sip his whisky, without looking up. Scots Robby bristled and looked away, muttering "fuckin' Sassenach" not quite beneath his breath. Blacklock glanced up sharply, his face hooded with sudden anger, but then he switched his gaze to the far corner of the room where Jane was sitting on a sofa next to two pale and nervous young men in their mid-twenties. The young men were busy rolling cigarettes while Jane gulped from a paper cup which she clutched in both hands. She met Blacklock's stare over the rim of the paper cup and her eyes widened, her cheeks twitching into a wan smile.

When The Professor shuffled into the room he was greeted with sporadic applause. Midnight Sam placed a bright red sleeve with a furry white cuff around his friend's shoulders and the two young men sitting on the sofa with Jane sprang to their feet.

"Sit 'ere Prof," said one, gathering up his smoking paraphernalia from the battered coffee table in front of him. The Professor, although embarrassed at the fuss, was glad of a comfortable seat. He nodded at the two men, who stood awkwardly at each end of the sofa, patted one of them on the arm and lowered himself next to Jane, breathing deeply with the exertion.

"You've been pretty busy, Midnight," The Professor looked around the room – a dense forest of paper chains, streamers, tinsel and holly (the mistletoe had been banned by Brian), in the midst of which rose a magnificent, ten-foot high Christmas Tree. It had been decorated with great enthusiasm: scores of multi-coloured baubles and bangles, thick with spray-on snow and dazzling with 160 flashing lights. And lashed to the top of the tree, in pride of place, was an 18-inch tall teddy bear dressed up as Santa Claus. Midnight thought it would make a change from the usual fairy or star and he was right. Beneath the tree were 32 presents, one for every guest, including Brian, who later thanked Midnight for the box of cigars, despite the fact that he hadn't smoked for nine years.

"Are you feeling better?" a timid voice whispered and The Professor turned to look into Jane's once beautiful grey eyes. They were now red-rimmed and criss-crossed with ruptured blood vessels. He noticed a small circular blister about the size of a one pence coin on her forehead. It looked like a burn. The Professor frowned inwardly but forced a friendly smile onto his face: "Yes thanks, I feel a lot better now. Feel a bit spoilt, to be honest. Don't know how long I'll stay at The Parlour. See how I feel."

He pursed his lips. He was warm, dry, comfortable, waited on by Midnight and even, albeit gruffly, by Scots Robby. But the comfort, the certainty and even the safety (despite having been nearly beaten to death) unsettled him. It made him feel restless.

Paddy burst through the door with a bottle of wine protruding from a coat pocket and fresh vomit on both lapels. He was very drunk and totally stoned – a normal condition for the 34-year-old Irish cocaine addict – and within seconds he fell into the Christmas Tree, became entangled in the fairy lights and sat down on one of the presents. He tried to disentangle himself from the fairy lights, pulled a shiny purple bauble from the tree, inspected it closely, and proceeded to scramble around in a circle on all fours. He cursed, apologised and giggled, roughly at the same time and Brian nodded to Splodge and Nobby (the unofficial bouncers). They hoisted Paddy to his feet and frog-marched him out of the room into the street.

"And don't you come back or we'll break your fuckin' legs." The gentle warning wafted from the doorway, just before the door was slammed shut and the key was turned in the lock. Brian closed his eyes for a second.

The turkey dinner was a success. Brian's wife and the wives of two other centre workers had joined forces to cook the three 15lb free-range turkeys proudly presented to them by Midnight Sam. They made a point of not asking where the birds had come from because, in a complicated fashion, Midnight was an honest man, and no doubt would have told them.

The only minor mishap occurred when Scots Robby overdid the brandy on one of the Marks and Spencer Christmas puddings. He managed to set fire to a festive-patterned paper tablecloth and singe his moustache into the bargain. The fire began to take hold until Splodge and Nobby (evidently also the unofficial firefighters) roared into action, armed with two jugs of water apiece, and managed to get some of it onto the flames.

Brian sat next to The Professor for the surprise carol concert. Handwritten, photocopied carol sheets were distributed by Midnight Sam, who made a strange, introductory speech before switching on a state-of-the-art CD player from Dixons, which still bore the security tag. They kicked off with Away in a Manger. The Professor shared a carol sheet with Jane, whose sudden radiant smile at the prospect of singing hit him in the pit of the stomach like a blow from a sledgehammer. It reminded him of somebody else a long time ago. Annoyed and shocked at his own weakness, he blinked the tears from his eyes angrily and rested his hand on Jane's shoulder, an innocent gesture of tenderness.

For just an instant, The Professor could see beyond the broken nose, the missing teeth, the scar, the haunted, frightened and bloodshot eyes. For a brief moment all was eclipsed by a fleeting but beautiful smile. For The Professor the smile filled the room, blotting out the tawdry tinsel, the unutterable pathos of the party. It was a flashback to a once-happy life, to a past full of promise and full of love.

But to Gordon Blacklock, scowling into his whisky on the other side of the room, what he saw was his woman getting far-too cosy with some doddery old fogey who spoke in a posh accent. *And* who had his arm around her shoulder.

Three-quarters of a bottle of whisky was dangerous fuel for the likes of this man. His eyes flashed and then turned cold as he bounced to his feet with surprisingly agility and strode purposefully across the crowded room. He knocked a couple of tables askew, spilling several paper cups, and kicked a chair out of the way. The voices belting out Away in a Manger faltered and petered out altogether and somebody turned off the CD player as Blacklock squared up to The Professor.

"Get your fuckin' hands off of her," he snarled, his arms half-bent by his sides and his massive fists clenched in readiness for violence. Taken aback and genuinely puzzled, The Professor dropped his arm from Jane's shoulder.

"Please Gordon, don't," Jane moved a pace forward, shaking her head and stretching her right arm protectively in front of The Professor.

Blacklock momentarily switched his glare to the woman, his face twisted into an expression of mild disgust and he cuffed her once, a measured but hard blow, across the side of her head. She fell to the floor but immediately staggered to her feet again and stood uncertainly but bravely in front of The Professor, with both arms outstretched.

Brian Davies fought his way through the now silent and uneasy crowd towards the troublespot as quickly as he could. But the floor was littered with overturned chairs, discarded paper cups, fallen paper chains and Splodge and Nobby, blissfully sound asleep in the middle of it all. A sudden commotion on the far side of the room stopped the centre manager in his tracks: Scots Robby, red-faced and fired-up with a mixture of whisky and indignation that anyone should contemplate taking a pop at The Professor, came with a rush, his orange paper party hat flying off, and gave Blacklock an almighty shove between the shoulder blades. The Professor and Jane only just managed to step out of the way to see the northerner plunge head-first, arms flailing like a windmill, into the Christmas Tree.

This time it was too much for the Norweigan Spruce – the tree crashed to the floor, narrowly missing a magnificent Christmas cake on a square trestle table. The teddy bear sailed from the top and the fairy lights flashed their last. Blacklock emerged from underneath the pole-axed tree, spluttering and spitting out obscenities, while The Professor ushered Jane to one side. Scots Robby, horrified at his act of heroism, vanished out of the front door of the day centre at astonishing speed for one so drunk.

"I want you out of here right now," Brian hissed, glowering at the back of Blacklock's head. "And you are not to come back. You're not welcome. Set so much as a foot inside here or the night shelter ever again and I will have no hesitation in calling the police." Blacklock stood up, brushed himself down, turned around and stepped towards the centre manager.

"You'd better watch out, taffy," he narrowed his eyes. "This fuckin' dump of yours might get burnt to the ground."

Brian, by far the smaller and much older of the two men, squared up to Blacklock without a shred of fear, white with anger: "That sounds very much like a threat to me and I have around 30 witnesses here. I want you gone, now, or I call the police. You've got three seconds."

Blacklock laughed nastily and barged his way across the room to the door, kicking out at the Christmas cake table as he went. The table rocked precariously but thankfully it did not fall over. Jane followed, chewing her lower lip and ringing her hands. The Professor, Brian and Midnight Sam tried to persuade her otherwise, but there was nothing they could do to stop her.

Brian blocked her path and rested his hands on her shoulders: "You don't have to go with him Jane. You can stay in the night shelter tonight and then …"

"He'd find me, he'd come and get me and then it would be worse," she interrupted wearily.

Brian tried again: "I can take you to the women's refuge, I can take you there now. He doesn't know where it is, he won't know where you are." Brian saw the deep resignation, the hopelessness in her face – she had been there before, he thought, many times – and he slumped his shoulders.

"He would find out, he would find out where I was ... he always does."

The Professor joined Brian, holding onto a table for support. The excitement had stirred up problems and he gulped for air. His ribs ached horribly and the deep devil inside his stomach flexed its painful muscles.

"I could quite easily move out of The Parlour for a while and you could stay there." His voice was soft and breathless. "He'd never know ."

She shook her head: "You're very kind, really kind, you all are." She walked over to Midnight Sam who was pretending to fuss over the felled Christmas Tree, the Teddy Bear Santa under his left arm. She raised a hand, a small wave, and Midnight acknowledged the gesture sadly.

"Thanks for a lovely party," she said without irony and left the room, closing the front door quietly behind her.

Brian clapped his hands: "Come on then ... pass the parcel." He shook Midnight Sam by the arm: "Come on, Midnight, this is your idea. Let's get those tables cleared away, let's get that Christmas Tree back on its feet." People started to move, started to relax, started to galvanise themselves back into action. "Stick a CD on the player, anything at all, it doesn't matter, and everyone on the floor in one bloody big circle. Come on, everybody, stop farting around!"

Thirty street-drinkers obeyed, with more determination than efficiency, and the 'bloody big circle' began to take shape. Splodge and Nobby, eventually awakened by the silence which accompanied the unpleasantness, but still sleepy-eyed and confused, took it upon themselves to deal with the stricken Christmas Tree, even managing to restore the Teddy Bear Santa to its rightful position. Midnight Sam stood guard over the pile of interestingly-wrapped presents (he had done the deeds himself the previous night after his fifth flagon of White Lightning).

The tables and chairs were cleared out of the way and The Professor, having selected Christmas Hits of the 1990s, assumed control of the CD player.

An unusual version of pass-the-parcel had been going on for around ten minutes when there was an almighty crash. The glass panel in the front door was in pieces and a half-brick skidded across the floor. A blast of cold air whipped into the room and The Professor turned off the CD player. Nobby, who was on a mission to win and was proud that he had mastered the rules of a game he had never heard of before, started to tear away at the wrappings of the parcel.

Brian, with Midnight Sam close behind, ran to the door, yanked it open and peered outside, jerking his head from left to right. They caught a fleeting glance of Gordon Blacklock scuttling around a corner, a six-inch length of silver tinsel dangling from his hair.

11

MARK Fenemore walked into The Mitre at four-thirty in the afternoon of Thursday, January 19. He had been away for five weeks.

Midnight Sam, The Professor and Scots Robby were sitting in the alcove and the landlord was watching a snooker match on a portable television set at the end of the bar, while he polished the same beer mug over and over again. Bobby had valiantly resisted Sky despite regular pleadings from locals. He was an old-fashioned and stubborn man.

Midnight and The Professor were drinking pints of Olde English and Scots Robby was experimenting with a drink he had recently discovered called 'snakebite' – equal portions of cider and lager.

Fen, his left arm in plaster and a tight sling, stood at the bar without a word of greeting. Bobby feigned not to have seen the surly Brummie and pointedly concentrated on the snooker match until the visiting player missed a difficult red. He then ambled back down the bar and faced the lean, hatchet-faced young man.

"What have you done to your arm?" he asked without an ounce of sympathy.

Fen shrugged: "Bust it. Give me a half of lager and get that lot another round." He waved his good arm in the direction of the alcove, tossed a £20 note onto the bar, pocketed the change without checking it and meandered over to the fruit machine. He pushed in the coins with casual violence and punched the buttons, barely bothering to wait for the results.

Ever the optimist, Midnight Sam got up and strolled over to Fen. He watched him play the fruit machine for a minute or two before he said, his tone kind and chatty: "So what have you been up to? Missed a good party at Christmas. Welshie let us have booze and all sorts. How d'you bust your arm?"

"Minding my own fuckin' business," Fen said nastily, not looking up from the fruit machine. Midnight turned around, picked up the three pints from the bar, not too confidently, and tottered precariously back to the alcove. He sat down with his back to Fen, facing the frosted window.

Scots Robby leaned across the table, grabbed his glass and took an exaggerated gulp: "Snakebite – cider and lager – fuckin' brilliant. Man's fuckin drink. None of your poxy, girlie, fuckin' sherry."

The fact that Midnight Sam was drinking cider, which he invariably did, made no difference to the Scotsman, who was never going to forget (or let anyone else forget) the Thursday before Christmas when his companion had fancied a schooner or two of Harveys Bristol Cream.

"Heard you got yourself worked over, Prof," Fen flashed The Professor a quick, sideways look before banging the sides of the fruit machine and growling: "Machine's fuckin' rigged … you all right now?"

"Yeah," The Professor called across the bar. "Bloody sods stole my watch though. That was the worst thing about it."

Although no words had been said and no explanation ever volunteered as to how a homeless street-drinker without two pennies to rub together had managed to hang onto a solid gold wristwatch, everybody knew what the timepiece had meant to The Professor. Its loss had offended them all and now it had even offended Fen.

"Fuckin' bastards," he spat, probably referring to the entire world and not just to the three thugs who had attacked The Professor.

"Mind your language," Bobby said sharply, peering over the rims of his glasses. Fen cleared his throat rudely, downed his half of lager and left the pub without a word, managing a rasping belch before pushing the swing doors open with both hands.

"Same old Fen," Midnight said, lighting up a generous dog-end which a woman, judging by the lip-stick on the filter tip, had left in the ashtray.

"Miserable fucker," Scots Robby picked up the pint Fen had bought him, downed a third and wiped his moustache with the sleeve of his anorak. "This snakebite's fuckin' brilliant, got a real bite to it."

"And you can mind your language and all," Bobby raised his voice irritably. "There's women gets in this pub and they don't want to hear your swearing all the time."

There wasn't a woman in sight and the sort of females who used The Mitre had vocabularies which were an easy match for the Scotsman's. And when the pub skittles team played a match in the back alley, Bobby managed more 'fucks' per sentence than Scots Robby and Fen put together. But the landlord disliked Scots Robby and Fen and, as it was his pub, he could afford to be a hypocrite.

"He's a dark horse, that one," mused The Professor. "I wonder where he goes. One minute he's here, moaning and moping about and as miserable as sin, and the next he's gone. Takes off without a word and, weeks later, waltzes back in without a word. Where the hell does he go?" The Professor addressed the question to himself.

"Always comes back on a Thursday, picks up his benefit and always buys us a drink," Midnight said in defence of the young man who racially abused him as a matter of course. "Always puts his hand in his pocket, the minute he gets back."

Scots Robby had to concede that point with a curt nod. "Miserable fucker though," he said, too quietly for the landlord to hear.

****

Mark Fenemore's earliest childhood memory was a violent and sexual one. He was three-and-a-half years old and shared a single bed with his 11-year-old brother Kevin in a crowded, three-bedroomed council house in Langley, a dreary suburb of Smethwick on the outskirts of Birmingham. His three sisters shared another bedroom and his mother, Sharon, occupied the third bedroom with her latest fellow, a 45-year-old lorry driver from Port Talbot, a restless man, small-framed but hard-muscled and strong. He went by the name of Owen Thomas, but there was some doubt whether that was his real name.

Mark was asleep, curled into Kevin's back for warmth, when the bedroom door clicked open. An orange-yellow glow from the naked landing light-bulb swept the room for a second before the door clicked shut. What had awoken Mark was not the door opening and closing but the acrid smell of tobacco coupled with the strong odour of alcohol. He lay perfectly still, his eyes wide open.

Thomas, breathing heavily and quickly, crept around the bottom of the bed and shook Kevin by the shoulders. Kevin, who was already awake, made a show of rubbing his eyes, shaking his head and turning over, away from his mother's lover. Thomas pulled Kevin back to face him, by the hair. Kevin stifled a gasp and swung both of his legs out of the bed, his head bowed.

Out of the corner of a narrowed eye, Mark watched his step-father loosen his belt and let his trousers drop to the floor. He couldn't see what was happening – he was too young to understand anyway – but, after a while, he heard Thomas let out a long but stifled groan, bend down clumsily and hitch up his trousers. Kevin, who had been sitting on the edge of the bed, tip-toed to a clothes-horse in the corner of the room and reached for a towel.

Thomas did up his belt, beckoned to Kevin, prodded the boy in the chest and waggled a forefinger in the boy's face. He cupped a hand behind the nape of Kevin's neck, tugged roughly so that the boy's face was less than an inch from his own and hissed some slurred and drunken warning. Still clutching the towel, Kevin nodded, wide-eyed, and wormed his way back under the duvet. The door clicked open and closed again and Kevin turned away from Mark and curled into the foetal position as if he wanted to become a ball which would get smaller and smaller until it would disappear altogether.

Even at such an age, Mark instinctively understood his half-brother's body language; he made no effort to move closer. Puzzled, disturbed but predominantly tired, the toddler snuggled down and drifted back to sleep, not sure whether Kevin was snoring or sniffing. It sounded more like sniffing. The smell of tobacco and alcohol hung in the air. In the morning Michael had consciously forgotten the incident, but it was stored forever in his subconscious. Kevin was very quiet as he got dressed for school and his eyes were red-rimmed.

Sharon Fenemore, Mark's mother, was a thirty-something, blowsy, peroxide blonde who found it difficult to keep her legs together when she had downed the requisite number of Badardi and Cokes. She found it equally as difficult to resist downing the requisite number of Bacardi and Cokes.

Sharon had five children by three different men. Her first-born, a boy, was of mixed race and the Jamaican father – a kind but violent man – stayed around until Sharon's second child, a daughter, was born. The baby girl was beautiful, blue-eyed, but unmistakeably white.

Sharon stubbornly refused to reveal who the father was, even when the incensed Jamaican took a hefty belt at her.

Kevin's father – an affable builder who broke into more homes than he helped to erect – was on the scene, off and on, for a number of years. Most of the time he spent at Her Majesty's Pleasure. He wasn't a very good thief, but then he wasn't a very good builder either.

During one 18-month stretch for breaking into the home of a prominent city councillor and carting off six cumbersome but relatively worthless paintings, Sharon rekindled the flame with her daughter's mystery father. It was only a one-night stand but enough to create Mark Fenemore. The builder was more understanding than the Jamaican (or perhaps he didn't care) and in one of his brief spells of freedom he gave Kevin a sister, Penelope.

Shortly after Owen Thomas moved in, the two eldest children moved out – one into a hostel for young single homeless and the other into a massage parlour in Bedminster, Bristol. Which left Kevin, Mark and Penny. Eventually they all fell victim to the persistent, sexual attentions of the Welsh lorry-driver, but Kevin was the first to suffer. And for two years he suffered, until one night his teenage body was found hanging from the rafters in a lock-up garage opposite the neglected block of council flats where the Fenemore family lived.

Some other kids, who had gone to the garage to smoke dope in peace, found him at 11.15pm. His face was quite blue, his eyes milky and half-closed. A small, plastic stool lay on its side underneath the dangling legs.

He was 16 years old. At the bleak inquest an open verdict was recorded. Coroners are often compassionate people. No suicide note had been found and there was the faint possibility that the lad had only intended a 'cry for help.' The coroner was kind enough to allow the family to grieve in peace without the stigma of a suicide verdict hanging over their heads. Many suicides are handled this way to spare relatives and friends of the deceased those unpalatable and inevitable pangs of guilt – if only we'd realised, if only he had said something, if only, if only …

Mark was seven-and-a-half and Penny three-years-old when Kevin killed himself. Penny was too young to appreciate the enormity of what had happened but the death had a profound effect on the boy. Images of those dark and dirty nights when Thomas had come into the bedroom and systematically abused Kevin while he lay curled, confused and frightened, feigning sleep, in the same bed, regularly came back to haunt him. He begun to have nightmares and would fight desperately hard to stay awake at night so that he wouldn't have to suffer them. But sleep inevitably won the battle and the bad dreams were laying in wait. Mark felt weighed down with festering guilt – somehow what had happened to Kevin was his fault.

Six months elapsed and the drab, dysfunctional household became, at last, peaceful. Owen Thomas was away for most of the time, driving long-haul on the Continent. He would be gone for weeks at a time and when he returned, Mark and Penny hardly ever saw him. He and Sharon would go out drinking, leaving the two children to their own devices, until the early hours of the morning. Mark began to blossom at primary school. When Thomas was conveniently out of the country, Sharon would bring the inevitable 'uncles' home after a night on the town, but Mark did not really mind: they were apologetically nice to him, treated mum nicely (perhaps too nicely) and would often slip a pound into his hand.

But things changed when Owen Thomas lost his job, leaving the haulage company midst a flurry of accusations and counter-accusations. Thomas turned even uglier than before, picking pointless but poisonous arguments with Sharon and shouting at Mark and Penny. And the drinking escalated, but now Thomas went out on his own, leaving Sharon to polish off a bottle of vodka at home. She would often have 'company' but it was always furtive and fraught, ears ever-listening for the sounds of Thomas returning home. Mark and Penny, upstairs in bed together, would hear the whispering, the giggling and even the orgasmic groaning, when their mother forgot to close the sitting room door.

On one occasion Thomas returned home early to discover a so-called mate of his (they played darts for the same team) in a state of undress asleep on the sofa, while Sharon was flat out on her back on the carpet, wearing only a bra and pants. She was snoring loudly and an empty bottle of vodka lay beside her.

After a scrappy and inconclusive tussle the 'uncle' pulled on his trousers, struggled with his jacket, forgot his shoes and tumbled out into the street. With more Stella Artois than jealousy in his veins, Thomas screamed for Sharon to get up and when she failed to respond, he kicked her with all his might but with limited accuracy. She rolled over, pushed herself up onto all fours, shook her head and staggered to her feet. Eyes blazing with sudden fury, she swayed her head from side to side until she focussed on Thomas.

"You bastard," she slurred, clambering to her feet unsteadily but with sudden agility. Despite her drunkenness and despite being caught *inflagrante delicto* years of experience had taught her that her best bet was to take the initiative and go immediately on the offensive. "You fucking bastard, you kicked me. That's assault. I'll have you done for assault. You bastard." Her voice rose to a scream, but she mistakenly kept her distance, bracing herself against a glass-fronted bookcase which contained no books. Her head lolled down to her chest but her eyes, wild with booze and rage, maintained their contact with Thomas.

Thomas realised his advantage (had she moved towards him he would have left) and he approached her very slowly but without trepidation. His fists were clenched, his body tensed and ready for violence, his whole being overwhelmed with a wave of pure sadism: "I'm going to beat the shit out of you, you fucking whore."

Mark, who had crept out of his bedroom and was hiding behind an overflowing laundry basket on the landing, raised himself to his full four feet. Unbeknown to him, his sister was cowering an inch behind him.

"Don't hit my mum, don't hit my mum!" he blurted, craning his head over the banisters. Penny instantly fell in love with Mark, who had, to her, become a giant of a man. She sidled up even closer to him and snaked an arm around his waist.

Owen Thomas froze. He sank his chin onto his chest, breathing heavily, and took a slow step backwards. Sharon, also breathing heavily, still glowered at the Welshman, but began to droop her head and stare stupidly at the floor. The heat vanished from the crisis and Penny dropped her arm from around Mark's waist. Mark wished it had stayed there, it felt good.

From that moment, on the surface at least, life in the Fenemore household appeared to take a turn for the better. Thomas became quieter, less argumentative and kinder to the kids, especially towards Mark. He never again raised his voice to Sharon or threatened her; he even stayed tactfully out of the way whenever she indulged her frequent need for male company. And when he volunteered to babysit for Sharon to have a "night out with the girls" Mark's mother could not believe her luck.

The casualties were of course Mark and Penny. Thomas was a clever and highly experienced paedophile. He was, as with most paedophiles, infinitely patient. He saw in Mark – accurately as it turned out – the perfect victim (Penny would be later). Thomas already knew that the boy must have been perfectly aware of what he had been doing with Kevin, but more importantly, he knew that Mark had kept it to himself.

In Thomas's eyes that meant that Mark was potentially compliant and it was that potential compliance he intended to test.

Sharon was unsurprisingly no problem. If she wasn't drunk she was trying, with varying success, to get into as many men's pants as possible. Whether or not she was aware of Thomas's sexual deviance was uncertain; whether or not she cared was equally uncertain. On one level she must have known or suspected that Thomas had "interfered with" her late son Kevin. Okay, she might have been as drunk as he was when the little man left her bed, crept across the landing and abused her young son, time and time again. But surely she was aware that something, something black and horrible, had been going on? On another level she had probably blocked her commonsense with a refusal to believe her partner could do such a thing. He was no angel, but there were limits.

To Sharon, Thomas was a drunken lout who shagged her when he was able (and when she was desperate), who put up with her children and who handed her sizeable wads of banknotes whenever he returned from one of his international trucking forays. And when the latter dried up she could still convince herself that he sort-of fancied her and, after all, he was "very good with the children." Of course he was.

Thomas began to spend more time in the council flat babysitting, while Sharon went out on the town. He never complained about her lateness, her drunkenness, even when she did not get home until the following morning. He volunteered to put the children to bed, read them bedtime stories (which nobody had done for them before), kissed them goodnight and turned off the lights. And when Sharon, on occasion, brought someone back home, giggling, in the early hours of the morning, Thomas would obligingly "get out of the way" and take his sleeping bag upstairs to the children's bedroom. Sharon could indeed not believe her luck, but then neither could Owen Thomas.

12

SPRING came early that year, bright and gay and even. Quick, light breezes loosened the grip of winter and daffodils boasted their golden display with gentle defiance. Rashes of crocuses, yellow, white and purple, brought the Park to life and a million taut and defensive buds on the trees and hedgerows heralded promise. The new season burned up from the ground, proud and childlike.

They met by accident, Lady Jane sitting alone on a park bench beneath The Tree, hugging her knees as usual and rocking slowly to and fro, and The Professor, who had ventured out alone, tempted by the kindly weather. Somebody had referred to her as 'Lady Jane,' probably Midnight Sam, and the name had stuck.

Lady Jane raised her eyes but not her head when The Professor approached. Gradually she relaxed the grip on her knees and straightened her back. She shifted from the middle of the bench to make room for him. An empty two-litre flagon of Tesco Strong Cider lay on the grass by her feet.

The Professor, breath rattling, sat down heavily, his chest aching with the effort of walking, and winced as the deep abdominal pains rippled a reminder. He was having a bad day and even the cider was not doing its job very well.

"You all right, Jane?" he asked, resting a hand on her wrist. They could be father and daughter, he 45 years old and she 27, although she looked older. But then so did he, a lot older. People aged quicker on the street and they died a lot sooner. The average life expectancy was 42, Brian Davies had said during one of his lectures, which put The Professor on borrowed time.

"I'm okay," she said in a dull, flat voice, speaking with difficulty out of the corner of her mouth. The Professor narrowed his eyes as he noticed caked blood on her upper lip. A small bruise on her left cheekbone was turning a sour yellow.

They sat together in silence for ten minutes and The Professor shared his cider with her. An unseasonably early cuckoo sang of summer from some secret place nearby – a dreamy, hazy, muffled sound which filled the world with wonder and joy but filled The Professor's heart with physically painful sorrow. The could-have-beens. The quintessentially English birdsong, though muted, possessed immense power and immense purity, while all he could see in front of him was the haggard, haunted and beat-up face of a once-beautiful young woman, bearing fresh scars inflicted by the current brute who was abusing her.

"Where is he?" The Professor asked. Lady shrugged and looked away, trying to hide her face and her soul from scrutiny. "Are you still in the bed-sit?" She nodded and The Professor noticed that her shoulders were fluttering. A large tear splashed down onto her lap and she cleared her throat quietly.

"You should go to the police …," The Professor trailed, not knowing what he could say that she had not heard before. "Before it's too late," he added ominously, without thinking, and instantly wishing that he hadn't. But Lady Jane acknowledged the warning with a calm "yes, I know I should" and flashed him a radiant but false smile.

"I was quite pretty once," she said, adding quickly, "can I have some more of your cider, please?" The Professor handed her the flagon. She did not bother to wipe the top before tilting it to her bruised mouth.

"Where did you meet him?"

It was a bold and unusual question. The street-drinking and homeless fraternity had an unwritten rule which decreed that you never inquired about past lives or past experiences.

"In Bradford. I was in a squat. Six, seven of us – all alkies of course – and about the same number of dogs. Vicious, foul things they were too, always fighting … the dogs, I mean," she added, with a flash of humour. Her face lit up and was pretty for a second. "Blokes were pretty nasty as well though. They used to slap me around a bit. You see, I was the only woman …" She left the sentence unfinished.

"And he was one of them?"

"Oh no. Gordon just happened to be passing by one day when there was this big fight outside the terrace. I'd been going with this one bloke for a week or so but his two mates wanted a slice of the action. I said that I didn't mind but my bloke went ballistic. Started to give me a good hiding. Other two blokes tried to get him off me and then suddenly everyone was at it." She paused and shuddered, her mouth twisted with disgust, disgust at the sordid scenario, disgust at what her life had become. "Gordon, who was passing by at the time, pulled my bloke off me, punched him on the jaw and then waded into the other two. I'll tell you something: Gordon Blacklock can certainly handle himself.

"I wasn't going to hang around anymore so I went into the house, gathered my bits and pieces and when I got back outside he was waiting for me. The others were nowhere to be seen. He took me to a pub for a few drinks and one thing led to another. We stayed in a B&B near the city centre for a week or two. He'd just come out of prison and some charity had fixed him up with temporary accommodation. After a while he said that he wanted to head south so I went along with him, as you do, and we ended up here. He's always got money, you know."

The Professor took a drink of cider, stifled a belch, patted his chest primly and leaned back on the bench: "It's none of my business …"

"You're right, Prof, it is none of your business," she interrupted gently, "but thanks all the same for caring … and I do think you care. I know what you were going to ask and the answer is 'I don't know.' I don't know why I stay with him, I don't know why I allowed those men in the squat in Bradford to do what they did to me, I don't know why … anything."

The Professor looked into her eyes and saw again that depth. He felt a surge of affinity for the young and wounded woman who sat beside him. In that instant he felt closer to another human being than he had done for ten years, ten dark and loveless years. Lady Jane felt the moment too and she moved an inch closer to him, an intimate inch. Her thigh touched his thigh and her shoulder was warm and comfortable against his shoulder. Nothing sexual but something deeper, more important.

"So what about you, Prof?" she asked mischievously. "So what's your story? Intelligent, well-educated gentleman like you living on the street. What's that all about?"

The Professor shook his head and realised, to his astonishment, that he was grinning. He could not remember the last time that had happened. Grinning? Now there was a rarity, a real rarity. He took an indulgent intake of breath (bugger the spasm of pain in his chest, he thought) and looked around the park. He saw the daffodils, the rash of cowslips underneath a splendid cedar tree, half a dozen boys in the distance kicking a football, above it all the unreachable white arc of a jet-stream across the pale blue sky. He closed his eyes and shivered with pleasure.

"What's the matter?" asked Lady Jane.

"Nothing," he whispered. "Nothing's the matter." The Professor flexed his neck muscles, left and right and up and down: "God, it really is such a lovely day. I say …," he curbed himself, aware of the boyish excitement in his voice. He marshalled his thoughts and attempted to level the tone of his voice: "I'm off to The Mitre for a drink. We go there every Thursday afternoon. I know it's not Thursday but would you like to come along? Landlord's okay." The Professor flinched, pressed his lips together and stared down into his lap: "Sorry, Jane, don't worry. I quite understand if you can't come. I really do … honestly. You'll be worried about *him*, I realise that. I'm sorry …"

"Come on then," said Lady Jane lightly, springing to her feet and feigning impatience. "But you'll have to pay. He never lets me have any money."

"My pleasure," The Professor got up, delighted, and opened his arm for Jane to link hers, which she did automatically. "Lady Jane," he said with a theatrical pause, "the drinks are on me." There was a gaiety in his voice, a gaiety which overcame the wheeziness.

"Lady Jane?"

"That's what we call you. Lady Jane."

****

It was during the long, school summer holidays. Sharon Fenemore had got a job in one of the fast-food restaurants in Smethwick. Money was tight since Thomas had fouled up his contract but he still had his HGV licence and picked up occasional freelance driving jobs. He suggested that Mark and Penny could come along for the ride –

company for him on those long-haul treks, something different for the kids and it would save Sharon a bit of baby-sitting money.

Since Kevin's death Mark had turned inward and become a silent, sullen boy, although he worked unusually hard at school and, being ever willing, capable and eager to please, he was popular with the teachers. But not so with his peers. They found him distant and different and they were frightened of him. Therefore they poked fun at him, bullied him and the girls, because he never responded to their pubescent flirting, labelled him 'gay boy.' Penny, on the other hand, was a bright and bubbly extrovert and was naturally popular with the other schoolchildren. But, unlike Mark, she was academically slow, unable to read or write until she was almost nine and then with painful difficulty.

Thomas put a selection of pornographic magazines in the glove compartment of his cab, not completely on show but tantalisingly half-hidden. And when he stopped to answer a call of nature he would take much longer than usual. He always knew if the magazines had been moved and invariably they had been. After a while the lorry-driver coaxed Mark into accompanying him to the toilets at lay-bys or motorway service stations: "Come on laddie, you must be bursting for a pee; two-three hours before we stop again." If the coast was clear Thomas would stand very close to Mark, feign the act of urinating and ensure that the boy had a clear view of his erect penis. At first Mark was shy and wary but he soon became curious and then fascinated.

Inevitably the looking graduated to touching and if the toilets were deserted Thomas would show Mark a pornographic magazine, flicking through the lurid pages while fondling the boy. This went on throughout the summer holidays and Mark, who had no friends, began to look forward to the trips. At least he was getting attention, which was more than he got at home. His embryonic sexuality had been awakened, albeit in an unnatural way, and he became more than willing to experiment further. And when he confided in Penny (who had also seen the pornographic magazines) she found it all rather funny.

After the school holidays the abuse escalated, but now at the council flat in Langley. Sharon – happy-go-lucky, drunken, inept and clinically stupid Sharon who thought that having casual sex with men would make them love her – made it so easy for Owen Thomas. She was either shift-working at Burger King, drinking herself senseless at some grubby back-street boozer or tarting it up in a nightclub in Birmingham. And when she returned to the flat in the early hours of the morning she was either too drunk to know or to care what had been going on in her absence or she was too intent on dragging her latest conquest to bed.

The paedophile's routine was as regular as clockwork. He put the children to bed, insisting that they both slept naked. He would often hide Penny's pyjamas and Mark, in any case, would encourage his half-sister to comply. Half an hour later, on the dot, Thomas would knock on their bedroom doors and get them to come back downstairs to watch a video.

He had stripped down to his boxer shorts and Mark and Penny would curl up either side of him to watch the film. He sexually abused them both and incited them to abuse each other, urging them to simulate scenes from the blue movie they were watching. And of course he kept them sweet (as all the most successful paedophiles do): trips to the cinema, designer gear, the latest CDs, gadgets, magazines, surprises and treats on a weekly, sometimes on a daily basis.

On the surface, Owen Thomas was an unbelievably tolerant and long-suffering partner – "that Sharon, she don't know 'ow lucky she is, she treats 'im like shit, she does, and just look at 'ow well 'e looks after them kids of 'ers.

"Spoils 'em rotten, 'e do, only hever gives 'em the best, 'e do, saint, that's what 'e is, a fuckin' saint."

****

Bobby was surprised when The Professor walked into The Mitre. Firstly it was not Thursday afternoon and secondly his once-a-week customer was with a young woman. Somebody he had not seen before but somebody he instantly deduced was a fellow street-drinker: unkempt, uncomfortable indoors, nervous and secretive. But she was with The Professor and that made it all right, despite the fact that his lunchtime trade was poised to commence. The landlord knew that The Professor would opt for his usual alcove, well away from the mainstream pub, and that he would keep himself to himself. And the young woman, trying to make herself invisible behind The Professor, was unlikely to pose a problem.

"Cider?" The Professor asked. Lady Jane arranged herself comfortably in the alcove, squeezing into a corner, and inclined her head to one side pensively. A slow smile warmed her face and she shook her head: "No ... no I'd like a glass of wine, I think. Dry white wine ... anything apart from Australian and preferably not Chardonnay."

The Professor raised an eyebrow and managed to suppress a smile, but Bobby was less successful. He shook his head and blurted: "Bloody hell, Prof, what the hell's going on? You'll be ordering a bottle of my finest Champagne next and I haven't got any."

Nevertheless, the customer was always right (even a street-drinker), and the landlord rubbed his chin, screwed up his eyes, turned and inspected the shelves behind the bar, peering studiously above the rims of his glasses. He stretched up, puffing and blowing, for two bottles and placed them reverently on the counter. The Professor studied the labels and turned to face Lady Jane, who was busy rolling herself a cigarette.

"Muscadet or Pinot Grigio?" he asked. "Not over-chilled, I'm afraid but I don't suppose Bobby would mind sorting out a couple of chunks of ice. Which is it to be?"

"The Italian," she replied, showing off and feigning a contemplative tone, but her sad eyes were sparkling. Bobby frowned, suddenly conscious that he was losing ground.

"She'll have a glass of Pinot Grigio please Bobby, if that's okay, and some ice. And I'll have a pint of Olde English."

"Thank Christ for that," the landlord mumbled as he rummaged about for a cork-screw.

The Professor found himself joining Lady Jane in the alcove before the drinks were ready and Bobby found himself carrying the drinks over to the couple, when they were. Waiter service was unique in The Mitre.

****

Owen Thomas brought Charlie Stanton home for a cup of tea one afternoon during half-term. Penny was staying with a schoolfriend for the day and Sharon was working, which left Mark alone in the flat.

Stanton was a fellow lorry-driver; he was also a fellow paedophile. And Thomas had told him all about his stepson. After forty minutes of three-way abuse, Stanton engineered a few moments alone with the 12-year-old boy, slipped him a £10 note and a scrap of paper upon which he had scrawled his mobile telephone number. He told Mark to call him anytime, promised him more £10 notes and suggested, with a wink, that it should be their secret: nobody, not even Penny should know. To a 12-year-old boy, again the intrigue was irresistible. But there was something else, something completely and terribly different about this new situation. Mark, already sexually marred, had been aroused by his encounter with Charlie Stanton. Past experiences with Thomas had been more naughty and mucky than sexual, but this was different.

Mark felt sexually attracted to and fascinated by his step-father's 27-year-old mate and he could hardly wait to see him again.

On the same day that Thomas and Stanton were abusing her brother, Penny confided in her older best friend and told her what Thomas had been doing to her in their soulless flat while their mother was away. For some reason, only known to the little girl, she only mentioned the abuse *she* had suffered – she said nothing about what had happened to Mark.

Penny's friend told her parents, who in turn contacted the police. They had never felt entirely comfortable about their daughter's friendship with Penny. Two hours after Stanton left Fenemore's flat, two police officers pulled up outside the block. Mark was in bed, Sharon had just got home fairly drunk and Thomas was watching television, almost asleep with a can of lager in his hand.

Thomas was arrested on suspicion of child abuse and Sharon proceeded to scream blue murder at the top of her voice, alternating between yelling "how dare you" at the police officers and "how could you" at her partner. After ranting for several minutes, during which the police very wisely remained passive, she ran out of steam. Exhausted and confused, she flopped into an armchair and began to wail. Spotting an ideal opportunity the officers hurried Thomas from the flat, along the corridor into the lift and out into the police van outside.

Thomas didn't bother to struggle, he didn't even protest. He had been arrested before and for similar offences. He did, however, deny any wrong-doing and pleaded not guilty at a subsequent magistrates court preliminary hearing.

After a sordid, unpleasant trial which necessitated Penny giving evidence by video link, Thomas was convicted of rape and of gross indecency with a child. Bearing in mind his previous convictions, he was sentenced to eight years imprisonment. Sharon was so distraught by the verdict that she called in at the nearest pub and got extremely drunk, forgetting that Mark and Penny were waiting for her at home. When she finally remembered and staggered into the flat with two bags of cold fish-and-chips, both her children were fast asleep in their bedrooms. Mark had made cheese on toast for himself and his sister and had then settled Penny into bed.

After the trial and conviction things changed for the Fenemores. At long last Social Services became involved but despite gentle, persistent questioning Penny never let on that Mark had also been abused. The little girl thought, for some reason, that if she kept Mark out of the equation, everything would be okay at home: Thomas was gone – forever as far as Penny was concerned – and the three of them could get on with their lives together. But the wheels of corporate care ground, albeit belatedly, into action and indignant social workers began charging about, waving admonishing fingers at everybody apart from themselves, holding case conferences, discussing action plans and soforth.

Penny was assessed as being "at serious risk" (bit late for that, some might have imagined) and she was whisked into care. It all happened very quickly, far too quickly for Sharon's slow and booze-befuddled mind to take in.

Mark was 'classified' less seriously: he was placed on the 'at risk' register and allowed to remain with his mother. A dedicated social worker was assigned to the case and would keep a close eye on things, which in practice meant a telephone call once a week and a visit once a month.

Three days after Penny was taken away, wide-eyed and terrified and heartbroken to be split up from her brother, Mark sent a text message to Charlie Stanton.

13

HE IMAGINED the sun of Africa on his upturned face and if he closed his eyes he could see the weighty palms rustling in the off-shore breeze, and the blue, blue ocean and the old hammock on the edge of the beach. But the instant his father's kind and strong face swam into the picture, he opened his eyes with a start to shut out a memory that was far too painful.

It was a lovely day in early June, gaiety was everywhere, and Midnight Sam had collected his batch of Big Issues from the one-roomed office in Canal Lane. He stood at the corner of the cobbled alleyway which wound its way to the Cathedral, leaned back against a wall and absorbed the peace of the early morning. Fat, unlovable pigeons fussed around his feet and half a dozen seagulls flew anxiously and aggressively low down the street, screeching angrily at nothing in particular. It was a quarter to seven in the morning and the city was almost empty. Midnight loved this time, it was a special time, his time: it reminded him of his father, quiet and dependable, of that battered old jetty at Barra, where he used to play as a child.

He watched Scots Robby striding up West Street on the opposite side of the road. The exaggerated, quasi-military gait was unmistakeable, even from a couple of hundred yards away. Scots, looking dishevelled and more flustered than usual, was coming from the direction of the police station. An aura of indignation and outrage was detectable even from such a distance. He was trying his best to march but exhaustion and probably a king-size hangover were taking their toll. When he drew level with Midnight Sam, the Big Issue seller raised an arm and called out. But Scots Robby was having none of it. Head down, jaw set and shoulders hunched he angered on, muttering to himself about the injustices of the night before. When he reached The Cross he couldn't resist a furtive glance back down the street, to make sure that it was Midnight Sam standing at the corner of the alleyway.

Midnight was awash with excitement: he decided it was going to be a wonderful day and the world was buzzing with promise. It was Thursday so he would pick up his benefit from the post office and meet The Professor, Scots Robby and possibly Fen in The Mitre for a couple of 'civilised' drinks in the afternoon. And he was looking forward to seeing Lady Jane in the pub. The Professor had told him a couple of days ago that he was thinking of asking her along, but he wasn't too sure how it would go down with Scots Robby or Fen. Or, perhaps more to the point, with Gordon Blacklock.

Since the Christmas party the northerner had kept a low profile, sheepish when encountered in the street or in The Park. One or two street-drinkers, notably Splodge and Nobby, had accepted invitations to his flat in Belgrave Road – a neglected, slovenly street of once-grand inner city homes occupied by doctors, lawyers and businessmen but now lost to the decay of DSS bedsits and absentee landlords.

The cider, courtesy of Blacklock, who always had more money than anybody else, flowed freely but the boys never did have much fun. They felt uneasy. They found the presence of Lady Jane – invariably nursing some fresh injury, some haphazard swathe of bandaging, some plaster, some bruise – deeply unsettling. She would always be there, curled up in the corner of the room, gazing unseeing at the far wall and never saying a word. Blacklock would place two flagons of cider on the floor in front of her and then ignore her. If she made a sound he would narrow his black eyes and silence her with a withering stare.

Midnight Sam sold a couple of copies of The Big Issue before eight o'clock, one pretty girl in a smart, 'executive' trouser suit giving him £5. He noticed the front cover headline: 'CHARITIES RALLY FOR BIG HOMELESS WEEK BOOST.' Midnight, who never normally bothered to read the magazine he sold, flicked through the pages until he found the article inside and, for some reason only destiny itself would ever be able to fathom, he gave it his fullest attention.

Shelter, Crisis, Housing Justice and Child Poverty Action Group were among an impressive array of charities joining forces to raise funds and awareness during National Homeless Week at the end of the month. And, still flushed with what he doggedly recalled as the success of his much-talked-about Christmas party, Midnight spawned a germ of an idea. As the morning progressed he became radiant with excitement, but he made a determined effort to keep his enthusiasm under wraps until he saw The Professor later that day. This time, a tiny inner voice had whispered a gentle word of warning. He had taken too much upon himself on his previous venture, so for his latest project he was determined to seek more practical help and advice. After all, the best leaders in the world delegated.

When Midnight Sam arrived at The Mitre, The Professor and Lady Jane were already in the alcove, deep in conversation. Scots Robby, who had been hanging about outside the pub waiting for the others to arrive, barged through the swing door less than a minute after Midnight. Fen, who had seen The Professor and Lady together earlier in the day, gave The Mitre a miss. Midnight was at the bar when Scots Robby blustered in, proudly wearing a Scotland soccer shirt generously stained with a variety of fluids. He strode up to where Midnight was standing and fired a disapproving glance over his shoulder towards the alcove.

Bobby poured three pints of cider and a large whisky and Midnight Sam ferried the four drinks, with difficulty, to the alcove. But Scots Robby remained obdurately at the bar, sulking at the unspeakable intrusion of a woman: "I'll have mine here." Midnight stopped in his tracks, returned with the Scotsman's whisky, placed it in front of him and rejoined The Professor and Lady Jane in the alcove.

"How you doing, Jane?" Midnight asked, his forehead creased with genuine interest. "You still living at Belgrave Road?" What he meant was 'are you still living with him, with Gordon Blacklock' and she knew that was what he meant. She nodded and clasped Midnight's arm affectionately. "And how about you, Sam? How are things with you?"

Midnight Sam took a long, luxuriant, vaguely sophisticated drink from his pint glass and assumed a serious, important pose.

"They're good, Jane, as a matter of fact they are very good indeed." He paused and turned towards The Professor: "In fact, Prof, I've had a bit of an idea."

"Not another of your crazy, fuckin' ideas," Scots Robby grumbled from the bar. Bobby put down the mug he was polishing and raised an admonishing finger. The Scotsman waved his hands in apology and fell silent, shaking his head.

Midnight Sam looked important: "At the end of the month it's National Homeless Week. Lots of charities doing things for the homeless, raising lots of money. They do it every year. I've just read about it in this week's Big Issue."

"You actually read the magazine?" Lady Jane asked, mildly surprised.

Midnight shrugged and continued: "Article says it wants people to do their own thing to raise money for the homeless. Well, I thought, why don't we – I mean us homeless here – why don't we all get together and do something ourselves? The homeless raising money for the homeless. How about that?"

The Professor felt his chest heave, his throat constrict and the burn of tears prickle behind his eyes. He saw Midnight Sam – clearly a once bright but now booze-ruined individual – brimming with enthusiasm, ever-eager to please, ever-caring, ever-unconditionally kind. And in the face of such massive odds, in the face of such hopelessness. He felt, not for the first time, humbled by the heroism of the human spirit.

"What have you got in mind?" he asked, managing to pull himself together, and Lady Jane leaned forwards, entering into the conspiracy. Scots Robby looked pointedly in the opposite direction but he listened to every word. He even bought another round of drinks, including one for Lady Jane, without being asked but with a great deal of fuss and grumbling largesse. Puffing and groaning and spilling a fair amount, he took the drinks over to the alcove and slammed the glasses onto the table. He nudged Lady Jane's drink an inch closer to her and was secretly pleased when she gave him a smile of thanks. He pulled up a stool as if he was doing them a huge favour.

"Well, Sam, what have you got in mind?" The Professor repeated the question.

"A sponsored walk, all the way around the city boundary," Midnight replied with an air of triumph. "In fancy dress."

****

Mark Fenemore no longer bothered with school. Well, to be accurate, he would leave the flat in the morning at the appointed hour in his school uniform, backpack bulging with books, and 'go' to school. He simply never got there. Instead he would detour to the canal or to the park or to whichever meeting place Charlie Stanton had arranged with him. Very soon he stopped bothering with the charade of donning his school uniform and he would leave his backpack in the wardrobe. And he would leave the flat at whatever time suited him. There was no problem with that because his mother never got up much before midday and was invariably too hung-over to know what time of day it was, let alone what her son was doing.

The truancy rate at Mark's grim and overcrowded urban inner city school was so appalling that it was three months before a council child welfare officer called. Warnings were issued, 'action plans' set up, regular home visits organised, but nothing changed. Mark Fenemore was one of many and the authorities didn't have the time, the will, the know-how or the resources to deal with him.

Sharon soon found out about Charlie Stanton – not that the man was regularly sexually abusing her son, but that he had 'befriended' Mark – and she absorbed the odd and unsavoury relationship into her sponge-like brain, along with the alcohol. It genuinely did not concern her that a 29-year-old man was spending days *and nights* in the company of a 12-year-old boy. Stanton took advantage of the situation: he showered Sharon with flattery, with alcohol, with money and, from time to time, with welcomed sexual advances. It was every paedophile's dream scenario – a trusted friend of the family – and he exploited the privilege mercilessly.

Mark and Charlie became inseparable, always together, always seen together and when this situation was made aware to the boy's assigned social worker by some public-spirited, gleefully nosy neighbour, the regulation confrontation led nowhere. Explanations were given and gratefully accepted, outraged denials of impropriety made, boxes ticked and effectively that was that.

Stanton had other uses for Mark, other than providing him with his own perverted sexual gratification. The vulnerable, impressionable and besotted boy fitted the bill perfectly as Stanton's young partner in crime. Stanton was an habitual thief and burglary was his speciality. To have a willing, small and agile accomplice like Mark was worth more than his weight in video recorders, CD players or whatever. And so, two or three nights a week, Stanton would drive his ageing Ford Transit panel van around to where Mark lived, pick up the boy and off they would go to any one of Birmingham's affluent suburbs.

He would park the van in some quiet, ill-lit side street and the two of them would make their way, in silence and keeping to the shadows, to whichever property the 29-year-old had been staking out. Of course the house would be empty (Stanton would have checked on that) and of course there would be no burglar alarm. And there would invariably be a skylight half-open which only the slender likes of Mark Fenemore could worm their way through.

After the burglary the two of them would go back to Stanton's four-berth caravan on a soulless and unregistered site a mile and a quarter outside Wolverhampton. Stanton would stash the night's pickings in a built-in wardrobe, ready for the fence, and have sex with the boy on a grey, unmade bed. He would drive Mark home the next day, with a £10 note or even a £20 note in the boy's trouser pocket. This routine continued for around 18 months until six o'clock one morning, when the knock on the door of Charlie Stanton's caravan door was sterner than usual.

Stanton, who was no stranger to court proceedings, was sent to prison for eight months, while Mark was made the subject of a referral order. The young offender found himself under the supervision of the youth offending team for the next six months. Well-meaning and passionate care workers embarked on a course of teaching Mark the difference between right and wrong, to become a responsible young member of the community, to 'reintegrate' into the school culture, to respect other people's property. Mark attended all the courses and all the appointments without fail; he was never late and never absent. He was a model 'student.' The youth offending team's final report was a text-book success story. Mark Fenemore had obviously seen the error of his ways and realised what a terrible influence Charlie Stanton had been. The risk of him reoffending was classified as "minimal."

However, during the months of Mark's rehabilitation, the 13-year-old had a success story all of his very own. He had managed to break into four private homes, two warehouses, two schools and a church hall. Well-versed in burglary but totally untutored in what to do with the stolen goods, he hid his haul in and on top of the wardrobe in his bedroom, with some vague notion that Charlie would sort it out when he was released from prison.

Sharon rarely went into her son's bedroom and even if she had and even if she had stumbled upon the evidence – video recorders, DVD players, jewellery boxes and various other stolen goods – she was extremely unlikely to have confronted her son. She had never been much use as a mother but now she was no use at all. She and Mark lived separate lives, neither showing the least interest in the other. The only thing they had in common was the occupancy of the same house. And Sharon's son was 13 years of age.

When Stanton was released from prison he caught a train to Birmingham New Street and then a bus to Langley. He was outside the Fenemore's third floor flat less than six hours after walking through the prison gates. Sharon was out somewhere, but Mark was waiting for him.

14

BISHOP John handed Midnight Sam a second schooner of Harvey's Bristol Cream and settled into his favourite armchair, well-worn from many years of exclusively his and nobody else's backside. Strands of unruly snow-white hair curtained the craggy, benevolent face, youthful and eager despite his age. Midnight sipped his sherry and put the glass delicately onto a place mat on the coffee table between the two men. Ever conscious of decorum when visiting the Bishop's Palace (he had tactfully left a flagon of GL cider with the housekeeper in the hall) Midnight was a model of etiquette.

"A sponsored walk, you say," the cleric took the pipe out of his mouth and inspected the empty bowl. He filled it with a couple of pinches of Old Holburn, tamped the tobacco down and fussed with three Swan Vesta matches before he got it going. A cloud of silver-yellow tobacco smoke swirled around his head
a shaft of sunlight which speared throug
Midnight sniffed the air and silently curs
any cigarettes or tobacco that morning. E
the gesture: "Would you like a cigarette?
on the mantelpiece. Benson and Hedges,

idea."

corr

Relieved, Midnight Sam walked carefully across the room as if he was stepping on hot coals, made a bit of a hash of opening the heavy, silver cigarette box, fumbled with the contents and, out of habit, popped one cigarette in his mouth and another behind his right ear. He rejoined the bishop.

"I think it's a jolly good idea." His voice croaked and slurred around the pipe stem glued to his mouth. "Homeless raising money for the homeless, eh? Jolly good idea Sam."

"Mind if I ask your advice, your honour?" asked Sam innocently, knowing that there was not a living soul on the planet who could resist such a question. The bishop shook his head emphatically and Midnight continued: "Only thing is, I'm not to sure how we go about getting sponsored."

Bishop John craned forward, staring at the carpet. He took the pipe from his mouth and rubbed his chin, his left knee twitching with concentration.

"The Evening News," he said, leaning back in his armchair. He patted both thighs with his hands and, forgetting that he had his pipe in one of them, nearly set fire to his trousers. He slapped the pipe into the ashtray and dusted himself down in a fluster. "Get the local rag to run a piece about your plans and then show the article to local businesses, shops, schools and soforth …," he trailed, still thinking. "I'll tell you what, I'll have a word with the editor, if you like. I know him, he's quite a nice sort of chap. I could make sure you get the right sort of coverage. (He too remembered the page three lead about from the Christmas party.) How does that sound to you?"

"You're a real gent, bish … sorry, I mean Bishop John," Midnight ⸻cted himself. "You're a real gent, your honour. That's a cracking

Seconds after Midnight Sam left, with much bowing and scraping and a crisp £20 note in his pocket, Bishop John reached for the telephone and rang the Evening News. The editor was very keen.

Brian Davies, on the other hand, was not. The headline, 'DRUNKEN CHRISTMAS PARTY BRAWL AT HOMELESS HOSTEL,' along with a photograph of Brian and an outside shot of the day centre, had not done his credibility much good. He had received several indignant telephone calls from members of the public and a curt letter from the city council (major funders of the charity) requesting an explanation. This had been followed with a 'casual' visit by the city centre police inspector and a thinly-veiled threat from the Salvation Army (who also funded the centre) that a repeat performance could result in "dire consequences."

Nevertheless, Brian took it all on the chin. He was used to dealing with 'ivory tower' benefactors. But he was professionally bruised and, worse, the reputation of the centre had taken a knock. He promised his critics and himself that he would not let such a thing happen again and he was about to let Midnight Sam down gently, when the latter played his trump card: "Bishop John has agreed to lead us around the city boundary himself, dressed up in all his robes and stuff. He thought it would help with the fund-raising. Bloody good bloke he is, Brian, a bishop and all that and he doesn't mind mixing with the likes of us homeless people. Bloody good bloke."

Brian's shoulders sank and he knew he was a beaten man (as did Midnight Sam): "If you've got the bishop's blessing then I suppose you've got mine as well, but Sam ...," he waved a stern forefinger, "I don't want anymore bad publicity. I'm only just recovering from the Christmas party." A hurt, almost indignant expression clouded Midnight's face and Brian relented: "It was a good party Sam, but there were repercussions and we must be careful. We are a charity, a vulnerable charity, and we depend on the goodwill of our funders. Without them we are finished, so we need to keep them sweet and ...," Brian recognised the blank look on Midnight's face and he stopped in mid-sentence. "But never mind all that," he continued, "just you make sure that nothing goes wrong. No Booze, no trouble and Sam ...," Brian paused for maximum effect, " ... nothing, and I mean nothing, with a security tag still attached. And I don't mean 'pull it off,' I mean nothing that is not honestly paid for. If you need a few quid for whatever reason then come to me ... please. No shopping sprees with light fingers and empty wallets this time, okay? Is that understood?"

Slightly disappointed – one or two outfits had already taken his fancy – Midnight pursed his lips and nodded.

With Bishop John's blessing (suitably publicised in the Evening News) getting sponsorship proved to be relatively easy. In five days they had collected pledges which amounted to around £3,000.

On the appointed day – Saturday, June 28th – resplendent in a leopard-skin loincloth, a North American Indian headdress, a faded Zulu shield and, for some reason, a pair of green Wellington boots, Midnight Sam cut an interesting dash. His face and bare chest were daubed liberally with bright red warpaint (lipstick from Pound-Stretcher) and a Winnie The Poo scarf was wrapped around his neck.

Scots Robby had also made an effort. Armed with £20 from Brian's fancy dress fund, he had headed for the Army and Navy Stores at the bottom of West Street, where a friendly, helpful but watchful shopkeeper was on hand to assist the Scotsman.

"I've got a couple of kilts, one minus the sporran, and both a shade on the worn side, I'm afraid," said the elderly man, bent almost double with arthritis and the epitome of greyness: grey hair, grey eyes, grey hands. He even wore a pair of loose-fitting, grey flannel trousers. He walked wheezily with a crab-like limp.

Scots Robby examined the kilts closely, fingered his moustache and picked his nose subconsciously: "My clan is the Sinclairs – the Sinclairs of Airdrie. And we go back hundreds of years, laddie, hundreds of years."

The considerably older man coughed with embarrassment at the patronising 'laddie' but said nothing.

"Now this one looks closer to the correct tartan," Scots Robby murmured solemnly, without having the slightest idea what the correct tartan was (if there was one at all, of course.)

A matching pair of socks could not be found so Scots settled for a garish pair of football socks boldly advertising Manchester United FC. However the assistant gently and apologetically but firmly refused to sell the eight-inch bladed Bowie knife.

"Scottish Highlander has got to have a dirk – that's a fuckin' knife in your lingo – he's got to have a dirk in his sock. It's part of the fuckin' uniform." While Scots Robby protested he edged closer to the knife, which was in a glass display cabinet to the right of the counter. But the storekeeper, ever genial, limped softly across his shop to stand in front of the counter and shrugged as if the decision was out of his hands: "No bad language, please sir … now is there anything else we can help you with?"

Headgear had posed a major problem – nothing remotely Scottish on offer – so a compromise had to be struck: military and authentic were the twin requirements. A First World War helmet was the result, beating a French Foreign Legion hat by a short head, so to speak. And an 1860s Confederate army jacket, with most of the buttons missing, completed the ensemble. From Bannockburn to the Somme to the American Civil War – Scots Robby had brought together a diverse selection of military history.

Sadly the bagpipes were way out of financial reach, but after some impressive argument (during which the Scotsman amazingly managed to avoid the word 'fuck') and after a quick telephone call to Brian at the day centre, the storekeeper decided to take a chance. For a deposit of £10, Scots Robby could hire the bagpipes for the day of the sponsored walk and, upon their safe return, he would be reimbursed with the money. Brian Davies got Scots on the phone (a feat in itself) and told him that he could keep the £10 afterwards, so long as the bagpipes were returned in one piece. The centre manager reasoned, correctly, that three or four flagons of strong cider constituted a serious incentive.

The Professor was not well enough to take part in the walk so he volunteered to be one of the three marshals needed to monitor the progress of the participants. The other two were Brian and Lady Jane. Brian would see the walkers on their way from The Cross in the city centre, while Lady Jane would be positioned outside the Great West Window of the Cathedral, where the walk was due to finish. The Professor had not taken much persuasion to agree to man the halfway post at The Mitre in South Street. Bobby (or rather Bobby's wife) had agreed to provide free refreshments for the walkers. Sandwiches and soft drinks only, naturally.

A pretty young reporter from the Evening News, along with a bad-tempered, middle-aged photographer, were waiting at The Cross to record the start of the historic event. They planned to cut across to the Cathedral, a quarter of a mile away for the finish which, taking into account stops to collect money en route and for refreshments at The Mitre, was estimated to be about three-and-a-half hours later.

Splodge and Nobby were the last to arrive at The Cross, in a fluster, seconds before Bishop John, resplendent in his robes, was preparing to lead his motley flock on their mini-Odyssey. The two latecomers had opted for a 'vicars and tarts' theme, not entirely meeting with the bishop's approval but undeniably eye-catching.

Nobby, a six-foot-tall beanpole of a man with a long, sad face, sported the dog collar, while Spodge, shorter by a good six inches and built like a tank, wore a gymslip, fishnet stockings and ruby red lipstick. Brian intervened sharply with regard to the cardboard signs hanging around his neck, front and back, partially obscuring the St Trinian's school tie: Help Homeless Harlots, it read. Although the alliteration was praiseworthy, as was the biblical term for women of easy virtue, Brian was adamant. The Evening News team, especially the photographer, breathed sighs of relief.

Seven homeless city street-drinkers set off - a ragged, self-conscious bunch - behind Bishop John, sombre and splendid in his full, ecclesiastical finery, holding his crozier like a latter-day Moses on his way down from Mount Sinai.

Paddy, the young Irish alcoholic junkie, caught up with them as they made their way along East Street. A gorilla outfit, minus the head, had come into his possession and he was strumming a guitar which had seen better days. Three strings and several frets were missing and the back of the instrument had come unstuck. The temperature was nudging 75 degrees and rising, but inside the gorilla outfit it must have been unimaginable. Paddy was awash with sweat, not helped by his decision to give the cocaine and alcohol a miss for three days leading up to the sponsored walk. He was suffering from a severe attack of 'cold turkey' but he kept going.

Scots Robby positioned himself inches behind the bishop, assuming the role as walk leader and frequently darting a disapproving glance over his shoulder to ensure that the others were keeping up and in order. He marched, rather than walked, holding his bucket to one side like a drum major, and puffing out his costumed chest.

When they reached a fork in the road, Bishop John correctly led his flock to the left down Dockside Parade, but an anxious tug on the sleeve of his surplice made him falter. Trying to march and skip in front of the bishop at the same time and nearly falling over, a red-faced Scots Robby blurted: "That's the wrong way, your holiness. We're going the wrong way. We need to take the right fork down Canal Road. I've studied the map, your grace, and we're going the wrong way."

"I don't thing we are, Robby," Bishop John stopped in mid-stride and looked down at the Scotsman. "I think you'll find that Dockside Parade is the right way, it follows the line of the Via Sacra."

Splodge, whose mascara was giving him problems, shouted from the rear: "Come on Robby, don't talk so much crap – oh, pardon me, your honour. The bishop's right, you Scotch prat, let's get going."

Scots Robby wheeled on the unlikely tart: "That's all you know, you bloody Sassenach, and you're bloody wrong." He turned back to the bishop and softened his tone: "Begging your pardon, my lord, but I'm going to stick to the official route."

Bishop John frowned and Scots Robby, bristling with righteous indignation, strode off resolutely along Canal Road, alone and wrong. The others, with Bishop John at the head, carried on along Dockside Parade.

The article in the Evening News had done them proud: more than the usual number of Saturday shoppers were about and generosity was in the air. Fifty pence pieces and pound coins rained into the walkers' buckets, especially into Midnight Sam's. And that had nothing to do with the African costume, complete with Red Indian headdress and Winnie the Pooh scarf. It was because everybody loved Midnight, especially the children.

Scots Robby, who was forced to admit to himself he was going the wrong way when an about turn was the only alternative to a lonely journey down the hard shoulder of the motorway to Bristol, retraced his steps to town, muttering, head held defiantly high. To his credit, as soon as he left the Green Belt behind and was back in the bowels of the city, he embarked upon a fund-raising mission of alarming intensity. His method was simple but effective. Eyes wide with barely controlled anger, he would march up to people in the street and demand money. If they tried to move politely aside he would move with them, obdurately blocking their path, bucket thrust menacingly under their noses. Dressed the way he was, he did very well.

The exceptions to his success involved children, never his favourite species. Having been wisely denied access to the Bowie knife, Scots had purchased a cheap, plastic knife from a toy shop. The retractable, silver-painted, six-inch blade looked fairly authentic at a glance and he took advantage of this. When approached by a youngster (his outfit was admittedly quite a magnet) he would bend down, whip the knife from a Manchester United FC sock and plunge it into the chest of the child, cackling with delight. He was the only one to see the funny side: the child would invariably burst into tears, the horrified parents would leap up and down and Scots Robby would scuttle off before the police were involved. Satisfied that he was doing pretty well financially, which he was, and convinced that he was ahead of the others time-wise, which he wasn't, he decided to pop into the Ship Inn for a 'swift half.' He had already worked out, accurately as it turned out, that the publicity in the Evening News would be a passport to a public house which had barred him forever two years ago.

"All right then, one drink and no trouble," a waspish barman, who had got the okay nod from the landlord, hissed reluctantly across the bar. Scots Robby scooped a handful of coins from his bucket, spilled them onto the bar and ordered a large whisky. Five double whiskies later, Scots Robby left the pub and headed for The Mitre. He had forgotten the official route but he felt justifiably pleased with the contents of his bucket (despite subtractions for refreshments). Although he would have been the first to deny it, he craved company. And, above all, he wanted to impress The Professor with his fund-raising prowess.

While Bishop John was leading Midnight Sam, Nobby and Splodge, Paddy and the others around the city and Scots Robby plodded an alternative route, Mark Fenemore was sitting morosely in the alcove of The Mitre with The Professor, who had on the table in front of him an array of sponsor check sheets. Without a word, Fen had bought The Professor a pint of Olde English. He sat on a stool, legs apart, staring passed the older man into the frosted glass window. His eyes were flat, his face without expression. He suddenly jerked out of his silent, secretive revelry, shook his head with quick anger and fumbled inside his shirt pocket. He extracted a £10 note and tossed it onto the table.

"What's that for, Fen?" The Professor asked.

"That sponsored walk crap," the younger man answered with a dismissive wave of the hand. He sprang to his feet and hurried out of the pub, without a 'goodbye.'

15

BOBBY stood to attention when the bishop walked into The Mitre, lowering his head and holding his crook so that it didn't catch in the doorway. The Professor, from the alcove, raised his pint of cider to the cleric (who knew him from a distant and different world) and Bishop John registered his acknowledgement with a kindly but sad nod. The mutual recognition went unnoticed.

Midnight Sam, minus the Red Indian headdress, followed the bishop into the pub, holding his bucket in front of him with both hands. It was already more than half full of coins and banknotes. Such was his popularity in town that he never needed to ask for donations. Men, women and especially children handed over their money willingly and the latter often benefited from a sweet or a piece of chocolate which Midnight would produce from an old canvas shoulder bag.

Nobby and Splodge, sweating profusely but in good spirits, were next through the door, masking their embarrassment with bravado. In Splodge's case this involved adopting a Marilyn Monroe, bum-swaying mince which he managed quite well. Bobby, who thought he had seen most things during his fifteen years in the downtown, dockside boozer, was visibly shocked.

Two other walkers and their three dogs arrived. Bobby shook his head, pointed at the dogs and then pointed at the door. No words were said but the animals were about-turned and tethered to a lamppost outside the pub. Paddy, whose wild eyes betrayed a blip in his temporary abstinence vow, brought up the rear.

The Professor, assuming an officious attitude with pen poised, recorded all walkers present, with the exception of Scots Robby. Paper cups of orange juice were handed out and gulped down. Nobody apart from The Professor noticed the litre bottle of Smirnoff vodka which Midnight Sam had produced from the recesses of his leopard-skin loincloth. The cups, with the exception of Bishop John's, were surreptitiously charged. But it was a stressful situation for Midnight and when Bobby produced three carafes of orange juice, each only three-quarters full, the Cheyenne Zulu was relieved. The twinkle in Midnight Sam's eyes troubled the landlord, who felt deeply suspicious of the whole affair. Call it a landlord's sixth sense if you like, but Bobby knew that he was being had.

"Thanks Bobby," said Midnight Sam genuinely. "It's pretty hot work out there." He wiped his brow theatrically, picked up two of the carafes, turned his back squarely on the landlord and, holding the bottle of vodka down by his knees out of sight, poured out the contents, without so much as a gurgle. Midnight had forgotten about the bishop, who proffered his paper cup for a refill. It was mighty hot underneath all his ecclesiastical finery. There was no going back for Midnight now and, to be fair to Bishop John, his face betrayed no surprise when he knocked back his first vodka and orange. Perhaps the faintest twitch of the eyebrows, a flutter of the shoulders, but, all in all, a perfect example of Protestant control.

Scots Robby burst in through the swing doors, bucket in one hand and plastic knife in the other. He stood in the middle of the room, chest heaving, jaw set and swaying, trying to focus. When he saw The Professor he zig-zagged over to the alcove.

"Corporal Robert Sinclair reporting for duty – sir!" he saluted, plunging the retractable toy dagger into his left temple. He placed his bucket on the table in front of The Professor, took a clumsy step backwards and saluted again, this time with his right hand. The First World War helmet had tilted forward at a comical angle, half-obscuring the Scotsman's face and something had gone wrong with the sporran: it was touching the floor. The Professor craned his head over the rim of the bucket and looked down. He closed his eyes for a second and grimaced. A Help the Aged charity box lay on top of the pile of coins. Scots Robby, misreading The Professor's closed eyes as a sign of approval, bristled with pride before lurching over to the bar, where the landlord, whetting his lips, was waiting for him.

"Large Scotch," he ordered, banging the counter with a fist.

"Orange juice only," Bobby growled, shoulders hunched in readiness for an argument, which he got.

"Are you fuckin' deaf. I said I want a large fuckin' Scotch and none of your fuckin,' namby-pampy orange juice."

Bobby did not move but he narrowed his eyes to mere slits: "One more word out of you, just one more word, and you're barred – for life. D'you hear me. For life."

Midnight floated onto the scene, edging in front of Scots Robby and pushing a carafe against the Scotsman's stomach: "Try some of this, Robby, it's pretty good stuff, very refreshing." Bobby frowned but turned away.

Scots Robby's face twisted with disgust: "I'm no drinkin' no fuckin' orange juice. I want a proper fuckin' drink."

Midnight Sam, who rarely displayed his physical strength but who was immensely strong, steered Scots Robby away from the bar, sat him down on a stool in the alcove opposite The Professor, filled a paper cup to the brim and handed it to him, with an encouraging nod: "Vodka and orange and there's more vodka than orange. Okay?"

The trouble started a few minutes later when Splodge crept up behind Scots Robby, a mischievous leer on his heavily rouged face, and knocked three times on the top of the First World War helmet with a clenched fist. Scots whirled around, the helmet fell off his head onto his lap and he lurched to his feet. The helmet dropped to the floor with a clatter.

"What the fuck are you doing?" he roared.

"Anybody in? Oh look everybody, its Scotch Robby dressed up like a Sassenach soldier.

Scots Robby looked Splodge up and down and sneered: "And just look at you, you fuckin' pooftah. Stockings, a wee skirt and fuckin' lipstick. A queer, that's what you are, a fuckin' bum bandit." He pushed Splodge backwards and one of the tart's bosoms, an orange balloon, popped out of his blouse. Splodge whirled his arms to stop himself from falling over, regained his balance and squared up to the Scotsman.

"You, you're a fuckin' tart," Scots Robby spat out the words with extraordinary venom.

"Of course I'm a tart, you Scotch twat. I'm supposed to be a tart. Vicars and Tarts – it's fancy fuckin' dress, you daft prat."

"Scottish, you pooftah, not Scotch," Scots Robby poked Splodge in the chest again, narrowly missing the other balloon. "Scotch is the fuckin' drink. I'm Scottish."

"You're a Scotch twat," said Splodge conversationally but he clenched his fists in readiness. "And if you poke me one more time I'll break your stupid, fuckin' Scotch face."

Scots Robby aimed a flailing blow at the shorter, stockier man and missed by six inches. The two then fell into each other and began wrestling, collapsing onto the floor in an untidy heap and thrashing about ineffectually until, out of kindness and to save them further embarrassment, Midnight Sam bent down and pulled them apart.

Not waiting to be told – Bobby had scurried around from behind the bar with a face like thunder – Scots Robby ducked through the swing doors, with commendable agility and ran off.

"Good fuckin' riddance," muttered Splodge, pulling up one of his fishnet stockings and fumbling with the suspender belt.

"And you!" Bobby bellowed. "Out!"

Splodge's feelings appeared to be genuinely hurt for a second, but for only a second as he accurately judged the expression on the landlord's face. He retrieved his bucket from the floor, kicked Scots Robby's helmet to one side and tottered out of The Mitre (surprisingly both red high heels had remained in place during the scuffle.) He waited outside for the other walkers, flushed and breathing heavily, a lonely and unusual figure leaning against the pub wall.

The sponsored walk resumed, minus Scots Robby, and, apart from an embarrassing quarter of an hour while a plain-clothed police officer 'stopped and searched' Paddy (to everyone's amazement without success) there were no more incidents.

Triumph was in the balmy, summer air when Bishop John, mildly flushed and more talkative after his four cups of orange juice, led his flock to the Great West Window of the Cathedral. And what a reception they were given: the mayor and mayoress; Brian Davies and several street-drinkers including Lady Jane; Doctor Dawes and the doctor's wife; the chairwoman of the Youth Housing Association; the area manager of the Big Issue; the reporter and photographer from the Evening News and around fifty curious members of the public.

When Scots Robby reappeared and swaggered across College Lawn, coaxing an incredible sound out of the bagpipes, Brian Davies swiftly intervened, glaring the Scotsman into the background, into silence and as far away from the Press as possible. The centre manager ushered the reporter and photographer towards Bishop John and Midnight Sam.

The interviews went well and the photo-shoot was a success – eventually. At first there were problems with Splodge and Paddy. Splodge had it in mind that a picture of him snuggling seductively up to Bishop John would take some beating and in some respects he was probably right. It took the physical intervention of Midnight Sam before he could be persuaded to abandon the idea. And Paddy's initial contribution to the photographs was to crouch down behind painstakingly-orchestrated line-ups and leap into the air with a King Kong war-cry to coincide with the click of the camera shutter. Again it was Midnight Sam to the rescue.

But the results were ultimately fine and the sponsored walk took up the whole of page three of the Evening News – four pictures and a glowing report. Brian was relieved and delighted when he picked up the newspaper in the evening. He was even more delighted a week later when the Professor and Midnight Sam called in at the day centre to see him, both men shining with triumph. Midnight, Splodge, Nobby and Lady Jane had collected all the sponsor money and, including the cash donated en route (minus a discreet and anonymous cheque to Help the Aged), a magnificent £3,247 had been amassed. The Professor paid the money into the HSBC bank on the corner of The Cross and obtained a certified cheque, payable to National Homeless Week.

Brian shook his head in wonder, reached for the telephone and called the Evening News. It made a great follow-up.

16

ON HIS release from youth detention, Mark Fenemore was sent to a secure special residential home for young offenders with severe behavioural problems. He was one of five residents, all aged 15 and all boys. The supervision was one-to-one, 24 hours a day, extremely costly to the State and in Mark's case a complete waste of time. Far too much, far too late. The intense counselling had no effect on the troubled youth.

Mark had grown more sullen, more inward, darker and more dangerous than before, frequently getting into fights with the other residents and, on two occasions, with members of staff. He had developed a sadistic streak, especially to those he could overpower easily. In one particularly ugly incident he waylaid an Asian resident in the communal kitchen, yanked down the terrified boy's trousers and underpants and calmly poured a mug of scalding hot tea over his genitals. What made the inexcusable attack even more worrying was the fact that, despite the inevitable internal investigation, no motive could be identified. But, in truth, the investigation was not particularly exhaustive. With £2,000 a week per resident at stake, the home administrators said nothing to the police and dealt with the matter themselves. Their contract with the local authority, only too pleased to abdicate responsibility at the taxpayers' expense, was a crucial piece of paper (for both parties.)

A covert but universal sigh of relief, by staff and residents alike, spread throughout the home when Mark Fenemore absconded. He left in the middle of the night after breaking into the principal's office, silently but thoroughly ransacking the room, urinating over the desk and smearing his own excretia onto the walls. He also sprayed 'FUCK OFF WANKERS' in bright red paint on the back of the office door.

A white Ford Transit panel van was parked in a narrow lay-by on a quiet lane less than a mile from the home and Charlie Stanton, smoking his third cigarette, was sitting patiently in the driving seat. Having run all the way, Mark pulled open the front passenger door, tossed his hastily packed holdall into the back of the van and swung onto the seat.

"Give us a fag, Charlie," he said breathlessly. Stanton placed a full packet on the teenager's lap, switched on the ignition and drove off quickly, a cigarette dangling from the corner of his mouth. When he had lit up his own cigarette, Mark leaned back in his seat, exhaled with eyes closed and, without moving his head, reached across with his right hand and gently squeezed Stanton's crotch.

"Later, gay-boy," Stanton murmured, squirming away from Mark's hand. "Wait until we get there." Mark frowned and looked sulkily out of the side window into the blackness.

"Where are we going?" he asked.

"Blackpool," Stanton said with a crooked grin, "and don't sulk. It's going to be a long drive."

The principal of the home went through the correct procedures, although he secretly crossed his fingers and hoped that they would all be in vain. Which they were. He contacted the police, the local authority which had referred Mark in the first place and he tried to get in touch with the boy's mother. But Sharon Fenemore had left the block of flats in Langley several months beforehand and her whereabouts were unknown. Vague rumours in some of the local pubs she was known to have frequented suggested that she might have ventured north to Hull with a merchant seaman she had met in Birmingham. But nobody knew for sure or appeared to care very much.

One or two local newspapers carried stories about the boy's disappearance, accompanied by a poor-quality police photograph of Mark when he was about 14. But there were only two months to go before the local authority's responsibility for him terminated so the corporate enthusiasm in his 'capture' was limited. At the age of 16 he could go where he liked and with whom he liked. And he did.

The police dutifully circulated his details to a number of surrounding forces and registered him as a missing person (one of the thousands who disappeared without trace nationwide every year). They did not hold out much hope but they went through the motions nonetheless. And press interest soon waned. Two or three fairly lame follow-ups, a cautious piece in the Kidderminster Times about care homes and an in-depth, pompous feature in The Birmingham Post headlined 'WHERE ARE THEY NOW?' which lived up to its question but offered no answers. Mark Fenemore, along with numerous others, had become another statistic (the sad story of his life) and was soon forgotten.

Meanwhile, Charlie Stanton had rented a small one-bedroomed flat in downtown Blackpool – a drab, depressing suburb on the southern outskirts of the town. He had used the name Nick Adams as a precaution: Stanton was wanted by Wolverhampton police in connection with a domestic burglary and there was also a warrant out for his arrest for failing to answer bail on credit card fraud allegations.

The landlady lived in Preston and she happily pocketed the deposit and three month's rent in advance without asking too many questions. Stanton didn't tell her about Mark, not that she would have objected: three month's rent in advance was a great sweetener. The flat was in the heart of sleazy, grey and loveless, housing benefit land. The sort of area where people kept themselves to themselves, where people harboured their secrets with ease, where community spirit and social responsibility were alien concepts. Where a promiscuous paedophile like Stanton could house his teenage 'sex slave' without fear of outrage or exposure. It was, for the older man, ideal.

Mark's relationship with Charlie Stanton was a complicated one. To Stanton, Mark was a sexual convenience, but to the young man, it was a case of total obsession. Mark's developing sexuality had been corrupted from an early age and detoured towards Charlie Stanton. It had become inextricably confused with largely unexplored filial instincts: he had never known his natural father and his temporary stepfather had ruthlessly and repeatedly abused him. As if that wasn't enough to cope with, he had never benefited from the protective love of a normal mother. Deep down, deep in his basic makeup, Mark was not a natural homosexual. True, his pubescent sexual appetite had been whetted by abnormal liaisons. He knew no better, no different and, in time, it became a *kind* of loving for him. He did not question what Stanton did to him and what he did to Stanton, because he told nobody and therefore nobody told him that it was wrong (or, more to the point, why it was wrong.)

Stanton had chosen Blackpool for two good reasons: firstly, the northern seaside resort was notorious for its overt and active gay scene. Gay bars boasting such subtle names as The Swinging Handbag; a gay sauna in Springfield Road, near the promenade, which publicised exhaustive lists of 'gay friendly' guest-houses on the notice-board; gay men opening cruising on foot about the streets at night.

But the second reason was more sinister. Stanton was well aware that Mark was potentially promiscuous and that he would do almost anything he suggested. So besides indulging in regular casual gay sex with strangers in town, Stanton began to seek out 'customers' he could take back to the flat and introduce to Mark – preferably affluent 'customers.' After three or four weeks of petty burglary and shoplifting, Stanton, sensing there were easier pickings from prostitution, broached the subject with Mark as they lay in bed together late one night.

"Couple of blokes I met today in The Swinging Handbag fancy coming back here for a few beers tomorrow night. Bit of a laugh, Markey, bit of slap and tickle. Okay with you?" Stanton nudged Mark in the ribs and sniggered.

Nothing adverse passed through the teenager's conscious mind; and even when he remembered Owen Thomas and the fellow lorry-driver he had brought back – Charlie Stanton – he saw nothing abnormal in that. Wasn't that the way things were, wasn't that the way of the world or at least, the way of his world?

"Yeah, okay," he mumbled, turned over and went to sleep.

And so a new routine began, a routine which made Stanton a lot of easy money. Mark had become a sexual commodity and, conveniently for Stanton, the young man was neither reluctant nor enthusiastic; he was the archetypal prostitute. He would make himself available whenever required and that entailed around three or four times a week.

Stanton would trawl the numerous gay haunts of Blackpool for punters. He was on the lookout for lone, middle-aged, financially well-heeled men who were clearly looking for action. And once engaged in conversation, it was easy to ascertain quite quickly whether an available, good-looking 16-year-old boy (and he had a photograph of Mark, naked, to prove it) would be an attractive proposition. Occasionally he would be rebuffed but Stanton was a good judge of bad character and his success rate was high.

Stanton was not stupid; he was a canny and calculating pimp. He knew that there would have to be something in it for Mark. He would need to keep his meal ticket sweet. He also knew that he would have to continually boost the boy's sexual ego. Because Mark never really enjoyed sex with anybody else other than with Stanton. He did not object to it - if it pleased his paedophile lover and earned a few pennies into the bargain, then so-be-it - but enjoy it? No. So Stanton shared his financial pickings relatively generously with the 16-year-old.

But there was a problem, a problem that was getting worse all the time. Mark was becoming paranoid with jealousy and Stanton had to keep reassuring the boy that he was faithful, which he was most definitely not.

So he wisely kept his numerous 'extra-marital' sexual liaisons a close secret from his young lover. Had he known what was going on in Mark's mind he would have stopped them altogether.

Mark had known nothing but abuse, neglect and exploitation during his short life and although this was what he had come to expect, some unidentifiable emotion deep inside him had started to stir. He began to feel cheated, angry, bitter and frustrated and yet he was not too sure why he felt those emotions. His mind was muddled, confused and contradictory; his life was solitary, dark, secretive. Something, and he had no idea what, was wrong, very wrong.

During the long and lonely afternoons, when Stanton was either sizing up 'customers' or thieving, Mark would trot down the wooden steps at the back of their first-floor flat, hurry into town and spend a couple of hours in one of the amusement arcades, playing the fruit machines. Something about the gamble, the remote chance of success, the vague notion of winning, of something going right in his life, drew him to the slot machines. Mark also took to striding up and down the promenade, hugging the sea wall, from pier to pier, in all weathers. In fact the wilder the better; it suited his smouldering mood. He would welcome the cruel and building rollers which drove in from the bleak, grey Irish Sea to crash violently against Blackpool's concrete defences, spurting thick and foaming water high into the air. He would welcome the stinging sea that soaked him and he would stand still, shivering but excited, and await the next surge.

Monstrous Blackpool Tower – spectacularly ugly and depressing – was his favourite haunt. Several times a week he would pay the fee and take the clanking lift to the top. Isolated from the crowds of chattering, invariably elderly or very young tourists who jostled him, he would stand, hunched, and gaze out to sea for hours. A rare snippet of information which had survived from his haphazard schooldays told him that America was out there, somewhere to the west. He would stare fixedly across the indifferent ocean, not really understanding what he felt but liking it. America, the United States of America, the USA – now what was that all about, what happened there?

But when he came down from Blackpool Tower, when he was finished with walking the promenade, when he returned to the grim and gloomy suburb to their flat, when his own sad reality kicked in, then the monster inside him began to grow. The green-eyed monster of jealousy. His unidentified yearnings and regrets, his total sexual confusion, the hopelessly mixed up emotional mess of the young man all focussed into an overpowering jealousy of Charlie Stanton. What was the older man (his pimp, lover and, he had to admit, his provider) up to? Where did he go when he was away, as he frequently was? What did he do and with whom? And the green-eyed monster continued to grow, consuming his every thought, infecting his mind, knotting his stomach with actual pain, eroding his reason, taking control.

Mark began checking up on Stanton's movements. He would inspect the older man's pockets, flick through the messages on his mobile phone, steam open envelopes, eavesdrop on conversations. Instead of his usual routines of frequenting Blackpool Tower and the amusement arcades, he began to dedicate his afternoons to following Stanton, to watching his every move. And of course it soon became clear to Mark that Stanton was regularly on the lookout for casual gay sex, whether in the gay sauna he was a member of or in the dreadful public toilets he hanged around or in the gay bars he visited. If Stanton was not out thieving, he was out 'cottaging.' Strangely enough this did not bother Mark to any great extent. He began to realise that he did not feel threatened by Stanton having sex with other *men*. After all, Mark was still very young, a teenager, and surely a far more attractive proposition than some ageing queen?

But what bothered Mark, what made him feel threatened, was the very thing which had brought the two of them together in the first place: Stanton's attraction to young boys, the fact that Stanton was, despite his adult sexual adventures, a predatory paedophile. And one rainy day in April, Mark's jealousy found a target, a deadly target. He had shadowed Stanton along the promenade as far as the north pier when, just as he was about to lose interest and give an amusement arcade a go, he saw a young boy, aged about ten or eleven, run across the tram lines and stand in front of Stanton. Mark watched as Stanton pulled out his wallet, briefly looked left and right, and then slipped a banknote into the boy's hand. They turned and walked off together, Stanton's hand resting lightly on the boy's shoulder. To most people they must have looked like father-and-son but Mark knew different and he recognised, even from fifty yards away, a familiar intimacy. He had no doubt (and he was right) what was going on.

Mark straightened up from behind the parked car and stood still, rain plastering his hair to his forehead and dripping from the tip of his nose and from the point of his chin. He gazed at the disappearing backs of Stanton and the boy, his arms braced by his sides, a furious jealousy pounding in his chest. After a short while the raw, red anger in his face changed into a crooked smile. He turned and walked calmly back along the promenade, even stopping off at the amusement arcade to squander £15 of Stanton's money.

Over the next two weeks, Mark witnessed five similar meetings between Stanton and the boy, but he said nothing. He also noticed a change in Stanton's attitude towards him. For on each occasion, when Stanton returned to the flat, much later than usual, Mark would suggest sex. And on each occasion Stanton would mumble an apology and decline, feigning tiredness or, believe it or not, a headache. And when Mark crawled into bed, Stanton's pointedly-turned back and demeanour displayed clear no-go signals. But still Mark said nothing and did nothing.

That all changed one Sunday morning. Stanton got up earlier than usual in order to drive to Preston "to sort something out." He was gone by eight o'clock and Mark was on the point of settling back into bed for a long lie-in when the doorbell rang. Sleepy and grumpy and thinking it was Stanton returning because he had forgotten his keys, he plodded across the room and opened the front door. The boy was standing there, wide-eyed and innocent and wearing a pair of skimpy, red shorts.

"Is Charlie in?" he asked, grinning and trying to peer around Mark into the flat.

"No," Mark snapped and slammed the door.

When Stanton got back later in the evening, half-drunk, there was a huge row. Mark screamed abuse at him, stamped his feet, banged doors and stormed around the flat in an uncontrollable fury. Stanton sat upright on the sofa, without saying a word but wearing a silly, vaguely embarrassed smile. But his expression changed to one of irritation when Mark called him a dirty old man at the top of his voice once too often: "Well, well, well, Markey baby, but that's what dirty old men like me do. They look for fresh meat. Nice, juicy, fresh meat, with the emphasis on fresh. Know what I mean? Plenty of young chickens out there, Markey *old* chap, plenty more fish in the sea, *old* boy."

Mark's tantrum stopped immediately. His jealousy and his anger appeared to freeze in an instant. He sighed, nodded, even smiled at Stanton and then went quietly to bed. He kept himself neatly to his side of the bed and when Stanton joined him an hour later, the older man instinctively knew that anything physical was out of the question.

Mark appeared to have gone to sleep and Stanton lay on his back frowning. He felt uneasy. Vibes of terrible strength radiated from the teenager and Stanton realised, to his surprise, that he was frightened of the boy. Mark was not asleep; he did not close his eyes all night. He stared across at the curtained window which failed to block out the orange glow of the street-light outside and he listened to the distant hum of the traffic.

****

In the morning Stanton tried valiantly to make amends; he made light of the argument; he put a kindly arm around Mark's shoulders and tried to jostle him back on to friendly terms. He told him that the other young boy meant nothing to him, was just a bit of fun, and he promised faithfully never to see him again. There was nobody like "Markey baby," nobody at all. But it was to no avail. Mark refused to speak. He dressed quietly, made himself a mug of coffee, sat alone at the small, kitchen table and smoked a joint. He then got up lightly and walked towards the front door. When Stanton blocked the door, with a pleading expression on his face, Mark stood his ground, holding Stanton's gaze until the older man dropped his eyes. The teenager's lithe body was rigid with cold strength and both his fists were clenched, the knuckles white. Scared and defeated, Stanton stepped aside and watched, troubled and bewildered, while Mark walked unhurriedly out of the flat. He tried to ruffle Mark's hair in a last-ditch attempt at reconciliation, but the boy ducked the paedophile's hand and was down the wooden steps and out on the street in one fluid movement.

Low clouds scudded across a fragmented, pale blue sky and flurries of rain swept in from the Atlantic Ocean. A strong and steady west wind whipped across the promenade. It was six o'clock in the morning and few people were about. A lonely and empty tram clattered around the corner where the Clifton hotel stood regally, overlooking the north pier and the grey sea. An elderly couple leaned against the sea wall, holding hands and looking down at the hard and virginal sweep of golden sand. The tide was out and distant seagulls wheeled low above a ragged line of small, receding grey waves.

Mark walked up and down the promenade several times, for nearly three hours, his face flat and stony, his eyes dull and without expression, his shoulders tight and hunched. When Wilkinsons opened at nine o'clock he went in and made some purchases. He then trekked across town, beyond the railway station, to a second-hand car salesroom, where he bought a blue Ford Fiesta for £550 (he had been saving Stanton's sweeteners). He drove the car back to the flat but parked a couple of hundred yards away from where he lived. It was 11.30am and Stanton had gone out. He sat on the sofa, hands clasped in his lap, and waited.

Three hours later Stanton returned, mildly drunk and full of beans. He appeared to have forgotten the argument.

"Hiya, Markey," he said, bending down to squeeze the young man's knee before swaggering into the kitchen. "Fancy a cuppa? I'll stick the kettle on. We can have a nice cuppa coffee." He busied himself with filling the kettle and swilled out two dirty mugs. "What a day I've had, Markey, what a fuckin' great day. Pinched this geezer's wallet in the pub. Old boy he was and as pissed as a fart. Easy as fuck. And you'll never believe it but he had over a hundred quid in tenners. What a fuckin' day I've had."

While Stanton clattered away at the sink, Mark levered himself up from the sofa very slowly and tip-toed across the living room to the kitchen, the claw-hammer he had bought from Wilkinsons in his right hand. When he was three feet from Stanton, he took a long, barely audible intake of breath and raised the hammer above his head. Either Stanton heard the intake of breath or he sensed Mark's presence or both, but it was too late.

Stanton stopped what he was doing and began to turn around at exactly the same time that Mark brought the claw-hammer crashing down on the back of his head. Stanton, eyes wide and mouth gaping, was facing Mark when the second blow was delivered, a tremendous sideways crunch to the left temple. Stanton staggered, holding onto a stool, blood pouring from his nose and mouth and blossoming black and sticky through his hair. He slumped to the floor, looking up at Mark with a glazed, puzzled expression on his face. Mark raised the hammer again, this time with both hands, paused for a couple of seconds and then brought it crashing down on the top of Stanton's head. Stanton collapsed forwards as if in prayer and his arms and legs began scrabbling and twitching. He groaned for a while and was then still. All colour drained from his face and his eyes were set half-open and lifeless.

Mark put the hammer on the kitchen table, opened a drawer in one of the cheap, ill-fitting units and selected a plastic-handled carving knife. He heaved the body over so that the dead man was lying on his back, knelt down, held the knife above his head with both hands and plunged it deep into Stanton's chest. He stabbed Stanton repeatedly until the blade snapped off. He then stood astride Stanton's mutilated body, legs apart and hands on hips. He surveyed the carnage for several minutes, gazing dispassionately at the body.

Mark removed his bloodstained clothes, bundled them into a black plastic bin liner, stepped over Stanton's body on his way to the bathroom, showered and washed his hair. He sidestepped pools of blood on the floor on his way to the bedroom, where he lay naked on the bed and waited for nightfall. He put his hands behind his head and stared up at the ceiling. In his short and ugly life, he had never felt so happy. Warm and comforting waves of that alien but delicious emotion washed over him like a large dose of morphine.

The sun sank and the orange street-light came on, bathing the room in an eerie glow. Mark swung both legs off the bed, put on fresh clothes and crept out of the flat. He made as little noise as possible on the wooden steps leading from the front door down to the tiny, overgrown back garden, even remembering to avoid the fourth step which creaked. He walked quickly down the road to where his Ford Fiesta was parked. He drove the car back to the flat, keeping the revs down, and parked it outside. A light rain had started to fall, a typical April shower, as he got out of the car, closed the door quietly, unlocked the boot and gathered up the purchases he had made from Wilkinsons earlier that day: a roll of heavy duty, black, plastic bin liners, a cheap hacksaw with four spare blades and a camping knife with an eight-inch serrated blade.

Back inside the flat, Mark closed the curtains and switched on the television set, turning up the volume. He went into the kitchen and dragged Stanton's body, by the feet, across the floor into the bathroom. Three streaks of blood traced their route across the linoleum and threadbare carpet. Mark stopped suddenly and let go of Stanton's legs, cursing himself for forgetting the chronology of his plan – namely stripping completely before touching Stanton's body again. He darted back into the bedroom, where he undressed. Luckily he had only managed to get one small bloodstain on the lower inside left leg of his jeans. He returned, naked, to the bathroom and manhandled Stanton's body into the bath.

It took him two-and-a-half hours to remove the arms, legs and head of the man who had systematically abused him for the past six years. Three hacksaw blades broke, the knife proved less than razor-sharp and the bin liners had to be doubled up to take the weight of the body parts. They also leaked. When he had finished five bulky bags were stacked in a row by the side of the bath and Mark was dripping with sweat and smeared in blood. He swilled the bath, took another shower, slipped on a pair of boxer shorts and began to ferry the bags out of the flat, down the wooden steps and into the boot of the Ford Fiesta. It was two-thirty in the morning and the streets were deserted.

With all five bags squeezed into the boot of the car, Mark forced the lid shut and locked it. He tested the handle with a sharp pull and crept back up the steps to the flat. He had another shower, got dressed, checked the £300 in his wallet, collected his car keys and left the flat, closing the front door carefully. He stood still on the little wooden landing at the top of the stairway and breathed in the soft night air. It had stopped raining, the clouds had spread away and a sickle moon burned white-gold, toy-like and beautiful. After a while he walked down the steps, got into his car and made himself a spliff.

His plans had come to an end and he had no idea what to do next. And for some unfathomable reason, perhaps a masochistic instinct, he decided to drive south, south to Birmingham, where the black horror of his life had begun.

17

LADY JANE wore a pale yellow, ankle-length, cotton skirt and a white, short-sleeved cardigan. She had washed and brushed her hair and it was swept back in a neat bun, tied with a bright yellow ribbon. She could not remember the last time she had used makeup, but a dab of powder toned down her facial scar and there was a touch of pink lipstick and a hint of mascara. She had left the grubby hessian bag at the flat, along with the ubiquitous flagon of cider. A small, brown handbag was on the table in front of her.

Early afternoon August sunshine blazed through the frosted front windows of The Mitre, picking her out in the alcove, like a spotlight. Her eyes flicked anxiously to the clock on the wall and she took a quick sip from her half-pint of Olde English. She concentrated to control the shaking. Bobby wore a puzzled, faintly amused expression.

The Professor walked in, out of breath, and laboured to the bar. He hadn't seen Lady Jane. "Pint of Olde English please," he said in a low, strained voice, his chest heaving. He flattened both hands on the bar and lowered his head, fighting to get his breath back.

"You've got company," said the landlord, inclining his head towards the alcove. The Professor looked up at Bobby and then across at Lady Jane. He smiled with surprise and pleasure: "Ready for a refill?" She shook her head but returned his smile.

The Professor took his pint of cider over to the alcove and pulled up a stool: "You look lovely."

She flinched, raised her eyebrows and blushed: "Not really. Half my teeth are missing, my hair is falling out and this," she fingered her scar and shrugged, but she was flattered at the compliment.

The Professor nodded, leaned forward and drank a third of his pint in one go. He stifled a belch, blinked the water from his eyes and shook his head briskly.

"Where is he?"

Lady picked up her glass again, steadier than before: "He's up north, Newcastle I think. Gone for a few days. He goes up there sometimes. Don't know why, don't know what he does, why he goes up there. Probably got a fancy bit."

"How are things, Jane?" He meant Blacklock and she knew it.

"So-so, I suppose. He hasn't hit me for a while, which I suppose is something. Shouts in my face, pushes me around, throws things at the wall of course, but, to be fair, he hasn't thumped me in weeks. Quite a bonus really."

The Professor shook his head and began to roll a cigarette, spreading Rizla papers, a pouch of tobacco (mainly from dogends) and a box of matches on the table in front of him. He had a brief coughing fit and the familiar old pain rippled across his belly, deep and frightening. He composed himself and sat back, a comfortable silence settling between them. Suddenly Lady Jane began to fidget; she rubbed the side of her nose and pulled at stray hairs from the side of her head, winding them around a forefinger. She shifted on the bench seat and chewed her lower lip. The Professor waited.

"I had a happy childhood, you know," the words came softly, almost a whisper and Lady stared wide-eyed into her glass. "Really happy." She paused and looked at The Professor. "Nothing but good memories. It always seemed to be summer or Christmas, nothing in between. Building sandcastles in the sunshine or in front of a log fire, warm and safe. Mum fussing about in the kitchen with her glass of wine and dad trying to get Julian's latest gadget to work ..."

"Julian?"

"My younger brother, three years younger than me."

"Where did you live?" The Professor felt comfortable asking her, breaking the unwritten rule amongst the homeless. Lady Jane had made it all right for him to ask.

"Cornwall, north Cornwall. Place called Padstow. Dad was manager of a bank down there and mum taught in the local infants' school. We had a house on the outskirts of town on the road to Wadebridge. Detached, red-brick house, quite old with a wooden, lean-to garage. Dad was forever creosoting or mending it, but it kept falling apart. Mum teased him about it."

She smiled at the memory, a warm smile that made The Professor shudder with longing. He pinched the end of his cigarette, rested it on the side of the ashtray, finished his pint and stood up. "Time for another drink," he said, picking up both glasses, pausing to catch his breath and turned towards the bar. He pulled a brown envelope from the back pocket of his jeans, unfolded a five pound note and placed it on the bar. Bobby refilled the glasses without being asked and ignored the five pound note. "On the house," he said gruffly and swayed wheezily to the far end of the bar, scratching his beer belly.

The Professor took the drinks over to the alcove, settled back on to his stool and waited for Lady Jane to continue, blowing the surface of his cider as if it were piping hot, before taking a small sip. It was a habit of his, but only with the second pint. His father used to do the same thing, or was it his uncle? He could never remember.

"I did okay at school, I really liked it. English and history were my best subjects. Rather fancied the idea of teaching. Probably had a lot to do with my mum being a teacher."

The Professor felt a lump grow in his throat; he began to wish the conversation had never started. This was getting too close to home.

"I had a boyfriend when I was sixteen. He was nice, you know. Kind and gentle. He was tall and very skinny and he had the most beautiful hands. Long fingers and his nails were long, too long for a boy. They were an artist's hands, the hands of a concert pianist. I can see them now. They were so beautiful …" She put her hand to her mouth. "I'm sorry, Prof, you don't want to hear all this. I'm sorry."

"Don't be," he said. "If you're okay with it then so am I." He paused and reached for his cider. "Actually I'd rather like to hear. Go on."

"He told me that he loved me and that one day we would get married …," she broke off again, her lips quivering. "And d'you know something? I can't for the life of me remember what happened. I don't know what happened to him. I can't even remember his name. Just his hands, his beautiful hands."

The Professor stretched across the table and folded his less-beautiful hand around hers. It was an instinctive act and Lady closed her fingers around his without thinking. She even placed her other hand on top of his and gave it a maternal pat.

"That's when it all started to go wrong."

"Why?" The Professor frowned, extracting his hand gently. He was interested. "What went wrong?"

"Funnily enough I remember when it happened, when it went wrong. I remember the exact day. It was a Saturday and my best friend was having her 18th birthday party. Her mum and dad had hired the backroom of a pub in Bodmin.

"It was a great party and I was having a really good time. Dancing, having a laugh with my mates. My boyfriend couldn't make it, can't remember why.

"Everything was fine until I went outside for some fresh air. These two blokes came up to me – they seemed okay, about my age, maybe a bit older. God I remember it so well," she shook her head at the memory. "One of them asked me if I'd like to have a bit of fun – I even remember the words – and I got quite stroppy and told him that I had a boyfriend. But he said not to worry because he didn't mean that.

"Their idea of fun was a little bit of brown powder. To cut a long story short they introduced me to heroin. And the next day I bunked off school, caught the bus back to Bodmin and met up with them in the park. They wanted twenty quid, which I gave them from my Christmas savings, and they gave me two wraps of heroin. In less than a week I was hooked."

"When did your parents find out?" The Professor asked, irrevocably drawn into the story.

"It wasn't long, a matter of weeks, I think," she said. "As soon as I started to steal from them. I didn't have the nerve to go out shoplifting – at least not at the beginning – and my mum and dad were such easy targets, bless them. Wallets and purses all over the place. A trusting household."

The swing doors of The Mitre opened and Midnight Sam strolled in, a bundle of Big Issues underneath his left arm. He raised a hand to The Professor and Lady Jane and treated Bobby to a less-than-subtle,

'I'm going to ask you a big favour' grin. The landlord waited for the inevitable. It was a tense moment.

"Scots Robby is outside," Midnight began. "I think he's a bit reluctant to come in."

Bobby straightened his body with difficulty, his hands gripping the edge of the bar. He bristled with indignation: "Reluctant, you say. I'll say he's reluctant. But he's nowhere near as reluctant as I am to let him back into my pub – not bloody now, not bloody ever. He's barred and he's barred for bloody life." There was thunder in his face but Midnight Sam was an expert in such situations.

"He's sorry about the other day, he just got over-excited. Come on Bobby, it was all for a good cause, he was only wound up because he wanted to raise as much money as possible." Midnight Sam scratched the back of his head and confided in the landlord how Scots Robby was appalled at his own behaviour and how it would never, ever happen again. Midnight's charm was a considerable weapon: it was a class act.

Five minutes later, Midnight Sam brought a sheepish Scots Robby into the pub and steered him directly to the alcove. The Scotsman pulled a face when he saw Lady Jane but thought better of saying anything about it. He sat down on a stool next to The Professor and blinked from the rays of smoky sunlight which angled through the pub window and lit up his face, highlighting the remnants of an ice-cream in his moustache.

"You look very nice today, Lady," Midnight beamed. He was drinking Stella for a change and was sipping the lager as if it was a fine wine. Lady Jane put her head to one side and mouthed a silent 'thank you.' They sat in silence for a while until Scots Robby, for some reason best known to himself, barked across the table at Lady Jane: "D'you like whisky?"

Lady recoiled for a second, composed herself and gave a small, serious nod: "I used to, not all the time, but on special occasions. Christmas, you know. It was my dad's favourite tipple. A good single malt, he used to like. Glenmoranje or Glenfiddich. Always kept a bottle in the house."

Scots Robby straightened his shoulders and puffed out his chest. "I knew it, I fuckin' knew it – sorry, sorry," he shot Bobby an apologetic glance and continued. "You, young lassie, you are from across the border. I knew it. You're a wee Scottish lassie, that's what you are. Didn't I tell you?" he lied to The Professor, who wisely chose to say nothing. "A wee bonnie lassie from bonnie Scotland." He leaned over the table and clapped her, too hard, on the shoulder, nearly knocking over her glass. Lady Jane, as bemused as The Professor, also chose to say nothing.

At that moment, Fen pushed through the swing doors, bringing his little cloud with him. He was wearing a grey anorak with the hood up, which curtained his pale, lean face, and light blue shell suit trousers. He bought himself a half of lager and started to play the fruit machine. Out of the corner of his left eye he saw Lady Jane and the permanent scowl on his face darkened a shade.

"She's from Scotland," Scots Robby shouted across to Fen, who took no notice. "A wee bonnie Scottish lassie. Knows her whisky, she does, and none of your blended rubbish."

Fen fed the fruit machine for ten minutes, picked up his drink and sat down at a table near to the alcove. Legs apart, he leaned forward and stared at the floor, holding his glass by the rim and weaving it from side to side. Every so often his eyes would lift for a fraction of a second and focus on Lady Jane. She was aware of the inspection and felt a little uneasy, although she didn't know exactly why. A smouldering aggression, a thinly-veiled anger, a dark resentment, the coiled ferocity of a cornered rat, all barely beneath the surface. Fen appeared to be ever on the edge, ever on the edge of exploding.

****

It was a beautiful, summer's day, hot but with a light, gay breeze from the south-west. High cirrus clouds streaked a heated and hazy blue sky. The Professor and Lady Jane met up again at The Tree in the park. Lady had changed into a pair of faded blue jeans and a new t-shirt (the folding creases were still visible).

Splodge was fast asleep on a bench, curled up like a baby, two empty flagons of Tesco's finest cider on the ground. Not wishing to disturb him, Lady Jane, to her own surprise, led the way over to the base of the magnificent oak tree and arranged herself, quite primly, on the ground.

The Professor followed awkwardly, carrying a plastic carrier bag bulging with three flagons of GL. Out of breath and clutching his side with his other hand, he flopped down against the gnarled tree trunk, pulled out one of the flagons and tried to unscrew the cap. What little strength he could normally muster had drained away. Lady Jane reached across for the flagon, unscrewed the cap and handed it back to him, without a fuss.

"Christ, I'm pathetic, bloody pathetic," he shook his head and tilted the flagon to his lips. "Can't even open a bottle of bloody cider anymore." He stared bleakly across the park, the flagon between his knees: "I feel as weak as a kitten these days, no strength, no strength at all; I feel drained, empty."

"You should go back to the doctor," said Lady Jane, "you're not well and you're not getting any better."

The Professor frowned and wriggled uncomfortably. He hated talking about his health. Lady sensed the no-go area and reached across his lap for the flagon of cider with a cheeky and clever grin. She took an indelicate swig and leaned back against The Tree, shoulder to shoulder with the older man.

"How old are you, Prof?" she asked.

"Forty-five."

"I'm 27 – I look a bloody sight older though."

The Professor gave her an appraising look, a kindly look: "You don't look too bad to me, not too bad at all. That dress really suited you today, you looked really nice, really pretty."

"Skirt," she corrected automatically, "it was a skirt. But thanks. Thanks for saying that. It's nice to hear."

"You don't take that stuff anymore, do you? You're clean now, aren't you?" The Professor hadn't meant to say that. It was her business not his and yet he couldn't help himself. He didn't wait for her to answer. He blundered on: "Why don't you go back to your parents? You're young enough, Jane, for God's sake. You don't have to live like this. You could start again, you know. It's not too late for you, you could start again …," he trailed. His heart was thumping and he started to cough. He also felt embarrassed. Where had all that come from?

"I made their life hell, absolute hell, for years and years," she stared into space, remembering. "And my brother Julian. I stole from them all, I lied to them, I brought every type of trouble to their doorstep. Dealers would come round to the house, at all hours of the day and night, banging on the door, shouting out my name, throwing stones at the windows. They threatened my mum and dad and they terrified Julian. My dad even gave them money to keep away. But I still took the stuff, I still ran up huge debts and the dealers still came back to the house. Time and time and time again."

Lady Jane shook her head at the horror: "I sold Julian's Christmas presents one year. The brother I adored. I sold his Christmas presents so that I could buy heroin. Can you imagine that? I *sold* his Christmas presents. And do you know what he said to me? He said that it didn't matter so long as it meant that 'those horrible men' didn't come round to our house anymore." She closed her eyes. "I sold my 12-year-old brother's Christmas presents."

"That's heroin, Jane. That's what it does to you . It wasn't you, it was the heroin. It takes over, it takes over completely. It gets right into your brain and there is nothing you can do. It destroys everything. I remember a couple of students in the Sixth Form ...," he stopped himself abruptly in mid-sentence, shook his head angrily and reached for the flagon of cider.

"What Sixth Form?"

"Never mind. It doesn't matter."

The subject was closed. The Professor began to cough; his face turned a bright red and his eyes watered. It was a bad coughing fit, it went on for a couple of minutes. He struggled to his feet, braced himself against The Tree with arms outstretched and fought to regain his breath. Lady Jane waited, hugging her knees, until she felt it was right for her to continue.

"I went into rehab – cost mum and dad a fortune – but I managed to get myself clean. And while I was there, you're never guess what they did, what my wonderful parents did. They sold the house in Padstow – and I know how much they loved that house – and they upped sticks and we all moved to Oxford. Dad wangled a transfer – actually it was a demotion – and mum managed to get a part-time teaching job in Witney, about ten miles from Oxford. We bought a much smaller house."

"And your brother? What about him, what about Julian? New school, I suppose."

Lady Jane stiffened and scrambled to her feet.

"Julian," she said quietly, chewing her lower lip and staring ahead. She got up, brushed herself down and walked away from The Tree. She held her head high and swung her handbag with a false gaiety. The Professor stared after her.

18

THE police officer took little notice of the blue Ford Fiesta parked outside a block of flats in Langley. He walked passed the car, looked down at the young driver smoking a cigarette, flicked his eyes over the tax disc, which had a couple of months to run, and carried on strolling down the pavement. But when he returned some three hours later he noticed that the young man had fallen asleep; he also noticed the dog-ends in the overflowing ashtray. Rather thick for conventional cigarettes. He tapped on the window. Mark Fenemore jumped at the noise and sat up straight, shaking the sleep from his head. He wound down the window and poked out his head. Still sleepy but calm and helpful. But the sweet and musky smell of cannabis was unmistakeable.

****

The assizes at Preston, in the heart of the high, windswept town, is a delightful relic from the past. A new and undeniably 'user-friendly' crown and magistrates courts complex has been built just over half a mile away, off a busy dual carriageway. A characterless chunk of concrete and steel. Functional but soulless, a place where the anachronistic but splendid wigs and gowns and pomp of the English justice system seem out of place. But Preston Assizes – where Doctor Shipton stood trial for murdering numerous patients and where the young killers of toddler James Bulger faced the music – is everything a court of law should be. Old, ornate, austere. A seat of judgement, a sombre institution of justice, of crime and punishment. The cold, uncarpeted, stone floors echo, the courtroom walls are intricately wood-panelled, the creaking furniture and furnishings ancient and uncomfortable. An air of high disapproval prevails: if you are found guilty you richly deserve the consequences and if you are found not guilty you are mighty lucky to have got away with it. The cramped press bench which faces the jury has long-unused sunken ink wells on the narrow and time-warped, wooden desktop. A huge wooden chandelier, with comically wonky yellow lampshades, hangs from the ceiling. Everything creaks, everything smells fousty and old.

Mark Fenemore stood in the dock, flanked by two security guards. During his nine months in custody at Lancaster Gate Young Offenders Institution awaiting trial he had put on weight, grown a goatee beard and shaved his head. He had just turned 18, his second birthday behind bars, but he looked older. In the raised public gallery sat Charlie Stanton's mother and father, Mark's mother Sharon and his sister Penelope. The two families looked understandably very uncomfortable, occasionally darting furtive glances at each other. Barristers, solicitors, plain-clothed police officers, Crown Prosecution Service clerks and probation officers fussed with thick files and bundles of papers, heads together for last-minute, whispered consultations.

"Court rise," an usher commanded in a loud, reverent and everso slightly theatrical voice (it was his moment of importance) and everybody did. The judge, a white-haired, diminuitive, busy woman in her early sixties, bustled into the raised dais from a side door, stood in front of her ornate chair for a second, bowed briskly and sat down.

Another court usher – a bent, grey-haired man with a hunched back and a pronounced limp – put one hand on the door handle to the jury waiting room and looked inquiringly across the courtroom to the judge. Her Honour Judge Carol Crowther nodded abruptly, eyebrows raised, and the usher opened the door and limped away to fetch the 'jury-in-waiting.' Seconds later 15 men and women, looking out-of-place and bewildered, crowded into a corner of the court. The court clerk explained the procedure, shuffled a pack of 15 name cards and called out 12 names at random. There were no objections and the chosen 12 jury members were duly sworn 'to try the case to the best of their ability and bring a verdict according to the evidence.' The solemnity of the occasion was already getting to them; it never took long.

Dudley Phillips QC, prosecuting barrister, stood up, arranged his papers on the lectern in front of him, placed his left hand on his hip, rearranged his robes with his right hand and opened the case: "Members of the jury, I appear for the prosecution and my learned friend, Jerome Burns QC, appears for the defence.

"The defendant in this case, Mark Fenemore, is accused of murder. His victim was a man by the name of Charlie Stanton. They lived together in a small flat in Grasmere Road, Blackpool. On the night of June 16th last year, Mark Fenemore battered Mr Stanton with a claw-hammer, stabbed him numerous times in the chest with a hunting knife, cut off his arms, legs and head with a hacksaw or knife, placed most of the dismembered body parts in black plastic bin liners in the boot of his car and, for some reason, drove down to a suburb of Birmingham, where he was soon arrested by the police. There is no argument about this sequence of events, no issue with these facts, no question that Mark Fenemore killed Charlie Stanton. The defendant has admitted this.

"But what this case hinges on, what this trial is about ladies and gentlemen of the jury, is the state of Mr Fenemore's mind when he killed Charlie Stanton. Did he intend to kill or to seriously harm Mr Stanton? Because if he did and if any argument of provocation submitted by the defence is not proven, then this young man is guilty of murder. But if the defendant only meant to cause Mr Stanton *some* harm and was provoked into doing so then he is not guilty of murder but guilty of manslaughter.

"There are points of law and Her Honour will explain these to you more fully in due course. It is my job, on behalf of the Crown, to outline the facts of this case and to call witnesses to give their evidence. You will then hear from Mr Burns, who will present the case for the defence. Mr Burns and I will then make our closing speeches and Her Honour will sum up the case and instruct you on your roles as members of the jury."

Dudley Phillips took most of the morning to open the case and the next four days to call his witnesses, which included a challenging and defensive landlady of the flat in Blackpool, the garrulous car salesman who sold Mark the Ford Fiesta, the police officer who arrested him in Langley, three interviewing officers, two doctors – one of them a psychiatrist – and a pedantic, humourless Home Office pathologist.

Judge Crowther adjourned the case at 4pm on Friday until 10.30am the following Monday, when Jerome Burns, a notoriously flamboyant barrister with a theatrically deep, resonant voice, was due to open for the defence.

Throughout the week Mark had sat motionless in the dock, displaying no emotion. He did not acknowledge his mother, who fidgeted nervously in the public gallery, but he did nod at his sister from time to time. She blew him a kiss once.

Burns faced the jury of seven men and five women, picked out whom he correctly deduced to be the most intelligent member – a sixtysomething man with thick-rimmed, owlish glasses and untidy, pure white, shoulder-length hair – and called his first and only witness, the defendant Mark Fenemore. He proceeded to address all his remarks, eyeball to eyeball, to the older jury member, who, his instinct had also suggested to him, would end up the elected foreman. He was correct on that count as well.

Through carefully orchestrated questioning (and Mark played his part perfectly) Burns described his client's life. The early casual sexual abuse, from the age of eleven, at the hands of Owen Thomas and others; and the sustained abuse at the hands of Charlie Stanton. The advocate left out no detail, however disgusting and however sordid. He built up an accurate picture of Mark's appalling childhood. Every single perverted, sexual abomination was brought up, every degradation painfully dissected and examined with clinical precision.

"Mark, please tell the judge and jury about that time when your mother walked into the bedroom and found you and Mr Stanton in bed together."

Michael replied: "He had just had sex with me …"

Burns: "What sort of sex Michael? What do you mean?"

"Anal sex, he had anal sex with me."

"So when your mother walked into the room what did she do?"

There was a mild commotion in the public gallery and Sharon Fenemore left at a run.

"She stood in the doorway and said nothing. Charlie asked her how she was and she said she was fine."

"How old were you at the time?"

"Eleven or twelve, I'm not sure."

The expression on Burns' face was one of astonishment: "Why on earth didn't you tell your mother what was going on?"

"I tried to but she didn't believe me – she didn't want to hear - and anyway Charlie used to tell me that it was all okay, that lots of kids did it. He said that if I told anyone he would say that I was telling lies and I would get into trouble."

And so the questioning continued, leading ultimately and inevitably to the night of the killing, and Jerome Burns' timing was perfect.

"What happened on that night, Mark? Why did you kill Charlie Stanton? What happened?"

Mark: "I don't know. I couldn't take anymore. I had had enough. He had sexually abused me for years, ruined my life. I just couldn't take anymore. Something happened that night, something went bang in my head. I couldn't think, I couldn't think of anything. All I could think of was that I wanted to make it stop, to stop him doing it to me. Nothing else mattered. I had to make it stop."

Burns left his bench, walked up to the witness stand and glowered up at his client, jaw set firm: "So did you mean to kill him, did you mean to cause him serious harm, Mark? A simple yes or no will do. Did you?"

The jury was mesmerised: it appeared that the defendant's own counsel was putting his client squarely on the spot.

Mark shook his head: "I wanted the abuse to stop. I had had enough. I just wanted it all to stop, that's all …, " his voice faded and he hung his head. Burns returned to his place, shoulders slumped, exhausted with the emotion. Seven men and five women – six of them with children of their own – ached with pity for the young defendant. What chance had he ever had? What terrible nightmares had plagued his short and dreadfully damaged life? Who could possibly blame him?

The cross-examination was clinically accurate: Fenemore had planned the killing and had carried it out with calculated efficiency. The inference was clear: Stanton was undoubtedly a monster but the defendant had, equally undoubtedly, intended to cause him serious harm. In fact, the defendant had clearly intended to kill him. And that equalled murder.

Dudley Phillips, who had sparred with Jerome Burns on a number of previous occasions and knew him to be a formidable adversary, stood up to make his closing speech in the quiet knowledge that he was probably fighting a losing battle. He knew, as Burns knew and as Mark Fenemore, more than anybody else, knew, that the killing of Charlie Stanton was premeditated, that it was in cold blood, that it had nothing to do with stopping the abuse. The prosecution barrister knew that the killing was murder, in the eyes of the law, and that there was no 'reasonable doubt' to suggest otherwise. But he also knew – or at the very least had a pretty good idea – that the jury had already made up its collective mind.

"Are we being asked to believe that this young man did not intend to kill or to seriously harm Charlie Stanton?" he waved a dismissive hand to the dock and shook his head in genuine amazement. "He went out and bought a hunting knife, a claw hammer, a hacksaw with four blades, a roll of black plastic bin-liners and a getaway car.

"He sat calmly in their flat in Blackpool and waited for his intended victim to come home. And when Stanton did return, this defendant, with cold-blooded savagery, smashed him over the head with the claw-hammer, plunged the hunting knife into his chest numerous times and then methodically sawed off his arms, legs and head. He placed the severed body parts in the bin-liners, crammed his grisly load into the boot of his car and drove away from the scene of the crime.

"You heard reference during this trial to an argument about another young boy who Stanton was becoming involved with. Although the defendant repeatedly denied this when he took the witness stand, it is a matter of record that he mentioned it in two police interviews. His 'love rival,' if I may refer to this unknown boy as such, has not been tracked down, but there is little doubt in my mind that he exists. So, far from having – as the defence would like you to believe – a crime of provocation, what do we really have here? What we are left with is a crime of jealousy, a crime of perverted passion. In short, Mark Fenemore feared that he was on the point of being replaced and, in a terrible but controlled fury, he planned and carried out the murder of Charlie Stanton. There is no other verdict, ladies and gentlemen of the jury: you must find Mark Fenemore guilty as charged."

Phillips did well but he was up against a monumental enemy: public outrage. A depraved paedophile had corrupted and systematically sexually abused a vulnerable young boy from the age of eleven and finally that young boy had turned on his abuser. Facts and legal definitions were going to struggle against that.

Jerome Burns, tall, immaculately dressed and debonair, rose elegantly to his feet, picked up the sheaf of papers on his lectern and was about to begin his closing speech when he appeared to freeze. He frowned and tossed his notes back onto the lectern with an element of disdain. A couple of sheets floated to the floor; he made no effort to retrieve them. Shaking his head gravely, Burns stepped out from his place behind the front bench and faced the jury. They were already mesmerised, in his hands, and he hadn't said a word.

"I'm sorry, members of the jury, but you are going to have to excuse my behaviour and be patient with me," he said, apology in his voice. "I had a carefully prepared speech, which has taken me a great deal of time to write. Most of last night as a matter of fact. And there it is …," he half-turned and waved a weary hand at the front bench, "...some of it on the floor." He shook his head again and continued: "I am not going to read it to you. I feel too strongly about this case to bury my head in a prepared speech. Instead – and I beg you to bear with me if I stumble, if I get a bit mixed up, if I get things wrong from time to time – instead, members of the jury, I am going to tell you a story and, when I have finished, I am going to sit down and leave the rest to you. It will be for you to decide whether this young defendant, barely 18-years-of-age, is a cold-blooded murderer or himself a victim. It will be your decision and not mine."

Dudley Phillips failed to suppress a wry smile and he scratched the side of his face. Burns and he were friends as well as occasional legal opponents and he had to admire the defence barrister's technique. The jury, especially the women members, were warming to his ostensibly clumsy approach. But every word, ever slip, every mannerism, every expression had been minutely rehearsed. It was a class act, a true performance.

"Mark Fenemore was born into a chaotic, totally dysfunctional family – various children by a variety of fathers. He never even knew his own father, but, oh yes, he knew a series of 'uncles,' he got to know them only too well. Mark's mother ...," he turned full circle and gestured to the public gallery where he knew Sharon Fenemore was no longer present, "... ah, but she's gone, of course," he held both hands out in supplication. "Mark's mother would leave her son and his sister Penelope to their own devices. And the result was that one of Sharon's more permanent partner's began sexually abusing both children. Fortunately he was found out, convicted and sent to prison and Penny was thankfully taken into care. But that left Mark, alone and vulnerable, in the foul clutches of the latest so-called 'uncle,' a man by the name of Charlie Stanton. A known paedophile and an habitual thief.

"The depraved sexual abuse by a much-older man on this child went on and on and on. Mark's childhood, his innocence, the purity and loveliness of his youth was destroyed, degraded, defiled. By the time this once-innocent, no-doubt once beautiful baby boy had reached the age of 17 he had been totally and utterly corrupted. He no longer knew right from wrong; he had never, ever had the chance to find out. His natural sexual urges had been twisted and warped into an ugly and foul deviation. He had fallen under the spell of this evil man.

"For years Mark Fenemore was provoked. Of course he was provoked. His deepest senses were, unbeknown to him, outraged, his instincts confused and contradicted. And he knew, in the centre of his being, that something was dreadfully, unacceptably wrong. And he began, subconsciously, to realise that that something was someone and that someone was Charlie Stanton. The sick pervert who had dominated his life, who had ruthlessly robbed him of his innocence.

"What happened on that dark day in June was inevitable, tragically inevitable. Oh yes, it all appears to have been premeditated, the act of a cold-blooded murderer. The prosecution would have you believe that. But come on, members of the jury, we all know the truth, we all know what drove Mark Fenemore to do what he did, we all know what finally tipped him over the edge. Years and years and years of constant provocation, until the young man snapped and his responsibility for his own actions was not just, in legal-speak, 'diminished,' it was smashed to smithereens. When this defendant killed the man who had ruined his life, he was in no way, by any stretch of the imagination, responsible for his own actions. How could he be?

"My client took a life and the Bible says 'thou shalt not kill.' And the Bible is right. My client took the life of Charlie Stanton and, whatever we think of that wicked man, my client was wrong to do so and he must suffer the consequences. But to say he *murdered* him? No, that is equally wrong. Mark Fenemore must be found guilty of manslaughter. But you must decide; it is your decision and yours alone. The buck stops with you."

Judge Crowther, who had heard Jerome Burns in action in the past and could easily see through the drama and emotion, smiled politely at the barrister and turned in her chair on the raised dais to face the jury. It was now her job to outline the evidence, to précis the cases of both prosecution and defence, to explain various points of law and to instruct the jury on how they should approach the thorny process of reaching a verdict.

However impartial judges strive to be, beneath the wig, the gown and the silk is another human being. Intelligent, intuitive, brilliantly versed in the letter of the law, sharp-minded, attentive, often intellectually well ahead of the field. But still another human being. With an opinion. And Judge Carol Crowther was no exception. She was certain "beyond reasonable doubt" that Mark Fenemore was guilty of murder. She had listened closely to the evidence, the arguments, the demeanour of the witnesses (especially the defendant) and she was quietly certain that provocation was not an issue and had not been proved. In her astute mind, Fenemore's responsibility was no more diminished than anybody capable of battering, stabbing and dissecting another human being. Nevertheless, with consummate fairness and professionalism, she neither voiced nor hinted at an opinion.

The jury bailiff was sworn, seven men and five women were sent out to the jury room to consider their verdict, the judge rose, bowed briefly and left the courtroom. Mark Fenemore was led back down to the cells to await his fate, three reporters compared notes, stretched their arms and gave their own verdicts, Jerome Burns and Dudley Phillips joked together and four people in the public gallery stood up uncertainly, not quite knowing what to do. An anti-climatic silence fell.

The British legal system is a quaint one. It weathers the storms of change which reshape most other walks of life on a daily basis (and not always to the good) with a gentle but fierce immutability. The case of Mark Fenemore is an example. Intensive police investigation; more than a year of legal preparation; numerous interviews and paperwork, with hundreds of thousands of words written and rewritten; the painstaking tracking-down of witnesses; vast amounts of taxpayers' money spent on barristers, solicitors, psychiatrists, doctors; numerous preparatory court hearings; the trial itself – hugely costly – lasting for two weeks. And after all that time, effort, expertise and expense the whole business is handed over to twelve totally inexperienced, randomly selected members of the public, who invariably listen with their hearts as opposed to their heads. A quaint system.

Mark sat in one of the austere and tiny cells below courtroom one with a talkative female warder for company. He answered her well-meaning but irritating chatter either with gruff monosyllables or with stony silence. His mind was numb, nothing seemed real. But then nothing had seemed real to him for years, least of all himself. He drank endless mugs of tea and smoked the kindly wardress's cigarettes and stared at the wall opposite. He wasn't nervous or anxious, he didn't cross his fingers or say a silent prayer. He felt nothing; he just waited. And when the announcement "all parties in the case of Mark Fenemore please return to courtroom one" crackled over the tinny, echoing tannoy system, he did not flinch, which was more than could be said for the wardress. But it was only to discharge the jury from their duty that day. They were not even close to a verdict and everybody went home.

It was mid-afternoon the following day before "all parties" were summoned back into court and this time the whisper which spread among barristers, ushers, court clerks and reporters was that a verdict had been reached.

Mark was ushered up the steps into the dock and the scene was complete: all the actors in one of the world's greatest theatrical performances were there, on stage, awaiting the final curtain. The raw, nerve-jangling anticipation was tangible, the sudden silence deafening. An usher, savouring his moment, gave the 'court rise' command in a deep and imposing tone as Judge Crowther, as ever vaguely irritated by the pomp and ceremony, marched in to take her presiding seat, businesslike and unflappable. She nodded across at another usher who was standing to attention by the door leading to the jury chamber. Seconds later seven men and five women, looking more important and more relaxed than when they first stumbled nervously into court on the first day of the trial, filed into their customary places. There was an intimacy among them now and a serious sense of occasion.

The court clerk stood up: "Mark Fenemore, please stand."

The clerk paused, turned to face the jury and asked, in a voice devoid of emotion (which made it all the more electric): "Would the foreman please stand?"

The 60-year-old man with thick-rimmed, owlish glasses and untidy, snow-white, shoulder-length hair stood up promptly.

"Members of the jury, have you reached a verdict on which you are all agreed?"

"Yes."

"Do you find the defendant guilty or not guilty of murder?"

"Not guilty."

"And do you find the defendant guilty or not guilty of manslaughter?"

"Guilty."

"And that is the verdict of you all?"

"Yes."

The jury foreman and the clerk sat down simultaneously and Dudley Phillips shot to his feet. He reeled off a daunting list of the defendant's previous convictions, followed by Jerome Burns, who gave an eloquent, if truncated, plea of mitigation (he had covered the same ground more than adequately in his closing speech) and requested a pre-sentence report. Judge Crowther refused with a polite "I don't think that will be necessary." She shifted her position slightly and looked across the court straight into the defendant's eyes.

"Mark Fenemore, you have been found guilty of manslaughter and it is now my duty to pass sentence upon you. The jury has decided that you are not guilty of murder and I have to respect that decision (it was obvious what she felt). Nevertheless you killed a man, albeit a man of bad character who had abused you for many years. You bludgeoned him with a hammer, you stabbed him a number of times and then you cut off his arms, legs and head with a hacksaw you had purchased earlier the same day for that very purpose. Whatever the provocation you suffered, it was an abominable crime, a crime for which you must pay. I sentence you to nine years in prison. Take him down."

****

Mark spent the first two years of his sentence in a succession of young offenders institutions. He was far from a model prisoner, ever picking fights with fellow inmates and with prison officers. He carried disruption and aggression with him wherever he went. When he was 20 he was transferred to Winson Green in Birmingham, an adult prison, where he found himself up against a far stricter and far less tolerant regime.

While Mark was languishing inside, Jerome Burns, miffed at having been out-manoeuvred by Judge Crowther, managed to successfully appeal his young client's sentence and win a two-year reduction of the prison term. Taking into account the time Mark had spent on remand before the trial and the automatic discount given, he was a free man less than four years after he had killed Charlie Stanton. Free but with nowhere to go.

On the evening of his release the 22-year-old made his lonely way to New Street station and bought a single ticket south. He spent most of the journey staring unseeing at his own reflection in the train window. He didn't really know where he was going or why and he certainly didn't care. He was heading for the wasteground.

19

DOC DAWES let the stethoscope around his neck fall to his chest. He patted The Professor affectionately on the shoulder. The Professor pulled down his shirt and fastened the buttons with some difficulty. Three were missing. He smoothed his hair – it had grown straggly and wayward again – and he remained standing with his customary stoop, half-inclined towards the door.

"For God's sake, sit down," the doctor said and The Professor, surprised by the stern tone, obeyed with raised eyebrows. "Have you any idea how ill you are? Yes, yes, I think you have, I think you know perfectly well how ill you are." Doc Dawes paused and slumped back into his chair with an even mix of frustration and weariness. He had been there before. He got up almost immediately and walked across the room to the window, with his back to The Professor. He looked out across The Docks, where the old warehouses had been faithfully restored – a combination of retail, residential and leisure uses – and where the estuarial waters of the river sparkled silver in the morning sunshine.

"Prof," he began, "or whatever your name is."

"Prof will do."

"Prof, we both know that you have stomach cancer. Just how advanced it is, whether or not it is operable, that we do not know. And we do not know because you, you stubborn old bugger, refuse to go into hospital and let them carry out tests." The doctor's voice had risen with irritation and he shook his head to bring down the volume. "But now I can actually feel the tumour. That means it is growing and that is not good news. But it is still possible that an operation could still save your life."

The Professor remained silent, his expression one of a defiant schoolboy who was being told off but refused to show any contrition as a point of principle.

"And this cough of yours, this breathlessness …"

"That's all it is, doc, a cough, a bloody persistent cough. I smoke too many cigarettes. Smoker's cough, that's what it is, nothing but a smoker's cough."

Doc Dawes hung his head in frustration: "It is not a smoker's cough." He emphasised the words clearly and separately, still with his back to The Professor. "I can assure you that is one thing it most certainly is not." He turned around and stood, silhouetted against the window, both hands behind his back, the stethoscope swinging across his chest. "I cannot be certain – you would need to have tests and before you say a word I know what you think about tests – but I can hazard a qualified guess. Your lungs are clearly the problem. They are weak and malfunctioning. I would say that you are suffering from pulmonary emphysema. The breathlessness is a tell-tale symptom as is the chesty sound in your voice, which, by the way, is getting worse. Obviously you don't help the condition by smoking or by living the sort of life that you do …," the doctor saw the look of impatience darken his patient's face and he decided not to go down that particular path. He had tried before.

"What is pulmonary emphysema?" The Professor asked with clinical interest. He had a vague idea but was not sure.

"The air sacs of your lungs are damaged and they become enlarged which causes the breathlessness – you cannot get sufficient air. It can be fatal and often is." Doc Dawes was being intentionally brutal but he knew it would be to no avail. Some people killed themselves with a noose, some with an overdose, some by hurling themselves from the top of a tower block. But a small number of people – and the 45-year-old man, who looked closer to 70, sitting on the chair in front of him, was one of them – committed suicide by deliberately allowing their bodies to fall apart. A hopeless silence rang out and The Professor got up with a struggle. He treated the doctor to a helpless, I-know-I'm-a-waste-of-time gesture and headed for the door.

Feeling guilty, The Professor turned around: "Is there anything I can do about it?" A serious expression, seeking the doctor's professional advice.

"Plenty of fresh air and give up smoking," Doc Dawes said lightly and with equally false seriousness. "Good, bracing sea breezes. Why don't you try Weston-Super-Mare?"

Midnight Sam was waiting for The Professor in the reception lounge of the day centre. He was smoking a roll-up cigarette and reading a copy of the Big Issue with consummate pride. It was two months since the sponsored walk and word had finally reached the national magazine, via Brian Davies. A well-written article, accompanied by two photographs supplied by the Evening News, occupied a whole page. Midnight, resplendent in his quasi-African get-up, featured in one of the photographs, along with a drug-crazed gorilla, minus the head. Bishop John and several dignatories shared the frame with a very red-faced Scots Robby in the other. Midnight put the magazine down as soon as he saw The Professor; he had already read it five times.

"How did it go, Prof?" he asked. Midnight had had to employ his considerable persuasive powers to get The Professor to see Doc Dawes in the first place.

"All I need is a bit of fresh air, some bracing sea breezes. That's what the doctor ordered. Weston-Supper-Mare's the answer, apparently." With more bounce in his step than usual, The Professor walked to the front door. "Come on, Midnight," he said over his shoulder. "Keep up."

"Where are we going?" Midnight Sam scrambled to his feet, rolled up his copy of the Big Issue and stuck it under his belt at the back of his jeans. He scooped up his donkey jacket (he wore it all year round, whatever the temperature), tightened the screw-cap on his flagon of White Lightning and followed The Professor into South Street.

"The wasteground?" suggested the older man, raising his eyebrows. "Haven't been there for ages. Lovely day, we could get a fire going, cook ourselves some sausages. How about that?"

"You're walking better, Prof, what's got into you? Hey, hang on, slow down." Midnight became entangled in his belt, which had a tendency to drag along the ground. "Doc must have said something. Are you feeling better?" Midnight's eyes widened optimistically.

"Yeah, I'm okay, Midnight. As I said, fresh air is all I need. Weston-Super-Mare. Just what the doctor ordered." The irony was wasted on Midnight Sam, who had far more important things, immediate things like sausages and where to get them, on his mind.

"I'll meet you at the wasteground in about half an hour," he said and then frowned. "You sure you're okay to get there – it's quite a walk."

The Professor stopped in mid-stride, valiantly fighting the wheeziness in his chest. "No problem, Midnight, I feel fighting fit today. But where are you off to?"

Midnight Sam sighed with mild irritation: "Sausages – you said that you wanted us to cook some sausages. We'll have some burgers as well. And of course we're going to need something to wash it all down with."

Midnight strode off back in the direction of town with determination – he was a man with a mission – while The Professor finally gave in to a rasping coughing fit before steadying himself and walking slowly in the opposite direction towards the wasteground. He was having a good day, both in body, mind and spirit, and the searing pain in his stomach had settled down to a dull ache. But there was something else, something wonderful, something which had flown in from nowhere. Something which suddenly swelled his being with exhilaration, which caused him to stop in his tracks, to rock his head back, to open his arms wide and to shout at the devil at the top of his voice. It was a day for defiance, a day for life. Midnight Sam and The Professor were going to have a barbecue and Midnight was going to steal the food and the booze and that was great. It was going to happen and nothing was going to stop it.

Of course Midnight excelled himself: two small packs of Bowyers pork sausages from Sainsburys and a box of four half-pound beefburgers from Marks and Spencer. But his piece de resistance was the wine: two one-litre bottles of Italian dry white, with – and this was the finishing touch – screwtops! The Professor, who was slumped on the ground against an Electrolux fridge-freezer which had seen better days, shaded his eyes from the slanting September sunlight and looked up. Midnight Sam paused for maximum theatrical effect and, with a flourish, produced a small frying pan encased in cellophane, shiny and cheap. The Professor burst out laughing.

"And where the bloody hell did you get that from?"

"Woolies. Only decided to get one after I got the burgers. It's easy enough to do sausages over a camp-fire – there's always something sharp around – but we'd have a problem with the burgers."

"We certainly would, Midnight." The Professor's eyes shone and it was nothing to do with the sunlight.

****

The following day, Midnight Sam paid Brian Davies a visit at the day centre. He had something on his mind and he needed to talk to the Welshman alone.

"It's fresh air that he needs," Midnight began earnestly. "Doc Dawes said so. He needs fresh air. He needs to go to Weston-Super-Mare. That's what the doc told him. Weston-Super-Mare. He said it would make him better."

"So what have you got in mind?" Brian's voice was cheery but with a trace of suspicion.

"A day-trip to Weston-Super-Mare, just for the day. I could look after him and perhaps Lady Jane would like to come too. Scots Robby, if he's around. Don't suppose Fen would be interested." Midnight started to turn the screw: "It would do him the world of good. Loads of fresh air down there in Weston, loads of it. Doc said The Prof needs fresh air, said it would make him better. Doc Dawes knows what he's talking about ...," he let the sentence hang.

Brian Davies pressed his hands together as if in prayer and lightly kissed both forefingers.

"National Express do regular coach trips – that would be your best bet," he said through his fingers. "I don't know how much it would cost but I could find out for you." He already knew that he would be buying the tickets, but he had to make an effort for the sake of pride. "What are you going to do when you get there, have you made any plans?"

Midnight shrugged and pulled a face: "Just to give The Prof a breath of fresh air. Loads of it down there. Splodge said he's been down there, said there was loads of fresh air."

"I suppose you want me to find out about coach times, tickets and that sort of stuff?" Brian asked wearily. Midnight said nothing, but then he didn't have to say anything. He knew what Brian was thinking and Brian knew that he knew. He got up, treated Brian to one of his extra-lovely smiles and walked towards the door.

"How many tickets do you think you'll need?" Brian asked, weakened and defeated.

"Four, to be on the safe side, I reckon," said Midnight.

The Professor and Lady Jane were already at The Tree when Midnight hurried up, excited and triumphant. They had been there for some time, sitting close together on the bench and deep in conversation. Midnight Sam stood in front of them, arms folded, commanding attention, which he got.

"We're going on a day trip to Weston-Super-Mare," he announced importantly. He nodded and waited for a response. Lady Jane and The Professor were temporarily stunned into silence but Lady was the first to recover: "Well Midnight, that sounds like a grand idea."

"I've just been with Welshie. He'll buy the coach tickets, no problem. It's all sorted. Weston-Super-Mare, here we come." He adopted a serious stance and looked The Professor straight and solemnly in the eye: "There's loads of fresh air, down there, Prof, absolutely loads."

Lady Jane touched The Professor on the arm but he swivelled his head away and stared across the park.

"Well then, Midnight," she said with unaccustomed authority, "we'd better get ourselves organised." And so they did.

Brian Davies bought three return tickets. It hadn't been necessary to include Scots Robby, who was otherwise engaged, spending a couple of weeks at Her Majesty's Pleasure. An argument with a Community Support Officer at the bus station about the Scotsman's flagon of White Lightning had ended unpleasantly, insomuch as most of the cider had found its way onto the officer's uniform. That plus a drunken but remarkably accurate kick to the poor man's shins. The accompanying remark – "you're not a proper fucking copper anyway, you Sassenach prat" – had less than helped the situation.

Word soon spread throughout the day centre and night shelter. Nobby and Splodge decided to organise a whip-round and within a couple of days – in 20p pieces, 50ps and the occasional pound coin – a total of £56.40p had been amassed. This figure was greatly and unexpectedly helped by a crumpled £20 note disdainfully tossed into Nobby's upturned bobble hat by a surlier-than-ever Fen. Brian rounded it up to a flat £100 and gave the money to Lady Jane.

The Professor and Midnight Sam met up again at The Tree the following day. "What are we going to wear?" The Professor asked without preamble: the day trip to Weston was the only topic of conversation. "We can't go dressed like this." He gestured to his torn, cider-stained, ill-fitting, grey flannels and a grimy, faded, red and black lumberjack shirt with a ripped back and no sleeve buttons. Midnight looked down at his own clothes and nodded gravely: "They'd never let us on the coach." He paused for a second and went on thoughtfully: "I think I had better get us some new clothes. We're going to need …."

"No, Midnight, that's too risky," The Professor interrupted. "You know how tight security is at clothing stores in town these days. And anyway you have had a bloody good run for your money lately. You don't want to push your luck. Last thing we want is you down the cop shop while we're swanning off to the seaside. Okay? Promise?"

"Okay, but I've got an idea."

"Christ," whispered The Professor.

Lady Jane joined them at The Tree. She kissed them both lightly on the cheeks, gay and silly like a schoolgirl, and squirmed on to the park bench between the two men.

"You don't want that bloke of yours see you do that," warned Midnight, but he touched his cheek where she had kissed him and wriggled with embarrassment and pleasure.

"Oh him," she waved a dismissive hand. "He telephoned me yesterday. He's still up north somewhere. I think he's gone to Bradford, I think that's what he said. Told me he'd be gone for at least a week. Suits me. Stay up there forever, for all I care." She grimaced as if the mere mention of Gordon Blacklock was an insult to the warm, late summer afternoon.

She stared bleakly across the park, shuddered and then giggled: "You two need sorting out if we're going to ponce around the Riviera. You can't go down there looking like a couple of tramps." Her hand flew to her mouth and The Professor laughed. "But we are," he said, chuckling. "That's exactly what we are. Couple of tramps, eh Midnight."

Lady pulled a face and then began rummaging around in her old, hessian sack (the handbag was reserved for the day trip). She produced a pair of scissors, a hairbrush, a comb and a battery-operated razor. Midnight and The Professor edged towards opposite ends of the bench.

"I hope you're not going to do what I think you are going to do," The Professor said cautiously. "You're not going to give us a haircut, are you?" He pulled at his matted, shoulder-length hair almost fondly and Midnight rubbed the stubble on his chin.

"Yes I bloody well am," she retorted. "And the razor's his – he left it behind. Now I want you both to sit still, completely still. I'm not sure that I'm any good at this. I've never done it before."

****

Bobby was visibly shocked when The Professor walked into The Mitre the following afternoon. He hardly recognised the man. It was Thursday – benefits day – and The Professor had already collected his £48.50p, folded the notes into a brown envelope, which he slid into the breast pocket of his lumberjack shirt, and dropped the four coins into a trouser pocket.

"Bloody 'ell," the landlord muttered to himself and pulled a pint of Olde English without waiting to be asked. The Professor leaned against the corner of the bar and took several deep breaths. His chest rattled and gravelled. He picked up his pint glass and struggled slowly across to the alcove, spilling a quarter of an inch of the cider on the way.

Bobby noticed but he didn't mind: the old linoleum floor, lovingly laid some 20 years ago, was now evilly-stained, burnt, ripped and battered and beyond help. But it was an integral part of the pub. Along with the wonky stools, the smoke-yellowed ceiling, the long bar where the varnish had worn down to the bare wood in parts, the cracked mirror above the fireplace and the temperamental 1950s clock on the mantelpiece.

The Mitre, thanks to a combination of stubbornness and laziness, had resisted the scourge of refurbishment which had swept through (and ruined) most public houses in the country. Bobby's single pride, however, was the brass foot-rail which ran the length of the bar. He or Hilda, his rarely-seen and formidable wife, would faithfully polish it every day, without fail. And it gleamed magnificently, easily as efficient as any mirror (not necessarily an advantage in a pub like The Mitre.)

The Professor was half-way through his first pint when Midnight Sam backed his way through the swing doors and lugged a bulging holdall into the pub. He dragged the bag over to the alcove and showed The Professor the contents with a proud flourish. It was full of clothes.

"For God's sake I told you not to …," The Professor began angrily, but Midnight put a finger to his lips and sat down.

"I didn't pinch them, Prof, honest I didn't."

"Then where the hell did they come from?"

"Charity shops. I got them from Save the Children and the Heart Foundation. Oh yes and a couple of pairs of jeans from that Sue Ryder shop in Whitefriars Street, the one that's recently opened."

The Professor frowned: "So how much did it all come to? You haven't blown your benefit on a load of second-hand clobber, have you?"

"Didn't cost me a penny," Midnight said. The Professor pursed his lips and waited. "I popped out last night. Lots of people leave their cast-offs outside these charity shops, you know. Boxes of the stuff. Clothes, books, bits and pieces, ornaments, all sorts. Boxes and boxes. It took me ages to sift through it all. By the time I was finished it was far too late for the night shelter. I had to kip at the underpass."

"Are you telling me that you stole these clothes from charity shops?" The Professor said, speaking slowly, disbelievingly. Midnight had anticipated the accusation and had prepared his response.

"Look Prof, I see it this way. People donate the stuff they don't want to charity shops. And these charity shops sell the stuff to raise money for those in need, for homeless people, for people like us. All I am doing is cutting out the middle man, saving everybody a whole lot of bother. It's not stealing, Prof, it's …," he searched for the right word, "… it's recycling."

215

"Go and get yourself a drink," The Professor said, a defeated man.

Midnight Sam let out a soft but satisfied grunt and strolled over to the bar, where Bobby was pretending not to have listened to every word. He was on Midnight's side actually: he couldn't see anything wrong with it.

Fen arrived and because Lady Jane was absent he deigned to sit with them. He sipped unenthusiastically at a half of lager, took one of The Professor's ready-made roll-ups without asking and stared at the floor.

"When you going?" he asked.

"Tomorrow morning, early," said The Professor. "We're catching the 7.15am coach. It'll take a couple of hours, at least, to get down there." He anticipated the next question: "We should be back around 10pm. Welshie said he'd let us in. We'll have to get Lady Jane home first, though."

"Why's she got to go with you?" Darkness in the eyes, resentment in the voice.

"Why don't you come?" The Professor countered, but kindly. "I'm sure we could get you on. We could have a word with Welshie tonight, if you like."

"No fuckin' fear," Fen snapped. "Don't want to go to no seaside." He finished his lager, got up with a jerk and loped over to the fruit machine. He won for a change but it made no difference to his mood.

When Midnight Sam and The Professor got up to go, Bobby, suddenly agitated, fumbled open the door behind the bar to his living quarters and yelled: "Hilda, Hilda, can you hear me? They're going now. Can you bring them boxes down?" He turned, rubbing his nose with embarrassment, and called across: "Hang on a minute, will you? Missus got something for you, something for your trip tomorrow."

Heavy footsteps creaked solidly down the stairs and a red, beefy arm thrust a carrier bag around the door into Bobby's hands. Bobby peered inside and checked the contents. He grunted with satisfaction, bunched the handles of the bag together and hefted it over the bar, where Midnight Sam had returned, sensing that something to their advantage was in the air.

"Missus fixed up your grub. Enough for a bloody army."

20

GEORGE Kilgour Sinclair sat on his usual stool at the far end of the bar of The Scottish Grenadier with proprietorial presence. He splashed a carefully measured amount of water into his whisky and flicked his eyes around the public house with instinctive disapproval. He inspected his watch – a stern and businesslike gesture as if the ageing timepiece was capable of lying – and tossed back the drink in one, practised swallow, replacing the tumbler neatly on the bar in front of him. He beckoned the barman by catching the young man's eye and wiggling a forefinger into his empty glass.

It was Friday evening and George Sinclair had finished his shift at Henderson's Electricals at 5.30pm on the dot, half an hour ago. He was into his second pint of heavy and his second double house whisky. Two more pints of heavy and two more double whiskies would follow and then he would gather up his tool bag, bid the barman a curt farewell and leave the pub not a second earlier or later than 7.30pm. It took him fifteen minutes to walk home to his council house in the grim and rambling Easterhouse district of Glasgow, which would leave him a further fifteen minutes to wash and change before dinner. Which would be on the table at eight o'clock sharp, along with a can of Newcastle

Brown. He never drank alcohol in the week, but his weekend started after work on Friday evenings.

George Sinclair was a very upright man, strong and wiry but short, barely five and a half feet tall. He wore a neat, jet-black moustache and kept his full head of hair very short. His steel-blue eyes were never still; they roamed restlessly. The dour Glaswegian had opinions on everything, unalterable opinions, and he would countenance no opposition. His reaction to disagreement was to snap "rubbish" and turn his back on the poor, misguided unfortunate who had dared to voice an alternative view.

He had few friends but he had three children – two sons and a daughter – and he had a wife, Mary, the nervous young girl he met two weeks after returning from Korea. He had utilised his Black Watch uniform to the full, but he didn't really have to. Mary was desperate to marry her way out of the slums she thought she was destined to live and die in (little did she know that she was never going to climb very high up the social ladder.) She willingly succumbed to the clumsy charms of George Sinclair.

The firstborn, Andrew George, was followed swiftly by Margaret, but then there was a five-year gap before Robert Kilgour came along. He was an unplanned addition and, if the truth be known, an unwanted one.

"He's a cuckoo, a cuckoo in the nest," George would say unkindly, with a pompous sneer in his voice, as he watched his wife breast-feeding his youngest son. Mary said nothing – she never did – because, after all, he was the man of the house. She kept her own counsel, a lonely and sad counsel.

Andrew George was a bright lad, good at everything. He excelled at schoolwork and secured a place at the much-respected Academy. He was also good at most sports. He played football for the school's first team and was later selected for the Scottish under-16s swimming squad in several international competitions. George Sinclair was proud of the boy and made no secret of it: he subjected his long-suffering fellow locals at The Scottish Grenadier to endless tales of his son's progress.

Margaret, a year younger than Andrew, was a nice-looking girl. Not pretty in the conventional sense but fresh-faced and pleasant on the eye. She invariably kept her light-brown hair tied tight back in a pony tail and her eyes were brown – a deep and speckled brown – like her mother's. She had her father's sharp and angular jaw. Margaret was average at everything at school, with one exception. Mathematics. George Sinclair boasted of his "little Einstein" in the pub but he was secretly slightly embarrassed: women were not supposed to be clever at anything apart from having babies, keeping the house clean and making sure there was a hot meal on the table when the man of the house came home from work.

After Margaret left school she qualified as an accountant and three years later she married a junior partner in a firm of accountants in Edinburgh, had two children, upped sticks and moved to New Zealand. Mary was quietly broken-hearted to see her daughter leave but George was awash with pride and consequently insufferable in The Scottish Grenadier for many weeks afterwards.

Naturally Andrew went on to university, in Durham, where he studied Law. After gaining a first class honours degree (the locals in The Scottish Grenadier were close to suicide) the young man became an articled clerk with a firm of solicitors south of the border in Harrogate. Sinclair senior was not too sure about his eldest son deserting the land of his father's and for a while the public bar of his local was blissfully peaceful.

Which left Robert. The youngest Sinclair spent his early childhood being alternately cosseted by his mother and older sister and ridiculed by his elder brother. And his father was a remote, terrifying and disapproving figure, who only ever spoke to him when criticism, correction or punishment were deemed to be necessary. It was a confusing scenario for the boy who was being brought up to believe that men were superior to women, but whose only solace, whose only warmth, whose only love came from the opposite, supposedly inferior, sex. Robert loved but despised his mother; and he hated but respected his father. Yet as he grew older he wanted, more than anything else, to earn the loveless patriach's approval. But it was never to be.

At school Robert found it difficult to keep up. He was of below average intelligence and most lessons were a forbidding and frightening fog to him. Hands would shoot up all around him, his peers would chatter enthusiastically about algebra, decimals, teutonic plates, the laws of supply and demand, the Russian Revolution, Macbeth and he would feel that he was drowning. Sinking deeper and deeper into a murky sea of ignorance, desperately trying to grasp the slippery lifeline of knowledge and inevitably failing.

If he found it difficult to keep up at school he found it impossible at home. With Andrew and Margaret gone, effortlessly scaling the dizzy heights of success, Robert was alone. Alone with a father who put him down ruthlessly at every opportunity, a father who mocked his failures, who compared him derisively with his two siblings, a father who made no secret of the fact that he was ashamed of his youngest child. But Robert also found himself alone with his mother, his long-suffering mother, a woman who had never stuck up for him, who had spent her entire life fussing around his father, making sure that the ill-tempered and severe man had everything he needed. Robert began to take out his frustrations on the woman.

The arguments started. Childish, let's-pick-a-fight arguments. Robert soon stumbled upon the realisation that his mother was a pushover. So instilled in her make-up that men (even 13-year-old apprentice men like her son) were the superior species, their every whim to be unreservedly pandered to, it was easy for Robert to bully her and use her as an emotional punch-bag.

Robert left school as soon as he was 16, without any qualifications and without the faintest idea what he was going to do with his life. So his father got him a job bottling-up at The Scottish Grenadier and Robert, gloomily and reluctantly, started work. He had to be at the public house at 7am every morning, when the landlord – a big, beefy-armed, red-faced man with an expensive beer-belly – would let him in, before puffing and panting his way back up the stairs to the living quarters. He left Robert to his chores and the young man soon discovered the perks of the job. He sampled his first glass of whisky, furtively and clumsily dispensed from one of the optics in the tiny snug bar at 8.15am one October morning. The fiery liquid slid down remarkably easily and warmed the pit of his stomach, magically quelling the nauseous anxiety which dogged him constantly. He had found a cure and the fact that he was stealing his father's tipple from his father's local gave him an element of satisfaction. In his clouded, troubled and nervous mind he was hitting back, albeit in a small way, at the tyrant who made his life such a misery.

The landlord never caught Robert in the act but he knew what was going on. The powerful smell of peppermint of the lad's breath was a dead giveaway. But the landlord was a kindly, if gruff, sort of man and felt sorry for the boy. After all, he knew Robert's father! And, anyway, it was only ever a couple of wee drams a day.

Besides bottling-up, Robert began to take on more responsibilities – polishing, cleaning the toilets, looking after the cellar, cleaning the beer lines, checking stock, even helping out with the staff rota. His confidence tentatively grew and his hours increased. The landlord had taken a shine to the timid, eager-to-please teenager and to some extent, he had taken him under his wing. He was beginning to realise that Robert was not as thick as he first thought he was or as his father would have everyone believe. Robert was becoming a real asset to his pub and the landlord began to think about the future.

"When you're 18 how do you fancy helping me out behind the bar?" he asked Robert at the end of a shift. Robert blushed but his heart swelled with pleasure. He nodded eagerly but before he could reply the landlord added, without criticism: "But no more wee drams from the house scotch, when I'm not looking, laddie. You can have a whisky or two after the shift, when we've closed, and I'll have a couple with you. Okay?"

Robert's blush turned bright red and he felt a panic rise from his stomach and the landlord noticed this: "Don't worry, laddie, just don't do it anymore. There's no need to."

Robert saw, with wonder, the humour and kindness in the landlord's eyes, where there would only have been cruelty and scorn in his father's, and the panic subsided. He felt safe.

But Robert never got to pull a pint of heavy from behind the bar of The Scottish Grenadier; his father had a different idea.

"Make a man of you," George Sinclair snapped, closing the subject as soon as Robert flustered a feeble, frightened protest. He always crumbled in the face of his father's authority and his mother had vanished into the kitchen on the pretext of doing the washing-up.

Robert joined the Highland Light Infantry six months before his 18th birthday. To say he was a reluctant recruit would have been an understatement, but the moment he left home and moved into the barracks on the outskirts of Glasgow, he experienced an enormous sense of relief. That ever-present tension was gone; that all-pervading atmosphere of disapproval and censure had lifted; the prison gates had been opened and he had left his gaoler behind. Even the screamed orders of the drill sergeant, the customary abuse from the sergeant major, the mindless rituals, routines and procedures and the systematic brutishness were nothing, absolutely nothing when compared to one word of scornful disapproval from his father.

Despite the physical and mental confines of army life, Robert Sinclair felt he was a free man. And, as often happens with young squaddies of limited intelligence, he had the makings of a good soldier. He found it easy to obey orders without question (his father had seen to that) and blind obedience is the key to being a good soldier. He also found himself surrounded by peers of similar and in some cases lesser intelligence than him, which was a unique experience. After having the prowess of his brother and sister rubbed in his face on a daily basis this was a novel and uplifting situation. Maybe Robert Sinclair *was* worth something.

Robert was of course destined to remain a private or at best a corporal for the whole of his army career. He was clearly not 'officer material' which suited him well: he didn't want to be. He was perfectly content to plod along standing to attention, marching in step, keeping his uniform and rifle spic and span, jumping through hoops, saying 'yes sir' at the top of his voice, being an ordinary soldier. Okay, it was not the Black Watch like his father and Scotland was not Korea, again like his father, but it was something and it was his.

A matter of weeks after joining the regiment, Robert made a remarkable discovery. It was on the day that the new intake – a dozen callow youths mainly from the deprived suburbs of Glasgow – were marched off to the rifle range to be taught how to shoot. A bored and bullish sergeant barked at them for a quarter of an hour about the dangers of firearms and the necessary safety precautions and then took them through the workings of their weapons. How to take the rifle apart, how to put it back together again, how to load, how to fire. He then instructed the 12 youngsters to lie down on 12 strips of cork matting on the floor of the indoor firing range with their rifles at their sides. He placed six rounds of ammunition alongside each rifle and ordered the rookies to load.

Robert managed the operation easily but two of the others jammed their breeches and another two forgot what to do altogether and worried the bolts of their rifles with potentially dangerous exasperation. The sergeant bellowed at the four youngsters, demonstrated the procedure again and ordered them to reload, softening his voice with simmering sarcasm.

Twelve cardboard targets were wound up into position and the 'take aim … fire' command was given. When the twelve targets were wound back to where the young soldiers were lying Robert was astonished with what he saw: six bullet holes an inch to the left of the bulls-eye and the grouping could be covered by a 50p coin. The sights needed adjusting but his grouping was impeccable. And it wasn't a fluke. Eighteen rounds later and Robert had improved his initial high score, instinctively compensating for the inaccurate sights on his rifle and hitting the bull on four occasions. His grouping was consistently spot-on and in marksmanship that is what really matters. Apart from a begrudging "good shooting, soldier," the sergeant said nothing. He did, however, make a note of Robert's name and number and a mental note to have a quiet word with his superior officer. Marksmen are born and not made and the sergeant realised that Robert Sinclair was undoubtedly a natural. And the Highland Light Infantry – a decidedly indifferent regiment – needed all the talent it could get.

And so the bemused but delighted 18-year-old found himself being given special treatment. He was excused many tedious, routine duties and instead allowed as much time as he wanted to hone his shooting skills. Robert was in heaven: he was gradually dragging himself out of the debilitating quagmire of his father's disapproval; he had stumbled upon something that he was good at, very good at, something which raised him above the norm; something which, dare he think, made him somebody, made him special, made him different and this time in a positive way.

But besides (or more accurately because of) his father, Robert had developed a problem, a problem which had begun when he was bottling up at The Scottish Grenadier in the mornings, a problem which had developed from the furtive 'wee drams' he purloined from the optics into a constant craving for alcohol. He would drink secretly and craftily, soon learning all the ploys, all the tricks, all the diversionary tactics of the alcoholic. Whereas in the early days the booze merely made him feel warm and safe, as time progressed the effects changed: alcohol began to give him confidence, a dubious sense of invulnerability, a quick temper and an increasingly foul tongue. His demeanour would become aggressive and challenging, very quickly. Drink had wormed its way deep into his inner self and dragged out, from hitherto hidden depths, parts of the psyche of his father. The new Robert Sinclair, the angry and contentious Robert Sinclair, found comfort and protection in his newly-acquired persona. Alcohol had built a force-field between him and the world, a force-field which kept the disapproving world at bay. People chose to avoid him, to back off, even to try to placate him. Alcohol protected Robert from his innermost self; the timid, terrified, innermost self of the man. It guaranteed his survival.

Robert Sinclair's young life began to revolve around alcohol and of course the tandem necessity of keeping his addiction a secret, especially considering his position as a soldier. He became clever at hiding his alcoholism from his fellow squaddies. Oh yes, they knew that he got roaring and unpleasantly drunk when he was off-duty; they knew about the chaotic and pointless fights he got into; they knew when it was best to creep out of the pub and leave him to it. But they knew nothing about the quarter bottles of whisky hidden underneath his mattress in the barracks or behind the rolls of toilet rolls on the deep windowsills in the lavatory cubicles or behind the dustbins. Robert had a number of hiding places and if he occasionally lost a bottle because somebody else had stumbled upon it, then so what? They never knew the booze belonged to him.

Peppermint became Robert's second best friend, with strong, minty toothpaste a close third. But his best friend by a long way was his new-found and unexpected talent as a marksman. Although most of his peers were easily fooled by his simple subterfuges and had not deduced that Robert was an alcoholic, his superior officers were well aware of his addiction. But this very average, young and disagreeable young private was capable of planting six rounds from his 303 rifle smack in the bulls eye, time and time again – and that was despite how much he had had to drink the previous day.

Word of Private Sinclair's extraordinary ability with a rifle (and of his ability with a bottle of whisky) soon reached the Commanding Officer of the regiment. The senior officer weighed one ability up against the other and decided, without much soul-searching, that regimental pride – and by God, the Highland Light Infantry needed some of that – was considerably heavier than the squaddie's propensity for Scotch whisky.

So, by decree from on high, Robert was left largely to his own devices, on condition that he practised and practised diligently for the forthcoming regimental shooting championships – a three-hander between the Black Watch, the Royal Scottish Grenadiers and the humble Highland Light Infantry. The Black Watch had won the previous three annual competitions and the Grenadiers the two before that. As the championships had only been in existence for five years, that left the

Highland Light Infantry with a less-than-impressive record. But that year, thanks to Private Sinclair and to two other members of the five-man team who had proved to be pretty useful, the Cinderella regiment stood a good chance of taking the trophy for the first time.

In one of his few letters home, which were always addressed to his mother, Robert mentioned the imminent competition, not boastfully but purely for something to say. Although the letter was addressed to her, Mary automatically handed it over, unopened, to the master of the house, who thumbed open the envelope disdainfully and frowned over the clumsily-penned contents. He said nothing to his ever-anxious wife (she had steamed the letter open, read the contents and resealed the envelope earlier that day, while her husband was at work) but he said a great deal to the clientele of The Scottish Grenadier that night.

"Pretty good shot myself, I was," he said. "In Korea, not in some arty-farty competition. The Real Mckoy, fighting for our lives, fighting for our country we were. Different ball game, that was. Real soldiering. None of your target practice nonsense. Moving targets: men, men with guns firing back at you. Different ball game, altogether." But a begrudging "he must be a pretty good shot though, suppose he's got to be good at something."

George Sinclair instructed his wife to write back to his younger son and tell him that his father intended to come and watch the competition. Mary felt a nervousness, a foreboding, an inexplicable sense of doom, as she posted the letter. Her conscious mind had no idea why, but subconsciously she knew only too well that disaster was around the corner.

Robert's first reaction to the letter was one of astonishment and delight. At last his disapproving father was going to approve of him. At last he was going to earn the respect of the man who had always mocked him, had always put him down. Andrew and Margaret could go hang. He, Robert Sinclair, was the marksman of the family, the genius of the rifle.

But in seconds the euphoria soured and sank into a deep and heavy pit of nauseous fear. He was terrified like never before, terrified that far more than his own pride, than the regiment's pride was at stake. His father's prowling disapproval was on its way, on its way to destroy the only thing he had ever amounted to, and there was nothing he could do about it. Or was there?

Two days before the competition, Robert – who had been given a week's special leave to prepare himself – went on a monumental bender. He bounced off the walls of a fair number of public houses, bellowing his prowess as a marksman to the rooftops, picked three fights which he lost and ended up in the cells of a local police station for eight hours, until he sobered up. He was charged with being drunk and disorderly and bailed to appear in court in three week's time. But he couldn't have cared less for tomorrow he was going to show them all, most importantly the person he hated and loved more than anybody else in the world, that he was worth something. He was going to show the bastard, make the bastard look at him, make the bastard approve of him.

On the morning of the competition, Robert's resolve weakened with every step he took back to the barracks. His father was making the effort for one reason only, he deduced, with more than a degree of truth: to see him fail. Robert looked bleakly at his watch – three hours before the shooting was due to begin, three hours for him to steady himself, to prepare himself for the contest. But also three hours to have one or two or maybe three wee drams ...

George Kilgour Sinclair never saw his son pull the trigger. A reserve was hastily drafted in and the Highland Light Infantry notched up their customary third place out of three.

Two weeks later, Private Robert Sinclair, at the age of 21, was dishonourably discharged from his regiment. He told his stony-faced commanding officer to fuck off before he swaggered out of the barracks and into the nearest pub. There were no friends to say goodbye to him.

21

BRIAN DAVIES met The Professor, Midnight Sam and Lady Jane at the National Express coach station in the city centre early in the morning. Miraculously they were there before him, standing self-consciously near the Weston-Super-Mare coach bay. It was 7am and the coach was due to depart at 7.15am. The trio stood some feet away from the other passengers who were waiting, but that was their choice as the only reaction they drew was one of mild curiosity and certainly not disapproval. For, apart from Lady Jane, who looked perfectly normal in a yellow summer dress and white cardigan, Midnight Sam and The Professor definitely caught the eye.

Midnight's charity shop haul had included several short-sleeved, floral shirts, a couple of Panama hats, two pairs of cream-coloured cricket flannels and three colourful, striped sports jackets. He had not had sufficient time to gauge the sizes accurately but he was not too far out. The results were interesting: The Professor cut an almost debonair dash (a definite touch of the Graham Greenes) in his over-length cream trousers with, thanks to Lady, knife-edge creases; an out-sized, blue, green and white striped sports jacket; and an incongruous pair of multi-coloured, Adidas trainers. Midnight Sam's image was more complicated: similar cream, cricket flannels but three inches too short; a pink evening dress shirt with bold brocade, which he chose to wear loose outside the trousers; and a bright green waistcoat with silver buttons. An ageing but resilient pair of Green Flash tennis shoes completed the ensemble.

Fellow passengers eyed the two men with interest. Midnight noted the looks with mild satisfaction and The Professor felt mischievous. He even played up to the audience with an aloof stance, hand on hip and a faraway look in the eyes. Lady Jane glowed between the two men but had to suppress a giggle from time to time. Brian feigned indifference to the spectacle as if he had accidentally happened upon the threesome, but a very small lump had formed in his throat. He coughed it away and swallowed.

"Now listen, you three," he turned on his 'I'm the boss' voice and frowned seriously at the three misfits in front of him. "I can't tell you what to do but, for your own sakes, no bottles of cider on the coach – it's against the rules anyway and they'd chuck you off. And don't get too drunk, please. Remember if you're out of your skulls when you're down there, they won't let you back on the coach to get back. And I'm not going to come and fetch you. No way!"

The three day-trippers nodded solemnly.

Brian pulled three folded ten pound notes from a trouser pocket: "Here's a little bit extra – you might as well make the most of it." He handed the money to Lady Jane as the Weston-Super-Mare coach swung into the bay.

Unwittingly they boarded the coach first, The Professor in front, flustering with the tickets, Lady Jane next, nervous and sticking as close as she could to the man in front of her and Midnight Sam bringing up the rear and feeling rather pleased with himself. After all, it was his idea, the weather was kind – cloudy but warm and dry – and The

Professor was going to get a king-size dose of fresh air. They made for the back of the coach and sat down in a row, Lady Jane in the middle. They felt self-conscious while the other passengers filed down the aisle. But as soon as everybody was seated, the driver had delivered his 'do's and don'ts' speech far too loud into his microphone and the coach reversed out of the bay, the back seat trio settled down and relaxed.

It was the first time that The Professor or Midnight Sam had left the city since they had turned up there many years ago. The two men had become part of the urban sprawl, part of the dark, sub-strata of the forgotten homeless, self-trapped within the city boundaries, for a long time. Seven-and-a-half years in The Professor's case and six years in the case of Midnight Sam. So when the coach purred down South Street onto the dual carriageway and rolling green fields spread to a ridge of hills on one side and a river glinted silver and lovely on the other side and the sky ranged high and mighty, they felt naked, exposed. Gone the claustrophobic comfort of the underpass or the bus station; gone the enclosed safety of the night shelter or the sad but friendly camaraderie of the day centre; gone the familiar streets and the back streets and the alleyways; gone the protective concrete and steel; gone the only life they had grown to understand and trust.

For the first half hour of the journey they were silent, lost in their own private but very similar thoughts. But gradually a rare and beautiful sense of excitement grew within them. The Professor was looking out of the side window, watching the distant river and Lady Jane nudged him. He turned his head towards her for a second before gazing back out across the flat and fertile river valley.

Midnight Sam, knees apart, peered around him like a jubilant schoolboy. He hadn't seen trees or the open sky for so long. A small herd of black-and-white cows grazing on the edge of distant woodland, picked out by the sun which had broken through the early morning cloud cover, stirred old feelings in the recesses of his mind. Distant memories fought their way through the swirling, alcoholic mists and shone suddenly bright, heartbreakingly bright. He no longer saw the plump, ungainly English cattle, waddling inch by inch through the meadow, spade-like jaws grinding methodically from side to side. Instead he saw the long-horned beasts of Paradise Island, lying languidly, heads held high, on the endless, virgin sand; he saw the malevolent crocodiles, evil eyes just proud of the shimmering powder-blue waters of the creek; he saw an occasional swift and ground-hugging leopard race fluidly back to the forests of Senegal, yellow eyes burning with silent fury.

Midnight stared out of the coach window and the green-and-brown patchwork quilt fields of England swam back into his vision, blotting out the beauty of the past.

"Are you okay, Midnight?" Lady Jane shot him a quick, sideways glance. She sensed a sudden change, a sudden sadness. He nodded vaguely, still looking away, out of the window, but he didn't turn and smile, which was unlike him.

"It's all a bit much, isn't it?" she spoke softly and patted Midnight's knee. He nodded again and this time he managed a smile. Not his best smile but a valiant attempt. The memories had made him melancholy, but more than that they had shocked him. For years, day-to-day, night-to-night, hand-to-mouth existence had left him no time for reflection, no time for nostalgia, no time for memories, no time for anything except survival. The next flagon of White Lightning, the next warm bed (if he was lucky), the next benefit pay-out, the next bag of soggy chips, the next night's drunken and welcome oblivion. And then suddenly, out of the blue, his beloved Paradise Island, his beloved Gambia and, most of all, his beloved father.

When they reached their destination and the day-trippers fanned out from the coach with the driver's return time ringing in their ears, Midnight Sam helped The Professor down the steps from the promenade to the beach. His breathing had settled but the pain in his stomach was bad. He sat on the bottom step and, with enormous effort, took off his trainers and socks and handed them to Midnight, who put them in his holdall. The Professor bent forwards again and rolled up his trousers to just below the knee, the exertion bringing about a modest coughing fit. Lady Jane took one arm and Midnight Sam took the other (despite The Professor's feeble protests) and they gently lifted him to his feet.

"You might as well put me down, put a gun to my head, useless old bugger that I am," he said with a grim chuckle. "Only bloody forty-five and I'm staggering around like some old fart in his nineties." But he straightened, arched his back, hands on hips and breathed in the sea air. Midnight grunted smugly. The tide was predictably out but the briny tang of the sea was carried across the expansive beach by a steady breeze from the south-west. The Professor inhaled the heady air as if it was his first cigarette of the day.

"What's that bloke selling over there?" Midnight asked, indicating a brightly-coloured stand, behind which stood a lanky teenager wearing a red-and-white striped apron and a white boater with a blue hat band.

"Toffee apples!" exclaimed The Professor with delight. "Christ, I haven't seen toffee apples for God-knows how long."

The Professor led the way and they bought three. Lady Jane held hers at arm's length, mildly disgusted, and Midnight inspected his at close quarters. The Professor, first testing his teeth with forefinger and thumb, took a cautious but successful bite. Midnight immediately followed suit but Lady settled for cautiously licking the crusted top of hers. She had fewer teeth than the two men and she didn't intend to lose any more.

The school summer holidays had ended and only a few children were playing on the beach. Rows of deck-chairs, canvassed in blue and white and red and white, stretched regimentally across the sand, mostly empty. The Professor made a beeline for the deckchairs, pushing the other two in the direction of the distant shore, where he knew they wanted to go. He waved them away and pointed at the deckchairs. They wandered off without a word and The Professor soldiered on across the sand, stopping occasionally to look down at his footprints. He flopped thankfully into a deckchair and realised immediately that it was so unbelievably comfortable he was destined to remain there forever, unless his mates came back for him.

The Professor lay back in the deckchair and savoured the sea breeze in his face. He ate half of the toffee apple and buried the remains in the sand. And then, looking around guiltily to ensure he wasn't being observed, he pulled out a quarter bottle of Dimple Haig whisky from the inside pocket of his sports jacket. The intermingled flavours of apple, toffee and whisky were interesting but surprisingly agreeable. He felt the sun on his face, the wind in what little hair he had left and the whisky in his belly. He was in heaven.

Lady Jane was the first to test the grey seawater which scuttled in busy little wavelets over the shiny sand towards the shore. The tide had turned and would shortly flow with deceptive speed. But Lady was having fun: she hoisted up her summer dress inelegantly, waded out into the sea until she was thigh deep, turned and beckoned Midnight Sam to follow. She laughed. Midnight had not heard her laugh before and the sound made him feel warm and safe. He followed, reflectively, idly kicking at the tiny waves and gazing out to sea, screwing up his eyes in the wind, deep in thought. They walked along the shore for the best part of a mile, Lady several steps in front. Neither spoke but the silence was comfortable. The scurrying tide, gaining momentum by the minute, eventually chased them back to town.

The Professor was snoring peacefully, an empty whisky bottle underneath the deckchair, half-hidden in the sand. It was a pity to disturb him but Midnight had spotted the pier – canned Sixties music and flashing lights – and he was determined that they should all sample the delights. On Lady Jane's insistence (and to the operator's amusement) they caught the toy train from the promenade to the pier. The Professor bought three 'kiss-me-quick' hats (he was astonished that they still made them) and three sticks of candyfloss, pink with blood-red streaks.

Midnight Sam was genuinely scared on the Ghost Train and could not understand what his fellow passengers, average age of around ten, found so funny about the experience. Lady Jane emerged at the bottom of the helter-skelter, ashen-faced and nauseous. She hadn't moved so fast in years. And The Professor? He toyed with the fruit machines and tried unsuccessfully to win Lady a cuddly toy with a .22 air-rifle which sported a barrel bent like a boomerang. He shuffled off to the end of the pier to watch the horizon. An angled September sun warmed his face and a firm and steady breeze ruffled his hair.

The Professor then suggested one of the numerous cafes which dotted the front for lunch, but he was out-voted. It was all right for him – he was half a bottle of Scotch ahead of them – but Midnight and Lady Jane were gasping for a drink. They bought fish-and-chips and found a quiet bench in a secluded little park. Midnight produced the cider – two bottles of Tescos finest and cheapest – took a generous swig and passed it down the line.

Midnight had to strike out twice for refills from a dreary, back-street, corner Co-Op he had discovered and The Professor fell asleep again, while Lady Jane wandered off into town. When she returned an hour later there was no sign of Midnight Sam. The Professor, who had evidently just woken up, was weaving from left to right in search of his Panama hat, which had fallen behind the bench. Lady retrieved the hat for him, plonked it on his head from behind and sat down. He rubbed his eyes, adjusted the hat to a rakish angle and stared out to sea, yawning. Midnight's clothes were strewn on the grass in front of them, clearly discarded in a hurry.

"Where is he?" Lady asked.

The Professor pointed at a lone figure in pale blue Y-fronts striding towards the in-coming tide. He strode with rare purpose, ignoring the giggles from a group of young girls in school uniforms, smoking brazenly but self-consciously on the beach. Midnight Sam was still wearing one of his socks. When the dingy water reached his buttocks he launched himself forwards and struck out in a graceful and powerful front crawl. The Professor and Lady Jane exchanged glances and sat back to watch.

"He won't drown, will he?" Lady asked, linking arms with The Professor and snuggling into his shoulder. The Professor shook his head with surprise and admiration: "I shouldn't think so, the way he's swimming. Regular Mark Spitz. Who'd have thought it …"

"Mark Spitz?"

"American swimmer, cleaned up at the Olympics. Years ago. Can't remember when. Long before your time, Lady."

Half an hour later Midnight Sam came ashore, swinging his arms fluidly and loosely, as he waded out of the water. The sun was low, casting an elongated, distorted shadow some fifty feet in front of him. He was completely in silhouette. When he was closer to his friends Midnight raised his right arm and waved. The lone sock had gone.

"Christ, he looks like Robinson Crusoe," The Professor mused.

"More like Man Friday," said Lady Jane.

22

THEY managed to secure the back seat again, all three a touch unsteady on their feet, a mite louder than before. The odour of alcohol hung around them like an invisible mist. These factors contributed to the distance the other passengers afforded them. The Professor and Lady Jane noticed the subtle alienation, Midnight Sam did not. As soon as he sat down he busied himself with the task of transferring cider from a flagon into a thermos flask he had brought along for that very purpose. Hidden from view behind the seat in front, he performed the task without spilling a drop. The concentration was palpable.

Dripping seawater onto his lap, Midnight handed the thermos flask to Lady, who poured a measure of cider into the plastic cup and drank it with great control. It could quite easily have been a cup of tea, from the way she pecked primly at the drink with pursed lips. Midnight struggled with his conscience, but reached a compromise: they weren't swigging booze from a bottle, so they weren't really letting Welshie down. The cider was contained in a perfectly respectable thermos flask and surely that made it all right?

The sun was setting behind them as the National Express coach filtered onto the motorway and headed north-east. The clouds had dropped down to the circled horizons, leaving a vaulted, deepening blue sky and the ground was already dark, full of the encroaching night. A few stars, lonely but bold, began to pierce the sky. The Professor looked through his own strengthening reflection in the window, into the sky and Lady Jane, catching his mood, followed suit. Midnight Sam was already asleep, snuffling and snoring gently and occasionally breaking wind, almost silently but with effect. The other two would hold their breath until the smell dissipated, hoping it wouldn't travel up-coach. Worrying moments.

"I don't seem to have seen the sky for such a long time," The Professor murmured. "I haven't looked up. Too busy grubbing about on the ground, I suppose." Lady Jane watched him closely, watched his sad eyes watching the night sky and she felt his loss, because it was her loss too.

"Do you want to know the rest of my story?" A small, nervous voice but an urgent one. The Professor waited, his silence and body language kind and expectant.

"I liked Oxfordshire, but I missed Padstow and I missed the seaside – very different from Weston," she began. "Mum and dad were so relieved to get away, they only had bad memories of Cornwall, all my fault, I'm afraid. The best thing of all, as far as I was concerned, was that I had managed to get clean. I mean really clean. And I've never touched the stuff since," she paused and tapped the thermos flask, clenched upright between The Professor's legs. "I've got a different problem now. It's bad but, Christ, it's not as bad as heroin. Nothing is as bad as heroin."

The coach settled into the soporific rhythm of travel, humming hypnotically up the slow lane of the motorway, cabin lights dimmed, virtual silence from the sleepy passengers, apart from the hushed voice, barely more than a whisper, of Lady Jane at the back.

"I was 21 and I'd totally messed up my education. Might have gone on to university, got a degree. Who knows? But I was okay. Guilty as hell, of course for disrupting my family and causing them so much pain, but back to my old self. And clean!

"Dad bought a three-bedroomed, terraced house in Longhanborough – that's a village about ten miles from Witney. A smaller house than the one we had in Padstow, but it was nice and it had a nice little garden. And we were in the country, virtually backing onto the Duke of Marlborough's estate, as a matter of fact. Dad used to make jokes about the palace at the bottom of our garden. Blenheim Palace," she added, by way of explanation.

"I know," The Professor said.

"I got myself a job at the local florists in Witney. Dad used to drop me off on his way to the bank in Oxford and pick me up on his way home. It was out of his way, but I think he was still edgy about the bad old days and wanted to protect me.

"Mum had a part-time teaching job in a junior school not far from where I worked and we used to meet up for lunch a couple of times a week."

Concentrating hard to compensate for the movement of the coach, The Professor carefully filled a plastic cup with cider and handed it to Lady Jane. She drained it and held the cup out for a refill.

"You're thirsty," said The Professor, tilting the thermos flask furtively, keeping an ever-watchful eye on the backs of the heads of the passengers in front.

"It's all this talking … haven't said so much for years. Not boring you, am I?" The Professor shook his head. A full moon hovered low over a darkened ridge of wooded hills to the right. The bottom of the bright silver orb appeared to brush the tops of the trees. A steady stream of vehicles crept by in the middle lane of the motorway and one or two cars sped silently passed in the fast lane. The coach purred along peacefully at a steady fifty miles an hour. The Professor looked down at the passing traffic, conscious of Lady's grip on his arm tightening a fraction.

"Julian got himself a job in a car showroom when he was 18 – he was always mad keen on cars – and he started to do jolly well. Prospective customers warmed to him. He was such an open, eager young man and so charming …," she trailed, fighting an inner battle to compose herself. She coughed and continued: "He seemed to be getting on fine. Plenty of sales, good money – commission plus a regular wage – and the boss had taken a real shine to him." Lady sighed and closed her eyes for a second. "He was getting on fine," she repeated. "Plenty of mates, money in his pocket, always out having a good time. Worked hard, played hard.

"Didn't have any regular girlfriends, but there was plenty of time for that …" Another pause and The Professor sensed that something about last remark troubled her. But she carried on.

"I remember the day clearly," her voice became flat and distant. "It was in the winter, middle of January, the 16th. Julian was soccer-mad and Oxford United was his team. They were playing an important game – Julian told me – I think it was an F.A. Cup match. A home game and Julian was very excited because he had managed to get tickets for himself and a couple of his mates.

"He asked dad if he could borrow his car to get to the ground. He wasn't going to drink and drive – he was always very good about that – but he was going to park the car, crash out with a mate in Oxford after the match and then drive back home the next day." She shook her head slowly and sighed. "And that was the last time I saw him."

Midnight Sam woke up briefly, heaved himself to an upright position, belched softly and reached across Lady Jane for the thermos flask, still between The Professor's knees. He shook it and frowned: it was empty. He leaned forward, rummaged about in his holdall and produced another flagon of cider. As he was facing the aisle and in full view he handed the flagon to The Professor, behind Lady's back. She instinctively leaned forwards to make room. The Professor did the honours and passed a plastic cup to Midnight, who gulped down the cider and promptly fell asleep again, his head virtually touching his knees.

"His mates waited for him in a pub near the ground before the match, but he never turned up. They tried his mobile but it was switched off, so they telephoned my dad. We started to get worried and called the police. And that was when the roller-coaster began. Photographs in the local newspaper, appeals on local radio and television, police officers calling round, asking endless questions. Was Julian depressed? Was he on drugs? Was he in trouble at work? Was he happy at home? Had he split up from a girlfriend? Questions, questions, horrible questions.

"It was a nightmare week – we all wandered around like zombies, panicking every time the phone rang or when there was a knock on the door."

The Professor handed Lady Jane a cupful of cider. She took it instinctively and held the cup on her knees, staring bleakly into the contents. She fell silent for a few minutes and The Professor felt her sorrow, her anxiousness.

"They found dad's car eight days later. Parked at a remote beauty spot in Gloucestershire, a place called Birdlip. Underneath some trees, down an unmade road. All the doors were locked. There was a hosepipe leading from the exhaust – you know the sort of thing."

"Why?" The Professor asked incredulously. "Why on earth did he do it?"

"It was my fault."

The Professor frowned and gave her a sharp stare: "Your fault? What the hell do you mean 'your fault'? How can it have been your fault?"

"I don't think he ever got over what I put them through in Padstow. I think it affected him, did something bad to him. I remember the way he used to look at me, tears streaming down his little face. He would stroke my forehead, wipe away the sweat with a handkerchief, and tell me that everything was going to be all right. Once, he even gave me the contents of his piggy bank …," her voice broke and two large tears welled up in her eyes and rolled slowly down her cheek. "He was eleven, a little boy of eleven. How could I have done that to him? How?"

"It was not your fault. Something else must have happened, something else which he, for whatever reason, found impossible to face. Something he could not bring himself to tell you, to tell anyone."

Lady Jane was not listening: "When Julian *killed* himself …" she emphasised the word brutally, masochistically.

"For God's sake, Jane, don't blame yourself," The Professor said almost angrily. She composed herself, brushed the tears away with the backs of her hands, gulped down more cider, handed the plastic cup back to The Professor and stretched, arching her back.

"… the police and the district coroner were as mystified as we all were. They issued press releases appealing for witnesses to come forward. They had been able to trace most of his movements by his credit card transactions. He bought petrol at various service stations, booked into a couple of small hotels and bed-and-breakfast guest houses. He drove all over the place, hundreds and hundreds of miles, before he ended up in this place called Birdlip. And why there? I'd never heard of Birdlip before, none of us had."

"He didn't leave a note? What did his mates say? What did they say at the car saleroom? Did he have any problems?" The Professor couldn't help himself. He was intrigued. But Lady Jane, who had heard all the questions before on numerous occasions, welcomed the academia of the mystery. It took her mind off the emotional ache of loss and the ever-festering sore of guilt.

She shook her head: "No, there was nothing. No note, nothing. His friends said that he had been in a good mood, laughing and joking the day before the match, and his boss could do nothing but sing his star employee's praises. He had even given Julian a pay rise the previous month."

"And he didn't have a girlfriend?"

"Lots of his friends were girls. But I don't think he had what you would call a girlfriend …," Lady was about to add something but she checked herself. "At least, not as far as I knew."

The coach left the motorway, slowed down at a roundabout, dropped a couple of gears and filtered onto the dual carriageway which led into the city. One or two passengers stirred at the change of pace, but Midnight Sam was not one of them. He continued to sleep like an angel, albeit a snoring and occasionally rather smelly angel.

"And that's where it all went wrong," The Professor said, a statement and not a question.

"Three months after Julian died, I left home. I couldn't stand the sorrow in my mum and dad's faces, I couldn't stand the look in their eyes, I couldn't stand the guilt, the dreadful, fucking guilt." The Professor started at the rare profanity. "I packed a duffel bag, drew out my savings from the building society, left my parents a pathetic letter – they deserved more than that – and caught a train to Newcastle. No idea why Newcastle. It just seemed a long way away – a long, long way away."

"And the rest is history," The Professor said, almost to himself.

Lady Jane snuggled into his shoulder and sighed with enormous relief. She had finally told somebody and that somebody had listened but had not judged. And had cared.

23

ROBERT Sinclair's bender lasted a week. He drank himself senseless every day and every night, got thrown out of an impressive number of public houses and waded into several fights, most of which he lost. And the Highland Light Infantry suffered the sharp edge of his tongue: it was their fault, their fuckin' fault. Best shot the fuckin' regiment ever had he was. Probably true. Could have won them the fuckin' trophy. Again probably true. Served them bloody well right. Probably not true.

Robert slipped back to his parents' home in the Easterhouse estate of Glasgow when he knew his father would be at work. His agitated mother clucked and oh-deared around him, suggesting that perhaps he should find somewhere else to live. But she was unable to force the issue: her son was a man (of sorts) after all and men were always right.

So Robert was allowed to climb wearily and drunkenly up the familiar stairs to his old room, throw his kitbag into a corner and flop onto the bed. He had a monumental hang-over, a seven-day hang-over and his head hammered with thunderous and agonising rhythm. Nevertheless he managed to crawl across the floor to where he had tossed his kitbag and retrieve a bottle of whisky. Soon he was asleep, snoring noisily; he didn't hear his father's raised voice downstairs or his bedroom door open a couple of minutes later. And he didn't see the man he feared more than death itself standing in the doorway.

For the six months that Robert lived back in his old home, father and son exchanged not one single word. It was stressful in the extreme for Mary Sinclair, who pretended that everything was all right and was forever trying to steer the two men into conversation. But what at the outset had been unbearable tension soon became dull emotional apartheid. Gloomy and cold and friendless, but no longer nerve-wracking.

Nevertheless Robert was desperate to leave the house where his father's disapproval, control and authority oozed from every pore and for once luck was on his side. One of his regular, desultory trips to the unemployment centre finally bore fruit. He was taken on as a labourer/'broom-pusher' at a heavy engineering factory on the outskirts of Airdree, some 12 miles east of Glasgow. The work was mind-numbingly boring, but then Robert's mental capacity was limited and the job suited him well. It was physically demanding and the shift-pattern was unforgiving, but then he was 23 years old and strong.

Robert left Easterhouse two months later, having found dreary lodgings in down-town Airdree. On the day of his departure his mother fussed over him and packed an inexpensive holdall she had bought, mail order, with neatly-ironed clothes. They sat awkwardly together either side of the tiny blue Formica kitchen table and blew the steam from their mugs of tea. Mary asked her son banal questions, pretended to be excited and Robert said nothing until he decided it was time to go. His father had gone to The Scottish Grenadier an hour earlier that evening, so that he wouldn't be around when Robert left. The feeling was mutual.

"Better be off then." And that was it.

Robert only spoke to his father once again and that was 13 years later when the stern, compassionless man lay on his death bed, eaten away by lung cancer. Andrew Sinclair had managed to track down his younger brother with the assistance of a private detective. The detective had been instructed to buy a return ticket, escort him to Scotland and to escort him back down south again, after the funeral.

"New suit and new shoes for the funeral?" the dying man had croaked, with a hard, humourless smile and Robert nodded bleakly.

Five weeks after he started work at the factory in Airdree, Robert met Betty, a thin, peroxide blonde with tarty good looks, the sort of features which would harden, hatchet-like, when her short pubescent flush of 'beauty' faded in the years to come. She worked in the factory canteen, forever cracking smutty jokes with the other girls and showing male customers her ample cleavage.

After three alcoholic dates which all ended up in the back seat of Betty's ageing Vauxhall Astra, Robert made her pregnant. She was a vague Catholic, whose religion suddenly strengthened when she realised she was with child. Abortion was out of the question and marriage the only answer. Robert was not bad looking, he had a job and he treated her well. Her expectations went no further than that.

Betty came from a violent family of six. Knocks at the door invariably sent one or more of the occupants scurrying out the back, over the garden fence and away. The police and social services were regular but rarely welcome visitors. Betty's brutish father had recently done time for assault occasioning grievous bodily harm. He had hit a neighbour across the back of the head with a coal shovel during an argument about a parking space. His eldest son had joined in the fun, kicking the stricken neighbour in the kidneys while the man lay on the ground. The son, whose first conviction it was, narrowly escaped a prison sentence, but the father, whose first conviction it was not, got 18 months.

The wedding was a hurried, disorganised and boozy affair. After the ceremony at St Catherine's Roman Catholic Church, the reception was held at Betty's father's local, a tough and notorious pub adjoining a derelict block of flats in the process of being bull-dozed to make way for a supermarket. The landlord, a close friend of Betty's father, had earned a good deal of respect a year previously when he broke up a fight between four locals with a four-foot-six Samurai Sword. Nobody reported the incident to the police and, when questioned by a suspicious doctor at the hospital, the injuries were blamed on a broken window.

Predictably Robert got monumentally drunk and tried to pick a fight with one of Betty's brothers, who, almost as drunk, was being aggressively protective towards his 'baby sister.' Fortunately Betty's father intervened and stopped his son (a promising light heavyweight boxer) from murdering the groom.

The best man, a casual drinking acquaintance of Robert's who had to be persuaded to perform the duty by the bride's father, seemed to be getting on rather too well with the bride. Fortunately it was another of Betty's brothers and not Robert who noticed the snog on the dance floor. A quiet word in the imprudent young man's ear clearly did the trick. Ashen-faced, he scurried out of the door unnoticed and was not seen again. Fortunately the speeches had already been made.

Robert's mother, father, brother and sister had been dutifully invited to the wedding but not one of them turned up. Andrew made some lame excuse concerning work commitments and Margaret made a legitimate excuse that New Zealand was a long way away and, in any case, she was due to have her second child in a matter of weeks. Robert's father did not make any excuse and did not even bother to reply to the invitation. Which naturally meant that Robert's mother would not be there either.

The couple moved into a one-bedroomed council flat in the suburbs of Airdree two months before the baby was born. It was cramped but it was home, their home and it felt good – at first. Alistair, named after Betty's father, was a good baby for the first six months of his life, hardly ever crying and forever grinning at the steady stream of uncles and aunts who came to visit him. Betty's father dropped in, unannounced, four or five time a week, gazing for hours on end at his first grandchild.

Robert took his responsibilities very seriously. Now the sole breadwinner, he volunteered for as much overtime as he could get and often double-shifted. He was on a pretty poor wage and money was always tight, but they managed – just. He had cut down his drinking drastically and idolised his son. And Betty was a good and natural mother, warm and patient, if a bit chaotic. The three of them were beginning to gel into an ordinary but close little family.

George and Mary Sinclair made the 'state visit' to see their grandchild six months after he was born. And only then on the insistence of their daughter Margaret, by letter and telephone, from Christchurch. Mary had ached to see the baby boy but had not dared to challenge the dictate of her unyielding husband. They arrived, by very formal prior appointment, at eleven o'clock on a Sunday morning. It was, to say the least, awkward. But Mary's maternal instincts overcame her subservience to her husband and she cooed and cuddled Alistair from the moment she set eyes on him. George, on the other hand, looked down dutifully into the carrycot and inspected the baby as if he were viewing a specimen of livestock. Betty registered the indifference but, to her credit, she held her tongue, which was a considerable feat for her. Alistair, sensing the change in atmosphere, screamed throughout the proceedings, especially when his paternal grandfather approached the carrycot, pompous and authoritative as ever, and prodded the baby's chest with a gnarled forefinger.

Robert did not speak to his father, but the sight of the unforgiving man touching his own son and glowering down at the baby boy with that all-too-familiar look of disapproval had a profound effect on him. A profound and devastating effect: disapprove of me, put me down, mock me, scorn me, laugh at me, oh yes, I'm used to that. But not Alistair, please not Alistair, not my own son, not your grandchild. Do it to me – you always have and you always will – but don't do it to Alistair. Please don't do it to him!

Something self-destructive clicked inside Robert's head and from that moment, from the moment his father's venom poisoned his little home, his sanctuary, the young family was doomed. Robert himself did not understand what was happening – maybe if he had he could have yanked it to the surface and dealt with it. He knew that his father's disapproval had reached his modest but potentially happy home and it was there to stay. He was helpless and defeated, so, of course, he turned to his old friend.

Robert spiralled down into a semi-permanent state of inebriation. Not at work (he had managed to avoid that) but the moment he trudged out of the factory gates after his shift he would head straight for the nearest pub, any pub, where he would drink for two or three hours before walking home. And when he arrived home, half-drunk and belligerent and demanding to play with Alistair, who Betty had just managed to get off to sleep, the inevitable arguments started. Pointless, spiteful arguments fuelled by pent-up frustrations, confusion, alcohol and the unrelenting undercurrent of financial worry. Robert stopped volunteering for overtime, he stopped double-shifting, but he started to spend more money, more money on drink.

On one occasion, a Friday, Robert did not get home until a quarter past ten in the evening. He was extremely drunk and the remains of an Indian takeaway curry stained the front of his shirt. He staggered into the flat, giggling, to be confronted by a very angry wife.

"Your tea is ruined and Ali has been screaming the fuckin' house down," she yelled at him. "And look at you, you're pissed again, pissed as a fuckin' fart, pissing what little money we've got against the wall."

Betty stormed into the kitchen, slammed the door and clapped her hands over her ears to shut out the escalating clamour from her son in the bedroom. Robert lurched into the room, where Alistair was standing up in his cot, rigid with distress at the argument and shrieking at the top of his voice. He lifted the boy awkwardly out of the cot, lost his balance and fell over backwards. Alistair rolled off his father's chest onto the floor. Betty heard the thump and rushed into the room. She picked up her son, who was silent with terror, held the baby close to her chest and snarled: "You get your fuckin' hands off him, you drunken, useless bastard. If you ever do that again, I'll get my dad and my brothers round here and they'll beat the shit out of you."

Robert thrashed about on the floor weakly for a few seconds, still giggling, before rolling over and pushing himself up into the kneeling position. He swayed for a moment, stiffened and then vomited onto the carpet. Betty sidestepped her husband and hurried out of the flat, clasping Alistair to her chest. She ran down the steps, her mobile phone clasped to the side of her head, and phoned for a taxi. When she reached her parents' house she had to beg her father not to pay Robert Sinclair a visit.

Robert retreated into himself and that was a dark place to be. He didn't 'talk things over' with his wife, try to get their foundering relationship back onto an even keel, but then neither did Betty. In her eyes he was a drunk and a bastard and that was that.

But there was an additional problem: Robert's drinking and his rekindled lack of self-esteem had combined to deal a savage blow to his libido. He had become virtually impotent. And Betty was a young woman with a healthy – some might say too healthy – sex-drive.

"Call yourself a man?" she would mock him. "You're pathetic, fuckin' pathetic. You can't even get it up, for what it's worth. You're useless. Piss all our fuckin' money up against the wall and you can't even do the fuckin' business. Call yourself a man? You're pathetic."

Robert had been working at the factory for seven years when he and 65 other employees were made redundant. They were paid the statutory amount, not a penny more, plus a week's notice and any outstanding holiday pay. Robert left the company with the princely sum of £2,534, but he didn't get home that night until gone midnight. The bedroom door was locked so he collapsed, dull-eyed and catatonic, on the sofa. The crumpled redundancy cheque was miraculously still in his back pocket.

For the next few weeks he made a pretence of looking for another job, allegedly setting out for the employment centre on most days but ending up in the nearest public house instead. Betty was barely on speaking terms with her husband and Alistair, who had just started infants school, had more of a relationship with his maternal grandparents, uncles and aunts than he did with his own father. He began to feel uneasy in his father's presence, a father who always smelt of alcohol, who always spoke with a slur, who was always inappropriately physical. A father who never kept his word. A present promised, and vehemently promised, in the morning never materialised in the afternoon.

It was a Saturday night and Robert was holding forth in the public bar of a street corner pub he occasionally frequented. Redundancy, that fucking factory, bloody women, the overwhelming unfairness of life. Having soon exhausted the patience of the other locals, he found himself alone, belligerently alone, at the bar. He smoothed the moustache he had recently grown (a carbon copy of his father's) and attacked his whisky as if that too were the enemy. The world was against him, nobody understood him, they (whoever they were) were all bastards, bastards intent on his downfall.

The long-suffering barman had run out of glasses to collect, surfaces to clean, customers to serve. So he stood, with an expression of dull defeatism on his tired face, and absorbed Robert's tirade of self-pity. His only relief came when Robert slammed his glass down on the bar, slid off his bar stool and stalked angrily towards the men's toilets, bumping into a couple of tables on the way.

He scrambled his way into a cubicle after a drunken tussle with the door handle, tore down his trousers and settled heavily but comfortably onto the WC. Head in hands, he sat there for a good five minutes before he was jolted out of his near-trance by the outside toilet door banging open and two men bursting in. One of them broke wind loudly, which they both found to be hysterically funny. Robert grimaced, shook his head and remained silent, staring down at his Y-fronts, which were stretched just below his knees.

"Did you hear him?" said one of the men in a high-pitched, incredulous voice. "Did you bloody well hear him? What a load of fuckin' crap. A woman's place is in the home, indeed. What the fuck does he know. His woman's place is on her fuckin' back – and that's not when he's around either."

"Who's she shaggin' now?" a younger voice asked. "Used to be that bloke in the bookies – coloured chap – can't think of his name."

The older man: "Wonder if it's true what they say …"

"Too fuckin' right, it is," replied the other. "Had one in our football team last season. Nigerian lad, I think he was. Dick down to his fuckin' knees, he had. Put us all to shame, I can fuckin' tell you." A pause and then: "So who d'you think she's shaggin' now?"

The older man: "I'll tell you who it is. It's that bloke they roped in to be his best man. Terry-something-or-other. He's been sniffing round 'er for fuckin' years."

Robert could just make out the younger man's parting comment as the two men left the toilets and walked into the passageway: "If that Robert, I-was-in-the-army, Sinclair wanker spent more time at home with his missus where he belonged, that Betty Bollocks of his wouldn't be out there shaggin' everything with a pulse, now would she?" The older man grunted sagely and belched.

Robert, heart thumping with outrage, strode out of the pub, his eyes bulging with rage, and lurched in the general direction of home, rehearsing the row-to-end-all-rows with every unsteady step. He fell over twice, vomited once, urinated inaccurately in the gutter but his indignant resolve held firm.

Betty and Alistair left home in the morning. Robert was still asleep on the sitting room floor, fully clothed, when his wife and son stepped around the inert body. He had been sick. Alistair shrivelled up his nose and his mother hurried the boy out of the flat.

That was when Robert Sinclair became Scots Robby.

24

A CLOUDLESS autumn sky was ablaze with stars and the distant city's neon glow a reminder of that other world, a world that was not theirs. But where the men gathered – a tiny clearing on the edge of the wasteground – the warmth and intimacy of their shared condition crackled within the small intense fire which Midnight Sam had created. They squatted close to the flames, warming their hands, not because they were cold but because it was the natural thing to do. The smell of burning wood filled their nostrils and smarted their eyes. Splodge coughed contentedly and scratched his ample belly and Nobby, squatting beside his friend, poked the embers of the fire with the base of his flagon of cider, not altogether a wise thing to do.

Midnight was very drunk, more drunk than usual. This was because he been to see The Professor earlier that day in the Parlour and had found his friend curled up in bed, red-eyed, wide awake and sober. Completely sober. An untouched flagon of White Lightning stood on the coffee table. And a plastic bag containing two further bottles stood by the door.

"Don't feel so good today, Sam. Why don't you help yourself to the cider. I can't drink it." The Professor spoke breathlessly, his chest heaving with the effort. Suddenly his face contorted with pain and his eyes enlarged. He turned towards Midnight Sam with an instinctive flash of pleading. Help me, the eyes said, but Midnight had no idea what to do to help. So he sat on the edge of the bed, rancid and soaked with sweat, and stroked The Professor's clammy forehead. He remained there, without changing his position, for two hours, until The Professor sank into a fitful sleep.

Midnight Sam stood up, reached for the plastic bag containing the two bottles of cider, leaving the other flagon on the coffee table in case The Professor rallied, tip-toed from the Parlour and closed the door quietly behind him. He made for the docks, sat on a bench overlooking the marina, established that there were no police around and started drinking. He watched the swanky power boats bobbing up and down at their moorings, listened to the rigging on the yachts slap against their masts, felt an unseasonably balmy breeze brush his face, but in his stomach there festered a sick and weighted panic: was The Professor going to die?

Midnight attacked the White Lightning with a vengeance, dropping the empty flagons into the water, one by one. By the time he reached the wasteground he was six flagons worse off. It was a miracle of pride that he managed to get the fire going.

Scots Robby had a new subject and he wasn't going to let such a captive audience off the hook lightly. Especially as he had bought two bottles of blended Jacobite whisky with his prison release money.

"What a fuckin' dump," he shook his head vehemently and gazed into the flickering flames. "Two of us to one fuckin' cell the size of a fuckin' matchbox. No room to swing a fuckin' cat. And the bloke I had to share the cell with? Fuckin' hell. He did nothing but fart – morning, noon and night. Fart, fart, fart. And he was forever on the bog, which was bang smack in the middle of the room. No privacy at all."

Scots took the lack of response from the others as an indication of their dumb-struck fascination with his story. The truth was a little different.

"You should have smelt it. It was horrible. Bastard must have had something wrong with him, cancer of the fuckin' arse I shouldn't wonder. Horrible it was."

Suffering from a rare attack of generosity, Scots Robby passed one of his bottles of whisky to Splodge, who took a serious swig before handing it to Nobby, who did the same. The Jacobite was passed over the inert body of Midnight Sam, who was asleep, flat on his back with his mouth wide open.

"Nice drop of Scotch," said Splodge politely. (He couldn't stand the stuff, but it was alcohol). Nobby nodded sagely, his mouth down-turned with the deliberation of a true connoisseur. They both stared into the fire and waited. Scots had been inside for three weeks and was desperate for company. The others knew that as surely as they knew that free whisky equalled company. The bottle came their way again.

Some instinct stirred Midnight Sam. He shuddered, rolled over on to his side, propped himself up on one arm and frowned disapprovingly at what was left of his fire. He staggered to his feet and faded into the encircling darkness, returning ten minutes later with an armful of wood. The exercise gave him a second wind and he busied himself with bringing the fire back to life.

The whisky did the rounds again and Scots Robby was midway into the graphic account of a male rape he had allegedly stumbled upon in one of the prison toilets when Fen materialised into the pool of firelight. A black-and-white mongrel dog padded along close behind him. A length of coarse rope had been looped into an all-in-one collar and lead. The dog, tail beating furiously, tugged at the crude leash and panted, pink tongue lolling out of the side of his mouth, red-brown eyes burning with excitement.

"And what the fuck's that?" asked Scot's Robby gruffly. Fen gave the Scotsman a withering look, yanked the leash savagely for no reason and sat down by the fire. The dog remained standing, jerking his head from left to right as he inspected the assembled group. Fen pulled a tin bowl and a box of dog biscuits from a plastic bag and fed the dog. Torn between the biscuits and curiosity, the dog kept looking up from his bowl to check on the new humans, whose faces glowed orange in the firelight.

"They won't let you keep that at the Lodge, no way," Scots Robby tossed his head back smugly and smoothed his moustache, which glistened wetly with whisky. "No fuckin' way," he added for emphasis, as if a sentence without the word 'fuck' in any of its impressive parts of speech would be incomplete.

The Lodge – Battersea Lodge in Park Road – was a large house divided into 16 bedsits. It was jointly run by the city council, Shelter and a small housing association. The residents were single males over 21 in receipt of housing benefit. Fen had moved into one of the rooms three weeks ago.

"Fuck off," Fen scowled at Scots Robby and ruffled the back of the dog's neck.

"Where d'you get him from?" Midnight, who was sitting opposite, spoke through the flames.

"Bloke I met on the bus, said he was going into hospital or sommat, had no-one to look after his dog." Fen shrugged his shoulders, pulled the hood of his jacket down to cover his forehead and kicked at the fire. Nobby blustered across, crouched down over the dog, belched and grabbed the animal's muzzle in an attempt to make friends. The dog growled, pulled his head away sharply and snarled, baring his teeth.

Nobby toppled over backwards, managed to stop himself from falling into the fire with an outstretched hand, inadvertently took hold of a red-hot ember and yelled. He scrambled to his feet, nursing the burnt hand and performed a little jig.

"You wanna get that fuckin' animal put down, you do – vicious, fuckin' bastard," he cried, blowing into the palms of his hands, trying to shake the pain away. "That bloody dog of yours comes near me again and I'll kick his fuckin' head off. Vicious bastard." Fen wore a small smile and continued to ruffle the scruff of his dog's neck. He rolled a joint, craned his head forward and lit it from the fire. He lay on his back, pulling the dog down on top of him. He gave a short, high-pitched giggle as the creature licked his face.

"Anyone want cider?" Midnight Sam's voice was hoarse and slurred. He waved a bottle in front of him. "Don't want anymore whisky, I'm going to have cider. Anybody want any cider?" He tilted the flagon to his lips and gulped clumsily. It went a bit wrong: the cider squirted out of both corners of his mouth and shot up his nose. He spluttered and gagged and exploded into a very messy coughing fit. The others took no notice of him but the dog stopped licking Fen's face for a second and half-turned his head.

Midnight collapsed face-down in the dirt and went back to sleep. Frothy bubbles expanded and popped on his lips. He dreamed of The Professor, with grey-faced, pinched cheeks, with huge sad and imploring eyes, and in his dream he saw the coffin and the hearse and the solemn faces of the mourners.

Fen finished his spliff, gathered up his plastic bags and loped off towards town without saying goodbye. He gave the leash a cruel jerk and the dog yelped but followed him obediently, tail dipped between his legs.

Splodge wriggled into a sleeping bag – the zip had long broken and the stuffing bulged from several mortal wounds – and Nobby, his injured hand bound with a couple of well-used handkerchiefs, was hidden underneath a dark grey, threadbare blanket with red piping around the edges. Scots Robby squatted by the fire with his eyes closed, coveting the two remaining inches of whisky in the second bottle.

****

A lavatory attendant found Paddy Maguire at 5.45pm in the evening, a quarter of an hour before he was due to lock up the public conveniences. The city council environmental services employee had already checked the toilets two hours previously and had noted that one of the cubicles was in use. The same cubicle was still locked when he made his final inspection.

The attendant, a sad and grey man in his early sixties, knocked on the cubicle door and explained that the place was due to close in fifteen minutes. There was no response. So he knocked on the door again and waited. After five minutes of intermittent knocking at the door, stage coughing and a loud display of swabbing the floor outside with his mop, the attendant finally ran out of patience. He knelt down with a degree of difficulty (his arthritis always played him up at this time of the year) and peered under the cubicle door. His heart skipped a beat.

Paddy Maguire had fallen forwards off the W.C. and his forehead had hit the floor half an inch from the door. Grotesquely and accidentally he had adopted the position of a Muslim at prayer, apart from the fact that he was not facing east. The syringe had snapped in two – it must have hit the floor very hard – and a puddle of vomit had spread, like a halo, from the dead man's head. The stench of faeces was overpowering and yet the expression on Paddy's chalk-white face was paradoxically angelic.

Shocked and shaking, the lavatory attendant scrambled to his feet, backed away from the cubicle and summoned the emergency services on his mobile phone. Pulling himself together, he took up his position in front of the entrance to the toilets, arms folded with sudden importance, and waited for the police and the ambulance to arrive. Two curious schoolboys, one devilishly cool with a cigarette dangling from the corner of his mouth, tried to edge passed him but the council employee held his ground stoically. An amiable tramp (Splodge as it happened) asked him for a light and "change for a cuppa tea" but he shook his head to both requests.

The attendant was mightily relieved when an ambulance, blue lights flashing, pulled up at the head of the narrow entrance to King's Lane, where the drab and dismal, detached toilet block was situated. A police car drove up the pedestrianised lane from the opposite direction. Two officers, one speaking into his radio, climbed out of the car and approached the attendant, not in too much of a hurry.

The police had to use a door enforcer to break into the cubicle, while one of the paramedics lay flat out, belly down on the damp floor, both arms stretched underneath the door to cradle Paddy's head protectively.

At the subsequent inquest the results of a post mortem and a toxicologist's examination established the cause of death to be a massive overdose of heroin. Due to fluctuations in the Class A drug market – cocaine had shot up in price and heroin was temporarily cheaper – Paddy had changed his tipple. But he was unfamiliar with heroin and had no idea that the batch sold to him at the bus station was virtually pure. He was also no expert with the hypodermic syringe.

Despite routine police inquiries and a personal investigation by Brian Davies, not a single relative could be found, in Ireland or England. Paddy Maguire, doubtless a fresh and innocent and unblemished baby at the beginning of his life 27 years ago, was totally alone in the world when he died in a public lavatory cubicle in King's Lane.

The city and district coroner recorded a verdict of death by misadventure and the young Irishman was cremated at the city crematorium on the edge of a vast and rundown council house estate. It was a bright and breezy October morning and Paddy's service had been slotted in from 11am until 11.30am.

Brian Davies, Splodge (who remembered trying to tap the lavatory assistant for money and felt guilty) and Midnight Sam were there to pay their last respects. The Professor was not well enough to attend, Scots Robby was too drunk to attend and Fen could not be bothered to attend, despite the fact that Paddy had regularly supplied him with cannabis. But Fen was Fen.

Midnight Sam had vaguely toyed with the idea of sprinkling Paddy's ashes over the Irish Sea, but Brian had talked him out of it. Instead, Midnight acquired a CD of some obscure folk band belting out a totally inappropriate version of When Irish Eyes Are Smiling. The service was all over in 17 minutes. They hadn't needed the full half hour.

****

Midnight Sam stood with his back to the wall in the Parlour and watched as Doctor Dawes, stethoscope plugged into his ears, listened to The Professor's chest. Midnight had broken an unspoken yet cardinal rule and he knew that The Professor was angry with him, but he was worried about his friend and didn't know what else to do.

"The emphysema has stabilised, miraculously, and it's not getting any worse, as far as I can tell," said the doctor, removing the stethoscope from his ears and letting it fall around his neck. "And I've got an inhaler for you. Easy to use. Instructions and all the usual rubbish on the box." He paused, took a deep breath and wagged a bossy forefinger in The

Professor's face. "Use it, for God's sake, use it. Take it from me, it will really help. When the breathlessness gets too much, give it a go. I promise you it will calm things down. Okay?" Doc Dawes craned forwards, eyes bulging, and glared at his reluctant patient.

"Okay," The Professor agreed wearily, his voice a barely audible whisper, "whatever you say, Doc."

The doctor turned to Midnight Sam: "Make sure he keeps the inhaler with him at all times. It's very important."

Midnight took a sharp step away from the wall and nodded solemnly, standing almost to attention by the side of The Professor's bed. "I thought that sea air would have done him some good," he said. "Hope it wasn't too much for him." Guilt and sorrow in his tone. And helplessness.

Doctor Dawes felt Midnight's helplessness too. What could he say? What was there to say? He took hold of Midnight's elbow gently and steered the man away from the bed towards the door.

"No, it wouldn't have been too much for him. I'm sure it did him the world of good. But you've got to remember he's not a well man, Midnight. He's going to have good days and bad days. And this is one of his bad days."

"So he'll be okay again, he'll be better?" Midnight Sam chipped in, nodding with encouragement.

"He'll have better days. Don't you worry. He'll have better days."

Doc Dawes ushered Midnight out of the door: "I need to speak to The Professor alone. Patient confidentiality, you understand. Nothing for you to worry about." Midnight nodded and left the room, raising a hand to The Professor, who propped himself up in the bed, both hands gripping the top of the duvet, and frowned at the doctor.

"You want to talk about the cancer. Okay, well ... ?"

"I'm going to have to be honest. I don't know how much it's spreading because you refuse to go into hospital. All I know is that it *is* spreading and, as I've told you, the tumour is growing. It's getting bigger and is probably malignant, which is not good news." The doctor gazed down at The Professor with a mixture of compassion and painful honesty and said: "Listen, you and I know that you are going to die …"

"We're all going to die, Doc," The Professor chipped in flippantly. "It's just a question of when."

Doctor Dawes closed his eyes for a second, then turned on his formal, doctor-patient voice: "Okay, but in your case I can give you a matter of weeks, months if you are lucky, but a bloody sight longer if you'd let me get you into the Royal." The Professor shook his head and waited for the doctor to continue. "Very soon now the pain is going to get bad and I mean really bad. It will become unbearable. So let me, at the very least, do something about that." Doc Dawes placed a bottle of pills on the bedside table and met The Professor's gaze. "Morphine," he said simply.

"When it gets too much take two tablets. It's no good me telling you not to drink, but please have something to eat. Anything – soup, biscuits, a chunk of bread – but try to eat something."

"Thanks Doc," The Professor managed to give a weary thumbs-up. "How many tablets have I got?"

"Don't worry about that," the doctor patted The Professor's hand, "as many as you need, as many as you want."

****

"He's back," Lady Jane said with a sigh, hunching her shoulders and staring at the floor. "Came back the day before yesterday. In a foul mood. I just keep out of his way. Best thing."

"The Prof's been ill," Midnight Sam said flatly, an element of challenge in his voice, and reached for his glass of Olde English. "He's been in bed these last three days. Doc Dawes came to see him. Gave him an inhaler thing and a bottle of pills."

"How is he?" Lady asked quickly, a flurry of panic in her face.

"He's better now. He got up and sat in his chair yesterday. He's breathing better as well." A pause and a disapproving: "Where have you been?"

Lady Jane shook her head and shrugged her shoulders: "He wouldn't let me leave the flat. Locked me in the other day. Followed me to the bathroom when I went to have a pee." She dropped her head into her hands and then looked up.

Midnight noticed a small bruise on her left temple but he said nothing. Lady followed his eyes, instinctively fingered the bruise and gave a helpless gesture with both hands. "He's a very jealous man, Midnight, a very jealous man. He heard about our trip to Weston-Super-Mare and he didn't like it. He didn't like it at all."

"He shouldn't hit you," Midnight Sam's tone would brook no opposition. He picked up the two empty glasses from the table in the alcove of The Mitre and took them to the bar, where Bobby was pretending not to listen to their conversation. Blacklock's violence festered inside Midnight's head while he waited at the bar and when he returned to the alcove he was an angry man, an unusual condition for him.

"Why does he hit you?" he demanded, his voice raised and his body tensed.

"Shush," Lady put a forefinger to her lips. "He just does, Midnight. That's the way he is. He just does."

Midnight Sam was not impressed: "A man should not hit a woman, not ever. When I see him next, I am going to tell him." He was speaking more to himself than to the young woman sitting opposite.

Fear flashed in Lady's eyes and her shoulders twitched nervously: "No, no, Midnight, please don't do that, please don't ever do that."

Midnight's face hardened imperceptibly and he exuded a subtle aura of power. Lady Jane had never experienced this side of the man before – Midnight Sam was always such a happy-go-lucky fellow – and the sudden transformation startled her, but at the same time made her feel extraordinarily safe.

"He doesn't frighten me, Lady," Midnight said quietly and Lady Jane knew that he meant it; she also knew that it was much more likely to be the other way around.

But she shook her head: "I know that, Midnight. He'd be scared of *you*. He's a bully, he only ever picks on women. No Midnight, it's me he would take it out of if you said anything to him. Not you. Me. He'd wait until you were out of the way and then he'd start, then he would hit me."

The pub swing doors burst open and Fen lurched in, dragging his dog behind him. The excitable animal's tail beat the sides of the wooden entrance porch and he immediately discovered an empty packet of crisps on the floor. The creature plunged his snout into the packet and snuffled at the crumbs. Fen yanked the rope and the dog scampered into the bar, crisp packet firmly clenched between his teeth, paws slithering on the greasy linoleum.

Bobby was a model of controlled outrage. He stiffened to his full height, beer gut to the fore, hands on hips, grubby tea towel dangling from his side. For a couple of seconds he was lost for words. Fen took no notice, swung a stool to face the alcove and sat down, legs wide apart, challenging the world. The dog had lost interest in the crisp packet but was tugging towards Lady Jane.

"You can't bring that dog in here," Bobby said, his voice trembling with indignation. "I will not have dogs in here."

Fen treated the landlord to a sullen and brooding look: "He ain't doin' no harm. He's on a lead. I'll keep him on a lead. He ain't doing no harm."

Bobby's face hardened and Fen noticed the danger. The landlord's initial anger quietened but headed towards violence.

"I am not having dogs in here, Fen. You'll have to leave …," Bobby opened the bar hatch and clenched his fists. Fen sensed the mood and sat bolt upright.

"I'll tie him up outside if you like," he said, getting to his feet.

Fen muttered something nasty beneath his breath and dragged the dog back out through the swing doors. The creature yelped as one of the doors clipped the side of his head. A minute later Fen was back, minus the dog. He sauntered up to the bar, ordered half a pint of lager as if nothing had happened and sat on the stool, facing Midnight Sam and Lady Jane.

"When did you get him?" Lady asked. Fen shrugged and pulled a dismissive face, but he warmed a shade.

"Week or two ago, I dunno. Bloke on a bus." A pause, then he scratched the back of his neck and stared at the frosted window. Pale October sunlight filtered through the translucent glass. "I like dogs," he added defensively.

"What's his name?" Lady Jane asked lightly.

A dark and secret smile flitted across Fen's face. "Charlie," he said, picking up his glass of lager. "I call him Charlie."

25

THE HEADMASTER'S study was situated on the fourth and top floor of the Old Bishop's Palace overlooking the Cathedral. A long, low-ceilinged room with a creaky, uneven floor. Three of the walls were panelled and the fourth boasted floor-to-ceiling book shelves, jammed with several hundred tomes of varying shapes, sizes, ages and colours. The head's desk – an ornate, very old and well-scratched, mahogany affair – stood in front of a leaded light window set in a deep stone arch, opposite the bookshelf wall. Behind the hopelessly untidy desk, littered with papers, books, unopened letters and three half-empty mugs of cold tea, sat Commander Eric Pankhurst MBE, headmaster and supreme ruler of King's College for the past 14 years.

At first sight Pankhurst was every bit the naval commander. He was a tall, upright man, well-manicured and impeccably dressed, military in demeanour, severe and stern. He oozed authority; he was the sort of man one instinctively called 'sir.'

Pankhurst was a firm believer in appearances: whenever his teachers were in the public eye he insisted they donned their graduation gowns, with coloured sashes denoting the quality of their degrees (his idea). Outside the hallowed halls of learning in the shadow of The Cathedral, boys were strictly forbidden to put their hands in their pockets while wearing their school uniform. Apart from sixth-formers who were permitted one hand in one pocket. It was also mandatory for boys to wear their school hats whenever they left the school grounds. Sixth-formers were again exempt.

The few girl pupils who had just been admitted to the school (Pankhurst's idea and one which had met with a certain degree of controversy) were also expected to wear their school uniforms neatly and with pride.

Pankhurst's thinking was clear and unequivocal: when his teachers and pupils entered the community of the city outside the hallowed portals of King's they were ambassadors of the school and they were expected to behave accordingly. But inside the school – in the classrooms, lecturing halls and debating chambers – it was an altogether different matter. Teachers were encouraged to conduct their lessons in their own way and not to stick to any rigid formula. They were expected to communicate, identify with and inspire the pupils in their charge. What happened within the confines of the classrooms was, within reason, the individual teacher's affair (so long as the results were good). But what happened outside the classrooms was very much the affair of Eric Pankhurst.

David Browning, the recently appointed Head of English, knew none of this when he knocked on the headmaster's door at the beginning of his first day at King's College. All he knew was that somehow, at the age of 32, he had landed his dream job.

Commander Pankhurst opened the door midway through David's second knock: "Come in, come in, come and take a pew, over there in front of my desk." David nodded, ducked into the room and followed the headmaster to the arched window.

When they had both sat down on either side of the headmaster's desk, Commander Pankhurst leaned back in his chair and said without preamble: "I love this school. I love the buildings, I love the history, I love our close attachment to The Cathedral. D'you know, I have been here for nigh on 20 years, 14 of those as headmaster, and my feelings for the place have never palled. The opposite in fact.

"This is a tough city, tough as old boots. Drugs, crime, homeless people on the streets, sleeping in doorways, gang warfare. It is a tough and troubled city. And yet here we are, King's College, an oasis of learning, of academia, of reason and of hope midst all the chaos and hopelessness. King's College soars above the grime, above the squalor, above it all."

David was surprised, confused and a little embarrassed by such instant passion – this was not quite what he expected from this first one-to-one, introductory chat with his new boss – but he felt obliged to respond. Commander Pankhurst's tone invited it.

"So do we detach ourselves from our surroundings, do we encourage our pupils to do the same?" The moment the words were out of his mouth he regretted them, but the headmaster's reply came as a surprise.

"Good question, Browning (David smiled inwardly at the anachronistic use of his surname). A very good question. And I like to think that I have a very good answer."

The retired naval commander swivelled theatrically in his chair and cast an arm upwards towards the soaring tower of The Cathedral, perfectly framed in the window behind him.

"No, we do the precise opposite, my boy. We encourage our pupils to live in the real world, to delve down into the so-called depths if need be, to take the knowledge, the education that we can hopefully instil in them, and pass it on to those who need it most. We have an obligation to spread the word, so to speak, to ensure that everyone has an opportunity. We have a duty to close the gap, to chip away at elitism."

"Sounds like old-style socialism to me sir," David ventured, still uncertain of his ground, unsure whether to speak his mind or to say what he thought the headmaster would want to hear.

"And what's so wrong with that?" the head asked sharply, resting both arms sternly on his desk and frowning at David as if he were a naughty schoolboy.

The new Head of English suddenly made up his mind: "Nothing sir, nothing at all. In fact it's what I believe, it's why I have always wanted to teach. Not just to convey information, to get good exam results and soforth, but to try to make a difference, a difference to the way my pupils think. Education should, in my opinion, prepare and equip young people for the real world. That's what I believe."

The commander's mouth twitched with a small smile: "I'm sorry to hit you with all this political stuff, Browning. I'm sure it's not quite what you were expecting from this meeting. I just need to know what sort of chap you are. Not what sort of teacher you are – your references and reputation indicate that you're a good teacher, job's yours and all that – but I like to bounce a few ideas off you new chaps and see how they do." Commander Pankhurst fell silent, almost brooding, and rubbed his temples with both eyes closed. He levered himself to his feet, turned and gazed out of the window, beckoning David to join him.

"Look down there," said the headmaster. Two tramps were splayed out on a bench in the Cathedral gardens below. They were drinking cider from two-litre flagons, half-heartedly concealed in brown paper bags, and they were both drunk. A litter of white, plastic bags surrounded them, the symbolic detritus of their despair. One of the men was trying to roll a cigarette, wearing the drunk's fixed expression of fierce, unco-ordinated concentration. The other was in the throes of a prolonged and evidently painful coughing fit. Passers-by were giving the bench a wide berth.

"What we see down there, my boy, at first sight are two street-drinkers, tramps, homeless vagrants, eyesores in this city of ours. An embarrassment. Dirty, untidy blots on the landscape, pretty damn disgusting.

"But what you also see down there are two human beings, no less or more than you and me. They were newborn babies once upon a time, no doubt beautiful and innocent and unblemished. On the threshold of life, with everything to live for.

"Do you seriously believe, as some would have you believe, that they want to be like they are now? Deep down 'want to' I mean. Of course they don't. No, something has happened to them, something which has sent them on a downward spiral, a spiral which is out of control and which they are powerless to reverse."

David followed Commander Pankhurst's gaze and nodded in agreement. He sensed that the headmaster was building up to a point and he waited.

"We have, in my humble opinion, a duty to people just like those two down there, a duty of care, of understanding. We should never pretend that they don't exist. Because they do exist. And if, as is so often the case, they are beyond our help or simply do not want it, then we should respect that too. First and foremost …," the tone had become that of the lecturer, the preacher, the man with a mission, the man in a pulpit, but David did not mind. He had already decided that he liked Commander Pankhurst. "First and foremost, we should practise compassion and understanding. Christianity with a small 'c.' The world, I fear is becoming a harder, less caring, less compassionate and less understanding place these days. Corporate and cold. That optimism of the Sixties has died.

"But in this school, in King's college, besides striving for excellence in academic subjects and in sport, here we strive for excellence in spirit and in humanity …," he paused, gave an embarrassed cough and withdrew from the window. "I do tend to get a bit carried away. Please excuse the lecture." He sat down stiffly and David returned to his chair in front of the headmaster's desk.

"When do you start, Browning?"

"Monday morning, sir. Mr Young (the deputy head) wants to see me at 8.30am."

Pankhurst shot to his feet, almost to attention, stepped around his magnificent desk and shook David warmly by the hand: "Good to have you aboard, Browning, good to have you aboard."

David let himself out and closed the door behind him. He hesitated for a second, reopened the door and poked his head back inside the room.

"I think I'm going to like it here, sir," he said softly and closed the door again quickly.

****

"He's quite a character, a real character, not at all what I expected," David said, sipping a mug of tea at the kitchen table. "An anachronism and yet, somehow, at the same time, a radical. He's a complete contradiction in terms and I really like him. He's full of passion, full of ideas."

David's wife made herself a cup of coffee and sat down at the table opposite her husband: "But you've met him before, at those interminable interviews during the summer holidays."

"Yes, I know, but that was all very formal and I never had the chance to be alone with him. There were always school governors in tow. You'd like him, Jan, he's a good man. I can't wait to start there."

David and Janet Browning and their nine-year-old daughter Louise lived in a modest but pleasant, three-bedroomed house on the outskirts of Bath, where he taught English at a run-of-the-mill comprehensive school. Janet, a qualified journalist, worked for three days a week at the Bath Chronicle. She looked after the features pages. A recent addition to the family was a lovable but totally uncontrollable cocker spaniel puppy, which Louise had named Skipper.

David started his new job, initially commuting from Bath daily and spending every moment of his spare time househunting. At weekends he would take Janet and Louise to the city to look over a selection of properties he had deemed to be suitable.

After a month they struck gold: a rundown, detached, black-and-white, 18th century cottage with a large but wildly overgrown garden in a village six-and-a-half miles from the city. Janet fell in love with the place at once and Louise gave her seal of approval with the words "Skipper will like it here." There was work to be done, plenty of work to be done, but the potential was there.

They moved in at the beginning of November, a particularly mild November, which was just as well: the only heating was a rambling and temperamental range in the long, kitchen-dining room and inglenook fireplaces in the two living rooms. David stocked up on logs and coal, Janet bought three electric heaters for the upstairs rooms and Louise nagged her parents into buying her a basket for Skipper, which somehow became an instant and irremovable fixture in front of the range.

David built a bonfire in the garden, which he had begun to clear, and Janet invited their new neighbours around for a combined November the Fifth/housewarming party. The obvious pun served as an ice-breaker. It turned out to be an old-fashioned Bonfire Night, with Guy Fawkes sporting a Roman Candle in a prurient position, potatoes in foil baked at the edges of the fire and a fair amount of wine.

The following weekend Janet's parents came down from Derbyshire to stay for a few days. Mother fussed over Louise and cast a critical eye over her daughter's desperately old-fashioned kitchen, making numerous notes to buy 'essentials,' while father organised David's garden (at least in theory) and endeavoured, with spectacular lack of success, to train Skipper. Both parents, however, were successful in insisting that David and Janet should take the opportunity to spend a couple of evenings out together. Although Janet's parents gave the impression they were doing the couple a huge favour, in truth they could hardly wait to have their grand-daughter to themselves.

"I'm so very happy, my darling," Janet looked across the restaurant table at her man through the candlelight and squeezed his hand.

"We've worked hard for all this, Jan. This is a good time for us, a really good time. You and me and Louise and, not forgetting, Skipper. We are a real family and things are going to get better and better."

David topped up their wine glasses and raised a forefinger to the hovering waiter: "Can we have another bottle of Chablis please? No, dammit, let's have a bottle of Champagne."

"David!" Janet frowned.

"Veuve Cliquot," he added defiantly. "Tears of the widow."

It was the beginning of three golden years for the Browning family – years that The Professor would remember for the rest of his life. David settled into his role as Head of English at King's College with relish and with great success; Janet managed to get a part-time job as a feature writer on the local paper, The Evening News; Louise flourished in her new school, soon making new friends and discovering a natural ability for ballet dancing, and Skipper grew from an uncontrollable puppy into an uncontrollable dog. And their new home began to take shape. David cleared, levelled, rotovated and seeded the overgrown garden, created borders, dug out a crescent-shaped pond, stocked it with ten goldfish and planted a variety of shrubs. He tiled the kitchen and bathroom floors, carpeted the living rooms and bedrooms, painted the cottage inside and out, paid for central heating to be installed and raised a second mortgage for the leaking roof to be thatched.

Commander Pankhurst asked to see David after school one Friday. The new Head of English had been in post for more than two-and-a-half years and he had made a significant impression. His predecessor had been a competent but plodding teacher, thorough but uninspiring. David Browning, on the other hand, had radical views and teaching methods and, more to the point, he was extremely popular with the pupils. His classroom always buzzed, was always full of energy, inspiration and challenge – and pupils. Very few chose to dodge his classes.

"How long have you been with us now?" the headmaster asked casually, although he, of course, already knew the answer.

"Soon be coming up for three years, sir."

Commander Pankhurst nodded, got up from behind his desk, turned and looked out of the window, pretending to be preoccupied. The Cathedral loomed with formidable, permanent and unforgiving might.

With his back to David he continued: "You've done well here, very well. You've turned the department around, made it buzz. The recent A-level results have been excellent and the pupils clearly like and respect you."

An embarrassed clearing of the throat and a lowering of the voice: "You, Browning, have become a credit to King's."

"Thank you, sir. I am very happy here. It's a wonderful school."

Feigning not to have heard, the commander continued: "Bertram Young, as you know, is retiring at the end of this term. He has been deputy head here for 22 years and has become something of an institution. But old Bertie Bollocks (David stiffened with a combination of shock and humour), as I know the pupils and, I suspect, you lot call him – behind his back I hope – is 72 years old. He is due a well-earned rest. Which leaves me with a dilemma."

The headmaster turned from the window, stepped around the desk, walked across the room, passed the seated Head of English and stood with his back to the book-shelved wall opposite. David shuffled his chair around to face him.

"How old are you, Browning?" Commander Pankhurst asked.

"I'm 35 sir, 36 this August."

The headmaster paused for a long time and returned to his desk, stroking his chin pensively, the other hand clenched behind his back. He sat down and leaned back in his chair.

"I'm considering putting your name forward to the Board of Governors as a possible replacement for Mr Young. It is by no means cut and dried, you understand, by no means a definite offer of the job. You are still very young and some of the governors will have a problem with that. But it's a possibility, Browning, a distinct possibility."

David Browning took the steps down the spiral staircase from the fourth floor three at a time, grinning and humming loudly but tunelessly. When he got to the bottom, he skipped through reception and out of the building.

On his way through the Cathedral Gardens, he noticed a Big Issue seller squatting on the ground next to a park bench. On one side of the gaunt, scruffy, ragamuffin man was curled an equally gaunt, scruffy, ragamuffin dog, fast asleep. On the other side lay a half-empty flagon of cider.

Poor bugger, he thought vaguely.

26

THE TREES in the park wore their autumn clothes with pride. Every imaginable shade of red, gold and brown – those bold and defiant colours of Nature's annual death – shone in the bright and slanted October sunshine, a chill but splendid sunshine. The sky was a pale, cloudless blue and the birds, forgetting what was in store, sang as if the season were spring.

The Professor sat alone on the park bench nearest to The Tree, which was reluctant to shed its leaves as if its great age gave it the right to choose. He was very thin now, very frail, and his eyes appeared to be too big for his face. The huge navy blue overcoat swamped his faded frame and the woolly hat he had taken to wearing flopped over his eyebrows.

He had lain, sodden with sweat and leaden with pain, in his bed in The Parlour for two weeks. Doctor Dawes had visited every other day, Brian Davies every day and Midnight Sam had to be forcibly removed from his 24/7 vigil periodically, so that The Professor could get some uninterrupted sleep and Midnight could be forced to get on with his own life, such as it was. The fever finally broke, the inhaler eased the breathing and the morphine tablets dulled the pain. He had come through, but at a cost.

It had taken The Professor half an hour to shuffle the 400 yards from The Parlour to The Tree, with the aid of two walking sticks which Midnight had acquired for him. In not much more than a fortnight The Professor had become an old man.

He fidgetted, checked his bottle of White Lightning, felt for his inhaler, frowned and put it back in his pocket. He jerked his head from right to left and glanced at his wrist. But the watch had not been there since the mugging. He was a worried man. Lady Jane had promised to meet him at The Tree at 3pm. They were going to have a chat before meeting up with the others at The Mitre. It was his first time out in two weeks and Lady had been very insistent and very bossy: "Be at The Tree at 3pm on the dot and I'll walk you to the pub." The Professor knew, from the chimes of the Cathedral bell, that it was 4pm and he also knew that Lady Jane was never late. While he was contemplating what to do and endeavouring not to panic, Midnight Sam, unable to keep away for very long, turned up, an enormous toy panda under his right arm, price tag swinging from the creature's left ear. Wisely The Professor chose not to ask where the panda had come from or where it was going to.

"She hasn't turned up," The Professor said flatly. "I've been here for an hour and no sign. I hope she's all right. She's never late." Midnight sat down on the park bench and placed the panda between them.

"Maybe she's gone straight to The Mitre," Midnight ventured, stroking the panda's head, before bending down to pull a bottle of cider from the white plastic bag he had dropped to the ground. The Professor shook his head and then nodded towards the flagon. Midnight handed it to him without a word. After taking a generous swig from his friend's flagon, The Professor lumbered unsteadily to his feet, clutching his two walking sticks as if he was about to go skiing. Midnight leapt up and fussed around The Professor, more hindrance than help, and the two men gravitated, crab-like, across The Park, slowly, in the general direction of South Street.

When they reached The Mitre, Fen's dog was already tethered outside the pub. He wagged his tail furiously at the sight of them and strained to reach The Professor with his outstretched tongue. Charlie was keen on The Professor but not so sure of Midnight Sam.

For once Fen was first in the pub, playing the fruit machine with a disdainful defeatism. His half pint of lager was on the table in the alcove, along with his tobacco pouch and a packet of green Rizlas. He didn't acknowledge Midnight Sam or The Professor when they walked into the pub but he nodded to Bobby, who understood the gesture and poured two pints of Olde English.

"Don't worry, Prof, she'll be okay, she'll be fine," said Midnight.

But The Professor said nothing. He fiddled with his walking sticks and waited, with silent but tangible impatience, for his drink. He had become more irritable, snappy even, in recent times.

"Prof, I've got a great idea," Midnight leaned across the table in the alcove, an enthusiastic gleam in his eyes. A sudden wave of relief swept over The Professor: whatever was coming was bound to be an enormous distraction from his own problems. Probably disastrous, possibly fatal for somebody or something, but doubtlessly a welcome diversion from the pain in his body and the worry in his mind. Thank God for Midnight Sam!

"Do you know what date it is Saturday week?" Midnight asked.

"No, not really, Midnight. November, isn't it? First week in November?"

"November the Fifth. Bonfire Night. Guy Fawkes and all that. Not this Saturday, but next. How about that?"

The statement hung in the air: The Professor mulled it over in his mind with quick and quiet delight; Fen, at the fruit machine, thought "so fuckin' what?" and made a mental note to be nowhere near the wasteground (where he correctly assumed events were scheduled to take place) on the night in question; and Bobby began calculating how much money he could charge Brian Davies (he knew it was bound to be the centre manager) for the barbecue he anticipated would be required of him – or, to be more accurate, of his wife.

The silence was broken by an outbreak of furious barking and then cursing, in a broad and indignant Scottish accent. Fen turned sharply from the fruit machine and glared at the door, while The Professor and Midnight Sam stared blindly through the frosted glass windows. Bobby, with a publican's sixth sense, waited for the inevitable altercation.

Scots Robby, face red with anger, burst through the swing doors, clutching his left hand, and stood in the middle of the room, chest heaving and teeth clenched. He turned, kicked the swing doors (in preference to the dog) and strode up to Fen, who was pretending to be engrossed in the fruit machine. Scots Robby made to tap the younger, coiled man on the shoulder but thought better of it, took a step back and shouted, with waning indignation: "Your fuckin' dog just bit me. Bit me on the fuckin' hand. And for no fuckin' reason. I've a good mind to call the police. Get the vicious little bastard put down. Fuckin' animal shouldn't be allowed on the streets. Just look at my hand …," Scots Robby took a tentative step forward and shoved his left hand under Fen's nose. There were two deep puncture marks either side of the thumb and dark blood was welling slowly from both wounds. It was a deep bite, but Fen could not have cared less. He chewed his lower lip and, with astonishing arrogance, turned back to the fruit machine without uttering a word.

"Let me take a look at that, Robby," The Professor said with a frown. He inspected the bite and shook his head: "You'll have to go to The Royal right away. You're going to need stitches and, more importantly, a tetanus jab. That's a deep bite."

Scots Robby bristled with pride and suddenly remembered to groan with pain. Bobby handed over several segments of kitchen roll to Midnight Sam, who gently wrapped them around the Scotsman's injured hand. Midnight then returned to the bar, bought a large whisky and plonked the glass in front of him. Scots grunted an acknowledgement, drained the drink in one go and gave off sufficient vibes for Midnight Sam to repeat the exercise. Fen, who missed nothing out of the corner of his eye, tossed a five pound note onto the bar to pay for the refill and continued to play the fruit machine. Ten minutes later he left without picking up his change and without saying goodbye.

"What's the panda for?" The Professor finally asked the question.

Midnight stroked the furry toy. "I thought Lady Jane might like it." A touch of defiance in the voice.

"Where did you get it from?" The Professor immediately regretted asking the question and reached for his cider, shaking his head at his temporary lapse. Appropriately, Midnight did not reply. "I'll have a couple more here and then I think I'll go round and give her the panda," he said finally. "See if she's all right as well, what with that bloke of hers being back."

"Yes, yes, I think that's a good idea," The Professor said gratefully. He had been worried about Lady Jane. He drew a painful breath and started panting, the wheeziness in his chest hoarse and malevolently deep. He pulled the inhaler from his coat pocket with a shaking hand and put it into his mouth, eyes closed. After a few seconds his breathing slowed and regulated. He reached for his cider and sipped the drink more cautiously than before.

Midnight Sam accompanied The Professor back to the night shelter. It wasn't officially open until six o'clock but The Professor had special dispensation and could come and go more-or-less whenever he pleased. He shuffled along, taking slow and small steps, stabbing two walking sticks at the ground as if spearing fish with a harpoon. Midnight, ever-patient Midnight, was ever at his side. Once satisfied that The Professor was safe and sound in The Parlour, Midnight Sam headed for Belgrave Road, the panda clasped underneath his left arm.

Forty years ago the street had been one of the most fashionable in the city. Grand and imposing red-brick, Georgian buildings. Four-storey terraced town houses and one or two large, detached mansions. Homes to doctors, architects, lawyers, citizens of substance. But that all changed in the 1970s. Multi-occupancy, bed-sit fever set in, fuelled by smaller families tempted into selling their inheritances for ready cash. And then by absentee and cynical landlords converting the houses into flats and bed-sits, interested only in easy money. And then again by local authorities interested only in farming out housing benefit 'problems.' So these once austere but beautiful buildings descended into unloved and decaying hovels, opening the floodgates to transient tenants who cared for their dark and loveless homes as little as they cared for themselves.

Midnight Sam pushed open the communal front door to the building where he knew Lady Jane lived, felt his way into the darkened hallway, unproductively flicked the light switch and began systematically knocking on doors. He didn't know the number of Lady Jane's flat so it was a process of elimination.

"Who is it?"

He recognised her voice and he cupped his hands to his mouth, accidentally letting the panda slip on to the floor. "It's me ... Sam ... Midnight Sam," he called.

A long pause and then: "Oh, it's you Sam. What do you want? I'm really tired. I was having a sleep."

"Prof's worried about you. You said that you'd meet him at The Tree. He waited for an hour …"

"I'm fine, Sam. Please tell The Professor that I'm fine. Tell him I'm sorry I let him down."

"Lady?"

"Yes, Sam, what is it?"

"Lady, why don't you open the door?"

Another long pause: "Please go now, Midnight, please go. Everything's okay. I'm just very tired."

"Is he in there?"

"No, he's not. He's gone out. I don't know where he's gone, but I don't think he'll be long."

"Open the door, Lady," Midnight's tone altered a fraction, but it was a paradoxically enormous fraction. And Lady found herself powerless to resist. She opened the door and backed away, head bowed, pathetically trying to hide the heavily plastered left arm and the elastoplast dressing above her left eye. Midnight stepped inside. Apart from a single candle in an empty wine bottle on the floor, the flat was in darkness. Lady stood still and allowed Midnight to inspect the damage.

When she sensed Midnight's anger she began to panic but then realised that the male anger was, for once, not directioned at her. It was that realisation that made her cry, very quietly, and Midnight held her in his powerful arms and stroked her head.

"My arm's broken," she whispered. "It's broken in two places. I was in the Royal most of yesterday. It hurts quite a lot."

Midnight pulled away gently, held her at arm's length and looked deeply into her eyes.

"You are coming with me now," he said softly. "Welshie will let you stay at the night shelter tonight. Go and get your things, Lady. I'll wait for you here."

Lady Jane nodded obediently, turned and shuffled towards the bedroom.

Midnight's eyes grew accustomed to the darkness and he looked around the flat while Lady stumbled about in the bedroom, gathering her meagre belongings. The flat wreaked of cigarette smoke, bad body odour – male body odour – stale urine and alcohol. Two cupboards, their tops littered with empty flagons of cider, stood, doors ajar, against a living room wall; a dreary sofa with the springs poking through in three places occupied the middle of the room; more bottles and ancient takeaway meals and a number of white, plastic bags, all empty, were strewn over the uncarpeted floor.

Midnight Sam shrivelled his nose in disgust: things were better on the wasteground, at The Tree, at the bus station, even at the underpass. Anything was better than this – this horrible cross-breed of two worlds, which contaminated both.

The front door opened with a clatter and Gordon Blacklock strode in, two carrier bags swinging from his hands. He didn't see Midnight Sam at first. He lowered the bags carefully to the floor, tried the light switch, cursed when nothing happened and yelled: "Jane, Jane, where the fuck are you? Fucking bulb's gone again. I can't see a fucking thing. JANE!"

He stood bear-like, chest heaving and his breathing loud. After a couple of seconds, when his eyes became accustomed to the gloom, he froze and then craned his head forwards.

"Who's that? Who the fuck's that?"

Midnight Sam took a step forwards and Blacklock braced himself for violence, narrowing his cold, black eyes and jutting out his bearded chin belligerently. Midnight held his ground and said nothing until realisation dawned on Blacklock.

"And what the fuck are you doing here? Where's Jane? What the fuck have you done with my missus?" He paused, eyes on fire and fists clenched. "You can fuck off, you half-breed bastard. You can fuck off out of here, before I beat the shit out of you."

Lady Jane appeared in the bedroom doorway, behind Midnight Sam. She was shaking and her eyes were wide with terror. When Blacklock saw her, pale in the flickering candlelight, he snarled like a dog and lurched towards her, trying to brush Midnight Sam aside. He was not prepared for what happened next.

Midnight side-stepped nimbly in front of Blacklock and gave him a mighty shove in the chest. The northerner staggered backwards and tumbled to the floor, stunned by the sheer power of the push. Midnight moved like a panther, soundless and swift, and pulled Blacklock (a heavy man) effortlessly to his feet. He locked his hands around Blacklock's throat and squeezed with tremendous power. Blacklock clawed ineffectually at Midnight's hands and quickly began to weaken. His shoulders slumped and his legs gave out altogether. But the dead weight made no difference to Midnight's stance – he held Blacklock upright while he throttled him. The only thing which prevented Midnight from killing Blacklock was the soft but surprisingly strong voice of Lady Jane.

"Stop now, Midnight. That's enough. Let him go. He's not worth it. Please, Midnight."

Midnight Sam relaxed his grip immediately, dropped his arms but stood his ground and stared at Blacklock with huge, murderous eyes. Blacklock collapsed onto his knees, scratched at his neck, coughed and gagged. He weaved his head from side to side, groaning with pain and fear. Midnight's shoulders slumped, he closed his eyes and hung his head.

Lady Jane read the situation and took immediate control. She hoisted her bag over her shoulder with her good arm and steered Midnight towards the front door, which was still open. Midnight bent down to pick up the toy panda and lumbered after her, trance-like, into the street. He was drained of emotion but in deep shock at what he had almost done.

Midnight Sam was an intrinsically gentle man and the realisation that he was capable of such violence – that he was capable of killing another human being – filled him with horror and shame. Lady Jane sensed this: she mothered him en route to the Night Shelter; she stroked his back and squeezed his waist. She wanted to stop and cuddle him, to draw him deep to her bosom with maternal protection, but her broken arm would not allow that. So she talked softly to him and told him that everything was going to be all right.

****

Lady Jane, on Brian Davies' insistence, moved temporarily into Prof's Parlour. It was against the rules (Brian's rules) but then there was a time and place for rules and this was not one of them. This was a time and the Parlour was the place to look after Lady Jane.

The Professor watched with bemused but secretly happy silence as Lady proceeded to 'make home.' She cleaned the flat from top to bottom, vacuumed the threadbare carpet, rearranged the paltry items of furniture, treated the piles of plates, dishes and mugs to their first experience of washing-up liquid and hot water, discovered a sofa beneath various items of dirty clothing and newspapers and filled several black, plastic bin liners with empty bottles of cider. Lady was in heaven: she was 'making home' for the first time ever.

Midnight Sam's confrontation with Blacklock haunted him for days afterwards. He was glad that he had taken Lady away from Belgrave Road; no regrets as far as that was concerned. But the murderous rage which had consumed him for those few savage seconds when there was no doubt that he would have strangled Blacklock had it not been for the intervention of Lady Jane? The undeniable fact that he was not only capable but was also willing to kill? He was terrified and ashamed at such a self-discovery and, what made matters worse, he knew that given the same set of circumstances he would do it again. Poor Midnight Sam – he did not know where to go with his sin.

But one morning a solution came to him while he was sitting on a bench in the gardens of The Cathedral, a small stack of Big Issues on one side and a two-litre bottle of GL cider, half-hidden inside a brown paper bag, on the other. Midnight was prone to such flashes of inspiration and they never failed to result in interesting consequences.

Bishop John listened patiently to Midnight Sam's dilemma, a small frown on his kind, craggy face. Two schooners of Harvey's Bristol Cream stood untouched on the coffee table between the two men and the bishop's pipe lay neglected on the heavy, cut-crystal ashtray.

"But Sam, there are times when our innate sense of goodness is so outraged by the actions of others that our basic instincts take over," said Bishop John, reaching for his sherry. Midnight Sam breathed a barely noticeable sigh of relief and swiftly followed suit. "You were reacting to the most primeval instinct of them all – protecting your woman ..."

"She is not my woman, your worship," Midnight interrupted quietly.

"Yes, yes, Sam, I know. But in a manner of speaking, at that time and in that place, she was. She was a woman you cared for, a vulnerable woman who you wanted to protect from violence. Look Sam, Jesus advocated turning the other cheek and it is a good and wonderful philosophy. And in 99% of life's crises it is the right thing to do. But this occasion was that remaining one percent and Jesus would have agreed with you. It was not you under threat, it was another human being. You were right to do what you did."

Midnight shook his head: "But I would have killed him, your honour, and I wanted to kill him." He rubbed his chin in furious concentration and hauled out a memory: "Thou Shalt Not Kill – that's one of those Ten Commandments, my lord, that's what God told Moses on Mount Sinai. He said 'Thou Shalt Not Kill.'" Midnight nodded smugly and inadvertently finished his sherry in one gulp.

Bishop John looked levelly across at Midnight and then leaned forward to refill his pipe. He nurtured the ancient briar back into life with the help of half a dozen Swan Vestas and disappeared behind a cloud of silver-grey smoke.

"So what is it exactly that I can do for you, Sam?"

A pious, almost ethereal expression crept onto Midnight's face: "I want to confess my sins, your honour. I want ablution."

"Absolution," the bishop corrected.

" 'Father, forgive me' and all that. You must know the sort of thing."

Bishop John leaned back in his chair and stared at the ceiling, pipe clenched between his teeth. Smoke drifted up through a thin shaft of sunlight which filtered into the room. He was rehearsing in his mind how to explain to Midnight Sam the differences between the Protestant and the Roman Catholic churches, but decided against it.

He removed his pipe and made up his mind: "You'd better come over here, Sam. You'll have to kneel."

Midnight Sam, a sombre and deeply religious expression on his face, got up and brushed himself down in preparation for the altar.

"Oh and you better move the coffee table out of the way," said Bishop John.

27

IT WAS Lady Jane's 28th birthday and The Professor bought her a silver-plated cigarette case, inscribed with the words 'Happy Birthday Lady Jane, Love Prof.'

Midnight Sam had been detailed to purchase four bottles of Chablis from the One-Stop Shop. They were on special offer – two bottles for a tenner. When Midnight handed over a £20 note to the shopkeeper, who knew this 'customer' only too well, the poor man thought that it must be a trick. But he could not, for the life of him, fathom out what the trick was. It played on his mind for the rest of the day and he even talked it over with his wife after he shut up shop at eleven o'clock and went home.

Lady Jane and The Professor were going to have a dinner party – just the two of them – in The Parlour. Prawn cocktails, chilli con carne, apple pie and cream. Lady bought the ingredients from Tescos (apart from the apple pie which Brian Davies' wife insisted on making for the occasion). Midnight Sam took a lot of persuading to desist from attempting a birthday cake; he was spotted poring over a tatty old cookbook in the day centre and scribbling copious notes. Brian and The Professor had an emergency meeting and came up with a compromise: perhaps Midnight would like to buy Lady a "nice bunch of flowers" instead.

A white bed sheet served as a tablecloth for the round, plastic, garden table; a tall candle stood at a slight angle from the top of an empty wine bottle; wine glasses, courtesy of Midnight Sam (more accurately courtesy of British Home Stores, had they but known it) awaited the Chablis; and two Christmas crackers, rescued by Midnight from the unforgettable Christmas Party.

"I can't remember cooking for a man before," said Lady excitedly as she busied herself, one-handed, in the kitchen. A flagon of cider stood on the draining board but she had only poured herself one glass and had hardly touched that. The Professor was curled up on the sofa, staring at the ceiling, engrossed in some deep and distant memory. He reached for his wine glass, twirled it between his forefinger and thumb, gazed into the crystal clear, lemon-green liquid and shook his head with a small sigh.

"I haven't touched Chablis for years," he said, out loud but really to himself. "It used to be one of my favourite tipples. Janet's too. She loved a glass of Chablis, more than one glass actually. But it had to be absolutely stone cold."

"Janet?" Lady appeared in the kitchen doorway, holding a tin of chilli beans.

"My ex-wife," he said, still inspecting the wine glass. "I haven't seen her for years. I can't remember how long it's been. I wonder what she's doing now?" He looked up at Lady Jane, who intuitively made light of the revelation, gave a nonchalant shrug and turned back to the draining board. It worked. "I've got a daughter, grown-up now of course, although I can't remember exactly how old she is," he continued. "Louise … Louise. It's her birthday next month. November 17th. The apple of my eye she was. Still is, I suppose, at least in here," he tapped the side of his head.

The Professor gulped at his wine, straightened and started to cough. After the fit, his chest heaved breathlessly and Lady Jane handed him the inhaler. He took two puffs, jammed the inhaler back into a trouser pocket and waited for things to calm down. Without a word, but with a pat on The Professor's shoulder, Lady went back to preparing the meal.

"I send Louise a birthday card every year," he went on. "No idea whether she ever gets them, of course – I've only got an old address. But I send them anyway. Every year, without fail."

He got up and shuffled into the kitchen, steadying himself on the furniture. "Is there anything I can do?" he asked, a wave of sudden and rare contentment washing over him. Lady swivelled around gaily and shook her head: "No, I'm fine. The one-armed chef is in complete control."

The Professor made a hash at opening another bottle of wine but he managed it eventually, even if he was forced to shove the splintered cork back down into the bottle. He filled both glasses, fished out a few pieces of cork with his fingers and, with concentration, lit the candle.

He weathered a deep spasm of pain across his stomach, surreptitiously swallowed a morphine tablet and waited, like a gleeful schoolboy, for his dinner.

"Do you know why they call me The Professor?" he asked, when they were through the prawns and one-and-a-half bottles of Chablis and had made a start on the chilli. Lady shook her head.

"Someone – I've no idea who and it doesn't matter anyway – found out that I used to be a teacher. Well, I was, and a pretty, damn good one at that, I like to think. I was Head of English, no less," he struck a mock superior pose. "Oh yes, I was destined for great things. My headmaster was even making noises about me being the next deputy headmaster when old … now what was his name? … Bertram Young – yes, that's it – when old Bertie Bollocks hung up his mortar board."

"What school was that?"

"King's College."

"There's a King's College here, isn't there? Very posh it is, I've been told."

"There certainly is," said The Professor with a teasing smile, watching the expression on her face change from polite curiosity to thinly-veiled astonishment. Lady placed her knife and fork beside her plate, placed both hands, palm-down, on the table and thrust her head forward.

"It was *here*, you were a teacher in *this* town, in King's College, *here*? Christ, Prof, what happened?"

The words – the forbidden words – were out before she could check herself. The words she had studiously avoided throughout the evening, the words no down-and-out street-drinker should ever say to another down-and-out street-drinker: what happened?

But The Professor was not offended; neither was he defensive nor secretive. He wanted to tell Lady Jane his story, while he was able to. He felt that he owed her that much.

"Melissa Carter," he said with a wry smile. "Melissa Carter happened."

Lady Jane could not resist squirming with anticipation; she prodded her glass forward for a refill and waited for The Professor to continue. He leaned back, tilting the chair, closed his eyes briefly, smiled thinly and chuckled.

Melissa Carter was 14 when she arrived at King's College. David Browning was her English teacher. She was a precocious and sexually advanced teenager, a dangerous young woman, who had gladly lost her virginity when she was 13. The 'victim' was one of the Jack-the-lad builders who were constructing a swimming pool in the grounds of the family home – a five-bedroomed, mock Georgian affair set in two acres of land in Surrey. After a fumbled fornication in one of the swimming pool changing rooms, for two weeks Melissa made the poor boy's life a complete misery. She took great delight in revealing her true age, then she threatened to tell her father that the luckless lad had forced himself upon her. Finally she hinted that her period was late. The poor young man was in pieces, totally at her command, and so the sexual liaisons continued wherever and whenever she chose. Not that the young bricklayer was reticent, for Melissa was a pretty and well-developed teenager who oozed smouldering, pubescent sexuality. He paid the required blackmail fee without too much of a problem.

The Professor shovelled a forkful of chilli con carne into his mouth and stared at the ceiling: "Melissa developed a crush on me – that's not unusual for teenage girls and their teachers, it happens all the time. An occupational hazard which teachers learn to cope with and the girls never really mean it anyway, just a harmless exercise of teenage fantasy. But in Melissa's case it was different. She meant it … she really meant it. She was a genius at engineering situations to be alone with me, ever 'accidentally' touching me, brushing against me, subtly but clearly displaying her sexuality.

"And when that didn't work she became more blatant, more emotional. She would tell me how much she liked me, how much she liked older men, how she couldn't stop thinking about me, how she was forever dreaming about me." The Professor laughed harshly: "Bloody hell, if she could only see me now, she wouldn't be having dreams about me, she'd be having bloody nightmares."

"So what did you do?"

"I tried to ignore it at first, laugh it off, make a joke of it. But that turned out to be a waste of time. Melissa was deadly serious and it was no laughing matter, not in her case."

"But that sort of thing must have happened to you before, surely. Weren't girls of her age always fluttering their eyelids at some teacher or other? Christ Prof, I remember having the most amazing crush on my French teacher. I used to dream about him, fantasise about him something wicked."

The Professor gave a quick nod and reached for the third bottle of Chablis: "Of course it happened before, but, as I said, it was never a problem. It was never serious, it was never going to materialise beyond the fantasy. The crushes always remained firmly locked in their teenage worlds of make-believe. But with Melissa, it was different."

Melissa Carter was on a mission: she would lie in wait for David after school, 'accidentally' bump into him, drop her books so that he would feel obliged to bend down and help her pick them up — a carefully orchestrated opportunity for her to show off her legs, her stockinged legs, and more.

But she was not content to keep things between David and herself. She was mischievous and manipulative and dangerous and wanted to involve her peers. So she began to drop hints, throwaway remarks, innuendos which led her friends to believe that it was David Browning and not the 14-year-old schoolgirl who was making the running.

"But then, all of a sudden, she changed towards me, she changed completely," The Professor went on. "Almost overnight she stopped flirting with me. She even apologised for being so difficult and promised that she would not embarrass me any more.

"I was taken aback, cautiously relieved but a bit suspicious at first, but as the weeks went by and she proved to be true to her word I thought that Melissa's schoolgirl crush had finally and thankfully burned itself out. It was a great relief, I can tell you."

The Professor topped up Lady Jane's glass, inspected the third empty bottle with a boyish frown and prepared to lever himself to his feet. Lady stayed him quite firmly with her good arm and got the last bottle from the fridge herself. She handed him the bottle and he made a better job of extracting the cork.

"Getting my old knack back," he observed with surprise and mild pleasure, filling both wine glasses.

The Carter family, who had been renting a large, detached, Cotswold stone house in a middleclass suburb two miles from the city centre, purchased a converted farmhouse with an orchard, small paddock, grass tennis court and an acre of grounds on the outskirts of a village six-and-a-half miles from town. Less than a mile from where David, Janet and Louise Browning and Skipper were living. It was a coincidence, a tragic coincidence as it turned out. And that was when the flirting stopped – the moment Melissa Carter learned who her new neighbours were. She had other plans.

"I bumped into her father – actually I think he engineered the meeting – but anyway, there he was in The Gardeners Arms, our local pub, 'absolutely delighted' to meet me," said The Professor with a wry smile.

"Has to be said Mr Carter was a charismatic man, flamboyant, engaging and with an amazing voice. Deep and resonant and with the most infectious laugh, if a little on the loud side. One of those people who is instantly popular and very persuasive. By God, I bet he was a bloody good barrister.

"We started talking (and of course he was very flattering to me) but he expressed concern that his daughter was falling behind with her

English studies. He was particularly concerned with her set Shakespeare work – Macbeth, I think it was…"

Lady Jane could not resist a rare interruption: "Don't tell me, Prof, he asked you to give little Miss Innocent Melissa whats-her-name some extra tuition at home." She shook her head sadly and sipped her wine.

"Of course and I found myself being talked into it. As I said, Mr Carter QC was a very, very persuasive man and, besides, he let it slip, accidentally on purpose, that he was going to be sitting on the Board of Governors next term. I was cornered.

"When I told Janet – who knew all about the Melissa business – she was far from happy. Not that she feared I would succumb to the young girl's charms but because she smelled danger, she sensed big trouble ahead. She warned me and God how I wish I'd listened to her. So I cleared it with the head, who saw no problem so long as Melissa's parents were always at home at the time."

"Did your headmaster know about the flirting and stuff?" asked Lady Jane.

The Professor heaved his shoulders and answered in a soft, guilty tone: "No, he didn't, I'm afraid. I didn't tell him. I should have done, I know, but I didn't. The damn infuriating thing is that he would have understood the situation better than me and he would have advised me what to do. I think he would have seen straight through the 'extra tuition' rubbish. But, oh no, I thought I knew best, I thought I knew how to deal with Melissa Carter on my own. How bloody wrong I was."

The conversation was interrupted by a commotion outside. Muffled cursing and then a clink of bottles, followed by the thump of something, body-like, against the door. "Fuckin' stairs," the slurred Scottish accent was unmistakeable.

Lady opened the door. Scots Robby was standing outside, breathing heavily and clutching a plastic bag in each hand. A small, recent cut at the top of his forehead just below the hairline oozed a trickle of blood and a large, orange stain on the front of his pullover betrayed the attempted consumption of a curry at some stage during the night.

"Nearly broke my fuckin' back on these stairs of yours," he grumbled, swaying but concentrating with alcoholic fury. "I could have broken my fuckin' neck."

Scots brushed a grain or two or rice from his moustache with the back of his hand and thrust the two bags in front of him: "A drop of the hard stuff, that's what a wee Scottish lassie like you needs on her birthday. Never mind all that poxy wine. A dram or two – that's what a bonnie lassie like you needs." He lowered the bags to the floor and backed towards the staircase, suddenly overwhelmed with embarrassment.

"Thanks, Robby, that's really kind of you, just what the doctor ordered," Lady Jane's smile was from the heart. "Won't you come in for a …"

"Sorry, Lady, no can do," Scots cut in with a fluster. "Prior engagement. But enjoy the whisky." He turned around and scrambled back up the stairs to the safety of the streets.

Precision planning went into Melissa Carter's revenge for having been rejected. It had never happened to her before. Although she was only 14 years old she had had a fair number of sexual liaisons, all with much older men, mostly her father's friends, and all on her own terms. Nobody she had set her sights on apart from David Browning had been able to resist those big blue eyes and those pouting lips. A woman's body stretching a schoolgirl's blouse; an ever-present aura of raw, young and seemingly innocent sexuality. But the new Head of English was having none of it. Melissa knew he found her sexually attractive — she could read the look in his eyes — but the pompous prick would do nothing about it. She remembered something her father had said while they were watching a television play one evening: "Hell hath no fury like a woman scorned." And so Melissa began to scheme her fury.

The Professor and Lady Jane were sitting peacefully on the sofa, contentedly tipsy but not drunk, despite four bottles of wine and a respectable inroad into the first of Scots Robby's two bottles of Scotch. The Professor's story was keeping them both focussed and sober. Lady was hooked and eager to know what happened and The Professor was consumed with an enormous relief in the telling, in the laying of a ghost which had haunted him a very long time.

"This was supposed to be your birthday party," he said, feigning an apology. He knew Lady was having a good time but he wanted her encouragement, her permission, to continue. "And all I've done is whitter on endlessly about me and my stuff, boring the pants off you with all my shit." Lady took the bait graciously and gave him what he wanted. But she wanted it too.

"Shut up, Prof. I want to hear it. I'm really pleased that you want to tell me. Go on."

"Have you got all night?"

Lady Jane nodded: "Yes, I've got all night."

28

MELISSA Carter arranged herself carefully on the bed. She lay back and hugged one knee, allowing her other leg to fall open, displaying her young womanhood. She was naked apart from a pair of black, fishnet stockings, a black suspender belt and her King's College tie. She wore bright red lipstick.

Her father's Polaroid camera, balanced on a pile of magazines on the dressing table stool, clicked dutifully after 30 seconds of the timer delay had expired. She posed for half a dozen photographs, shifting her position each time, before she took off the stockings and suspender belt, secreted them at the bottom of one of her bedside cabinets, returned the camera to her father's study and washed off the lipstick. She slid the six prints in a plain brown envelope and slid the envelope into a 'secret' compartment of her satchel.

Three weeks later she began confiding in her best friend, Angela Douglas, that Mr Browning had been 'taking advantage' of her during the extra tuition sessions at her home. He had squeezed her bottom, stroked her legs, brushed his hands across her breasts and pushed his crutch against her, clearly in a state of arousal. Melissa quelled her friend's protective indignation ("Report the dirty beast," had been the girl's words) and told Angela that on no account was she to tell anyone: it was their secret and she would deal with it. Her best friend of course confided in her best friend and before too long it was common knowledge among the pupils of King's College.

At about that time, Melissa invited Angela and two other girlfriends to spend the weekend with her. Unbeknown to anybody, she had planned what was to happen next with military precision. After school on Friday, Melissa, Angela and the two other girls stood outside David Browning's study. Melissa knocked on the door. She knew he was in.

"What's all this, then?" David had asked. Melissa looked sheepish and embarrassed. She appeared to pluck up the courage and take a deep breath: "I'm everso sorry, sir, but we've got a real problem. I wondered if I could ask you a huge favour?" She pulled a nervous face and stared at the floor for a second. David waited, mildly amused at the theatricals.

"You see, sir, we've missed our last bus home and we're going back to mine for the weekend. Dad's in London on some big case or other, so he can't pick us up. I've tried ringing my mum but she's turned her mobile phone off and nobody's answering the land line. I don't know what to do, sir." A scary, little girl pause. "I don't suppose you could give us a lift, sir?"

David could see no problem. Melissa had thankfully cooled her fantasy designs on him and there were, after all, three other girls in tow. So he agreed, albeit with slight reluctance. Melissa waited until they turned into the long drive leading to her home, knowing that her friends would be too preoccupied with taking in the overt opulence to notice what she was up to. She slid the brown envelope containing the six Polaroid photographs down the gap between the back rest and the seat. She pushed it down until it was out of sight. One element of circumstantial, but damning, evidence had been successfully planted.

Two weeks passed before Melissa had an opportunity to obtain the next piece of 'evidence.' It was a warm, summer evening in August – deep in the heart of the school holidays – and David had called round at the Carter's home to treat his extra-curricula pupil to an insight into the contemporary relevance of Macbeth.

After exchanging pleasantries with Mr and Mrs Carter, he hung his jacket on a coat-stand in the hallway and joined Melissa in her downstairs 'den' where the tuition took place. It was simplicity itself for the teenager to excuse herself for a few minutes to answer 'nature's call' and rifle through David's jacket in the hallway until she found his comb. She extracted a few hairs, wrapped them in a tissue and popped the little package into the back pocket of her jeans. Simplicity itself but, as it turned out, devastatingly effective. She returned gaily to her tuition, asking pertinent questions about Lady Macbeth's role in fuelling her husband's ambition.

The village tennis club committee was having its annual general meeting in The Gardener's Arms public house and the Carters, keen members, would not have missed it for the world. Mr Carter was going to make a determined bid for the chairmanship. And so, unbeknown to David, on one August evening the Carter family home was empty, apart from Melissa, and he did not discover that disturbing fact until teacher and pupil were a good half hour into their tuition. Mr Carter had left his Mercedes in the driveway, along with his wife's Quattro, and first impressions, not allayed by Melissa, indicated that mum and dad were at home. Melissa had taken a chance with the weather and with her knowledge of her parents and she turned out to have struck gold. It was a lovely evening and the Carters decided that the evening merited a drink or three. They were going to walk to the pub and enjoy themselves.

Ever a faithful, if covert, student of her father's legal pontifications, Melissa had 'briefed' another potential witness (even if he didn't know it). With a furtive kiss and a fumble in one of the outbuildings and the promise of a lot more later that night, she had secured the services of the gardener – a lank, spotty 18-year-old with more testosterone than brains – to mow the tennis court. She made sure the lad saw David arrive and saw him leave in somewhat of a hurry three-quarters of an hour later, much earlier than usual. She also ensured that the lad saw her run out of the house and fling herself onto one of the garden benches in floods of tears. When the ever-hopeful teenager tried to console her (with only one thing on his mind) she also made sure he heard every word she said: "I hate men, I hate them, I hate them all. You're only ever after one thing, that's all, just one thing. I'm only fourteen, I'm still a child. I thought he was a nice man. Oh my God, I hate him, I hate him. I hate you all." She wrenched herself out of the young gardener's 'comforting' embrace, got up and ran back into the house. It was an Oscar-winning performance.

****

"I must say the police were very thorough, I'll give them that," said The Professor. They were sitting comfortably side by side on the sofa, The Professor drinking Scots Robby's whisky and Lady Jane (who was neither Scottish nor a real lover of whisky) reverting to a dependable glass of Olde English. "And quick. My God, they were quick. Melissa waited three days before she supposedly broke down and spilled the beans. She told her mother that I'd raped her and mum told dad and dad telephoned the police. Within an hour they were all over the place – my home, my car, my study at King's and me."

Lady closed her eyes briefly and gripped The Professor's arm: "Christ, it must have been a nightmare."

"Everything happened at such speed and yet, paradoxically, in slow motion. I felt like a bystander, detached from the frenzy, almost as if it was nothing to do with me. Numb. I suppose I was in total shock. I existed day-to-day, on auto-pilot. My emotions shut down, refused to accept the unacceptable. I went through the motions of living like a robot. Eat, answer questions, sleep, answer more questions, go to the lavatory, sleep, answer even more questions – all the same bloody questions – on and on and bloody on, day after day after bloody day.

"I was suspended from school immediately, on full pay of course. Poor old Commander Pankhurst – he was almost as shell-shocked as I was. I remember the day well. He stood with his back to me, hands on hips, gazing bleakly out of his study window at the Cathedral. He couldn't bring himself to look me in the eye. I remember feeling sorry for him, really sorry. He made all the right noises of course, you know the sort of things. 'Don't believe a word of it,' 'we'll get this sorted out, old chap, don't you worry,' 'this is all a dreadful mistake,' 'soon be cleared up,' and so on. But I knew that deep down he was not completely convinced of my innocence. I could sense there was a nasty little shred of doubt which was gnawing away at him. And I couldn't blame him for that; I would have probably felt exactly the same if our roles had been reversed.

"Janet was wonderful. Totally behind me, one hundred per cent, never a doubt in her mind that I was innocent and that justice would ultimately prevail. She referred to Melissa Carter as 'that wicked little witch' and she, more than I, was confident the police would soon realise what a terrible mistake they had made, give the young troublemaker a serious ticking-off at the very least and drop the charges."

Lady Jane kept shaking her head at the unfolding horror: "So what did the police do? Did they arrest you? Did they charge you? What happened, Prof?"

"I was arrested on suspicion of the rape and indecent assault of a child, spent a degrading night in the cells and, in the morning, was granted police bail. But that was only the beginning of the nightmare, only the bloody beginning."

The Professor leaned back on the sofa, resting the whisky glass on his knee, and closed his eyes. Lady was perched on the edge of the sofa; she turned towards him and watched his face anxiously, her heart in her eyes.

"While I was in the cells they got a search warrant and raided my home. And that's the right word – 'raided.' Four detectives barged into the cottage, waving a piece of paper in Janet's face but offering her no explanation whatsoever. They were rude and threatening and the poor woman didn't know what the hell was going on.

"They searched the house and my car and took away our computer. Janet was in shock, totally traumatised, and poor Louise … the girl was terrified. They found nothing in the house or on our computer, but – surprise, surprise – they found the Polaroid photographs down the back seat of my car.

"They also found several of my hairs in Melissa's bed. Forensic analysis obviously matched them with DNA samples taken from me.

"A week later I was formally charged with rape and with 'making indecent images of a girl under the age of 16' – I think that was the wording."

The Professor topped up his glass (he was halfway down the first bottle of whisky) and he smiled wistfully at Lady Jane: "Please don't look so sad, my dear, it was a long time ago and I've grown used to it over the years. And, I can't tell you how bloody, damn good it feels to tell someone after all this time." He paused, stroked his chin and corrected himself: "No, what I mean is, how good it feels to tell you."

Lady didn't know what to do or say so she looked down at her hands, which were clasped on her knees.

****

The jury comprised eight women and four men and the time estimate for the trial was two weeks. Prosecution witnesses were to include Melissa's best friend Jackie Mitchell, the 18-year-old family gardener, several pupils from King's College, the investigating police officers, a forensic scientist, Melissa's mother and father and, of course, the alleged victim herself. Defence witnesses were the defendant, with character witness back-up from the headmaster of King's and Janet Browning. From the outset, it was an uneven contest.

Melissa and her school-friends, all being under 16-years-old, gave their evidence by video link. The school-friends were honest, in that they only repeated what Melissa had told them, but they were not particularly articulate. On the other hand, Melissa was outstanding. A trembling lower lip, an occasional tear angrily brushed away, catches in the voice and even – and this was inspired – a clumsy, heart-rending attempt to blame herself for the outrage. Bless her. And the genuine anguish of Melissa's parents: they should never have allowed Browning to spend so much time with their daughter. Maybe it was partly their fault as well …

The prosecuting barrister's closing speech was a masterpiece of carefully-constructed understatement, almost apologetic, as if it was so obvious the defendant was guilty that the whole trial was an embarrassing and costly waste of time and public funds. But in the interests of justice …

"It is every defendant's right to plead not guilty, members of the jury, and it is also every defendant's right to have a fair trial," he began courteously. "And it is up to the Crown to prove to you, beyond reasonable doubt, that the defendant – in this case David Browning

– is guilty as charged. Nothing less will do, as His Honour will no doubt instruct you when he sums up the case.

"You have heard all the evidence, you have listened to and seen all the witnesses, both for the prosecution and for the defence, and you have heard from the defendant himself and from Melissa Carter, the 14-year-old schoolgirl, we say, he sexually abused and raped.

"I am not going to go through the evidence again; His Honour will be covering that aspect. But what I am going to do is to highlight the most important planks in our case. Important, ladies and gentlemen of the jury, because, in my mind, they leave no doubt – let alone reasonable doubt – that this man, a senior teacher at a well-respected public school, took gross advantage of his position of trust, gross advantage of one of his pupils. A vulnerable, impressionable young girl, whose innocence he corrupted, whose virginity he stole, whose life he damaged beyond repair.

"It is clear, is it not, members of the jury, that this defendant, David Browning, was determined to have his way with Melissa Carter. Her friends have had the courage to give evidence that she confided in them, told them how the Head of English was pursuing her, touching her, making suggestive comments. And, to Melissa's mistaken credit, she swore them all to secrecy and tried to deal with the situation herself.

"And then all this 'extra tuition' business in her own home. What a golden opportunity this must have been for the man. Alone with a young girl who was clearly falling more and more under his spell.

"Circumstantial evidence, unsubstantiated opinion, flights of fancy of a teenage girl with an overactive romantic imagination – the defence has continually and eloquently made these suggestions during the course of this harrowing trial.

"Okay, so let us draw a line under this so-called circumstantial evidence. Instead, let us consider the evidence of the Carter family's

young gardener. Not a very articulate witness some might say, but an honest one, I suggest. He saw Mr Browning arrive, he saw him leave early, he witnessed the obvious distress that Melissa Carter was in.

"Let us consider the explicit photographs of Melissa which were found hidden in the defendant's car. Let us consider the hairs, forensically proved to the tolerance of one billion to one to belong to the defendant, discovered in Melissa Carter's bed."

The barrister tidied the papers on his lectern and scratched the back of his neck: "Members of the jury, in legal circles I am well-renowned for making particularly long, verbose and detailed closing speeches. I make no apology for that, but on this occasion, you may be relieved to hear, my closing speech is relatively short. In fact it is virtually over. The reason for this is simple: what more can I say?

"David Browning succumbed to a temptation which is placed before most teachers — the evidence is overwhelming — and not only did he violate a young girl in the most vile and self-gratifying manner, but he grossly abused his position of trust and, incidentally, dragged the name of a fine school, a very fine school, down into undeserved disrepute.

"Members of the jury, it is your decision."

****

Lady Jane winced: "Christ, Prof, you didn't stand a chance, did you? What did your guy say?"

The Professor shrugged: "She — it was a she. Always a good idea in a rape case to be defended by a woman, I was told. She did her best. The odd thing was that she really believed me, she knew I was innocent and that really upset her.

"During the trial she would get frustrated, almost tearful at times (and she was a tough cookie) but we both knew we were fighting a losing battle. Of course we worked out from day one that Melissa had set me up. Hell hath no fury and all that. Shakespeare, ironically," he gave a short chuckle. "We knew that she must have planted the photographs – and I remembered the lift home – and my hairs, but how were we ever going to prove it?

"We also found out – and this was the result of my legal team digging away – that Melissa Carter had a reputation at King's College for having an insatiable sexual appetite."

"She was the school bike," Lady muttered bitterly.

"But she was only 14 and my barrister knew only too well that to attack her character openly in court would be emotional suicide. The jury would be outraged. So she had to restrict herself to subtle hints and innuendo, most of which were wasted on the jury."

The muffled, resonant toll of The Cathedral bell struck two o'clock. They could just about hear it and they glanced at each other like two schoolkids way passed their bedtime. Lady Jane smiled encouragingly and The Professor continued.

"The jury took two days to reach their verdict – longest two days of my life – and when those twelve people filed back into the courtroom, studiously avoiding my face, I knew what they had decided.

"Janet, who hadn't missed a single day in court and had far more faith in justice being done than I had, gasped when the foreman said that one word. She looked at me and I will never forget the expression on her face. Despair and compassion and horror.

"I remember feeling completely numb, detached from the proceedings. I could hear the judge's voice but I had no idea what he was saying. I had to ask one of the prison guards who led me down to the cells what the sentence was. He told me seven years. I served four."

****

When the initial shock of the verdict and sentence wore off, the sheer, unmitigated horror of what had happened to David Browning's life burned like the cancer that several years later was to invade his body. At first he could not stop crying, quietly but constantly, and he developed chronic diarrhoea (not a pleasant condition in an eight foot square shared cell with an unshielded WC in the middle). He did not sleep for four nights and was placed on 'suicide watch.' Which was good as far as David's safety was concerned, but invasive, to say the least, when it came to his privacy. The cell door crashing open numerous times throughout the day and night; the spy-hole clicking open and a disembodied eye peering in to make sure the inmate had not strung himself up.

The first week was a living nightmare, the second week horrible, the third miserable and, from then on, David settled into the grim and boring routine of prison life. Being an intelligent man, he soon learned the secret to survival behind bars: go through the motions, the routines, the mindless regulations, without question; assimilate, fit in, never rock the boat, become grey and invisible; live life day-to-day and never, never think of those bleak years of incarceration which stretch out in front of you; never cross off the days on a calendar; be a number and do your time.

Commander Pankhurst, ever the honourable man, came to see David, a fortnight into his sentence. Stiffly but with pained compassion, the headmaster handed his once-star teacher an official letter terminating his employment. Neither man knew what to say. What was there to say? So they said nothing and David's ex-boss got up awkwardly, practically stood to attention, nodded and marched out of the visitors hall, his eyes burning with fiercely-restrained tears of regret. The two men never saw each other again.

Six months later Janet sold the cottage. It was impossible to live in the same village as the Carters anymore and, besides, she could no longer afford the mortgage. She also resigned from her part-time job on the

Evening News. Given the publicity her husband's trial had engendered, her position on the local newspaper had become untenable.

And poor Louise was naturally and systematically put through hell at the village school: bullied, taunted, shunned, punished for the 'sins' of her father. She tried to be brave, she tried to stick up for her dad, but she was in a minority of one and, like all children, she wanted to be liked, to be accepted, to fit in. She learned that the only way she could counter the torment was to collude with her tormentors. She found that if she took their side, betrayed her own father and joined in his condemnation, life in the classroom and the playground became tolerable.

But Louise paid a huge and irrevocable emotional price for that betrayal and guilt rode heavy on her shoulders, hung darkly on her young heart. The girl turned in on herself, shaped a protective shell and became a different person.

Janet took Louise and Skipper to the small market town of Bromyard in Herefordshire, where her mum and dad lived in a converted barn with a two-bedroomed annexe. They made home in the annexe and Louise went to the local school where nobody knew about her father. He was working overseas – that was all the other children needed to know. And, with mum and dad more than willing baby-sitters, Janet managed to get a full-time job on the Hereford Times, a well-established weekly newspaper.

Janet remained completely loyal to her husband, writing to him twice a week, encouraging Louise to do the same, keeping his memory alive in both their minds, never allowing him to fade from their thoughts. However the prison visits became increasingly awkward and neither Janet nor Louise were to blame for that.

"I couldn't bear either of them seeing me there," said The Professor, lying flat out on the sofa with Lady Jane curled up on the floor beside him. "I didn't want them to see me, I wanted them to carry on with their lives, I wanted them to be happy. I began to resent their visits and I even began to write to Janet and urge her not to come."

"But why?" asked Lady. "She stuck by you, she believed in you, she must have really loved you."

The Professor continued, as if he hadn't heard her: "I'd already switched off my life, my previous life. It was the only way I could cope. I knew that nothing was ever going to be the same again. And, quite frankly, I couldn't bear the thought of dragging Janet and Louise down with me. They had been through enough and they had a right to their own lives."

"So did you," Lady Jane snapped, a rare flash of anger in her eyes. "What the hell about you?"

"It was all over for me, Lady. Something happened to me in gaol; something happened to my self-respect, my pride, my self-belief, my self-esteem. I lost faith in myself, just as I had lost faith in the world. Strange thing though, as the months turned into years, I began to feel safe in prison. It was the outside world that frightened me."

The Professor reached out shakily for his glass of whisky and Lady leaned over and handed it to him. She stroked his hair and neither was embarrassed: it seemed the natural thing to do. He patted her hand.

"I began to pester Janet for a divorce. I kept on and on and in the end she gave in. I wanted her and Louise to be free, but to be brutally honest I wanted to be free myself. Free to forget about my former life, free to fade into the background, free from that great big ugly world out there. It was not my world anymore, you see. My world was an eight-foot square prison cell, an exercise yard, a loud and disgusting canteen and a sad little prison library, where I worked."

Lady gazed at The Professor's closed eyes and said: "And when you got out, your world was here."

29

A SHEEPISH and dishevelled Gordon Blacklock knocked on the door to the Parlour. Arms folded across his chest, Brian Davies, stern and watchful, stood on guard behind the northerner, who had promised he would cause no trouble and only wanted to apologise. Nobby and Splodge had materialised at the top of the steps, just in case.

Blacklock was less than a pretty sight: two toggles on his duffle coat were missing and there was a bloodstain on the left sleeve. His black hair was unkempt and one of his front teeth was missing. A bruise yellowed his right cheekbone.

He was clutching a cellophane-wrapped bouquet of flowers, not in pristine condition, when Lady Jane opened the door. His quick, mean eyes darted over Lady's shoulder to The Professor, who was sitting at the table, blowing onto the surface of a steaming mug of tea. A quick eye-contact between the two men but no words were said.

"I forgot your birthday," he mumbled and tendered the flowers tentatively towards her. She took them and mouthed a soundless 'thank-you.' "Can we talk?" he paused and stared at the ground, "in private."

Lady took a step back; The Professor stiffened in his chair and braced both hands on the arm-rests. Blacklock raised his hands submissively and cleared his throat: "I only want to talk, I promise. I want to try to make it up to you ... how is it?" he nodded at her broken arm.

"Not too bad now," she raised the arm and wiggled her fingers. Raw rage welled up inside The Professor but he said nothing. "Another three weeks and I can have the plaster off ... I'll get my coat."

Lady turned and left Blacklock on the doorstep. She looked helplessly at The Professor, touched him lightly on the shoulder and picked up her coat from the back of the sofa. It was an old-fashioned, wide-lapelled, vivid green garment which Midnight Sam had acquired for her from outside the Save the Children shop a couple of weeks ago.

"I'll be back soon," she said gaily.

****

Over the next few weeks The Professor's condition deteriorated. Winter was beginning to snap at the heels and Midnight got into the habit of picking up his friend's benefit money for him. He visited The Professor twice every day, mornings and afternoons, supplied him with cider and generally fussed over the sick man. Doctor Dawes, as ever exceeding the call of duty, popped in at least three times a week and Brian Davies never missed a day. But there was no sign of Lady Jane.

The Professor would lie on the sofa, curled up in the foetal position, wide awake with his eyes closed, waiting for the morphine tablet to kick in. The pain was getting worse now, gnawing away at the efficacy of the medication, gradually making inroads into the welcome, numbing wash of the drug.

The Professor, who had never fared well in the cold weather, was using his inhaler more but with lessening effect. The breathlessness had become a permanent state, escalating to a choking coughing fit perhaps a dozen times a day. And he was beginning to cough up blood.

Doctor Dawes was in despair: "We both know that you're going to die and there's very little I can do for you. But for Christ's sake let me get you into a hospice. I can get you into Sue Ryder tomorrow, no problem. At least you'll have some comfort, some full-time care ...," the doctor paused, "...some dignity."

"You want me to die with dignity?" The Professor's face, grey with pain, twitched whimsically. They had had the same conversation many times and it had always ended the same way.

"Yes, dammit, I do. Don't you?"

"No," said The Professor, "no, I don't."

And that would be that.

It took Midnight Sam and Scots Robby 45 minutes to walk The Professor to The Mitre, less than a third of a mile away. One either side, arms around his skeletal shoulders, the two men had to virtually carry him there. And God help anybody who got in their way; they would have the colourful edge of Scots Robby's tongue to contend with. Once they reached the pub, it would take The Professor a further ten minutes to recover sufficiently to tackle his first pint of Olde English.

"No Fen?" Midnight asked, standing at the bar and scanning the empty pub. Bobby shook his head and shrugged.

"Nope, I haven't seen him for a couple of weeks. Done one of his famous disappearing acts."

Nobody mentioned Fen again; he would turn up eventually – sullen Fen and Charlie, his happy-go-lucky mongrel – and he would glower and snarl at everyone (Fen, not the dog!) But the surly Brummie would put his hand in his pocket, without a word, and buy them all a drink.

The Professor was worried about Lady Jane. He hadn't seen her for more than two weeks. He was used to bumping into her every day, either at The Tree, the wasteground, the day centre, the Parlour or, on Thursday afternoons at The Mitre. True he was not as mobile as he used to be, but he was either going to be in his flat or in the pub, and Lady knew that.

Having made a solemn vow not to lose his temper again (he was doubtful of Bishop John's willingness to administer another 'ablution'), Midnight went to Belgrave Road the following morning. He was nervous and noticed that his hands were shaking, and this time it wasn't the booze. He knocked on the door.

Almost immediately he heard the rustling, clinking sound of a security chain. He was puzzled: there hadn't been a chain before. The door opened a fraction, barely an inch, and the moon-like face of an Oriental woman, a very short woman, peered up through the gap at Midnight. Her hair was tied back in a tight bun and she frowned with undisguised suspicion. Her face was smooth and shiny, like plastic, without a single wrinkle, and yet she must have been at least seventy years old.

"What you want?" she barked, narrowing the gap between the door and door jam even more.

"My friend lives here. Jane. She lives with a man called Blacklock." It was more question than statement; Midnight already feared what the answer was going to be.

"No flen live here. No Jane. They go 'way. They no live here no more. You go 'way." The door closed with a sharp click and the bolt slammed back into place.

Midnight stared at the closed door for a long time before he turned around and walked out of the dingy building. He left the communal front door as he had found it – wide open. He couldn't face The Professor straightaway so he called in at the One Stop Shop and bought a two-litre flagon of White Lightning.

Hunching his shoulders against a chill November wind, he walked across the park to The Tree and sat on the bench next to Splodge, who was fast asleep and snoring mightily. Midnight unscrewed the top, took a long drink, replaced the cap carefully and placed the bottle upright on the ground. His heart was heavy and a knot of anxiety, fear almost, twisted in his stomach. He looked down at the flagon, grabbed it violently, tore off the cap again and gulped with defiance, spilling a good deal from the corners of his mouth on to the lapels of his donkey jacket.

Splodge awoke with a splutter, broke wind and belched at the same time, shook his head and noticed Midnight Sam sitting beside him. Midnight instinctively offered Splodge the bottle and Splodge instinctively accepted.

"Still on for that Bonfire Night of yours – only a few days away?"

Midnight shook his head sadly: "Afraid not, Splodge. Maybe next year, maybe we'll have one next year, but not this time, not now. Prof's pretty bad and Lady Jane's gone. Don't know where …"

Splodge was shocked: "Lady? Gone? Where's she gone to? Not with that bastard Blackie?"

Midnight Sam got to his feet wearily, like an old man, and walked away aimlessly: "Maybe next year, Splodge, maybe next year." He left the cider behind, much to Splodge's relief.

****

The following morning, The Professor made an early start to what was going to be an important day for him. It took him half an hour to get dressed, an operation frequently interrupted by savage coughing fits. But he managed to be climbing the steps from the Parlour to the street above, albeit painfully slowly, as the Cathedral bell started to strike ten. He needed to be particularly early because he did not want to bump into Midnight Sam and, besides, he had certain things to do. It was November 17th.

Swaddled in his over-sized, navy blue and voluminous overcoat and armed with a good supply of the morphine tablets he had been hoarding and with the support of two walking sticks, The Professor shuffled towards W.H. Smiths. Once inside, pursued politely by a security guard in his late teens, the former public school Head of English chose a birthday card for his daughter Louise. He picked the card carefully: the photograph on the front was of a little girl hugging a Golden Retriever. They didn't have any cards of 23-year-old women hugging Cocker Spaniels called Skipper, but it was as close as he could get.

He left the store, still observed by the young security guard, and made his way through the shopping arcade to the Post Office, where he drew out his Incapacity Benefit, bought a first-class stamp and sat down gratefully at a long, oblong table to write the card. Five minutes later he struggled to his feet and inched his way painfully out of the Post Office. Once outside he kissed the envelope and posted it through the postbox on the wall. Nobody saw the tears in his eyes or felt the sorrow in his heart.

He made his way to Sainsbury's, where he bought two bottles of Chablis – they weren't on offer anymore and it cost him £22 – and a corkscrew.

Bobby was surprised to see The Professor alone and even more surprised to see him so early. It was barely midday when the street-drinker struggled through the swing doors, the tops of the two bottles of Chablis protruding from each overcoat pocket.

Four builders, their overalls smeared with plaster and magnolia paint, were loud at the bar and a middle-aged couple had taken up residence in the alcove. And three young men, swigging from colourful bottles, were grouped around the fruit machine.

"Usual, Prof?" Bobby put down the pint mug he was polishing and swung the tea-towel over his shoulder. "You're a bit early. On your own?"

The Professor nodded: "Got a hospital appointment this afternoon. Thought I'd have a swift one beforehand. Bit of Dutch courage. I think they want to keep me in overnight. Tests and things, you know."

Bobby looked puzzled: "I thought you didn't go in for all that hospital stuff."

"Well, there you go, then."

The Professor had two more pints before asking Bobby to ring for a taxi. The landlord obliged, but raised an eyebrow: he had never known The Professor to use a taxi before. When The Professor asked if he could borrow a wine glass until next week, Bobby obliged but raised his eyebrow a second time.

Half an hour later a dull-faced man in his early twenties poked his head around the swing doors, shouted 'taxi' to the room in general and disappeared. The taxi door slammed and the driver revved up the engine pointedly.

The Professor eased himself from the bar stool and handed Bobby three five pound notes: "Get them a couple of drinks apiece when they come in. Tell them 'cheers' from me." He waved goodbye with one of his walking sticks, narrowly missing a tarty teenager in a mini-skirt who was mincing into the pub, jabbering into her mobile phone.

The taxi-driver looked The Professor up and down rudely. His eyes fixed on the two wine bottles protruding from The Professor's coat pockets, registered the creased, brown corduroy trousers with frayed turn-ups which stopped short of his ankles by two inches and ended up studying the black, laceless boots with worn-out heels.

"You got any money?" the cabbie asked, curling his upper lip in disgust.

The Professor nodded and crabbed his way painfully towards the back door of the vehicle. He fumbled with the handle, dropped one of his walking sticks and got into a muddle trying to pick it up. The taxi-driver did nothing to help.

"Where are you going?"

The Professor banged his forehead when he finally ducked into the back of the taxi. A tiny trickle of blood dribbled into his left eyebrow. "Mile and a half down South Street, please, just beyond the old gasworks. There's a road to the right, signposted for the canal. Couple of hundred yards down that road and I'll tell you when to stop."

The taxi-driver half-turned and swivelled his eyes to fix The Professor with a cold, suspicious stare: "What d'ya wanna go down there for? Fuck-all down there. It's wasteground."

The Professor smiled at the flat, grumpy face in the rear-view mirror: "Exactly."

"It's your money," the taxi-driver shrugged and added, "and that'll be a fiver." He flicked an index finger and thumb impatiently: "Money up front or you can walk."

The Professor pulled a brown envelope from a trouser pocket, fumbled with the two remaining bank notes and handed over five pounds. A 50p coin fell on to the floor and The Professor made no attempt to retrieve it.

A light drizzle swirled from heavy, low cloud banks which marched in from the south-west. It had turned very cold.

****

Midnight Sam found The Professor at twenty-five to eleven the next morning. A sixth sense had told him where to go; he knew where to find his friend.

The Professor was propped up against a rusted old gas cooker which had long lost its door. His chin was resting on his chest and his overcoat had fallen open to the waist, where a length of coarse string had been wrapped around a number of times to form a crude belt. His unkempt, straggly grey hair danced in the gusts of wind. One empty bottle of Chablis lay between his outstretched, open legs and the other bottle, with two inches of wine remaining, stood inside the oven of the doorless cooker, behind The Professor's head.

Midnight kneeled down and carefully fastened the buttons of The Professor's overcoat. He removed the empty wine bottle, straightened the legs and gently covered them with the skirts of the overcoat.

Oblivious of the rain, which was sweeping hard across the wasteground, Midnight Sam stepped back and gazed down at The Professor for a quarter of an hour, before he bent down and kissed his friend on the forehead.

He eased the bottle of Chablis from behind The Professor's head and drank the remains of the wine.

Midnight Sam picked his way through the flotsam and jetsam which littered the wasteground until he reached South Street and the growl of traffic and the people of the city.

He quickened his pace, tears streaming down both cheeks – a man with a mission – as he made his way to the Bishop's Palace.

By God, it was going to be one hell of a funeral.

END

author's note

The characters in Wasteground, bar one, are fictitious but their stories are based on truth.

In the case of 'Midnight' Sam, his nickname is borrowed from the late 'Midnight' Steve Long to whom this book is dedicated.

These two men have in common an innate kindness and goodness, but there the similarity ends. Their backgrounds are, as far as I know, entirely different.

'Scots' Robby owes his nickname to a street-drinker called 'Scots' Andy, whose body was found in an inner city churchyard many years ago. His death was originally treated as suspicious but was later put down to natural causes. The nickname is the only thing which links these two men. The rest is fiction.

Lady Jane is an invention (well, sort of) as is The Professor, although people similar to them both do exist.

Mark 'Fen' Fenemore is a loose amalgam of two real people although the young man's name and background are fiction. The crime he committed, however, is not.

And the likes of Paddy Maguire, Nobby and Splodge? Sadly such characters populate the wastegrounds of our world and maybe they always will.

Bishop John is an imaginary character and yet it is a matter of record that one previous incumbent at Gloucester Cathedral regularly entertained 'Scots' Andy to tea at the Bishop's Palace and later officiated at the street-drinker's funeral – in the cathedral!

Although Gordon Blacklock is not real, unfortunately his type is.

Which leaves the 'bar one' character.

Brian Davies, the long-suffering good guy who runs the Day Centre and the Night Shelter, is unashamedly based on a real person: Brian Jones, the man who penned the foreword for this book. In his case the *stories* are fiction but the man is not.

To my knowledge, there is no pub in Gloucester called The Mitre.

But the wastegrounds of our cities and towns do exist, along with the unfortunates who dwell there.

Spare them a thought, for as far as what matters, this is a true story.

Dennis Apperly, August 2007.